IN THE MOOD

CHARLES GRANT

A Tom Doherty Associates Book New York

IN THE MOOD

A Forge Book
Published by Tom Doherty Associates, Inc.
175 Fifth Avenue
New York, NY 10010

Forge® is a registered trademark of Tom Doherty Associates, Inc.

Design by Patrice Sheridan

Library of Congress Cataloging-in-Publication Data

Grant, Charles L.
    In the mood / Charles Grant. — 1st ed.
        p. cm.
    "A Tom Doherty Associates book."
    ISBN 0-312-86277-6 (acid-free paper)
    I. Title.
PS3557.R65I56   1998
813'.54—dc21   97-34386
                                                          CIP

First Edition: February 1998

Printed in the United States of America

0 9 8 7 6 5 4 3 2 1

For Wendy,

magician of smiles, patron nurse of bruised egos;

who knew just what to say when the
famine hit too close to home.

Part 1

1

A comfortable night in the city.

Clouds, but no rain; warm enough to sit on the stoop after sunset, a pleasant chill on the breeze in case someone forgot it was only a day shy of October. No sirens, no screams.

Harsh light and traffic at both ends of the long Chelsea block made the area seem much darker than it was. Trees lined the curb, most of them short, most of them still full enough to shatter the streetlamps' glow and drop shifting speckled patterns onto the tarmac and pavement. A glitter of broken glass in the gutter to mark the remains of a broken bulb. A few windows still lit.

The buildings were more brick face than brownstone, and a few still had the weathered grimaces of gargoyles and stone lions above their narrow lintels. A handful of false balconies on the upper stories, studded with potted plants; bars on the lower windows, hidden by the night.

No music; no shouting; and the voice of the city so constant it was silent.

Midway down the block, on the wide top step of a four-step stoop, two men sat on folding lawn chairs on either side of the wood-and-glass-door entrance. A dim light in the foyer gave them outline, without substance.

They had been there for two hours, as they were most every night, watching the occasional pedestrian, sneering at the cars cutting through from Eighth Avenue to Ninth, speculating on the few silhouettes they could see on the shades across the way. Long stretches of conversation broken by long stretches of silence. Staccato condemnations of the Yankees and the Jets, dirges and sighs for the Giants and Mets. Neither cared about hockey, so the Rangers were ignored; both thought basketball an overpaid game, so the Knicks were never mentioned at all.

Best friends for half a century, in this neighborhood and others, with too many birthdays and funerals between them to bother counting.

"I think," said Tony Garza, "I'm going down to the Korean's for something to eat."

"Eat? What are you, nuts? It's nearly midnight, for God's sake."

"I'm hungry."

"You'll get heartburn."

"I never get heartburn."

Ari Lowe shook his head, rolled his eyes. A short man in loose dark trousers, white shirt, open vest, open cardigan. A slight triangular head that deepened his cheeks and pointed his chin, with wavy white hair he touched once in a while as if to make sure it was still there.

"Heartburn," Garza told him, "is for little men like you, who don't trust their stomachs."

Lowe was short, with a genteel paunch; he was seventy-four and looked it.

Garza was not tall, but everything about him made it seem so. He was large without a suggestion of fat, his long heavy face barely marked by wrinkles. Far less hair than his friend, still dark and combed straight back from a high forehead. A deep voice somewhat rough; a smile that always exposed his still-white teeth. Even when silent, he talked with his hands.

"I trust my stomach to tell me I'm an idiot for eating so late at night."

"Bah." A sweep of an arm. "Live, Ari! You got to live, otherwise what's the point?"

"I've been living. I need a vacation."

"You went to Florida in June."

"You call that a vacation? You ever been to Florida in June? Don't answer. Hot as hell, bugs you wouldn't believe, and they got more old people down there than pelicans, for God's sake. They depress me."

Garza wore a collarless pinstripe white shirt rolled up twice at the cuffs. His pants were baggy. Lowe wore regular shoes with laces; he wore running shoes with the laces wrapped around his ankles.

"What you need, you know, is to go see that woman up on Thirty-first."

"What woman?"

"You've seen her." Hands moving, sketching. "Chest and hips, legs to crush your ribs if you give her half a chance. Mabel, or Miriam, something like that."

"Oh. Her."

Garza laughed. "What's the matter?"

"Sex."

"Sex? What's the matter with sex?"

Lowe scowled as Garza lit a cigarette; he had quit twenty years ago, when the doctor told him it would kill him. "Sex is the matter with sex. I see all those movies on the cable, I keep thinking, is that the way it was? I sure don't remember it that way."

"That's because you never got any."

"Hey. I was married, remember?"

Left hand in the air, right hand with the cigarette. "So was I. Five times. Believe me when I tell you, that's not sex, you old bastard. That's producing progeny, doing your duty. When the honeymoon's over, it's something you gotta do so your wife won't keep nagging you all the time."

Lowe muttered, "You're crazy."

"Now, sex. Sex is . . ." He squinted his concentration. "Sex is feeling each other up in the movies, in the car, running up the stairs and not even making it to the bed. Sex is sweat, Ari. Sex is fun."

Lowe snorted.

"You're jealous."

"Of what?"

"That I still get it and you don't."

"Jesus Christ, Tony, you're damn near eighty! How the hell can you still get sex?"

Garza thumped his barrel chest, then leaned over and poked a finger at Ari's stomach. "Eighty-one, and I get it because I don't give up, my friend. I don't give up just because I'm getting old." He tapped a finger to his temple. "All in the mind. All in the mind. You think you're too old . . ." He snapped his fingers. "Poof, no sex. All in the mind, Ari. All in the mind."

"Yeah, well, you're outta yours."

Garza laughed again, loudly, stretched out his legs, and folded his hands across his stomach. Sighed. Sighed again. Looked to his left and saw a little woman on the sidewalk, wearing a scarf over her hair and a long black coat. She puffed behind a small dog more hair than meat that insisted on checking out every tree on the block and every section of the wrought-iron fencing that fronted most of the buildings. She had a newspaper tucked under her arm, and as she passed he cleared his throat.

"Good evening, Mrs. Lefcowitz."

She didn't stop, but she looked over. "Mr. Lowe. Mr. Garza."

The dog yipped and tried to climb the stairs.

Lowe nodded toward the paper. "They catch him yet?"

"No," she snapped, and hurried away.

Another killer loose in the city. Nothing new, Garza thought; comes with the territory, even in the suburbs. Even in the country. This one cut throats, Slasher they call him. This one showed up all over the damn place, from Chelsea to the Village. No one had seen him yet. The cops didn't have a clue.

"You remember that thing last year?" Ari said, scratching between the buttons of his shirt.

"Which thing? I'm a mind reader now?"

"In Jersey. When it was hot. Some gang took out practically a whole town?"

He remembered.

"Jersey, Nebraska, who cares?" He flicked the cigarette into the street. "The place is going to hell in a handbasket, we got troubles of our own." He patted his breast pocket, decided it was too soon for another smoke. "End of the world is coming, my friend. And I'm still hungry."

Ari, who never sagged, always sat straight, shook his head in disgust. "Are you talking that Millennium thing again?"

"When it happens, you'll be sorry."

Ari chuckled, sniffed, pulled a folded handkerchief from his hip pocket, and blew his nose. "My daughter says she can't wait, she hopes it's true. That Millennium thing happens, that what do you call it—the Rapture?— then all you damn Christians will go away and leave the rest of us alone."

Garza drew himself up, mock indignant. "Did it ever occur to your daughter that if it's true, there isn't going to be anybody left to be left alone?"

Ari grinned. "Sure. She says she'll take that chance just to get rid of you."

"Bad influence."

Ari nodded. "Corrupting me, she says."

Garza wondered what the chicken-leg bitch would say if she knew that her father was in charge of a traveling gambling show, which, no thanks to her and her cheapskate husband, was the only way he could stay here on that damn pension he had.

"Then get off your ass," he said, "and come with me. You want corrupting, I'll give you corrupting. We'll find Mabel, or Miriam, and get laid."

"Again the sex."

"Again and again, my friend. As many times as I can."

Ari flapped his hands in lieu of something to say, stared at the sidewalk and shook his head. His voice was soft: "I'll tell you, Tony, we got the cable and the goddamn Madison Square Garden and the goddamn . . . the goddamn . . ." Frustrated, he let his hands drop weakly into his lap. "People starving, Tony. People dying all over the place, it ain't fun anymore. It ain't fun getting up anymore."

Garza kept silent.

A lone figure down at the corner, the way he was shifting, he wasn't sure whether to use this block to go crosstown or go up another one.

"How many kids you got, Tony? Six, seven?"

"Maybe more." He grinned. "You never know."

"One daughter, two grandkids." Ari blew his nose again. "You'd think they'd come up to see me once in a while, instead of the other way around."

Two or three times a week lately Garza heard the same song, and he began to wonder if his old friend was getting ready to die.

"How many grandkids you got now, Tony?"

"I can't keep track."

"You count the adopted ones?"

"Kids are kids, Ari."

Ari paused before he said, "Not all of them, Tony. Not all of them."

Garza looked at him sideways, just a glance.

"Go to bed, Ari," he said gently.

Ari shrugged wearily.

"Go to bed. Tomorrow we'll go up to Times Square and watch them arrest hookers."

He could see the man fighting against a smile.

"They got rid of the hookers, Tony. Disney's buying up the whole damn place. It ain't no fun up there anymore."

"Then we'll watch somebody mug Goofy." He reached over and briefly grabbed his friend's too-thin wrist. "Go to bed."

The figure at the corner had decided this block would do.

A long moment passed before Ari nodded. He stood, groaning, and folded his chair. "You coming?"

"I'm hungry. The Korean will feed me."

"Heartburn."

"Screw the heartburn."

"Mazel tov, you bastard."

"Same to you."

They shook hands, and Ari went inside, the old glass in the door distorting him before he was gone through the heavy inner entrance.

Garza rubbed his stomach and stood, stretched his arms out sideways, and yawned. He rubbed his stomach again and checked the figure coming toward him, not very fast. For a second he wondered if he should bother, shrugged, and decided he would let Fate do all the thinking. If it worked, it worked; if it didn't, it didn't.

What the hell.

By the time he had folded his chair and propped it up against the door, then stepped down to the sidewalk, it looked as if the timing would be right.

Then again, maybe not.

What the goddamn hell.

There were blocks, he knew, scores of them all over the world, that had blind spots, like that place in the rearview mirror where a car in another lane comes up on you and you can't see him. On many blocks on most neighborhoods, all the conditions being right, it was the same principle—walk along, reach the spot, and no one can see you from any window on any floor in any building.

He walked down toward Ninth, right hand in his pocket, left swinging loosely. Maybe he would get roast beef for a change. It was expensive these days. Cows dying all over because the grain wasn't growing right, and they had to ship the meat in; he read someplace it came from Argentina or Australia, he couldn't remember which. Some kind of riot down in Philly because a guy was accused of hoarding, even though it wasn't illegal. At least not yet.

It didn't really matter when you could barely afford it, anymore.

Even bread cost too much, for crying out loud.

The figure passed under a streetlamp. A young man in a sweatshirt and fatigue pants, his boots slamming on the pavement like he owned the place.

Garza couldn't figure out why kids just didn't wear ordinary clothes anymore. What was so wonderful about looking like you were in the army? He grunted softly.

He checked over his shoulder; his stoop was quiet. Ari hadn't come back out.

For most buildings, like his, the iron fencing was less decorative than to keep people from falling down the flight of concrete steps that led below-ground, to the basement apartment. Trash cans were stored there, under the main steps. Litter was tossed there. He smiled as he remembered a time a couple of years ago when he and that blonde he'd met at St. John's had a little fun down there, just to see if they could do it without getting caught.

The dance of danger, he had called it.

He did the dance again now, because the timing was perfect and because he had never done it on his own street before.

His right hand left his pocket and pressed lightly against his leg, thumb caressing the mother-of-pearl handle tucked in his palm.

The young man heard him approach, looked up, didn't even nod a hello.

Garza, however, smiled.

As soon as they were abreast, the dance began.

Four easy steps.

Silently, smoothly, he turned as his left hand grabbed the young man's hair and yanked the head back; his right hand brought up the straight razor and slashed it deeply across the exposed throat; he shifted the razor hand to the back of the kid's neck, grabbed the seat of his pants, hoisted him effortlessly over the fencing, and dropped him into the well.

Into the dark.

Not a sound but a startled grunt, and the dull thud of the body landing.

Not a single wasted motion.

Not a single pause.

He stood for a moment, staring down, absently folding the razor into his pocket.

Then he blinked, once, and walked away.

When he reached the streetlamp, he didn't look down, didn't check for blood.

He didn't have to.

It was never there.

Horseradish, he thought then as he headed for the corner; if he was going to have roast beef, he couldn't forget the horseradish.

And maybe he'd bring a little something back for Ari.

2

The rain had already been through once that night; not a steady shimmering sheet, but a vicious barrage of pebble and stone that ricocheted off cars, smacked against cobbles, stung flesh, and raised twisting specters of steam along sagging side-street gutters.

And it had, just for a moment, made the night a bit cooler.

It didn't last.

As water dripped from ironwork railings, hanging ferns, sagging eaves, the temperature crept back out of the shadows and made it all much worse than before.

Lightning still forked on the far side of the Mississippi.

And ghosts filled the hotel room, two at a time.

Their voices were soft, unnervingly clear.

Outside, there was thunder. Distant, little more than a grumbling, just loud enough to be heard through the large windowpane and the dark, heavy drapes.

Inside, there was nothing. The TV was off. On the nightstand beside the double bed the clock radio was silent. Nothing from the adjoining rooms, nothing from the hallway.

Only the voices.

Over a round darkwood table near the double bed, a hanging lamp dropped a faint spray of white, illuminating the table, its chair, and turning everything else to hulking shadow.

Only the voices.

*   *   *

Thanks for taking the time to talk to me, Stan.

Yeah, right. Like I've got other appointments, huh?

You could have said no.

I could have said a lot of things, but it won't make any difference. So, you going to let me see the . . . whatever you call it?

The transcript?

Yeah. Sorry. I knew that. I just couldn't think of it.

Sure, if you want. I don't know if it'll be done in time, though.

Breaks of the game. So what do you want to know?

Why you killed them.

That's it? Boy, you don't fool around.

What do you mean?

Half the people who come in here, they want to know if I hated my mother, if my father hit me, if I ran away from home a lot, things like that. It takes them forever to get to the good stuff.

I've already read the court transcripts, the police records, the profiles, and the evaluations. Not to mention the magazines and papers. I already know the answers, so why waste time and tape?

Because time, Mr. Bannock, is all I've got left. And not much of that, either.

Well, if you want to talk about them, be my guest. It's your show.

It's your book.

Whatever.

Okay. Hell, why not? No skin off my nose. No, I did not hate my mother. She did the best she could with what we had, which wasn't much, but she tried. My father was pretty strict. He spanked me now and then, like maybe three, four times a year, but only when I did something really bad. You know, deliberately smashed something up, stuff like that. Other than that, it was just rules of the house, you know? Curfews, chores, things like that. He did right by us, me and my sister and my mother. I never ran away, I never screwed my sister, I don't even remember getting detention more than once or twice.

Basically, an ordinary kid.

You got it.

So why did you kill those people?

IN THE MOOD

You want to know the truth, I've been thinking a lot about that these past few years. It'll sound funny, but the best thing I can come up with is—it seemed like a good idea at the time.

I don't . . . wait a minute . . . maybe that's the wrong question.

Nope, it's right all right. I mean, what else matters? You want to know why, I told you why. It's not all that complicated. I felt like it, that's all.

Eight times?

Look, Mr. Bannock, you can believe me or not, I really don't care. I felt like it. I did it. That's about all it is.

John stood in the bathroom, watching his reflection listen to the ghost. Stanley Arlington Hovinskal. A thirty-four-year-old man whose death-row cell had been vacated sixteen months ago. Nothing quite so dramatic as lights dimming or smoke drifting from beneath a specially made cap banded in iron or fingers convulsing or lips screaming.

He had died.

Period.

Only the voice remained.

You look a little confused, Mr. Bannock.

I can't help it, Stan, I'm sorry. You had a decent life, a decent job, you were getting ready to start a family, your fiancée had the wedding all planned . . . I'm sorry, but I just don't get it.

Well . . . things change.

Forgive me, Stan, really, but . . . let's face it, you pushed someone in front of a subway train in Washington, you cut the throats of three women and two men in the Midwest, you threw a teenager off a bridge in San Francisco, and you ran a traffic cop over four times with your car in Pennsylvania.

Yes. But it took me three years to do it all.

Is that important? The timing?

Ask the shrinks, Mr. Bannock, I wouldn't know. You know, one of them actually said I had spells? Like I was some kind of old Southern lady with the vapors or something? Some kind of state, I don't know what the word is.

Fugue.

19

Yeah, maybe. Another one, she wanted to tie it all up with the anniversaries of my parents' deaths. Didn't work. She had charts and everything, but she couldn't make it work.

Stan, I—

Look, Mr. Bannock, there's nothing all that complicated about this. I keep telling you. When I felt like it, I did it; when I didn't, I didn't.

No voices.

Nope.

No messages from another dimension.

God, no.

No seeing your parents' faces superimposed over those of your victims.

Are you kidding?

No demons.

Stan?

Stan?

John held his breath. The reflection cocked its head, waiting.

Are you scared, Stan?

No, not really. Not of dying, if that's what you mean. It's going to happen, and nothing I can do is going to stop it. Before, I kind of was, when the appeals were going on. Not now, though. I'm not going to like it, I wish it wasn't happening, I wish I could have more time to do things, but . . . you know. Price is price. I gotta pay it, no way around it.

But you are scared of something.

Oh yeah. Oh yeah.

You want to tell me what it is?

I don't have to, Mr. Bannock. I think you already know.

He exhaled loudly and lowered his head, hands braced on either side of the porcelain basin. A minute passed, and another, before he straightened and rolled his shoulders, feeling the joints pop softly. An unexpected yawn made him grin. His watch was in the other room, but he had a feeling it was close to midnight. He sniffed, rubbed his nose, and wondered if he was up for another ghost tonight.

This time he laughed aloud. Shortly. Sharply.

Hell, no.

Then maybe it was time to hit the downstairs bar before it closed. Something to help him sleep.

"Yeah," he whispered. "Right."

He stretched then, and strained to reach the ceiling with his fingers.

He almost made it.

He had always been tall, but never quite tall enough. Even in high school, the basketball players had tended toward giants, and he had never had enough weight to make it in football, or coordination for baseball. His hair was just long enough to cover his ears and his neck, dark hair flecked with early silver that seemed to sparkle in the right light, add years where they didn't belong; stray waves in front refused to stay off his forehead. In college he had tried dramatics, his soft rasping voice an oddity there, but the first time they slapped a beard on, his thick eyebrows and deep eyes, the high cheeks and prominent nose, made him look like Abraham Lincoln.

It gave him "Prez" as a nickname that lasted all four years.

"Fourscore," said the reflection.

"Up yours," said John, gave the face a grin and a lazy two-finger salute, and walked into the other room, picked up his wallet and key from the low dresser, reached for the suit jacket thrown on the bedspread . . . and stopped.

He stared at the tape recorder on the table.

That drink would be nice.

The company, even if it was only the bartender, would be nice.

But it wouldn't be just one drink. The first, taken quickly, would choke him and water his eyes, hardly any taste at all; the second, sipped, but not too slowly, would eventually numb his throat; and he wouldn't be able to keep track of those that followed. Certainly not the way he was feeling now. Certainly not if history were any kind of teacher at all.

With a grunt part relief, part regret, part sneering gratitude at this display of false strength, he dropped wallet and room key onto the bed and went to the window, pulled aside the drapes and looked out at the city, his hands still gripping the edges of the stiff cloth.

A few droplets shimmered on the wide pane, catching fragments of neon as they slipped down toward the sill.

He could see up a fair portion of Canal Street six stories below, watched a handful of pedestrians turn into the Quarter, watched two more leave, holding on to each other as they crossed the empty street. They were too small, however; they weren't real, just clumsy clockwork figures that would vanish when he looked away. The Quarter itself was little more than a hazy glow that turned the buildings around it black.

You need sleep, Patty scolded gently from the farthest darkened corner. *You'll drop if you don't rest.*

"I don't want to." He let himself sag a little, and the drapes held him up when he tightened his grip.

You've been here over a week, John. What are you trying to prove?

He didn't answer. This particular ghost was his own, and she could read his mind. Always could. From the first day they had met, she had known more things about him than he thought he knew about himself.

Then what are you going to do? Stand there all night until you fall through the window?

He chuckled, but he didn't move.

Come on, Ace, don't be stupid. Not now.

She was right, of course. He did need the sleep, he did need the rest, he did need some time away from all those ghosts. A duck of his head and glance under his arm, and he saw the briefcase set beneath the table. It was filled with tapes, the tapes filled with voices, the voices filled with words that had once been his dream—to put them all down in a book.

Conversations with the Dead, some such nonsense like that. The title, like the purpose, had long since fallen behind.

But like Stan had said, it seemed like a good idea at the time.

Until, at last, he had actually listened to the words. Not heard them, not transcribed them, but listened.

Really listened.

John? John, honey, what's the matter?

He looked down at the city, humidity blurring the lights, trails of aimless mist crawling across the river. The air conditioner kept the room cool, but now he felt cold.

A deep breath before he said, "I don't know, Patty. I don't know."

IN THE MOOD

*   *   *

He stands at a crossroads in lower Custer County, right in the center of the intersection. He has never seen land so flat in his life. Two lanes in four directions all the way to the horizon a million miles away and nothing on them but dust drifting out of the fields, out of the roadside ditches, lazily swirling across the blacktop. The wind isn't strong enough to lift it into clouds and not cool enough to dry the running sweat that stains his shirt. He knows he should be looking at horizon-deep corn waiting for the harvest; he knows he should be listening to the sound of giant machines that roll through the rows and take the stalks and swallow them; he knows there ought to be something out here but nothing.

There isn't.

The corn, what's left of it, what little has grown despite irrigation and prayers, is the color of the dust.

So is the sky.

So is the sun.

And the machines are still back in their sheds, in their barns, unused for the most part because there's little for them to do.

But right now, in this place, he doesn't care.

He's waiting for his son.

His hands cup his mouth and he calls, "Joey!"

A crow answers.

"Joey!"

A wobbling dust dervish patters and dies against his leg.

"Joey!"

In the heat and the dry air his voice doesn't carry.

He looks down all the roads, stares across the dead and dying fields, even checks the sky.

Damn, he thinks; how the hell can I find out—

He sees them.

Eastward, walking down the center line away from him—two figures, one not much taller than the other, holding hands, the shorter one every few steps playfully bumping into the other and dodging a playful slap.

He runs.

"Joey!"

Sweat blinds him and pebbles stab at his feet through the wafer soles of his worn shoes and the heat rests on his shoulders like a boulder made of cooling lava.

"Joey!"

They don't turn, and they don't get any closer.

This time, he swears to himself; this time I'll get them, this time I'm not going to lose them, this time I'll find out where the hell they've—

He runs.

"Joey!"

Two figures, black in the pale, hot sun, cutouts with legs and arms and heads and nothing else.

"Joey, damnit!"

A crow flies beside him, off his left shoulder. It's joined by another on the right, and he feels like some World War Two bomber on a suicide mission, escorts on the wings, and that makes him run faster because these escorts, these crows don't have the dead black eyes such birds usually had.

They're blue.

Startlingly vivid, almost blinding blue.

"Joey!"

Silent wings.

Silent feet.

"Joey!" he cries.

And finally yells, "Patty, wait up, it's me!"

While the crows with the live blue eyes edge closer, and begin to laugh.

John opened his eyes and groaned at the sunlight that made him squint. He had forgotten to close the drapes last night, and a glance at the clock radio told him it was barely past dawn. He supposed he could get up, but there wouldn't be much point. He had no desire to listen to the news this early in the day, and the hotel's coffee shop wouldn't be open yet.

More sleep would be the best thing, even if only for a couple of hours.

As he moved stiffly off the bed, he didn't bother to dwell on the dream. He had it at least three times a week in one form or another for what seemed his whole life. Last night he had been in Nebraska; a couple of nights ago he had been in Montana; the time before that he had been standing in Times Square, and the crows had been two taxis with dead men at the wheels.

Blue-eyed dead men, who laughed just like his son.

Just like the crows.

"You're cracking up, Ace," he muttered as he yanked the drapes together, leaving nothing left but a dusty slant of sun that cut across the foot of the bed.

But he wasn't crazy.

He knew it.

Cracking up would be too easy. In fact, it would be better if he did. That would make it all much more simple. Crazy equals safety. No one listens to a nut except other nuts. Safety in numbers.

He dropped back onto the bed, cupped his hands behind his head, and closed his eyes.

After a few moments, he began to laugh. Just a little. Deep in his throat.

At an image of his mother, standing on the back porch, hands on her skinny hips, glaring at him without anger, strands of graying hair dancing around her face, the face that eventually became his.

Good Lord in His fiery chariot, Johnny, she would say, what have you gotten yourself into now?

Fallen out of another tree while trying to swipe yet another apple; covered with smears and clots of weedy dirt like those creepy mud people in that old Flash Gordon movie; hair mussed and clothes ripped after wrestling with his friends; scraped and bruised after crawling through the drainpipes that burrowed under the road.

Nothing, Ma, he would answer lamely, and brace himself for when she would grab him by one ear, even when he was a teenager and taller by a head, and haul him inside, shove him toward the stairs with a sharp swat to his butt, and demand he clean himself up. Now. No arguments. Don't let her see him again until he was decent.

And while you're in the shower, John, pray that the Good Lord doesn't ride that fiery chariot up your miserable excuse for a spine and leave tracks.

He would laugh then as he ran for his room, and he laughed now as he turned over and tucked his hands under the pillow.

He would indeed pray while he was cleaning up, not so much that the chariot wouldn't leave its mark as for the hope that his father wouldn't find out he'd been in trouble again.

Knox Bannock wasn't a cruel man, but he was prairie hard. No nonsense, few frills. A well-liked, competent member of the Nebraska State Police who seldom relaxed that same mental discipline at home. Willing to allow John his youthful exuberance only as long as it didn't upset his mother.

Son, he would say, one tear from your mother's eye and you won't sit down for a week.

Praying in the shower was one way around it.

John smiled as he drifted, dozed, for no reason he could think of suddenly feeling a whole lot better.

Drifting.

Thinking that when he got up again, he would shower, change clothes, and have a decent breakfast for a change. No liquor, just food. Good, healthy food, even if it killed him. After that he would take a break, walk the riverfront, breathe some fresh air, eat a good healthy lunch, and maybe, just maybe, he wouldn't have to listen to the ghosts tonight.

Maybe, just maybe, he would finally find his son.

And the woman who took him away.

3

The Royal Cajun was an old hotel, lost amid the newer construction near the Quarter and along the river, with no real desire to call attention to itself. It had the requisite ironwork filigree and hanging ferns for its balconies, tall shutters for its windows on the lower floors, and a peeling weathered facade for those who didn't want the pretensions, or the glitter, or the constant noise of constant travelers.

The lobby was small, of hardwood and scattered fringed rugs, potted plants and brass spittoons; ceiling fans and squared mahogany pillars, gaslight fixtures on paneled walls, and low glass-top tables beside brocaded Queen Annes and upholstered club chairs faded and low and comfortably worn.

At the back was the registration desk, at least one clerk on duty at all times, seldom more, never less. To the left, in front, was the Bayou Café, open to the lobby, and beside it, behind dark paneling punctuated with etched tinted glass, the Cajun Lounge. To the right were two elevators and a gift shop. In the center, angling down in front of the elevators from the right, a wide carpeted staircase that led to the mezzanine, the meeting rooms, banquet rooms, and a restaurant where "proper attire required" justified its high evening prices.

John had gotten into the habit of taking the elevator to the mezzanine because he liked walking down the stairs, one hand gliding lightly along the curved bannister. A descent into silence and color. No matter how many people sat or waited in the lobby, all voices seemed muted. They nodded greetings rather than calling out; they conversed with heads or chairs close together, and the occasional burst of laughter was swallowed by the plants and the carpets, scattered by the fans.

On the bottom step he paused.

A glance left to the entrance showed him a white glare through which traffic shadows darted. The heat had returned, yesterday's rain already turned to steam. It made him uncomfortable just thinking about it. It definitely helped him decide not to go out to eat.

The café was nearly empty just an hour shy of noon, and for that small miracle he was grateful. There was something about him—the Lincoln Factor, he had once called it sourly—that made perfect strangers want to pull up a chair and tell him their life stories. All the details. All the miseries. Things, he guessed, they wouldn't even tell their shrinks or spouses. It both amused and appalled him, and he seldom had the nerve to tell them to go away.

The room was done in shrimp and white, with swampland depicted in murals on all the walls, complete with Spanish moss and gators, herons and knobby cypress. He took the booth farthest from the entrance, touched his hip pocket to be sure he still had his wallet, and reached over to a neighboring table to grab a newspaper a patron had left behind.

"Morning, Mr. Bannock," the waitress said. A medium-size woman made tall by her hair, a mass of rich auburn all sweeps and curls. A pink-and-white uniform with a skirt that only flirted with her knees. A pleasant face, whose angles would sharpen as she grew older. "Usual?"

"Please, Lisse." He smiled up at her. "Heck of a rain last night."

Thin lips pouted. "Shoo, ain't going to do nothing. Too hard and too short." She giggled. "Just like my ex."

He laughed as he was expected to; as, as a matter of fact, he didn't mind doing. She was far from beautiful, but attractive just the same. The joke about her ex was just that—a joke. As best he could figure, she didn't even have an ex-boyfriend. They had flirted since that first morning last week, a courtship safe and distant until, two days ago, she had deliberately mistotaled the bill in his favor. He had a feeling that if he asked her out, she'd be naked before they reached the elevator.

She leaned over and tapped the front page with her pencil. The scent of fresh soap and perfume; a view, if he chose, of what lurked between the two open buttons of her top.

"Bad stuff there, you know?"

IN THE MOOD

A story below the fold, yet another harrowing account of starvation in central Africa, deprivation and cannibalism in southern India, and China's continual denial that its people were desperately short of food. Calls for humanitarian aid; demands for relief.

She tapped the paper again. "I heard someplace in Europe they were rationing meat, can you beat it?"

"Germany," he said absently. And added, "Which reminds me, I'm hungry."

"Oh . . . you!" She rapped him on the skull with the pencil, giggled, and walked away.

He didn't dare look. She was a little too thin for his taste, but what she had she knew how to move. And she knew he enjoyed it.

His eyes closed briefly before he switched to the sports section. I must be getting old, he thought, checking baseball's countdown to the World Series; it's getting too easy to pass something like that up.

Out in the lobby a telephone rang softly.

His stomach grumbled, obscenely loud, and he looked around quickly as if there were someone to overhear. He should have come down as soon as he had gotten up, but the ghosts had been too strong. He had already taken three hours to continue transcribing the latest tape into his laptop, not listening this time. Just typing the words. A woman awaiting execution in Angola who had poisoned thirteen people. Her lucky number, she had said with a half-hearted grin. Fourteen, and she was sure she would never have been caught.

You know, Mr. Bannock, I ain't a stupid woman. I know better, you know what I mean? Thirteen, fourteen, ain't no difference but one, but I just knew deep down that one more would make it all right. Wouldn't though, would it? Would have been just another notch, so to speak.

Ruesette, the way I read this, you didn't even try.

Nope.

Why not?

Didn't feel like it.

*   *   *

Lisse poured him a cup of coffee.

A heavyset elderly man in a Panama hat and rumpled white suit waited patiently at the hostess station until Lisse finally noticed him and brought him to a table on the far side of the room. Once he was settled, she pushed into the kitchen, returned a few seconds later with John's meal—sausage, scrambled eggs, hash browns, orange juice, a side order of toast fairly soggy with fresh butter.

Without invitation she sat opposite him, scribbling on the bill. "That stuff's gonna kill you, you know."

"My heart can take it."

"You still working on that book?"

He nodded.

His first mistake happened on the second morning, when he'd brought his laptop down so he could work while he ate. She had been impressed, and he had been in need of impressing someone. Before he knew it, she was clipping murder stories from the papers, from magazines at the beauty parlor, and telling him stories she had heard from the friend of a friend who had a cousin in Baton Rouge who knew this guy in the sheriff's office.

It passed the time, but it drove him nuts.

Yet she had been genuinely concerned when she found out he was interviewing a serial killer at Angola.

"Lord, that's dangerous work," she called it in a hushed voice. "They all know each other, you know. You got to be real careful around people like that."

For a change he had kept his comments to himself.

She finished the bill, turned it over, and slid it across the table. Leaned back and looked at him through eyes half closed.

"You're going soon?"

He kept chewing, holding up a hand to tell her to hang on, he'd be done in a second. The question had startled him. He hadn't really thought about it, but it was true. With Ruesette's interview over, there was really no reason for him to stick around much longer. There was the money, for one thing; he didn't have much left. For another, there was the book.

What was left of it, that is.

He swallowed, took some coffee, and finally, reluctantly, nodded.

She sighed without making a sound, folding her arms under her breasts.

"What's the matter?"

She shrugged with a tilt of her head. "I don't know. Kind of used to having you around, that's all, I guess." She glanced over to the old man in the Panama hat. "Folks come here, they don't stay very long. You're kind of a treat, you know what I mean?"

He forced a laugh. "My ex-wife didn't think so."

Another shrug, this time with her shoulders. "Her loss."

"Damn right."

Her lips almost smiled as she slid out of the booth. "So you let me know when's your last day, huh? I'll fix you something special. My own self."

No innuendo; just a promise.

"I'll do that."

The smile was there, rueful and resigned, before she walked away. No sway this time.

John stared at his plate. Well, he thought, you have a real knack, don't you. She's not looking long-term, you dope. If the choice is between you and the guy in the white suit . . .

He finished, Lisse poured him another cup, and he sat back, watching the languid motion of guests in the lobby. Like watching a fish tank, different species drifting here and there, more than likely ending up at registration for a quick question, a search for messages, and drifting again. Once in a while vanishing into the glare.

Lisse fussed behind the counter at the hostess station, changing the breakfast menus for lunch, absently making change for the old man who clearly wanted to talk, picking up the phone there to take an order for room service.

He couldn't stand it any longer.

When she finally turned in his direction, he lifted a hand.

She ignored it.

He waggled his fingers.

She ignored him.

He warned himself he was making a huge mistake. There was no need, no reason to pursue this. She was a waitress, he had been a steady customer, that's all there was to it. Feeling guilty was dumb. It made no sense. For God's sake, he had spent the past two years practically living with people who killed other people in bunches, in droves, just so he could see his damn name on the cover of a damn book his own mother probably wouldn't buy.

What was the point?

He blinked.

The point of what?

Ruesette, a man I talked to—

For the book?

Yes.

He gonna be in it?

I think so.

Me, too?

I would say so, yes.

Wow. Hope I'm around to read it.

I do, too, Ruesette, I do, too. But hang on a minute, okay? This man I talked to, up in Michigan, he told me that while he was . . . waiting—

Death row, Mr. Bannock. You can say it. It's okay.

Yeah, well . . . he said something that has me wondering. He said he wasn't afraid of dying because he knew God knew it was all right. A woman, not much older than you, she said almost the same thing. In New York. I know from talking to you, from reading your files, that you were a church-going woman. You think God is all right with you, too?

Oh, sure.

Why? I mean, Ruesette, you killed all those people. Do you mean you've made your peace and you think God has forgiven you?

Well, I don't know about the forgiveness part, Mr. Bannock, but I know it's all right with Him. I mean, it was all part of the plan, right? I mean, that was the whole point.

He blinked again, angry that the ghosts should be visiting him now. Out here. Where he wanted nothing more than a little respite, a little peace. Somehow it just didn't seem fair. No one had told him it would be like this.

No one had told him there would be something wrong with the project. A flaw. He knew it was there, he could sense it, but he couldn't pin it down. Probably, as his mother often complained, it was right there in front of him, plain as the nose on his face. But he couldn't see the damn thing.

He just couldn't see it.

Unless, of course, he was wrong, and it was only all those men and women waiting to die that was getting to him.

Making him crazy.

What he needed was a major diversion, something to keep the ghosts at bay until he could think more clearly, gain some decent perspective.

What he needed was Patty and Joey.

But he, and the book, were the reasons they were gone in the first place.

He stared at the dregs of the coffee in his cup and grunted when he saw liquor there instead. Could taste it. Could smell it. Could feel it in his belly. Doing its job. It would be a diversion, all right. It would certainly get him focused on something else.

He looked away in disgust—you're pathetic, Bannock, really pathetic—and was distracted by soft insistent voices. It took a moment before he saw the old man standing at the counter, hat in both hands, smiling at Lisse. It wasn't a pleasant smile. It was the smile of a man who always got his way and brooked no refusals.

Without thinking, John grabbed his check and hurried over.

"Really, sir," Lisse said, and shook her head emphatically.

"We all have options, my dear," the old man said. Insisted. Politely.

"Hi," John said, dropping his check onto the counter.

"Enjoy your meal?" she asked with professional politeness, ringing the charges on the register.

"Absolutely. Thanks."

"My pleasure."

The old man watched him.

John could feel it.

"Shall I put this on your bill?"

"Please, thanks."

"Young lady," said the old man, scolding. "Please. We were talking."

John turned away, and turned back. "Oh, and don't forget tonight. You think seven, seven-thirty will be okay?"

Lisse didn't falter. Her professional smile became a personal one. "Sure, John, that'll be just fine. Make it seven-thirty, though, give me some time to get ready. Nothing fancy, right?"

"Absolutely." He touched her arm, said, "Good afternoon," to the old man, and walked toward the staircase. He heard nothing behind him, but he felt it again—the old man's stare. He was tempted to check over his shoulder; he was tempted to head straight for the desk and tell them he was leaving now, get his bill ready; he was tempted to head straight for the river and wade in until the current took him.

Instead, he felt a curious giddiness that fluttered around his stomach, and a familiar but long dormant grin fighting to shape his lips.

Jesus Christ, he thought in a rush of panic and delight, there's no way out of it now. I'm going on a date.

Halfway up the staircase he couldn't help it—he looked back.

The man in the white suit was gone. Lisse was out of sight. The clerks were gone. The lobby was deserted.

On the registration counter the telephone rang softly.

No one answered.

4

Dorina Castro wondered what it would cost if, the next time she was offered, she refused to attend an industry conference. Not that it would be a realistic option. But assuming, just for kicks, they came to her and gave her the opportunity to decline. What would it cost her? What harm would it do? Everyone knew these four- and five-day exercises in corporate education were only excuses to get out of the office. Everyone knew that once the day's activities were over, the watchword wasn't study, it was party. As fast and as hard as you can without throwing up on one of the execs.

Be honest, she told herself as she dried the sweat from her legs; what would be the worst that could happen?

For the first time that day she laughed. Genuinely laughed.

She was alone in the hotel's health spa, the training tables and machines deserted, the only sound the rippling of the pool on the other side of the translucent glass wall. It suited her just fine. As soon as the attendant trainer realized she knew what she was doing, and didn't much care for his muscles and smile, he had left her alone, fussing instead over the others, praising form and correcting technique while they panted on the treadmills that did most of the work for them, lifted free weights that nearly popped their neck muscles, or bragged about the laps they were able to do at home.

They also spent a lot of time glancing at her. Checking her out in the mirrors that lined two of the walls, making small talk, asking if she needed help, and posing as if they had something to pose with.

She laughed again and draped a towel around her neck.

Actually, it was kind of flattering, all that attention, all those signals only a baby wouldn't understand. She didn't mind it because her attitude more than anything she said drew the lines clearly. Flirting was all right; anything else was out of the question. The best ones knew it and abided; a couple of them, however, were either too stupid or too full of themselves to pay proper attention. They were the price she had to pay.

And that was all right too.

She slipped into her flip-flops, drew on her robe, and after making sure she had replaced all the equipment she had used, she hurried out into the hall. Shivered when the air-conditioning slithered over her bare legs. Wished again she had remembered to bring her sweatpants with her. It wasn't far to the elevator alcove, but she hated being seen like this—leotards cut high, legs gleaming, long brown hair pulled back in a ponytail that emphasized her high forehead, and her large dark eyes. The flush on her cheeks. The bead of sweat she could feel in the hollow of her throat.

In the spa that was okay; out here, it made her feel much too exposed.

It didn't make sense, she knew it, but she was glad when the elevator arrived in a hurry and she was able to step in without anyone seeing.

That lasted to the tenth floor, when Chet Rainer joined her, slacks and polo shirt and a leather briefcase for his laptop. She stared at the doors, could feel him beside her, checking her over. One of the Gonad Boys.

"Going to the presentation, Dorina?"

She nodded. "Soon as I shower and change."

He chuckled deep in his throat. "You only have five minutes, kiddo. Why don't you just go as you are?"

She smiled. "I don't think so."

"Tell you the truth," he said, voice lowered to invite her into a conspiracy of two, "it'd be a lot easier watching you than old Sanborn playing with those damn slides."

"Well, thank you, sir," she said, ducking her head in a mock curtsy. "I do appreciate the compliment. But I'm still going to change."

At fourteen he left, reached back suddenly and held the doors open with one hand. "Sure you won't change your mind?"

She couldn't believe it; he actually waggled his eyebrows.

She stared; he shrugged; the doors closed, and she muttered, "Prick."

A slow ride to twenty-three, just her and the red numbers ticking off the floors.

The strange thing was, she honestly didn't mind going to these things.

True, it did get her away from the office; true, it didn't hurt to have participation noted in her folder; and true, she found most of the seminars and conferences, the lectures and presentation boring to the extreme, especially since she already knew most of what she heard.

Yet she also, once in a while, actually learned something new. Something she might use. Something that would give her the edge over the men who patronized her and figuratively patted her on the head and suggested by innuendo and subtle deed that the only way she would break through the glass ceiling was by rising toward it on her back.

So far it hadn't happened.

So far she had done all right for herself.

So far it gave her great pleasure to show those blow-dried sons of bitches a hint of T and A while, at the same time, she dug their corporate graves back home. She supposed that made her something of a bitch.

She also supposed she didn't give a damn.

At twenty-three the doors slid open and she stepped out, feeling good, loose, breathing easy, muscles tuned, brain oxygen-fed and ready to go. She turned left and strode out of the alcove, listening to the sounds of the hotel rise and fall around her, muted and distant, moving on automatic and automatically moving as far right as she could without actually touching the wall.

Ten paces later she stopped.

This was stupid.

There was nothing to be afraid of.

The hotel was built around a central atrium that rose twenty-five floors before it reached its first ceiling. Each floor had a gallery that overlooked the atrium, with rooms and other corridors on three sides, the fourth side mostly slanting windows that let in the sun.

She was alone. No housekeeping carts, no one leaving their rooms, no one strolling around the gallery, leaning over, and calling to someone they could see on the floors below.

Deep breath, Dory, she ordered; deep breath.

When she finally moved again, she allowed herself to drift toward the gallery's inside wall, thick and chest-high, with black plastic planters fastened to the outside. To see straight down she would have to lean well over the planters or find a gap between them.

Every morning, twice every afternoon, twice each night, she did her best to look, trying to ignore the chill that grew in her stomach and the way her legs wobbled and the way her heart doubled its rate.

Five times a day, telling herself that unless she was monumentally stupid, there was no way she could fall over and fly to the lobby floor. No way the wall and planters would collapse beneath her. No way she would die. No way at all.

As she reached the first corner, turned left and allowed her left hand to trail along the top of the wall, she heard the ping of an elevator stopping on her floor.

Another thirty feet to the next corridor.

She stopped and looked across the gap, watching the inside, glass-walled, bullet-shaped car glide away without a sound. Down; trailing cable behind it, the tiny white bulbs that outlined its form making her dizzy just watching them disappear.

Down.

She saw him then.

Chet Rainer, ambling toward her, smiling broadly, a hand lifted in a tentative wave. The other hand making sure all those blond waves were in place, that the polo shirt was adequately molded to his torso. Casual gestures, designed to encourage her to look him over, it's okay, we're all adults here, and we all know what we want once the boring crap's over.

He would say he had been sent to make sure she would be there, that her presence, while not required, would certainly be noted by those who counted.

He had tried it once before. He had let her know that while he was, in fact, a homeboy and she was on his turf, he didn't hold it against her that she was from the North. An offer, after the meeting, to show her around town. A drink, perhaps, or dinner. Southern hospitality, in the flesh.

She had turned him down, politely, and he had taken it well. "Maybe next time," he had said.

In your wet dreams, she'd thought.

"Hey," he called softly, voice not quite echoing across the gap. "Dorina, wait up, okay?"

She hadn't moved.

She wasn't about to.

At the corner he leaned over, shook his head as if amazed at the view, and came on, grinning shyly. "Don't mean to rush you," he said, letting that Georgia accent turn to syrup before her eyes. "Being Saturday and all, and knowing damn well we're not up for this crap, they're cracking the whip."

Her eyes narrowed as he approached, pausing again to lean over at the hip, shaking his head again, then looking sideways at her. Baldly. Appraising. Straightening slowly as she unbelted the robe and let it fall open.

"I won't be long," she assured him.

"No problem." He leaned back against the wall. "I'll wait here, if you don't mind."

Invite me in is what he meant.

"Man, you're still sweating," he said, a gesture with his right hand. "You work out hard." Admiration. "It shows, too, if you don't mind me saying so."

She smiled and made a muscle with her right arm, looked at it, then looked at him sideways. "I try."

He laughed silently. "Want to arm wrestle?"

She took a step toward him, then away and went to the wall. "Maybe." Looking straight across the gap was all right. Even glancing down a couple of floors wasn't all that bad. Her fingers poked at each section of the empty planter. "They need flowers, you know? Everything's white around here; it needs a little color."

He moved to stand beside her. Not too close. He was very good. "It's that redecorating they've been doing. Haven't gotten up this far yet, I guess."

"Ah." She nodded. And let herself shudder.

"What . . . ?" His turn to nod, as if exposing her secret and telling her he wouldn't spill it to the others. "Can't take the height, huh?"

"No." She folded her arms across her chest as if abruptly cold. "I can fly, I can cross bridges, but this stuff . . ." She shuddered again.

"There's a trick," he said, winking at her. "As long as you can feel the wall against you, it's okay. Like a psychological thing, you know?"

She frowned. "I don't get it."

He shrugged. "You know. Like this." He made a show of bracing his lower body against the wall, gripped the inner edge with both hands, took a deep breath for show, and leaned out, stretching hard so he could see over the planter. "As long as you're in contact with the wall, you feel grounded. No, anchored."

His voice drifted as if he were whispering.

"You want to try it? I'll hold you. No funny stuff, I swear."

Then he laughed and raised his left leg. "See? No sweat."

"Right," she said.

It didn't take very long, almost no effort at all.

She reached down and grabbed his right ankle, snapped it up as she shoved against on his left shoe.

The planter cracked and splintered under his weight.

He didn't start screaming for almost two full seconds.

She walked down the corridor to her room, unlocked the door, stepped in, and frowned. "Damn," she said. "I'm going to be late."

5

"So," Lisse said, "you're a writer, huh?"

John grinned. "Actually, I'm a CPA."

A small place off St. Peter, open to the street, barely large enough for its seven tiny tables, barely large enough for its bar. No band, just a cleared space against the bare brick wall in back for a stool, an amplifier, and an old steel guitar resting on its stand.

A perfect place, if only because it was clear neither had expected the other to make good on the charade for the old man in white.

She stared. "You're kidding. A CPA?"

The sun was down, the sky not quite dark. In the streets a few people, not many but growing, walking without haste from corner to corner, plastic cups in one hand, plastic plates of food in the other. Standing a while and listening to the rock and country and Dixie and lounge that pounded and drifted from the open-face bars. Applause and laughter and moving on to the next, lingering here and there, stepping inside for a while, listening, always listening before moving on.

But at a distance, over the voices, beyond the running lights of the strip shows and the melodramatic lights of tourist voodoo, never quite tempting, never quite repelling, there was always the blues.

A harmonica's cry, a clarinet's call, a bass guitar vibrating softly like a silk and sticky web; more at home here than the other sounds, the other songs, no matter what the posters said; more at home with paint peeling from moldy plaster walls, soggy litter on the streets, broken cobblestones, canted doors, a single lamp in a high window blurred by rippling muslin curtains.

John heard it.

He almost felt it.

"Hello?" Lisse reached over to touch his arm. Her hair was down, spilling over her shoulders, her white linen shirt. She was older in here. Pleasantly so. "I say something wrong?"

"No, sorry." A brief, apologetic smile. He looked at his empty plate, glanced at her, and forced a shudder.

She laughed.

He hadn't expected to have to pull the legs and heads off the shrimp he had ordered, and her teasing hadn't made his stomach feel any better. Finally she had done it for him, deftly, chattering the whole time about absolutely nothing that mattered and making him feel welcome.

It was an odd sensation these days.

"So, you going to tell me, or do I have to guess?"

"Not much to tell. I did mostly taxes—"

It was her turn to shudder comically, hair rippling, her eyes giving the lie to the scowl at her lips.

"—and one of my clients was this guy, he's about sixty now, who used to be a librarian until he figured he could write better than some of the books he had to buy. He studied it, you see. He figured he could make more writing nonfiction than fiction." He spread his arms. "And he did. Started with some articles for magazines and such, then wrote a book that did all right, wrote another, and the next thing you know . . ." He snapped his fingers. "The man's got more money than he knows what to do with."

"That," said Lisse solemnly, "would never be my problem."

For seven years John had watched the receipts and forms cross his desk, watched the blanks fill in, watched the refunds flow, and three days after his thirtieth birthday, tax season over and a chance to breathe for a change, he told George Trout he didn't think he could stand doing this for the rest of his life.

George claimed he knew how he felt.

John didn't doubt it. Not for a second.

Patty, on the other hand, told him it was only turning thirty that had made him think that way. It would pass. He was good. The money was there and getting better. Besides, Ace, what the hell else are you good for? She hadn't put it quite that way, of course, but the meaning was the same.

"No kids?" Lisse asked as she raised a hand—two fingers, two beers.

"Not then, no."

"She have a job?"

"Real estate shark."

She frowned.

"That's what I called her. She had a way . . . I don't know how to explain it. She had a way of spotting people who were ready to spend without really thinking. Like a shark circling, see? Her commissions were amazing. She had firms all over the state and down into Kentucky begging her to come with them."

"So . . . so you could have quit for a while, no trouble?"

He could have. He hadn't. That wasn't how he had been raised. Old-fashioned, without question, but he knew no other way.

Until, one afternoon, George had presented him with a challenge. Take some notes he had, write an article, he was in the middle of a book and couldn't take the time and couldn't pass up the money. George would show him the ropes, give him all the help he needed.

It worked.

It worked four times.

But four times do not a career make.

The beers arrived, and John lifted his bottle in a silent toast. Lisse didn't respond.

"What?"

She nodded, and he twisted around just in time to see the old man in the white suit, standing on the sidewalk on the other side of the narrow street. The pedestrian traffic had increased dramatically, and it took a moment before he realized it was indeed the same man from the hotel.

There, in a gap, hat in one hand.

There again, in another gap, hat on his head.

And gone.

He turned back. "I guess he has a crush on you, huh?"

Lisse cupped her hands around her bottle, frowning, staring at the label. "No, I don't think so."

"Oh, come on," he said lightly. The way he was hitting on you? The guy ought to be ashamed of himself."

A hesitation; a debate.

"He wasn't," she said at last. "He was asking about you."

John heard approaching music and shifted his chair until he was beside her, the better to hear her.

On the street a moment later, a walkin' band headed down toward the river, taking its time, no marching. Black men in fresh white suits, just horns and clarinets, with a tall white man in back, base drum with no lettering strapped to his chest. Several women, mostly black, in fancy white dresses glittering with rhinestones, winding in and out of the band, strolling to the beat, snapping their fingers, grinning at the pedestrians who began to tag along.

John recognized the tune but didn't know the name. He was pretty sure it was Glenn Miller. Maybe "Tuxedo Junction." Maybe "String of Pearls." It didn't really matter. It just didn't seem right for this place, this time.

"He wanted to meet you," Lisse said quietly, forcing him to lean closer, smelling the beer and the perfume and the lingering spice of their meal. "That was before, when he was sitting down."

"You should have sent him over."

"I told him, just go on over. He's a nice guy, I said, you can just go over. He won't bite your head off.

"He didn't want to. Said he was shy. Said he wanted to meet you. I didn't push it. I had work to do, and besides, he gave me the shivers. I didn't like those eyes. It's like you can see right through them, you know? So he tries again, and I ignore him, pretend like I don't hear him.

"Then he's up there paying his bill, and he says he wants to talk to you. I tell him, it ain't my job to go around introducing folks to each other. Not my job. You want to talk to him, you go right ahead. No skin off my nose.

"He says, that ain't right, not the way he does things. He needs an introduction. He tells me I have to do it. I say, didn't your momma teach you any manners? I don't have to do anything, especially not for someone I don't know.

"He gets mad, you know? He looks at me, gives me a look that really gets me going. Like, I'm a somebody and you're nothing but a waitress, you mind your place, young lady, and you do what you're told. He calls me young lady, but I know that tone. I've heard it all my life. It doesn't say young lady, it says child. Go on, child, obey your elders, that's a good girl.

"So I told him flat out, I said, I don't have to do anything I don't want to, y'hear? Besides, I already told you, it's not my place. You want to meet him so bad, you got two good legs, use them and do it yourself.

"He gets this look, then, like he smells something bad, and he tells me I'm making a mistake.

"I say, look, it comes down to it, I don't have a choice, okay? It ain't my job to bother the customers. I ain't going to get fired just for you.

"That's when you come up, when he tells me we all have options, or some such nonsense like that. Man about drove me crazy, acting like that. Just about drove me crazy."

The walkin' band was gone.

The music faded.

John tapped a finger on the table, thinking, wondering who the hell that guy was. He had never seen him before in his life. Unless he was a lawyer for one of the convicts he'd been talking to. But he'd met most of them, little more than simple intermediaries to get him into each prison.

He sniffed, rubbed a finger under his nose. "I wonder how he knew I was writing a book."

Lisse shrugged. "I don't know. I didn't ask."

Until she answered, he hadn't realized he'd spoken aloud. He checked the street again, then felt a grin playing with his lips. He looked at her and said, "So Lisse, you up for an adventure?"

"What?"

He stood quickly, signaling the waiter as he drained the rest of his bottle. "Come on."

"Where?"

"Where else? The guy wants to meet me, he's following us around, let's go find out what he wants."

She shook her head quickly. "I don't think so."

He put a hand on her shoulder and let the grin out. "Oh, come on, why not?" He pulled lightly, and reluctantly she got to her feet, waiting stiffly while he paid the bill, drawing back when he took her elbow and led her to the sidewalk. "Okay, which way?"

To the left the street was mostly residential. Apartments, he assumed, with garages on the first floor he figured must have been stables in the old days, however long ago they had been. Jackson Square was to the right, two blocks down. Not crowded, but enough people to prevent him from seeing very far. It shouldn't be all that difficult to find a chubby old man in a white suit and Panama hat.

But at Bourbon Street she balked.

"What?" he said, trying to see over the heads of the pedestrians wandering in the street. The walkin' band had finished, and most were against the fence that walled in the central garden. White suits and dresses all over the place.

"I can't do this, John. Please, let's go somewhere else."

Smiling, he grabbed her shoulders. "Listen, Lisse, for the past couple of years I've been all over the damn country, talking to people, most of whom have been executed by now. That may sound interesting or exciting to you, but believe me, it's not. This," and he swept one hand out, "is something else. This is an adventure."

She didn't smile back. She moved her shoulders slightly, just enough to free them, and shook her head. "I can't. I got a bad feeling. I can't."

He pleaded with her with a look, but she only shook her head again and hurried away without looking back.

"Lisse!" he called.

Nothing.

A step to follow her, a step toward the sidewalk, and he cursed the choice she had forced him to make. A slow turn; nothing. When he looked back toward Canal, she was gone, and so were most of the tourists.

"Damn," he muttered, knowing that even if he caught up with her, there'd be nothing for him with her tonight. The old man had spooked her, and he, with his usual ham-hands, had completed the process.

He walked for over an hour, checking around the Square, walking along the levee, finally deciding there was no sense trying to find him in any of the bars in the Quarter. The old guy, for some reason, didn't seem the type. It wasn't until he was on his way back to the hotel that it hit him:

Maybe he was a lawyer for Patty.

That almost goaded him into a trot, until he reminded himself that she already had a lawyer, back up in Illinois. And he wasn't old, and he wasn't fat, and he claimed, like everyone else, that he didn't know where Patty was.

Or even if she still had the boy.

His son.

He had also suggested, in tones not at all bothering to coat the condescension, that John give up on the book and get his butt back behind his desk and make a few bucks for a change. There was no guarantee, but that might bring his family back together again.

John stopped at the foot of Canal, looked up, looked at the river, and said, "The hell with it."

He crossed over, moving slowly, feeling the evening's heat on his shoulders, the sweat that chilled his chest and spine. When he entered the hotel, he had decided it was time to move on. One more stop, in Texas, and he would be done.

He would go home.

He would call George and let him know all the talking was done, it was time to get to work.

He had one hand on the banister before he realized he was alone.

The lobby, dimly lit, was empty.

No one in the café, no muffled music from the lounge, no one behind the front desk. No voices from the mezzanine.

He took a step up, and the telephones rang.

The phone at the cafe, two on side tables, the one at the desk. Not in unison; each one different, each at its own pace. The result was less cacophony than carillon.

They rang softly.

Puzzled, he waited a few seconds, thinking one of the clerks would soon pop out of the office, or the hotel operator would pick up, or someone would hurry out of the lounge, or the kitchen.

They rang softly.

He shrugged when no one appeared, took another step up, and stopped, turned, listening to the ringing.

Another adventure, he thought; pick up the phone and see who's there.

Without bothering to tell himself he was being an idiot, he hurried over to the desk, leaned over, saw no bodies on the floor, called out once in hopes a clerk would hear him, then shrugged and picked up the receiver.

"Hello?"

All the phones stopped ringing.

No one answered, but someone was there.

"This is the Royal Cajun hotel, there's no one here to answer. You want me to take a message?"

Someone was there.

"Hello?"

"Well, hello there, Ace. You having fun yet?"

It was Patty.

He yanked the receiver away from his ear, gaped at it, and returned it to his ear.

"Give it up, Ace. Give it up, it's too late."

And the phone went dead.

6

1

He knew he was sitting down, and he knew he was floating.

An old sensation, a comfortable one.

He widened his eyes as far as they would go, narrowed them into a squint, and focused on the glass between his hands. There were colors in there not in any rainbow, and he tried like hell to put a name to them, until they blurred and he had to look away because they made his eyes water.

Floating.

Slowly he moved his head, looking around, trying to make sense of the shapes and the lights. Listening to a honky-tonk piano in the corner, soft and sad.

Floating.

He didn't bother to check his watch; he knew he wouldn't be able to read it.

Hours, maybe, since he had spoken with Patty.

No; since Patty had spoken with him.

Hours, days, who cares, it was all right despite the scare because he was floating now, away from it all, and wouldn't have to think about it until he was ready. He wouldn't have to wonder how she had known where he was, wouldn't have to wonder where she was now, wouldn't have to wonder why the Patty who had called on all those phones was so different from the ghost Patty who followed him from state to state, hotel room to hotel room, keeping him sane.

Floating.

God, he loved floating.

Everything made sense up here. The Truth Of It All drifted past him like puffed lazy clouds on a soft summer day. He recognized it. He memorized it. He watched kaleidoscope rays from the fat prism sun illuminate it all and show him the Way.

It made him laugh at its simplicity.

It made him angry because he could never remember it once the floating was over. Only hints and glimpses of what he had learned, like hints and glimpses of a dream that came and went just before waking.

It made him grin when fingers touched his shoulder and slid away.

"John?"

Voices, too. Once in a while there were voices, celestial, singing words he couldn't always understand but it didn't matter because they were so beautiful.

So indescribably beautiful.

Like the music, that piano, playing somewhere in the clouds. Not chamber, not classical, but a soft insistent honky-tonk sound, a blues sound, a fitting sound that required no words because there were no words for a sound like that, for the simple chords and the simple beat and the way they fit into the kaleidoscope like glittering pieces of small bleeding jewels.

Beautiful enough to make him want to cry.

Beautiful enough to make him want to scream.

Something cool closed around his wrist.

He stared at it for a long while before he recognized it as a hand, long fingers and no rings. Carefully, because it wasn't easy to stay afloat if you made sudden moves, he tracked the hand to a wrist to a flowing white sleeve to a narrow round shoulder to a cloud of intense auburn that sent wisps of itself across the face of an angel.

She spoke.

He couldn't hear her.

She spoke again, and he wanted to weep.

An arm around his waist.

The angel would guide him, he knew that, and he let her.

Floating.

Music fading.

Floating.

From wherever he was to a new place now, forced to use his useless legs, swimming through the air that was at once warm and cool.

She spoke to him. Gently. Sadly. The arm still so strong at his waist that he leaned into her and felt how soft and hard she was. A true angel. An angel who would sift through the kaleidoscope and show him the sense of it, the patterns of it, the melody and words of it.

He licked his lips and tried to answer when he heard her ask a question, but his tongue wouldn't work and his throat wouldn't work and all he could do was grin while a single tear made its way down his cheek.

Floating.

Using his legs to propel him. Concentrating so fiercely he felt an ache in his chest and a tiny stab behind his eyes.

But he wouldn't let her down, this guardian guiding angel. He couldn't. It would be wrong. It would be as wrong as what he had done to Patty and his son. His fault. It had to have been his fault, or they wouldn't have been gone that morning in May, a note on the kitchen table beneath his favorite coffee mug. His fault, or Joey would have called him before now and told him that he loved him.

The bizarre thing was, the thing he couldn't understand despite the Truth floating with him, was why she had left. Why she had taken the boy. One year, maybe less, that's all, he had told her. They had plenty of money, and she was still working, but as soon as he had showed her the proposal Trout had prepared, she had freaked, had declared that she didn't know him anymore, that he wasn't the man she had married, that this wasn't negotiable.

He wouldn't do it, and that was that.

She wouldn't allow it.

His fault.

All his fault, because he had yelled for the first time in their marriage, losing it completely, demanding to know what was so wrong if money wasn't the issue.

His fault, because Joey started crying.

His fault, because he had done it anyway.

Sinking. Slowly sinking.

The angel sang then, and he tightened his neck and he tightened his jaw and he heard her sing, "Hang on, hang on, it won't be but a minute."

Floating again, upward now and slowly, smelling the scent of the angel and wondering if that was blasphemy, if angels were supposed to let others know how they smelled, how they felt, how amazingly powerful they were to keep men like him floating for what seemed like forever.

And drifting, his legs back in use, his eyes without focus, dim light and bright light, and the angel singing constantly, like a lullaby, like a hymn that made him want to sing along, but all he could say was, "Angel. Angel."

While the angel sang, "That's right, John, that's right, just a few more steps, that's right, that's right."

A moment's new drifting, almost sinking, that frightened him because her protective arm left him, and he flailed until she sang again and took him again and guided him into a darkness, floating while she sang, and falling while she held him, and staring up at absolutely nothing while her hands fluttered over him and a miracle happened.

What once was weight was now weightless.

What once was wrong was now perfectly all right.

And when she sang in his ear, "Sleep now, get some sleep," he grinned and sang back, "I think angels are God."

2

It didn't take very long.

One minute he was saying something weird about God, the next he was sound asleep, or passed out; it didn't make much difference to her as long as he was all right.

She fussed for a few minutes. Turning on the bathroom light in case he needed it. Draping the coverlet over him because the room was too cold. Dropping his clothes onto the chair by the table without, she hoped, wrinkling them too much. Adjusting the drapes to keep as much light out as she could. Picking up her purse where she'd dropped it when she came in and putting it on the table where, she saw, he had a tape recorder and one of those portable computers.

Then standing at the foot of the bed and wondering what in God's name she was going to do next.

Dumping a drunk into his bed wasn't exactly what she had had in mind for tonight.

Of course, coming back here hadn't been high on her list of how to spend a Saturday night, either. That had just sort of happened. She had left the Quarter in a hurry, upset that John hadn't paid any attention to her unease, and had gone straight to her car in the barely adequate parking lot behind the hotel. Where she had sat with the key in the ignition, telling herself it was time to go home, shower, and count herself lucky she hadn't gotten involved with a freak like John Bannock.

He had to be a freak, right?

Had to be, because who else would be writing a book about people who were mostly already dead? People, for God's sake, who killed other people.

Who else would have spooky old men in spooky white suits following him around, talking to her like that?

And who else would want to talk to a nobody like her?

By the time she had started the car, she had worked herself into a real fit of righteousness; by the time she was halfway home, she had begun wondering about him, if he was all right, if he knew there were certain parts of the city down there that no one ever entered without some kind of protection. Wondering if maybe she had overreacted.

The wonder turned to concern, and that made her angry.

The concern, and the anger, had turned to guilt, and she'd nearly run a delivery truck off the road making a sudden sharp U-turn.

The guilt made her angry again.

The anger made her guilt stronger.

By the time she reached the Royal Cajun, she felt so ridiculous shifting from one emotion to the other that she had begun to giggle.

And when she saw him in the bar, barely able to sit upright, she had nearly walked away.

I don't need this, she had thought.

"I don't need this," she whispered now, and without thinking about it, slumped into the armchair in the corner, between the TV and the window. She crossed her legs. She wiped the back of her hand under her nose. She gave her hair an impatient shove away from her face.

"So now what?"

John mumbled something, but he didn't move.

If experience had taught her anything, that man was out for the duration.

Of course, if experience had done its job like it was supposed to, she wouldn't be here in the first place. He was a customer, for heaven's sake. She saw him, at most, twice a day. Flirted a little, and thought nothing of it when he flirted back, nothing serious, nothing that made her believe he would ever do, or want, anything else. Not even when she had given him that gift—deliberately screwing up his bill.

Then he went and saved her ass tonight, stepping in with that other freak.

Okay, so John's not a freak.

The old guy, though . . . he was something else.

First, he wasn't as old as he looked or made out to be. The face was creased, the hair white, the hands with dark spots across the knuckles, but he wasn't old. Or ancient. She couldn't help thinking he just wanted people to think that.

His accent, too, had given her the creeps. Deep South. Old South. The South where power never met the spotlight, but did its job, whatever that would be, like an alligator on the hunt in the swamps. Drifting just below the surface. Hardly a ripple. Nostrils exposed to catch the scent of prey and corruption, eyes watching. Always watching.

Except his eyes were so pale, it was like looking at the dead.

Yes. Definitely. He was a freak, and he scared her, and when she had seen him outside the bar, she couldn't help the way everything inside her contracted as if drawing away from a snake.

And John had saved her.

From what, she didn't know; she only knew he had saved her.

Okay, she had done this thing, it was too late to do anything about it now, so . . . what next?

That was easy. Beside the chair was a pole lamp, and she switched it on. Damned if she was going to sit here in the dark.

The light was directed by a large lamp shade, and its glow was more like dusk by the time it reached his face. He didn't even twitch. She looked around and saw nothing to read. Turning on the TV was out of the question. So the smart thing would be to wait a bit, make sure he wasn't going to toss and choke himself to death, then get the hell out and get the hell home. It was already way past ten, and she had to be back in at six-thirty. The very thought of it made her yawn. A second thought had her checking the width of the queen-size bed.

"Oh, no," she said. "Oh, no, you don't. You out of your mind?"

It was like those dopey cartoons—on one shoulder was her in a tight red devil's costume, waggling its eyebrows, swinging that forked tail, suggesting that even if he did wake up and found her lying there, there wasn't a whole lot he'd be able to do. Even if she wanted him to. Which she did, right? After all, it's been a while, Lisse, you can't deny that. You have needs, dear, don't you? And he's not that bad looking. Not a movie star, but not a pig, either. So who cares if he's married, with a kid? Ain't nothing gonna happen, all very innocent, and you'll be up and out before he knows you've been there.

And who knows?

Maybe you'll get lucky.

On the other shoulder, her in an angel's costume complete with halo and wings, telling her that this was the story of her life and when was she going to get hold of herself and be a real woman for a change? When was she going to stop catting around just because she felt lonely? Lots of women, good women just like you, feel lonely, for crying out loud, and they don't pick up customers, right? They don't wear that half-size-too-small shirt, and don't think I don't know why you did it. And they definitely do not stoop to praying a married drunk will wake up in the middle of the night, suddenly sober and grateful, and—

"Okay, okay," she snapped, and shook her head sharply.

This was no big deal.

Simple, really. Just go downstairs, talk to Fannon, the night manager. He would get her an empty room—God knew there were enough of those these days—and let her sleep without anyone being the wiser. It had been done before, lots of times, and not just for her.

Simple, really.

The best possible solution for all concerned.

John sputtered.

"Angel," he whispered.

Suddenly she felt passing strange, and she gripped the armrests tightly, uncrossed her legs, and set her feet flat on the carpet.

It didn't help.

Floating.

She felt as if she were floating.

She closed her eyes so hard she felt a twinge of pain, but she held her breath and waited . . . floating . . . until the sensation passed as abruptly as it had begun.

When it did she stood immediately, grabbed her purse, and headed for the door. Screw it. She didn't need this. She didn't need any of it. Fannon would take care of her, he wouldn't put on the moves because she wasn't his type, or even, for that matter, his favorite sex, and tomorrow morning she would wait to see if John remembered anything.

Like being undressed by his waitress.

That made her smile.

That made her look back.

That made her sigh when she saw the light was still on.

Leave it, the angel warned her; it's a signal of your strength.

You got to be kidding, the devil said; don't you believe in signs?

"Ah, screw it," she said, rolled her eyes, and walked back. Stood at the foot of the bed and added, "You try anything, bud, I'll cut off your balls."

He didn't move.

The purse went to the chair. Her jeans were draped over the back. Her shirt, one of the few decent ones she had left, she hung in the closet beside his suit jacket. Her skin dimpled with the cold, and she hurried to the bed's near side, pulled back sheets and thin blanket, and slipped in. Keeping as close to the edge as she could.

But feeling him.

Definitely feeling him.

She smiled as she closed her eyes. Well, child, he asked if you wanted an adventure, right?

"Angel," he whispered just before she fell asleep.

"Damn right," she whispered back.

3

Floating.

She was floating.

Not quite like flying, because she was on her stomach as if she were still in bed, head resting on her folded arms, one strand of hair tickling her cheek. If she opened her eyes she knew she would see clouds, she would see the ground, she might even see her building, one of six in an aged complex that fought the good fight but couldn't keep itself from dying.

Floating.

IN THE MOOD

Hell, maybe she was an angel after all.
She smiled.
She stirred.
She opened her eyes and saw the bird flying beside her.
A large sleek crow with bright blue eyes.

7

Lisse opened her eyes.

No passing from dream to coasting to awake.

She opened her eyes and something was wrong.

It took a second. First she had to remember where she was, then why she was there and obviously not in her own bed. A heartbeat later before she realized the light was all wrong. It was still fairly dark in the room, but the dark felt strained. Slowly she lifted her head and looked over her bare shoulder toward the window. Tiny flares of white poked around the edges, much too bright for simply dawn.

No, she thought, and brought her wrist close to her eyes, squinting at the tiny watch her sister had given to her on her last birthday.

Nearly seven-thirty.

She didn't move; she didn't believe it.

She checked again, choked off a cry, and moved as fast as she could without making a racket. Grabbed her clothes and purse. Into the bathroom and out. A look, but John was still on his back, still sound asleep. Into the hall that was silent but awake, half-skipping toward the elevator while putting on her flats. Into the car. Down to the lobby and through the café just a step short of running, feeling the desk clerk stare, waggling her fingers at him over her shoulder.

It didn't take all that long.

Taped to her locker was a hotel envelope. It wasn't pink, and the paper inside wasn't pink, either. They didn't have to be. The note was simple: "See me." Signed by the manager. Not Fannon.

No "I'm sorry, Lisse."

No "You're late for the last time, Montgomery."

Not even a sympathetic smile.

He sat behind his goddamn big desk in his goddamn fancy jacket and handed her a paycheck, said, "You're fired," and looked pointedly at the door.

She would have killed him if she had been able to think, but it all happened so fast, all she could do was nod, turn, walk out, and stand motionless in the lobby watching a young couple head for the café, watching two men climb the staircase, watching the new doorman rub sleep from his eyes.

Deep breath, girl, she cautioned when she felt herself blinking rapidly; deep breath, it ain't the first time, it won't be the last, deep breath, deep breath.

A swallow, a straightening of her shoulders, and she walked behind the staircase to the elevators, rode to the sixth floor, stood in front the door halfway down the hall and stared at the number without seeing it. Then she reached into her jeans pocket, pulled out the electronic key, opened the door, stepped in, slammed the door behind her, switched on the lights, walked to the window and yanked the drapes open, walked to the foot of the bed and threw her purse at John's chest as hard as she could.

He started, opened his eyes, saw her, and smiled painfully against the light.

"You bastard," she said, swaying against the temptation to scream, "I don't have a job, I don't have much money, it's your fault, you son of a bitch, so what the hell are you going to do about it?"

Then she took a swing at his feet, the edge of her fist clipping his toes.

She wanted to take a swing at his jaw when she saw the bewilderment on his face; she wanted to take up that damn computer thing from the table and bash it over his head; she wanted to cry but snatched up her purse instead and dropped heavily into the armchair, crossed her legs right knee over left, and demanded, "Well?"

Maybe it was funny the way he struggled to sit up, left hand raised in a wait-a-minute gesture, fell back and sat up again; maybe it was funny when he realized he was naked except for his briefs and widened his eyes as memory and realization set in somewhere amid the hangover fog; maybe it was funny the way he swung unsteadily out of bed, muttered, "I don't think I'm dead, right?'' and staggered off to the bathroom and closed the door behind him.

Maybe it was funny, but all she could do was stare out the window at the impossibly bright sky and swallow, and swallow again, and swallow a third time while her right foot bounced sharply until she felt the beginning of a cramp.

That didn't stop her.

The cramp took her arch and brought the tears, and she let it stay until she could stand it no longer; then she pushed out her heel and closed her eyes and waited. Ignoring the toilet's flush, water spitting into the basin, the sounds over it all of his barely controlled groans.

Then she wiped her eyes with the heels of each hand, fumbled a tissue out of her purse, and blew her nose.

When she heard the drumroll of the shower, she almost got up and left. It was stupid, sitting here. What the hell can he do for me, this is nuts. I shouldn't have stayed. I'm a grown woman, it's my fault, it's sure as mud not the end of the world.

But it might as well be.

It might as well be.

"Oh, Lord," she sighed, leaned her head back and closed her eyes. "Oh, Lord."

His voice sounded like the creak of an old door, his natural rasp accentuated, rougher: "I'm sorry, Lisse."

She didn't look.

She sensed his weight moving around the room, disturbing the air, sitting on the bed and dressing.

Her own voice was hoarse: "I was late. Again. It's not your fault."

But she didn't open her eyes.

She knew that if she saw him, his hands would be flapping around for something to do, that his old-young face would look like Daddy's bloodhound, that he was probably trying to figure out how to take it all on his shoulders. Just like Daddy used to, before he slipped into the bayou and never came out.

Her left hand rose and waved and fell again. "I'll get another job."

"Sure you will, no problem."

"I was tired of working here, anyway. Hardly anybody comes, and they're all lousy tippers."

"Okay."

He was afraid to say the wrong thing, and that made her mad, for no reason she could think of.

When she opened her eyes, he was on the far side of the table, the computer in front of him, the tape recorder on top, as though he were building a wall.

"Well," he said, trying a smile that looked more like a grimace, "at least your mascara didn't run."

That did it.

Before she could stop herself she was on her feet and across the room, leaning over the table.

"I don't *wear* mascara," she yelled. "There ain't nothing fake about me, you son of a bitch!" She pointed at her eyes with a trembling finger. "These are *my* goddamn lashes." Pointed. "*My* goddamn eyebrows." Pointed. "*My* goddamn boobs." Pointed. "*My* goddamn . . . *my* . . ." She faltered, glowered at his sudden grin, straightened, and said, "Honey, you put that grin away or I'll slap it away so fast your eyes will roll into your goddamn ears."

He did, instantly.

A sharp nod, and she stood at the window, a hand on one hip, rapping a knuckle lightly against the pane. "I hate this damn city."

He cleared his throat cautiously.

"Shreveport," she said, looking down at the river, the tankers, the ferry, the sidewheeler churning at its dock and not moving.

"Huh?"

"You were going to ask where I came from. Shreveport. Near there, anyway." Her forehead touched the glass, cool from the air-conditioning and warm from the sun. Suddenly she was tired; so very, very tired. Her knuckle slipped down to the narrow sill. A shrug with her eyebrows. "There wasn't a whole lot to do for someone like me up there. High school diploma, barely. Didn't want to end up like my girlfriends, marrying straight out of graduation, a couple of kids before they was even twenty." Another shrug, this one with her shoulder as her hand left the sill and buried itself in her hair. "It was either here or St. Louis, and no offense, but I had no desire to see St. Louis." She glanced at him, half-smiled. "They talk funny up there."

He smiled back, with one eye in a partial squint as if he wasn't sure he had to take it back.

She turned her back to the pane and folded her arms across her chest, studied the floor while she bit softly on her lower lip. "I am on the wrong side of thirty, got no skills to speak of . . . hell, I'd even make a lousy whore." She laughed, more a grunt. "I'm not about to jump in the river, understand, but the idiot that called this town the Big Easy was a jackass. It ain't easy. It ain't easy at all."

"Why . . ."

She looked at him.

"Why don't you go back home?"

"What for?"

He wouldn't meet her gaze. He moved the recorder off the computer, eased the computer to one side, pulled it back, pushed it away again, and sat back. Stretched his neck. Scratched the side of his nose.

"Hey," she said softly. "Are you a preacher or something? One of those guys who don't wear that collar?"

He almost laughed. "No. Why?"

" 'Cause I'm telling you stuff, that's why. I don't know you from anybody, I just got my ass fired, and I'm telling you stuff. Something about you, I guess." She shook her head in quiet amazement, shifted a little against the heat that warmed her back, and narrowed her eyes, lifting a finger to her lips. "You know, you look like somebody."

"Oh, God," he said, raising his hands to shoulder level. "Please. Don't."

She leaned forward, peering at him. Nodding. "You know what I'm talking about, huh?"

"Yes," he said flatly. "They called me Prez in college."

"Maybe," she said, "I'll just call you Abe."

"Maybe," he answered, "you could just stick to John."

Strange, she thought; strange guy. Not in a bad way, not like that white suit. Just . . . strange.

A quick smile—sort of—and a hesitation in case he had something to say, and she pushed off the sill and picked up her purse.

"I'm sorry," he said. "Really. I didn't mean . . . you know."

"Don't worry," she told him, checking to be sure the paycheck was still in there. "I'll manage." Mentally crossing her fingers, wishing on a star, avoiding cracks in the sidewalk, running from black cats. "No problem. I'll be all right."

She looked out at the city again, shaking her head slowly. Nothing down there. What the hell had she been thinking of?

"And thanks, Lisse."

"For what?"

"You know. Getting me home. Here, I mean." She heard him grunt. "A heck of day yesterday. Weird."

She held the purse against her chest, watched the ghost of a cloud head down toward the Gulf, and spotted a quartet of pigeons wheel over the water, taking their time.

It all moved so slowly.

"You know," she said, "I had the strangest dream last night."

Silence; he was listening.

Her eyes half closed, warmth on her face, chill on her back—as if she were sleeping again.

Sleeping, and floating.

"I was flying. Kind of flying. Just drifting along with the current, nothing to worry about, nothing up there but me and the clouds and all that soft air. . . . Lord, I think I could have stayed up there forever. I think . . ." Cocking her head, listening for him listening. "I don't know. I don't know what it was. It was nice, until the bird."

His chair moved.

She didn't look.

She didn't want to lose the warmth on her face.

"I was drifting . . . floating, I guess . . . and I looked over and there he was. Big old crow flying beside me."

He whispered, "I know."

She frowned, at the words and the image. "I'm not sure, but I think he scared me. Crows aren't . . . they don't scare me. I mean, I don't have a thing about them, you know? But this one, he looked at me. He flew along, and he looked at me. And—"

"Blue eyes."

She snapped around, warmth gone, breath nearly gone. "What?"

John's left hand nearly covered his mouth. "He had blue eyes."

*　*　*

She batted away the obvious question with an abrupt frantic gesture. She did not . . . she absolutely did *not* want to know how he knew that. She didn't get it, she did not want to get it, and as she headed for the door, she refused to look at him. There was a life to get on with here, such as it was, and she was not about to get involved with bull like this.

When she opened the door, he didn't stop her.

When she stepped into the hall, he did not call after her.

But when the door swung slowly to, she let her right heel catch it before it closed.

He had said something in his sleep, that's what it was, and she had heard it and had let it influence her own dream; or he had said something while she had labored with him to his room; or the world was filled with bizarre coincidences and this was just one of them.

Nothing more; nothing less.

But she didn't move her foot.

Face it, Lisse Gayle, your life needs serious repairs and you don't have the hammers and nails and what all else you're going to need to get the job done.

Far down the hall she saw a housekeeper's cart parked outside someone's door, its laundry bag already packed with dirty sheets and towels, a rag hanging over a bottle of glass cleaner. She heard the faint hum of a vacuum cleaner.

You could do that, she told herself; you could get a job doing that.

Lord, Lord, what the hell am I doing?

She went back inside; John was still at the table, slipping a tape into the recorder. He looked up, but said nothing, eyes red rimmed, cheeks taut, hair still drying from the shower. No question about it—he was a mess-and-a-half.

"Patty's your wife?" she said.

"Ex-wife. Yes."

"Joey's your son?"

"Yes."

"You're writing that book about executed people?"

"Yes."

"You get paid for it?"

"George Trout pays the expenses."

"Who's he?"

"One of my tax clients. He writes books. The one I told you about, the one who used to be a librarian."

"So?"

"So he wants me to do the work, and he'll show me how to put it together."

"Somebody's going to print it?"

"It's already sold, yes. On his name."

"Those are the tapes of those people?"

"Yes."

"What's the computer for?"

"I have to type in all the conversations first. Word for word. So I know what I have, so I can take out what doesn't seem right."

They stared at each other.

"You going to talk to any more dead people?"

"One. Maybe. I don't know. I may not have to."

She tapped her foot.

"You going to stay here until you're done with that stuff you already have there?"

"No."

She looked to the window, to the city washed out by the sun.

"Okay," she said, not feeling nearly as strong as she sounded. "I can type."

8

1

A twilight room, with filtered light through thin white curtains. Two single beds whose plywood headboards are bolted to a pale plaster wall. Trailer-truck traffic makes the floor vibrate, and in the distance, a church bell.

"Mom?"

"What is it, Joey?"

"Mom, what are you doing?"

"I'm tired, honey, I have to rest. It's Sunday, remember? A day of rest? You should know that."

"I'm not tired."

"You're never tired."

"So?"

"So sometimes, dear, big people, like me, have to rest. I'm hungry, I need some sleep, one more step and I'm going to drop."

"Mom?"

"Now what?"

"What about Dad?"

"Later, Joey. We'll talk about him later."

2

The armchair was too comfortable, but John didn't want to move. The air-conditioning was on low, the sunlight was pleasantly warm, and his head had finally stopped feeling as if it were going to sink beneath his shoulders. Or explode. Or implode. At Lisse's insistence he had managed to keep down a light breakfast; at Lisse's insistence he had poured the Jim Beam down the bathroom sink. The fumes had come close to bringing up the food, but he had managed. Just.

"Are you an alcoholic?" she had asked.

"Nope. Just a sometimes drunk."

He didn't think that made her feel much better, but it made him feel a whole lot better than he'd felt when she had hit him with the purse. Damn, she must have an anvil in there. He rubbed his sternum at the memory, yawned, and watched her at the table.

Although he wouldn't admit it, he had been surprised at how fast she had taken to the computer. A half hour's instructions, a few answered questions during the next sixty minutes, and now she sat there with earphones on, transcribing yet another section of tape. It was tedious work at best, yet she seemed more proficient at it than he was. She claimed it was from being a waitress, having to listen to ninety people all talking at once, all demanding special orders, all wondering if this thing here could be substituted for that thing there, and not mixing anything up.

She listened better, she said, that's all.

Watching her work, he didn't doubt it.

He shifted, stretched out his legs, and stared at the notepad lying in his lap. Things to do before he left New Orleans.

First, he had to contact George and make sure it was all right to hire Lisse. He didn't think there'd be a problem, but with Trout footing the bills, paying the credit card charges John rang up every month, he wanted to be sure.

Then he had to get himself one of those portable printers. A yeoman machine, not a luxury item. It was one thing seeing all those words on a screen, or listening to the ghosts for hours on end, but something bothered him. Something he knew was in all that talk, and he suspected he was too close to it, had heard it too often, and he wanted to see it right there on paper. Black and white. Something he could touch, feel, move around, stare at.

Put side by side for comparison if he had to.

What he needed was to focus.

He hadn't realized it before, but he had become scattershot. The ghosts, the actual prisoners, Patty and Joey . . . he hadn't understood how depressed all that had made him, how it had dampened his mind, turned his brain to a slug . . . hell, no wonder he'd been drinking like it was going out of style. Anybody would, listening to those people, and worrying about his son, and waking up every morning with nothing more but the same old same old.

It was enough to make a man not give a damn.

He stretched and yawned, twisted around to face the TV set bolted to a swivel base on the low dresser. He used the remote control to turn it on, winced at the faded colors and colored static, and made the rounds.

"Damn," he said.

"What?" Lisse said, looking up, distracted.

"Nothing." He used the remote for a pointer. "Practically every channel's got some preacher on it."

"Honey, this is Sunday and it's the South, remember? Now hush, I'm almost done with this part."

The array fascinated him, made him lean forward as he lowered the sound so he could listen without disturbing her. Six programs in all, ranging from a man and woman preaching from a set made to look like someone's living room, to a man in flowing sacramental robes in what appeared to be a huge cathedral made of gold and silver.

A choir of six; a choir of more than one hundred.

Congregations in fervent prayer, in vibrant song, attentively listening to a full-throated sermon; some eyes closed, some hands raised, swaying with the music, nodding with the exhortations, bobbing and bouncing in their seats as the minister grew more heated, more excited, roaming the stage or the aisles, Bible in one hand, the other fisted or pleading or sweeping the air ahead and above him.

He knew those places.

He had been there, and he had left.

"John?"

"Wait." He slipped out of the chair and swiveled the set around to face the bed. "Here." He sat on the edge and patted the mattress beside him until she joined him. "It's . . ." He frowned and changed the channel. "It's all the same."

"I don't—"

IN THE MOOD

"Listen," he said, free hand covering his mouth, fingers drumming on his cheek. "Listen."

"He will take those seven gold vials and one each will he give to each of seven angels, and make no mistake about it, they *will* be opened, and they *will* . . ."

". . . seven seals which will be broken one by one, until the last, which will be the last, my friends, and . . ."

"The Beast. We cannot forget the Beast."

"Riding! Riding among the heathen, scythe and sword, to smote them, to smote *us,* my brethren. Us! From the throne, across the void, and whether we want it or not, they will be here. They are here. They cannot be . . ."

"All it takes . . . all it takes is an acceptance of the Lord as your personal Saviour. A whisper in the ear of God is all it takes, dear friends, for . . ."

"There will be no quarter for saint and sinner alike."

"The trumpet. The trumpet."

"The end of the world," he said in quiet amazement, muting the sound, letting the remote dangle between his legs. "Did you hear it? Every single one of them is talking about the end of the world."

Lisse shrugged. "So? It's all that Millennium stuff going around. Isn't that when we're all supposed to die and go to heaven or something?"

"So they say," he whispered.

She took the remote from his hand and turned the set off. "Another thing you got to remember, these preachers, aside from the fact that I think most of them are crooks, they've been dooming and glooming ever since they all worked out of tents." She laughed, and bumped his shoulder with hers. "Not that I blame them." She looked to the window. "Out there . . . the way things have been, they're just using what they got, I guess."

He stared at the blank screen, seeing Lisse's reflection, a wavering ghost watching him watching her.

Scattershot.

Still, he took the remote back and ignored her scowl when he switched the set on again.

"Don't tell me," she said wearily, "you're going to watch football. The Saints suck, I'm hungry, and in case you haven't noticed it's just about noon." She pinched his arm. "You could use a couple pounds yourself, by the way."

He nodded, not really listening, rocking slowly as he watched the ministers blur into one another, all Scriptures and song, until he found himself at CNN, and stopped.

"Damn," he said.

A large crowd, more than a hundred, marched behind police barriers outside the capital building in Baton Rouge.

"Hey, look," he said. "Take a look."

They carried placards and banners, wore sandwich boards and special T-shirts, held up crosses and rosaries, chanted and sang, and used bullhorns and cardboard megaphones.

"But nobody's in there," Lisse said. "All the government people are home. It's Sunday."

"A slow news day," he explained. "If you really want airtime, you try to do your thing on a slow news day."

She squinted, moved her lips. "Executions? Oh. They're against the death penalty, huh."

"There," he said, pointing to one placard. "Ruesette Argo's name. I'll be damned, she has fans." He noticed Lisse's puzzlement and nodded toward the recorder. "She was the one I talked to this week. Poisoned over a dozen people. Thirteen, to be exact."

Lisse shuddered. "Lord, she must be nuts."

He leaned back on his elbows, the remote resting on his stomach. The protesters marched in a ragged circle. Chanting. Singing. Apparently led by a pair of young Catholic priests, augmented by at least a half-dozen nuns dressed from the traditional to the contemporary. The commentator noted the abrupt increase in state executions over the course of the last two years, to such an extent that death chambers, in some states, were now being used as much as once a week. And they still couldn't keep up.

Thanks to the Supreme Court, the average stay on death row now was little more than two years.

The camera panned to the street.

There were no hecklers, and the light traffic didn't slow down.

The police on duty looked monumentally bored.

If there was any public support, it wasn't in Baton Rouge.

"No," he said at last.

Lisse started. "What?"

"Ruesette Argo. I don't think she's crazy."

"She has to be." She jerked her chin toward the screen. "All those people dead? You can't do that and be normal."

John tucked his lower lip between his teeth and considered for a moment. Then he said, as if surprised himself, "Yeah. Yeah, I think you can."

3

The room is silent except for the faint buzz of cartoons on the TV. A fly caught between the curtains and the pane buzzes angrily because it can't find a way out. Outside the warped door, a neon sign buzzes, four letters missing.

"Mom?"

"Hmmm?"

"These cartoons are silly."

"I know, dear. That's what makes them fun."

"They're not fun, they're silly."

"Then find something else to watch. Better yet, young man, turn the set off and read."

"There's nothing to read."

"I bought the Sunday paper. Read the comics."

"I don't want to. They're silly, too."

"Then go outside and play."

"In the parking lot?"

"Joey, you're the one with the cowboy suit, not me. Pretend . . . oh, pretend it's a prairie and you're hunting for Indians, or guiding a wagon train to the mountains. Or . . . or you're a lawman on the trail of a real desperado."

"What's a desperado?"

"A badman. A crook. Pretend he's robbed a bank and you have to bring him in."

"Do I have to kill him?"

"You're the one with the gun, honey. You have to do what's right. Maybe he'll come quietly, maybe he won't. You have to decide what to do."

"But it's not a real gun."

"I know. That's why you pretend."

"I don't have to pretend, Mom."

"Yes. I know. So then what do you want to do?"

"Maybe . . . go home."

"Are you sure?"

"I think so."

"But . . . Joey. Honey. What about your father?"

The fly; the neon.

The TV switched off.

"Joey? . . . Joey?"

4

John knew he wasn't making a whole lot of sense, but he couldn't help it. A rare charge of surprising energy galvanized him to his feet as he said, "Yes, of course you can be normal. Of course you can. It's . . . Jesus, there's stuff I have to do. God, this is amazing. This is—" and he grabbed her by the arms, pulled her to her feet, kissed her quickly on the lips, and said, "You are a genius, Miss Montgomery. Come on, we're leaving the batcave, I need fresh air."

He laughed at the stunned look on her face, but was not so carried away that he didn't remember the taste of her lips.

"Do you know someone down in the office? Someone who isn't above making some extra cash on company time? Kind of under the table?"

Stunned she nodded.

"Good. Great. That's great." He shut down the computer, closed the lid, and stared for a second at the tape recorder before shaking his head once. "No, that's silly."

"What's silly?"

"Nothing, nothing, don't worry about it." He tucked the laptop under his arm, looked around the room as though checking to be sure he hadn't forgotten anything, then took her arm and led her to the hall.

IN THE MOOD

"Key?"

She patted her jeans. "Still have it. But—"

"You'll see, you'll see."

Scattershot.

Maybe. Maybe he was still a little drunk. Maybe, when he really thought about what he was doing, he'd realize what an idiot he probably was.

Still . . .

Avoiding the day manager was easy. At the Royal Cajun, on a Sunday in October, there wasn't a whole lot of things to do, and the man apparently spent most of his time in his office. With the door closed. Sometimes locked. Nobody had ever asked; nobody had ever really cared.

It didn't take long to make arrangements for some of his computer files to be printed. He didn't think about the cash he paid out or the cash he would have to give if it was all done by dinner. That wasn't his problem; he would square it with George later.

Once that was done, Lisse, still bewildered but giggling at his infectious excitement, agreed to put together a lunch for them both. To go.

"A picnic," he said.

"A picnic? We don't have a basket."

"Use a paper bag."

"Some picnic."

"It's the thought," he said sternly, pushing her gently toward the kitchen. "And I thought the thought was, you were hungry."

As soon as she left, glancing at him over her shoulder, he sat in the lobby. Stood. Sat again and stared at the ceiling fans.

He had no real idea why he felt the way he did. He only knew there was an urgency, that whatever he was doing had to be finished soon. Very soon. And he didn't think it had anything to do with completing the book.

He stood, took a few hesitant steps toward the café, and sat again.

His fingers tapped his thighs; he counted the number of revolutions a ceiling fan made in sixty seconds; one heel tapped the floor; he stared so long and so hard at the bank of telephones by the front desk that his eyes began to water, his vision began to blur.

He neither lowered his gaze nor dried the tears.

Floating.

He was floating.

Voices murmured, footsteps were muffled, a giggling couple on the mezzanine sounded like tiny bells, the hushing slide of an elevator's doors sounded like surf, and the shadow that suddenly stood in front of him terrified him so much he scrambled out of the chair, nearly knocking it over.

"John!"

Panting, he held up a hand.

"John, are you crying?"

"No." He shook his head, blinked rapidly, finally used a sleeve to dry his face. "No."

Lisse held a large, bulging paper bag in her arms, mounds of wax paper rising from the top. "Are you okay?"

"Yeah." He looked from the phones to the entrance and back again. "Yeah."

Uncertain, she hefted the bag. "I'm ready. I've got—"

"Good," he said. "Great." His left hand pulled at his neck; his right hand slapped his leg nervously. "Yeah. Great."

"Now wait a minute," she said angrily. "If you're—"

He walked away.

"Hey!"

"A call," he said over his shoulder.

"But I thought—"

"Lisse, it won't take a minute. I have to make a phone call."

5

There are dents in the walls where bottles and fists have been thrown by previous tenants. Near the bottom of the door is a splintered gouge where a kick landed. The headboards are scratched. Flakes of dull paint drift into the bathroom sink.

On the floor beneath the window, the fly twitches silently as it dies.

At the foot of the single bed farthest from the window a young boy stands, shaking the covered feet of the woman lying facedown on the mattress. He wears faded jeans tucked into a pair of gleaming tan boots, a dark leather belt around his waist with a plastic gun in a tasseled holster, a dark shirt perhaps a half size too large, and a hat that hangs down his back by the braided strap around his neck.

"Mom! Mommy! Mommy, come on!"

The woman groans as she rolls stiffly onto her side, propping her head up with one hand. Her face is creased where it pressed against the pillow, pale from lack of sleep. Her shirt and jeans are on the floor, her socks balled up in her dirt-smudged sneakers. She pulls the thin sheet up under her chin, and stares at him blearily.

He shakes her feet again until she swipes at his hands ineffectually, until she focuses.

"Mom, get up, get up!"

"Oh, Lord," she moans, "what is it now?"

He steps away from the bed, hands at his sides. "We have to go, Mom."

"What?"

"Come on, Mom!"

"Now?"

"Now, Mom. We have to go now."

"Oh, but Joey, I'm—"

"Now, Mommy. Come on."

6

"His name," said John, "is Casey Chisholm."

In an admittedly feeble attempt to mollify her hurt feelings, he let her choose the site for their lunch. It had been a toss-up between Jackson Square and the Canal Street ferry, but she had finally opted for the river instead of the tourists. There were chairs and benches scattered around the top, deserted open deck; without discussion they pulled two to the railing, propped their feet up, and watched a pair of tugs nose a cargo ship into the channel downriver.

"A friend of yours?"

"No. Not really. I met him only twice, at Rahway State Prison, in New Jersey."

"Lord, he's not one of your killers is he?"

"No. He's a priest."

7

Joey stands outside the door, beneath the corrugated plastic overhang that runs the length of the motel. Ten feet to his left is the office, its neon vacancy sign still buzzing. On the far side of the narrow, empty parking lot, the ground rises to a weed-cluttered embankment; on the top a freight train lumbers past, clanking, creaking, its cars peeling and old.

Impatiently he says, "Mom, come on."

"Just hold your horses, cowboy," she snaps. "I'm not leaving anything behind, okay? I don't want anything here they can use to trace us."

He looks at her over his shoulder, grinning.

"Yeah, yeah, okay," she says, smiling for the first time in several days. Then she shakes a mock-severe finger at him. "But just because they haven't yet doesn't mean they won't."

He turns away as he whispers, "Yes, it does. Yes, it does."

He watches the train. He waits. He doesn't move when Patty steps out of the room and closes the door behind her.

"Joey?" A soft voice. "Honey?" She smoothes his impossibly blond hair with a palm. When he looks up at her, she smiles. "Home, right?"

He doesn't answer, and the smile dies as she closes her eyes.

He takes her hand, and they walk toward the highway.

He doesn't speak.

But he smiles.

8

John felt the boat's vibrations through his rump and soles, watched the city's tourist center lurch away to the left as the ferry barged through the water toward the opposite bank. A faint breeze worked across the deck, and on it he could smell exhaust and food and the warmth of the sun and something Lisse wore that he couldn't put a name to.

The bag was on the deck between them, and as she handed out the food, he told her about Casey.

A fascinating man, he said. Big. Not fat, but big. Tall. Wears black all the time, as far as I can tell, even when he isn't wearing his white collar. I was there to interview a guy named Mercer. Mercer Prince. Who wasn't one, believe me. He had robbed a convenience store in Trenton, shot the pregnant clerk through the head when she didn't deliver fast enough, then took the police on a high-speed chase clear down to the Delaware River. There was a gunfight on the bridge there. He shot four cops, two of them died. He was . . . evil, believe it or not, is too good a word for him. Pure nasty, that's all I can say.

Anyway, Casey was there visiting a relative of one of his parishioners, and we kind of fell into talking a little, before and after visiting hours.

You have to know this, Lisse: I am not a terribly religious man. My mother used to take me to revivalists. Whoever was in town, it didn't matter who; they came, we went. I grew up thinking the world was doomed, I was doomed, and nothing I could do was going to change it. I was not, you might say, the most sunny kid on the block. That changed when I was a teenager. Mom took to going to the nearest church—Presbyterian, as it happens—because her legs weren't so good anymore, and my father took the car when he walked out. Meanwhile, all these guys—Swaggart and Baker, guys like that—were going down for the count, and that just proved to me that no one, especially preachers, had a clue, you know what I mean?

But this Episcopal priest, he was something else.

I can't tell you what it is even now, but he impressed the hell out of me. So to speak. He's special, Lisse. I don't know why, but he's really special.

Anyway, you remember last year, part of the year before? Everything seemed to be going to hell? Towns exploding, violence all over the place, people blaming terrorists and gangs and the Mafia and whatever?

Well, Casey got caught in it. I don't know what happened, exactly, but the town he works in became part of the pattern. He ended up in the hospital, nearly died. I call him now and then to see how he's doing. Most of the time I get the doctor, or his lady, whose name is Helen.

But the last time I talked to him—not today, about two months ago— he was in some pain, physical therapy was almost worse than his original injuries, so we couldn't talk very long. I asked him how he was, we talked a little about getting together if I got back East again, and then he was quiet for the longest time.

For a change I didn't say anything, I just waited.

Then he said, "They're here, John. I know because I saw one. I was marked, and I saw one."

That's all. I didn't get a chance to ask him who he was talking about because the nurse took the phone then.

Then today . . .

Now understand this, Lisse, if you can: He is a priest and a big man, like I said. But he has this voice that . . . I wish I could tell you . . . describe . . . a voice, Lisse. He has a *voice.*

His doctor was there today and didn't want me to talk to him. But I could hear Casey in the background, arguing, and when the doctor finally let him talk, all he said was,

"You're marked, John.

"God help you, you're marked."

With that voice, Lisse.

With that *voice.*

9

1

Lisse took a bite of her sandwich and said nothing.

To the left, a hundred or so yards downriver, she watched what seemed to be a tour group gathered on the broad top of the levee, taking pictures of the water, the three spires of St. Louis Cathedral behind them, maybe even the chugging ferry. A shay with a tasseled cover rode past them, drawn by a mule whose ears poked through a straw hat. Cameras swiveled. Tourists taking pictures of tourists.

The ferry docked with only the faintest lurch. The handful of cars below instantly gunned their engines, waiting for the ramp and barriers to accommodate their leaving.

It was . . . normal.

Nothing out of place.

City life as usual on a Sunday afternoon.

She ate the last of the sandwich and reached down beside her for the can of soda she had set on the deck.

This was supposed to be normal, too. A clear, comfortable day with an easy, sometimes tickling breeze. A makeshift picnic—his idea, not hers—on a ferry on the Mississippi. Not exactly first class, but it wouldn't take much pushing to even call it a little romantic. Which, she thought, is just about the story of my life since there ain't nothing else normal going on.

She felt him flicking glances at her, waiting for a reaction as if it actually mattered to him.

This, she decided, is just too damn weird.

He may not be a freak, but he's damn sure turning into a fruitcake.

Voices distracted her. John paid no attention, but when she looked, she saw two women settle on a bench against the wheelhouse, loaded shopping bags between their feet, while a young man slumped in a chair near the stairs. The women were fat and swarmed by unashamedly vivid clothing, intent on their conversation while fanning themselves with white handkerchiefs. When one looked up and gave her a quick wave, she realized it was the Grudeau sisters, Giselle and Pandora, housekeepers at the Cajun. It was the first time she had ever seen them not in their hotel whites.

The kid, on the other hand, she had never seen before. He wore a bandanna around his head pirate-style, a silver cross dangling from one ear, his hair in an unkempt ponytail.

As if even an inch would make a difference between privacy and eavesdropping, Lisse smiled politely at the sisters and scooted her chair closer to the railing so she could fold her arms on it and rest her chin on the back of her hand. Then she turned her head and said, "Are you . . . ?" Her right eye nearly closed as she tried to work it out as she spoke. "Are you in trouble with, like, the Mob?"

"I . . . *what?*"

"That guy you talked to, he said you were marked, right? You do taxes and finances, right? Moving numbers around, things like that? So maybe you're skimming a little here and there, they find out, they mark you for a what-do-you-call-it, a hit, right? I mean, you're a CPA, for crying out loud, no offense. Maybe you're not really writing a book at all, maybe you're just getting a little information, you know what I mean? Something to keep them off your back. Or . . . or for the Feds, you know?"

She shrugged.

He started to laugh, changed his mind, started to laugh again, and finally said, simply, "No."

She didn't move, didn't smile, didn't frown; but she believed him. "Then what are we talking about? I mean, what did he mean by you're marked?"

He shook his head. "I don't know, Lisse. Honest to God, I don't know."

"Well, something's the matter," she said, not accusing, only wondering. "You get all bent out of shape over some TV preaching, then all of a sudden you're running around like crazy needing to get some stuff printed, then you're acting like somebody just told you it's going to rain for the next hundred days and you ain't got anything to keep your shorts dry."

She raised her eyebrows—*so what is it?*—and did frown then when all he could do was shake his head again and shrug helplessly, his expression marked by fearful confusion. It was the look, not the lack of an answer, that bothered her, and she concentrated on the water as the ferry nudged away from the dock.

"Then I don't get it. I mean, I'm grateful for the job and all. I won't say that I can't use the money, especially now. But I like to know what I'm getting into, you know? And I have to tell you, I don't like this at all. It's too . . ." She shuddered, and wished she had brought a light sweater or something.

When he draped his jacket over her shoulders, smoothed it down her back, she wanted to cry.

Maybe she would have, but a voice said, loudly and belligerently, "Hey."

When she looked, she saw the pirate a few feet away, hands in his pockets, one hip cocked.

"I know you, kid?" she said flatly.

He jerked his chin at the picnic bag. "Looks like you got enough there for an army. I ain't eaten today. Wanna share?"

She rolled her eyes, not bothering to answer.

John shifted around to sit sideways in his chair, looking up at the kid, who had cocked his other hip, making it clear Lisse didn't exist.

"Just give me something," the kid said, pointing languidly as if they were wasting his time with a foregone conclusion.

John smiled tolerantly. "Looks like you could use more than just a sandwich, kiddo."

"It'll do for now."

Lisse stood slowly. She didn't like the way his right hand bulged in its pocket; there was something more in there than just a fist. "Hike it," she said, scowling. "We got nothing for you."

"Tell him, child," one of the sisters called, and her companion laughed.

The pirate shook his head slowly as if to say that he had tried, he had really tried to be civilized about all this, and took a step to his left. "You know, bitch, you got a mouth."

"Hey," John said softly.

81

Lisse faced the kid squarely. John's jacket slid from her shoulders, hit her chair, and slithered to the deck. "You got a name, boy?"

He sneered. "Yeah. They call me Levee Pete."

One of the sisters hooted.

Lisse grinned. "Well, listen here, Mr. Levee Pete, my friend and me, we got ourselves a private conversation going here, and we don't need you bothering us, okay? So why don't you just—"

The step forward and the punch came so swiftly it was only instinct that made her lean away from the brass-knuckled fist, feeling the wind of it pass just under her chin. But his momentum half-turned him, and before he could recover, she grabbed his ponytail with both hands and yanked it as she dropped to her knees, slamming him hard onto the deck on his back.

The sisters hooted and applauded; one put thumb and forefinger in her mouth and whistled appreciation.

Then a hand grabbed the back of her shirt as she got to her feet and jerked her to one side so hard she came up against the railing. She didn't feel the collision; all she felt was a cold tremor in her muscles that wouldn't let her legs hold her until she leaned hard against the top rail.

That, she thought, was the dumbest thing you ever did in your life, are you out of your mind?

John stood between her and the pirate, head slightly cocked. "Levee Pete," he said evenly, as the kid rolled to his feet, "is a dumbass name, and you're just as dumb for swinging at a lady. Move on, kid, before somebody gets hurt."

The pirate swayed, leaning forward, panting to catch his breath, grinning the whole time, wide enough to expose a mouth of stained teeth. He held up his right fist, and Lisse's eyes widened when she saw the filed edges ranged across the knuckles; no wonder he had aimed for her throat.

"John."

John gestured quickly—*I know, I see it*—but didn't move. "Go on, kid," he said gently. "Go on, this is silly."

Swaying. "Ain't nothing silly about it, mister." Never taking his eyes off John. "Said I could ride with him, John, so I'm gonna ride." His grin widened, gums exposed. "Gotta eat first, though, gotta eat. And you got the food."

John shrugged. "Then take it. Hell, take it."

"Too late," and he lunged, swinging, darting back when he missed and John tried to grab his wrist.

Lisse looked to the sisters, thinking, praying, one of them was on her way to fetch someone, a crew member or the captain or whoever ran this damn boat. But they hadn't moved; they were watching intently, handkerchiefs fanning.

Not real, she thought; this isn't real.

The ferry reached the other side, engines sputtering.

The pirate lurched at the docking, and swung again, but from so far away John didn't even have to move. Then the kid snatched up a chair and flung it at his head. It was wide of the mark, and John turned as it went past, using one hand to keep it going, over the rail and into the river.

"Oooh, that'll cost you," one of the sisters said. "That'll cost you."

Frenzied, muttering, the pirate grabbed a second chair and threw it so wildly it went directly behind him. Muttering. Wide eyed and panting. Finally uttering a desperate shriek and charging.

John met him without flinching, easily grabbing both his wrists. Chest to chest. Face to face. Arms fully extended, outward and up.

Not a sound.

Lisse looked down and saw the kid was on his toes, saw the legs trembling; when she pushed away from the rail, she could see the kid's face—covered with sweat, absolutely pale. While John simply stared.

Not a sound.

Then she saw John's lips move.

And the kid screamed. Once. Short. Before he sagged, unconscious.

Still John held him, still stared at him, until Lisse hurried over and touched his shoulder. "It's okay, John," she whispered urgently, "it's okay, let him go."

Slowly he lowered his arms, opened his hands, and the kid slumped to the deck. Lisse knelt beside him, suddenly afraid he was dead, holding a hand to his chest until she felt a shallow rise and fall.

A bubble of blood quivered at the corner of his mouth.

His eyes were open, but she suspected he didn't see the sky.

2

The depot is small and freshly painted. A bus is parked at the curb, gleaming wetly as a man in coveralls hoses it down. From a small patch of bright grass between the sidewalk and the building a flagpole rises out of a round garden ringed with bricks. Rope slaps against the pole, the hollow ring of an aluminum bell.

Patty sits on a bench just outside the entrance, a worn suitcase between her feet. There are tickets in her right hand; in her left hand is a cigarette she seems to have forgotten she's lit.

The little cowboy paces up and down the concrete walk to the bus. He looks at the sky. He looks at the flag. He stops in front of his mother and says, "Mom?"

She blinks and smiles. "Yes, dear?"

"Soon?"

She leans forward and twists around to check the round-faced clock above the doors. "Fifteen minutes, hon."

"Thank you."

She winks at him, and crushes the cigarette out beneath her sole. "Is there something wrong, honey?"

He doesn't answer. He walks back to the bus, tips his hat back, and stares up at the closed door. He bounces a little with impatience, with impotence. The rawhide strip at the bottom on his holster slaps lightly against his leg.

The man with the hose grins at him and suggests he step back or he's going to get an early shower.

Joey retreats a few steps, then turns and walks back to his mother. "Mom?"

"Joey. Honey. I'll tell you when, okay? You just have to be patient."

He squints as hard as he can. "Dad."

Patty turns her head, looks at him sideways. "What about him?"

"I think he's in trouble."

"How do you know?"

He puts a hand against his stomach and rubs it. "My tummy hurts."

"Well, maybe you're just hungry, what do you think about that?"

The little cowboy giggles. "Mom!"

Patty smiles, and reaches for her son's hand just as the bus driver steps out of the depot.

Joey hurries to his mother's side and looks up at the man, and whispers, "Is he going to take us home?"

"If you want, honey, if you want."

A few seconds pass before the boy nods.

3

"Do you know," John said with mild astonishment, "I have never been in a fight in my life?"

"Could've fooled me," she told him. She took hold of his arm and hauled herself to her feet, holding on because she was still shaking. Her side hurt where she had struck the rail, and she refused to think what would have happened if those filed brass knuckles had even brushed across her throat. Unconsciously her hand went to her neck, and she swallowed a sudden surge of nausea.

The sisters paused on their way to the exit, shopping bags in hand, handkerchiefs gone.

One of them looked down and said to the pirate, "Child, you the pure definition of trash," and spat at him dryly.

The other nodded at John with gratitude. "He was following us around, scared us half to death. Thought he was one of them drug boys, you know?"

He took in her girth and the clear strength in her hands, and said, "Well, I think he was lucky he didn't tangle with you."

"Oh, you right about that," the first woman agreed emphatically. "But it's nice having a man do all the work for a change."

He laughed softly, ducking his head in embarrassment.

The second sister reached across and patted Lisse's arm. "Don't you worry, honey. I saw what you did. But you let this man take the credit, it be good for his male mind."

And they were gone, and Lisse couldn't help it, she shifted until her arms were around him and her cheek was against his chest. "You know," she whispered, "you Northern boys haven't a clue how to run a proper picnic."

When finally he held her, too, she allowed herself to relax, sensing the still unconscious kid behind her and not really caring. However it had begun, this was nice, and she didn't even mind when the police met them onshore, asking questions, nodding, not really paying much attention when ambulance attendants took the pirate kid away. A few notes; a caution to John to come to the station for a statement, although it was clear they weren't going to make this a priority; a suggestion to her that she be careful with her mouth if she ever came up on a drugged-out idiot like this; a handshake all around; and they were gone, too.

Now, alone again, she felt awkward and uneasy. She guessed that, given half a chance, John would bolt the city so fast his shadow would have a hard time catching up. He looked up Canal, and she could see him trembling, catching himself, and trembling again. He kept licking his lips. He blinked too fast.

She knew how he felt.

The adrenaline had drained, and reaction had set in, the realization of what could have happened instead of what did.

She whirled toward the river and stamped her foot. "Damn, we left the food on the ferry."

"The hell with food," he grumbled. "What I need now, what I want now, is a stiff cold drink and I don't care what time it is."

"John," she warned.

"It's all right, I don't mean getting drunk." His head swiveled toward her. "Although that sure sounds tempting."

She didn't know whether he was kidding or not, not until she saw the lines around his eyes deepen. "Okay. Where?"

"Not the hotel. The Quarter. I want people, Lisse. Lots and lots of people."

Yet he didn't move until she took his hand, and they drifted toward the Square. Edges sharper, colors brighter, reminding her of the time she'd fallen from her bicycle and whacked her head against the pavement. All sound had an edge.

They turned the first corner, the gardens on their right, and there they were—the people watching the sidewalk artists, the people drifting in and out of the shops, the people walking past them and paying them no mind.

She squeezed his hand as they crossed over Bourbon Street, looking for a place that would hide them for a while. "John," she said, tugging his arm until he looked down, "why did the kid scream?"

He shook his head, and said, "His eyes."

IN THE MOOD

Oh, Lord, she thought, moving closer, holding tighter.

Everything had moved so fast, it hadn't registered until it was all over, until she'd watched them load the kid into the ambulance.

At the time she had thought it had only been her imagination.

He had the crow's eyes.

Bright, and blue.

And watching.

10

Bullé Pete's was on Burgundy, one of the few bars John had seen that wasn't open to the street. A sun-faded wide-plank facade, no windows at all, not even in the door propped open by a thick wedge of wood. They didn't have to go in to see that it was crowded.

"You wanted people," Lisse said after sticking her head in, stepping back and grinning. "There you go."

"People, not a mob," he answered sourly. "Hang on, I'll be back."

Inside, there were ferns hanging and potted, faded jazz festival posters on the back wall, lazy ceiling fans, and a jukebox that played zydeco and country almost loud enough to be heard. From the look of it, he figured most of the patrons were local, with just enough tourists to keep the prices decently high. A beer-and-a-shot place; asking for a margarita here, or even a hurricane, was an unspoken taboo even the newcomers sensed.

He ordered two beers in tall styrofoam cups; anything stronger, he decided, would crush his resolve.

Once outside, he handed one of the cups to Lisse and leaned against the wall. "To mysteries," he said, raising his drink to his lips.

"I hate mysteries," she answered. "How about to a kid who can't throw a punch worth a damn."

"Whatever," he said, drank, sighed, and wondered how he could have ever complained about the winters at home. The afternoon temperature had climbed, the breeze from the river didn't reach this far, and the beer wasn't all that cold.

It wasn't all that good, either, but it wasn't the brewer's fault.

He kept seeing the eyes—crow's eyes; pirate's eyes.

Joey's eyes.

He drank again.

Across the street was a dusty-paned antique shop. Above it, a balcony on which sat two black men, dressed in black, reading newspapers, smoking cigars.

Crows, he thought.

"Let's walk."

"Where?" She rolled her eyes. "Never mind. I know. People."

It wasn't hard to catch the strain in her voice, or, when he glanced over, to miss the taut muscles in her neck.

Then she shifted her cup to her left hand, hooked her arm around his left elbow, and said, "It is possible, even in this city, to talk and walk at the same time."

"And?" he said cautiously.

She hugged his arm more tightly. "What happened out there, John? I mean, I know what I saw, but . . . what happened?"

He didn't have the vaguest idea.

He hadn't been lying when he had told her he had never been in a fight before, but when that kid had regained his feet, those eyes suddenly big and glaring, he had moved without thinking. All he had wanted to do was keep those filed knuckles from slashing his throat; grabbing the wrists was pure self-preservation, not part of some plan.

He had heard nothing but his own breathing, felt nothing of the strain as he pulled the kid to him and spread his arms; but he did feel the kid's struggling, his head down, grunting, snarling, trying to outmuscle him. John's fury wouldn't allow it. He was more than ready to pull those arms out of their sockets, more than ready to toss the kid into the river.

Then the kid had raised his head, and John had seen the eyes.

He couldn't help it—he had whispered, "Joey?"

Then the kid screamed and passed out.

John stared into the cup, drained it, and tossed it into a city trash bin. Lisse threw hers away as well, but he noticed she had hardly drunk any beer at all.

They walked, and her hand drifted away from his arm.

They walked, and she reminded him they had to make their statement to the police.

She found them a taxi, and they said nothing on the way; two hours later they were on the street again, officially forgiven, the only information they were allowed was that the kid had suffered a concussion when Lisse had yanked him to the deck. He would be fine. They could go, with another warning about taking on street hustlers and thieves.

Again she found them a cab, and again they rode in silence. But once they reached the hotel, she stopped him before he went inside. Her head shook as she tried to find the words, and the expression to go with them, and after a few seconds he couldn't stand it anymore.

"It's all right," he said, forcing a knowing smile. "If I had been with me today, I wouldn't want to be with me anymore, either." Before she could make any gestures of protest, he held her shoulders and kissed her cheek, winked, and stepped back. Then he held up a finger. "Nuts, I forgot. When the banks open tomorrow, I'll get your money. I can . . . I'll put it in an envelope and leave it with your friend in the office there, all right?"

She nodded, gave him a quick wave, and hurried away.

He didn't watch.

As soon as she turned, he went inside, stood in the empty lobby and stared at the bar, its double doors open, soft music inside. The air-conditioning made him rub one arm slowly. His stomach told him he was hungry. His eyes told him the clerk at the front desk was trying to get his attention, waving with one hand while pointing to a stack of paper with the other.

But it was the man in the white suit and Panama hat that got his attention, sitting in a fan-back rattan chair beside the staircase.

Watching him.

If I go over there, he thought, I will probably lose my temper; if I don't go over there, I'll probably never know.

The old man tilted his head in greeting ever so slightly, crossed his legs, put his hat on his knee, and folded his hands in his lap. Patient; he was in no real hurry.

John considered his empty room, the dim comfort of the bar, the demands of his complaining stomach; there was no real competition, no true debate. The way things had gone today, they sure as hell couldn't get any worse.

He started across the floor, and changed his mind when he reached the fringed edge of the carpet. "I'll be with you in a minute," he said quietly, and as the old man nodded, he went to the front desk.

"Your printing, Mr. Bannock," the clerk said. "I had to get more paper, but it's all done."

John glanced at the closed manager's door. "Any problems?"

The clerk snorted.

"Can I leave this here for a minute?"

"Sure. No problem."

John picked up the top page and scanned it, leaned his elbows on the counter and said, "That man in the suit back there."

"Yes?"

"You know him?"

"Yes, sir."

John pointed at the page. "So who is he?"

There was a hesitation before the answer: "Lanyon Trask."

"Oh, really? Who's that? Somebody important?"

The clerk grunted a laugh. "He thinks he is."

"Politician? Hotel management?"

"Hell, no, a preacher."

John didn't react. He replaced the page on the stack, pulled a folded twenty from his pocket, and slid it across the counter, not bothering to blink when it vanished before it reached the other side.

The clerk slid the stack to the end of the counter. "Just pick it up when you're ready, Mr. Bannock. I'll see that nobody touches it."

"Thanks." He straightened, used one hand to pat his hair into a semblance of neatness, and said, "Well, guess I'll go see what he wants. Maybe get saved in the process."

He hadn't gone three steps before the clerk muttered, "Not in this lifetime."

John didn't look back, but he stifled a laugh and walked over to the old man, who pushed himself smoothly to his feet and held out a hand. "Lanyon Trask, Mr. Bannock. Reverend Lanyon Trask."

John shook the hand without speaking, pulled an armchair over and sat facing him, doing his best to breathe evenly as not to betray his nervousness. Trask was stout indeed, but unless that tailored suit was a miracle of concealment, there wasn't much soft about the man. His face was creased and wrinkled in just enough proportion to the natural smoothness of his cheeks and chin to signify age and wisdom, without losing strength. His hair was thinning, as white as his suit, professionally tucked in gentle sweeps around his ears and above his collar.

And his eyes were as Lisse had said—gray and pale, disturbingly so, as if they were, for the right people, transparent.

"What do you want, Mr. Trask?" he said evenly.

Trask didn't blink at the deliberate avoidance of his title. "You, sir. You."

A professionally trained voice as well, John figured; professionally deep, professionally Southern. Modulation on command, to suit the climate or the pulpit. He suspected the man had never played good ol' boy in his life.

"Meaning what?" he asked, just shy of being rude.

Trask set the Panama on the table beside him, a deliberate movement, as was easing back in his seat, settling himself for comfort, clasping his hands loosely across his abdomen. Inhaling slowly, deeply.

John had little patience for the display, but he hoped his irritation didn't show. He had had enough for one day. Enough, he figured, for a lifetime or two. He felt battered, immensely weary, and the only reason he was here, now, was because he was too tired to do anything else.

"You probably don't know me," the minister said. A self-deprecating shrug. "I am not the kind of man who seeks the limelight."

John waited; the man was lying.

"Oh, I do have a small following, of course. I do find myself on occasion appearing in the media. But—" A vague wave; a dismissal. "It is, as they say, of no consequence."

Suddenly John pointed. "Television. I saw you on television this morning."

Trask nodded modestly. "One of many, I'm sure."

This, John remembered, was the one who spoke of the Beast. White robe, huge church, several hundred in the congregation, a monster pipe organ ranged behind him.

He couldn't help it: "You don't seek the limelight?"

"No." Trask smiled, carefully. "My forebears in the ministry used wagons and tents, then radios and auditoriums. No one listens to the radio anymore, so I use the next generation of communication, Mr. Bannock. Can't be faulted for that, now can I."

"What do you want?"

"I already told you, sir."

John closed his eyes briefly, wishing he could sleep, wishing he could open his eyes and find himself in his room, in bed, packed and ready to get out of New Orleans and get home again. Wishing he could open his eyes and see Patty and Joey standing on the lawn, waiting for him.

Four men and a woman hurried into the lobby from the outside, heading loudly for the front desk where, loudly, they demanded directions to the best casinos in town. Their voices echoed.

John watched them for a moment.

"Are you a believer, sir?"

John bridled as he turned back. "Don't start," he warned.

The minister's palms snapped up high. "I didn't mean offense, Mr. Bannock, not at all. Just asking, that's all."

"It's none of your business."

Laughter from the five at the desk.

"Perhaps not, sir, perhaps not. But I think, believer or not, that I can help you in your quest."

It was as if a plug had been pulled. Strength and energy drained, and John sagged, grinned, chuckled as he shook his head. "I haven't the slightest idea what you're talking about, Mr. Trask, and frankly, I don't care. You've been following me around, asking questions about me, and I want to know why. If you're going to tell me, fine. If not, I'm on my way home."

Trask seemed maddeningly unperturbed, so much so that John had a frightening urge to throttle him. Instead, he drew a heavy hand over his face and said, "Good-bye, Mr. Trask."

Trask held up a hand. "Your work."

John sighed. "What about it?"

Trask moistened his lips, glared at the commotion at the front desk, and bowed his head for a moment. "First, I must apologize for seeming to know more about you than perhaps I should, considering we have never met. I have . . ." He looked up at the ceiling, two floors above their heads, lips moving as he sought the right words. Finally: "My congregation, Mr. Bannock, is rather ordinary in terms of size. Certainly not when compared to the . . . let's say the more high-profile 'stars' of my profession. But what my people lack in numbers, they more than make up for in their undying belief in the Gospels.

"They trust me, Mr. Bannock. They trust me not to betray that trust. And because of that trust, they tell me things. In confidence, of course. In the certain knowledge that what they tell me will be put to good use."

"Spies," John accused before he could stop himself.

"Gatherers," Trask corrected.

Right, of course, how foolish of me, John thought, and refused to meet the man's gaze. Those pale eyes disturbed him, and for no reason he could think of, he was relieved when he finally saw the man blink.

Yet he couldn't move, couldn't leave.

A part of him commanded his legs to take him up, his voice to say farewell.

Yet he couldn't move.

A part of him shrilled that Lisse was right, that he was only a CPA, for crying out loud. A man who worked numbers. A man who figured taxes. Nobody special; just a guy who wanted to get his butt home and get his family back together and get himself a life again. A real life. No books, no articles, just numbers on a form.

Yet he couldn't move.

The guests left the lobby as noisily as they had entered, one brushing against the back of his chair, apologizing, and moving on in the wake of his friends' laughter.

The chime of the elevator.

The clash of plates in the café as a busboy cleared a table.

"Mr. Bannock," said Reverend Trask, "you've been talking to murderers, listening to their stories."

John blinked rapidly, hands gripping the armrests tightly.

"I have no doubt you have seen firsthand the devastation in our heartland. The empty fields, the flooded fields, the fields that no longer produce what we as a nation require."

John swallowed.

Trask leaned forward, hands on his knees, lowering his voice as if in fear of being overheard. "Believer or not, John Bannock, I know that you know this isn't natural. This isn't right. This isn't the plan our Lord has put forth."

John swayed as he sat.

"Tell me, John," Trask whispered. Smiling kindly. Grandfather and preacher rolled into one. "Tell me, John. Tell me you do not believe the Antichrist walks among us."

John stared at him, gaped at him, felt a bubble of giggles expand in his throat.

"I can help you, John."

John forced his gaze away from those eyes, concentrating on the ceiling fans, picking a single blade to follow its revolution.

"I can help you, John."

Swallowing the giggles, feeling back in his legs and arms.

"Tell me."

You know something, Ace? Patty said from the staircase; *this guy's not all there, you know what I mean? Looney Tunes, man, he's Looney Tunes.*

He nodded, swallowed again, and stood quickly, so quickly the lobby tilted for a moment.

"Tell me."

When equilibrium returned, he looked at the preacher and shook his head slowly. "No."

Trask sat back. Still smiling. Still confident.

"There's nothing to tell, Mr. Trask. You're barking up the wrong tree."

Trask raised an eyebrow. "I don't think so, Mr. Bannock."

"Good for you," and he walked away, taking his time, making sure his knees weren't about to buckle, making sure he didn't laugh in the man's face.

And he didn't turn around when Trask said to his back, "We'll meet again, Mr. Bannock. We'll meet again. Because the truth is . . . you need me."

Part 2

1

The sky was clear over Vallor on Monday morning, such a regular occurrence over the past three months that letters to the local paper were almost taken seriously whenever they suggested sending to South Dakota for some Indians to do whatever it was they did to bring back the rain. Most of the leaves on the great oaks and maples had already turned and fallen. Water wasn't close to being rationed, but the restaurants no longer served glasses of it automatically. And there was a peculiar fondness for stories of the good old days, two years before, when the Ohio rose, the Mississippi flooded, and Oakbend Creek left its bed with a vengeance for the first time in forty years.

Vallor was not, even to its most fervent boosters, a particularly unique community. It had begun as a crossroads for wagons and stages west, and a place where area farmers could buy their feed and food. Large enough now to be found on most maps, not so large that it couldn't handle itself. The early-nineteenth-century founders had laid the streets out in a simple grid, the north-south streets all numbered, the east-west streets all, for reasons unknown, named after the presidents. Two high schools that were able, barely, to manage the student population. A downtown that thrived because there were no cities or shopping malls close enough to siphon off the customers. A railhead for produce and a few cattle to be sent northeast to Chicago, northwest to St. Louis. The original farms long since consolidated into a handful, those that were still in business after the floods, and now the drought. A dozen churches and a synagogue.

And dust.

Grit.

It rode on the breeze and sifted into everything, covered everything, made everyone who went outdoors want to brush their teeth four times a day.

When the breeze strengthened, there were thin clouds of it, rising from the farmland like a sickly fog. Not very high, and they didn't travel very far, but it was clear to those who bothered to pay attention to such things that a windstorm would be all it would take to carry the topsoil away. Like Oklahoma. Like Texas. Like half the Midwest over the past half decade.

The difference here, some tried to point out, was the not-quite-flat land. Knobs and knolls rather than hills, trees and still-flowing creeks would all keep disaster to a minimum because the dust and grit wouldn't go very far before landing on something. Unlike Oklahoma. Unlike Texas. It would have to be, they claimed, the Windstorm from Hell to do anything more than wipe out a few farms and make a few cars extra dirty.

A few preachers pointed out that Hell was already here; all they needed was the wind.

2

1

Sharon Gillespie stood in front of her open locker, ignoring the bedlam around her, the jostling, the cracks, the plans being made for after school. She pulled on her quilted jacket, rolled her shoulders to settle it, then grabbed her notebook, history and English texts, and her purse. She answered no questions, acknowledged no calls, gave no one a smile as she made her way down the crowded hall and out the side door. It was lunchtime, but she wasn't hungry; she had modern civ next, but she had no intention of going back. She walked to the corner and turned right, heading west on Jackson. Taking her time. Books hugged snugly to her chest. Staring hard at the sidewalk, using the cracked and dusty concrete to keep the images at bay, using the sound of her shoes to keep the narrator's voice from filling her head, using every trick she knew to keep the tears where they belonged.

And failing.

Failing badly.

"Hey, Sharon!"

No need to look back; only Mag Baer had a voice like that. Husky, with the occasional unexpected crack to a pitch as high as an excited child's.

"Hey!"

She walked on, not turning her head until Mag hustled up beside her, puffing, frowning, finally bumping her with her shoulder.

"What's going on?"

There was no need to answer.

It was supposed to have been a simple exercise in Communications that day—watch the noon headline stories and come up with ten questions per story the news anchor or reporter didn't answer, and how they might be answered in a newspaper or newsmagazine. They did it at least three times a month; most of the time she could do it without even watching.

First there was a heavily wooded West Virginia hillside, then a narrow road that ran along a shallow creek more stones than water. Houses— shacks and shanties, really—clustered back in the trees; pickups and rusted cars; a tire swing; a refrigerator on its side, the door gone, porcelain chipped; several gardens with nothing in them but weeds. The camera was the reporter's eye, moving up a worn path toward one of the houses, veering away from the porch to go around the side to the back. The reporter's voice was hushed, almost whispering, as she described what everyone could al- ready see—there no was no one here, no dogs, no chickens, no birds, not a thing.

When she finally stopped talking, they could hear the crunch of footsteps and the rattle of a breeze through the bare branches. Nothing more.

The backyard was empty. A clothesline strung between two canted poles held a child's dress, a man's shirt, a set of long underwear that made some of the boys laugh until Mr. Willyard shut them up. A stake in the ground off to the right had a chain leash attached to it, but there was no sign of a dog, or whatever had been kept there. To the left, near the house, was a lean-to that protected a meager stack of chopped wood.

The camera panned across the yard, stopping when it discovered an outhouse back near the treeline.

That's when Kyle Dovinsky said, "Hey, Gillespie, looks like they got your place by mistake."

The laughter was equal parts cruel and embarrassed, and Sharon could only stare blindly at the screen while fire burned through her cheeks. Even Mr. Willyard grinned a little, and she hated him for that.

Then the reporter said, "Oh my God," and the class shut up.

At first it didn't look like much—a basic outhouse, unpainted and narrow, with its door slightly open, something like a piece of wood caught at the cor- ner. Nothing to get excited about until the camera zoomed in, and the piece of wood blurred for a moment, the lens focused, and they could see it.

IN THE MOOD

The bare foot.

A child's emaciated bare foot.

Sharon had shut her eyes then, and several others weren't able to stifle a gasp, a half sob, a startled curse.

She didn't dare look again until she heard the anchor's voice: ". . . which brings the unofficial total to just over nine hundred. Authorities both here and in other states speculate it could easily reach twice that before the Appalachian sweep is over."

And Kyle Dovinsky, astonishing everyone with his outrage, said, "How the goddamn hell can a thousand people starve to death in this country? What the hell's going on?"

Mr. Willyard didn't even give him detention for his language.

He didn't have an answer, either.

"Shar, come on," Mag said, bumping her again.

"No. I'm not going back." She looked down at her friend. "I can't. Not after . . . I can't."

"Okay." A shrug. "Whatever. But Willyard's gonna be pissed, you know."

"Like I care."

Mag giggled. "You will when the grades come out."

"Sure. Right."

Of all the things she had to worry about, grades were pretty much down near the bottom of the list. She wasn't valedictorian material or anything, but it would take practically World War Three to keep her from graduating with anything lower than a 3.5. After that, she was out of Vallor, out of Illinois. For good. Forever. Applications had already gone out, not a single college closer than six hundred miles. If she didn't get in, she'd leave anyway. The only regret, and it wasn't much of one, was that she hadn't stuck with basketball. As tall as she already was, and as popular as women's basketball had grown across the country, an athletic scholarship would have nailed her escape. As it was, she had to work like a mutt to keep those grades.

As it was—

A sharp tug on her ponytail made her blink.

"Hello?" Mag said. "You still in there?"

Her answer was a jab with an elbow, provoking an outburst of outrageous indignation that carried them for the next two blocks. By the time the insults and mock threats had run out, they had also just about run out of town.

Two blocks to the tracks.

Here, there were ordinary houses on ordinary lawns under ordinary trees that seemed as old as the town itself; here, there were shrubs and small flower gardens and signs of children scattered over the grass; here, there was Vallor West High School, faded brick and white trim and too small for its student population, even with Vallor East, a place twice as big, siphoning the extra.

There, on the other hand, was . . . there.

"I'm gone," Mag announced, heading north on Second Street. "One thing I don't need now is Poppa Bear catching my ass on the street instead of in class."

"Call you later," Sharon called as her friend hurried off. The answer was a waggling finger over Mag's shoulder just before she broke into a hasty trot. For a deliciously evil second, Sharon was tempted to imitate a police car siren, just to see how fast the girl could run. But that would be too mean. It was hard enough lugging a policeman around as a father, without her adding to it. Still . . .

She grinned and walked on, in no hurry at all. That morning had been cold, a touch of frost on the ground, but the afternoon sun had sucked up most of the chill, and her jacket, even unzipped, had grown too warm. By the time she reached the house, she'd be lucky not to be drenched in sweat.

And a voice said, *perspiration, dear, perspiration. Men sweat, women perspire.*

The grin flashed again. For all that her mother had grown up during the sixties, hippies and communes and equal rights and like that, she was way too much like Grandma, anymore. Demanding she be ladylike at all times, despite her half inch shy of six feet, despite the undeniable fact that the only time she ever felt like a lady was when she was in the shower and could see that she was. Which wasn't exactly what Mom and Grandma meant, but it was all Sharon was willing to give them.

Maybe if she had a father, things would be different.

But she didn't, and they weren't.

Not, however, as bad as butthead Dovinsky made out.

She sighed loudly, considered taking off her jacket before she roasted, and trudged on, daring someone to stop her, to demand to know why she wasn't in school, so she could take her anger out on someone, anyone, it didn't matter who; so she could let them know what she had just seen and heard and demand answers she already knew weren't there.

She wished Mr. Bannock were here.

He wasn't a teacher or anything, but he was a pretty cool neighbor who liked to help out once in a while, especially when her mother pretended she could do everything herself. Most of the time it worked out pretty good; sometimes, though, she needed more help than her daughter could give her, and Mr. Bannock was pretty reliable, most of the time, when he didn't have to work.

"Yo! Gillespie!"

She looked up quickly, as if whoever it was had been reading her mind, which made her blush, and that made her angry. She hated blushing, a condition that happened far too easily, far too often.

A blush is becoming, her Grandma said; *it adds a lovely color to your face.*

Which, as always, only made it worse.

"Gillespie, you still on this planet or what?"

"Very funny, Kyle," she said. "And why aren't you back in class?"

She stood on the last corner. To her right was an old warehouse, windows and doors boarded up, sparkles of broken glass amid the gravel at the foundation. Across Jackson, on the other corner, was Hummaker's Feed and Grain, its two large display windows tinted and blind, a pair of pickups and a dump truck around the side nearest the tracks.

The tracks here, as they were all along their route past town, were higher than street level by a good five feet for no reason anyone could think of; the land along the route didn't climb naturally, it was a man-made rise. Dovinsky, in jeans and flannel shirt, worn western boots, a denim jacket draped over one shoulder, leaned against the near striped gate, arms folded across his chest, a disgusting smirk on his, if she were to be honest about it, not too disgusting face.

He didn't answer. Instead, finally pushing a hand back over his brushcut, he jerked his head—*come on, I'll walk you.*

She almost balked. If Mag had stuck around, she would've made some excuse about studying at her house, and they would have turned around and walked away.

It would be kind of obvious she was lying if she made the excuse now.

"Come on, Sharon," he said, gesturing for her to get a move on.

She pointed at him, frowning. "No funny stuff."

He laughed. "Yeah. Right." But to her surprise, he sounded a little disappointed.

Stuck on you, Grandma said.

And Sharon whispered, "Grandma, I love you but you're dead, go away."

2

The main part of Vallor stopped at the tracks. Beyond, along Jackson and the three other streets that crossed over the rails, were a handful of farms, isolated stands of what was left of the original woodland, and Les Burgoyne's spread, up near Oakbend Creek—seven hundred acres of paddocks and pasture for the three dozen horses he and his wife raised or boarded. It had originally been a dairy farm, but competition and weather had finally been too much, and the family made the decision to change over almost fifteen years ago.

It had worked.

Les wasn't wealthy, Fran didn't wear fancy clothes or drive a fancy car, but there was enough in the bank and enough coming in to tide them over these hard times. That the horses weren't skin and bone was due mainly to an irrigation system he had installed himself, the water drawn from three wells he had sunk with equipment rented from Horst Hummaker. Still, it hadn't been an entirely successful. The grass still died, and during the worst of the drought he had had to ration his own supply; the water table had dropped and he had no ready cash to drive deeper wells.

What bothered him most today were the horses.

They wouldn't keep still.

Those few he kept in the barn for various reasons—injuries and minor aches—were uneasy in their stalls; those in the field, nine of them today, were in constant motion from one fence to another. Walking sometimes, trotting most of the time. Like a herd that knew a bad storm was on the way.

The problem was, the forecast was as it had been for a week, and there was nothing in the sky to call the weatherman a liar.

And so they moved.

Back and forth.

Without making a sound.

3

Jackson west of the tracks was shaded, when there was shade, by massive oaks whose branches more often than not interlaced over the worn blacktop road. Here and there behind them were houses built on large plots purchased from farmers who needed extra cash. Sharon's out-of-town relatives thought the rich had to live here, the houses were so big, the land so lovely, and she had given up trying to explain that the rich had chosen the east side of Vallor, primarily to stay away from the pungent odors of the farms and the Burgoyne ranch.

"You know," Kyle said, shaking his head at the ground, "that stuff in class."

"Please, okay? I don't want to talk about it."

They were half a mile past the tracks, not bothering to hurry, walking on the edge of the blacktop, since sidewalks out here had never been laid down, and no one had ever asked for them. The houses were farther apart now, older, not quite as large or quite as well kept.

"I didn't mean it, you know. Really. What I said. In class, I mean. I mean—"

She couldn't take it anymore. "What do you want, Kyle?"

He stumbled in his surprise and looked at her as if she were from another galaxy or something. She had a feeling she had just made a major mistake, but she wasn't sure which one it was. Nor did she know how to apologize again—for the hurt look on his face still touched with tan, for the way his hands kept trying to stay in his pockets, for the way he'd look at her and try to speak, shake his head and try again.

It didn't occur to her until he picked up a birch switch and began to whip everything in his path that he was embarrassed.

Shy.

Kyle Dovinsky was, right there in front of her, actually and unbelievably shy.

She blinked so rapidly she feared she'd make herself dizzy.

My God, could this mean he—

"Listen," he said, one shoulder up, tossing the switch away. "The Kentucky thing this weekend."

Which was what half the school had been in an uproar over since the fall session had begun. Vallor West had arranged to play a home-and-home football series with some school in Kentucky, some forty miles or so south as the crow flies, just across the Ohio. Although, as her mother once said, no crow would bother to take the trouble. None of her friends knew why such a deal had been made, since it was obviously going to cost a bundle to send kids, band, and the team down. But it definitely gave the grown-ups something to talk about all day. According to the newspaper, other communities were watching closely, mainly to see if Vallor made any money off the visitors once all the bills were in.

This weekend was the first game.

"You know?" he said.

"Sure, sure, I know." Oh no, she thought; oh please no, he's not—"What about it?"

"You going?"

"I don't know. I hadn't really planned on it."

"Really?"

"Really."

"Wow," he said quietly, as if not going were unthinkable. "Well . . . wow."

She didn't offer him any help. She couldn't. It wasn't that she hadn't dated before; it wasn't that she believed she was an ugly duckling, although her face was a little long, her mouth a little too wide; it wasn't that she thought Kyle was ugly, because he wasn't.

It was—

"So," he said, walking backward ahead of her, the switch still in his hand, "Leuman and some guys, you know what I mean, he's . . . we were going to drive down, you know? I kind of figured maybe . . . you know?"

—because too many of them thought she was something like a trophy. Something to show off because she was so big. A few cracks, a few giggles, not a whole lot of fun.

She stopped. "Take off your boots."

He gaped. "What?"

Her head cocked, her expression hardened. "Take off your boots and ask me again."

He sputtered and looked around as though asking an invisible audience if they knew what was going on because he sure didn't. Then, to her astonishment, he checked behind him for traffic, looked back toward town, stood in the middle of the road on his jacket and took off his boots.

Awkwardly.

But he took them off.

Doing her best not to smile, she listened to his grumbling, wondering what his father would think if he could see him now. Marcotte Dovinsky owned Dove's Department Store, on the corner of Fourteenth and Madison, smack in the middle of downtown, practically the geographical center of Vallor. The oldest, largest store in town. Three-piece suit, pocket watch, hair that looked like it had been slicked back with oil, and an attitude that did its best to make everyone else feel small.

Kyle, as far as she could tell, was exactly the opposite, most of the time.

When he finished, he walked straight up to her, the top of his head near level with her eyes. She had never realized how short he really was. Compared to her. And how round his face was, pleasantly so. How big his eyes were.

Watch it, she warned; watch it.

He looked up and grinned. "So? This some kind of power thing or what?"

"Are you still asking?"

"Sure I'm still asking."

Stocking feet, looking up at a girl, that dumbass grin on his face, no embarrassment at all. And definitely not his father.

She shrugged. "I guess."

Satisfied, he nodded once, walked back to his boots, sat on his jacket, and pulled them on. "You're crazy, Gillespie, you know that, right?"

"Could be."

He waved off an offer to help him to his feet, dusted off the jacket, slung it back over his shoulder, and said, "Come on, I'll walk you the rest of the way. At least to the creek."

"It's almost a mile," she answered, not really protesting.

"No big. I need the exercise."

Two miles out total, two miles back; she figured he'd be dead on his feet by the time he got home.

"Okay."

"Just do me a favor, okay? Let's not stop to watch the horses."

4

In the late 1930s someone in Vallor got the idea that Roosevelt's WPA should pay for the new town hall and police station. Although few believed it would happen, it did. Now half the town wished it hadn't.

It was a rococo monster of large-block granite and pillars and high windows and ornate lintel inscriptions better suited to a community three times the size. The vaulted hall immediately inside the triple front doors was tiled in swirled marble, inlaid with the state and town seals, lit by a chandelier that would have been more at home in a French palace whose owner never gave a thought to practicality. The city offices were down a corridor to the left, the police offices down a corridor to the right; directly ahead, a fan-shaped staircase leading up to the second level where the courts were. And the mayor.

Even crowded it sounded hollow.

Arn Baer stood on the sidewalk, just around the corner on Seventeenth Street, out of the flow of the lunchtime secretary and clerk flow. A few nodded to him, a few called him by name, none stopped to pass the time. He never wore a uniform, braids and studs and belts and sharp creases. He let his men do all the strutting and posing. After ten years as chief, he believed that his suit was uniform enough. They knew who he was. Hell, everyone knew who he was.

Which was why he couldn't decide what to do now.

The call from the school had torched his temper, and he was out of the office and on his way to his car before he had even figured out how, exactly, he was going to handle Margaret. Skipping school in the middle of the day. Bold as brass, walking right out without even looking back.

Did she really think no one would notice, that no one would call him?

He glared at the traffic, glared at the miserable clear sky, glared at his polished shoes and figured maybe this wasn't the time to confront her. Step through the front door now and he'd probably throttle her. No sense talking to her mother, either. Working at the bank like Vonda did, until she dropped that job quick to take on a partner and open that bookstore, Vonda believed in independence for women, and that included their teenage daughter.

He stuck his hands in his trouser pockets, and slumped back against the wall.

Women, he was positive, were going to be the death of him.

Five minutes later one of his deputies ran up to him and said, "Chief, you'd better come with me."

"What now?"

"We've got another one."

Suddenly the afternoon wasn't so warm anymore.

5

"You weren't supposed to do this," Kyle complained.

The entrance to the Burgoyne ranch was a whitewashed split-rail arch. The driveway went some fifty yards in before forking at the base of a large willow—to the right, the drive led to the back of the ranch house; to the left, to the stables and barns. It would not have been out of place in Wyoming.

"Oh, stop it," she scolded lightly.

The split-rail fence extended eighty yards or so east and west of the entrance, and when they reached the westernmost corner, she leaned on the fence, Kyle fidgeting behind her. Through a smattering of tall broad pines to the left of the house she could see someone perched on a white paddock fence just beyond the stables, probably Mr. Burgoyne by the white western hat, and the horses chasing each other across the grass.

Back and forth.

She frowned.

Back and forth.

Kyle finally came up beside her, hands in his pockets, nodded toward the animals. "You ride, huh?"

"Sometimes. I help Mr. Burgoyne once in a while. The stables and all."

He chuckled. "Must be easy, huh? You're as big as they are."

When she glared, he brought up his hands. "Hey, I didn't mean that. I meant tall, you know? Easier to get on and stuff." He shrugged and put his hands back. "That's all I meant. Jeez, Gillespie, you're touchy."

I wonder why, she thought. Years of jokes and tricks and people exaggerating when they look up, trying to look me in the face. How's the weather up there, kid; you must be a hell of a basketball player. I wonder why?

Then, for the first time in a long time, she muttered, "Sorry."

"No sweat."

She pushed away from the fence and led him up the road. A glance to her right to check the horses again, but she couldn't see them now. They were blocked by the willows and birch that lined the crooked Oakbend Creek bed. It was kind of weird though, the way they moved. Keeping in a bunch, not kicking up their heels, not trying to nip one another's flanks.

A glance at the sky, but no sign of a storm.

"You know," Kyle said, "for all those horses, they sure were quiet."

6

Les couldn't take it anymore. The damn things spooked him, and he swung stiffly to the ground, told himself he was being an idiot, and took his time walking over to the stables—two, parallel to each other, a dozen stalls in each. Once inside the first, he checked on an old roan Fran had taken in out of pity when the owner wanted to put the poor thing down because she couldn't gallop much anymore. As if growing old and getting slow was a crime.

The roan poked her head over the stall gate and whickered at him.

"Hey, girl," he said, opening the gate and easing his way in. "Let's take a look at that leg, okay?"

The left hind leg was lightly wrapped, a sprain when the animal had tried to turn too quickly last week. It was, in more ways than one, a pain, but she was lucky, at her age, the bone hadn't snapped.

She stood patiently while he stroked her flank, stroked the leg, and wrinkled his nose against the pungent smell of the ointment.

It took a moment to realize the wrapping was too loose.

"You been trying to break out?" he asked, and shook his head. It didn't take a minute to strip the bandage away, but it did take a minute for him to believe what he saw.

"Damn," he said.

The swelling wasn't down, it was gone, with no discoloration or, when he passed a hand over it, apparent tenderness.

"Now how," he said, "did you manage to pull that trick off, lady?"

7

She was on her front lawn, the old woman was, long gray hair loose and flying, wearing only an old pair of panties and a bra.

She danced across the grass, scrawny arms high, legs stiff, face to the sky and her eyes closed as she sang.

Chief Baer stood on the sidewalk and shook his head sadly. "What's that, Rafe, eight? Nine?"

Deputy Rafe Schmidt checked the notepad he kept in his breast pocket. "Fourteen."

"Jesus, that many?"

He didn't wait for confirmation. Rafe was a little short on the personal touch, but no one ever argued with his record keeping. A sigh, a glance at the folks gathered on neighboring lawns despite admonishments to get back inside, and he stepped onto the lawn.

"Mrs. Grauer?"

The old woman ignored him. Still dancing. Singing quietly to herself.

"What the hell is that song?" Rafe wanted to know. As far as he was concerned, if it wasn't rock 'n' roll, it wasn't worth remembering, much less listening to.

" 'So Rare.' " Baer answered. "One of the Dorsey brothers. I ain't heard that one in a hundred years." He took another step. "Mrs. Grauer? It's me, Chief Baer. You want to stop a moment and talk to me?"

He counted to five.

She stopped, out of breath but still singing.

He counted to five again.

She opened her eyes, saw him, and screamed.

8

Just beyond the Burgoyne ranch, Jackson Street rose over a low bridge so unobtrusive that motorists who didn't know the area seldom realized it was there. Ten feet below was Oakbend Creek, twenty feet wide and running shallow.

Kyle leaned over the chest-high wood guardrail. "Sucks, doesn't it."

Sharon agreed. There were places, though not here, where the creek used to be deep enough to swim in. Now it was shallow enough all over that walking across barely got your feet wet, even in the pools. She turned away and hugged her books closer to her chest.

Across the bridge on the other side of the street was a low and wide two-story house whose front lawn needed mowing, whose wraparound porch needed a good sweeping. A small, gold-and-black-lettered sign near the road told passersby that taxes and estates and other financial services were available inside.

Used to be, anyway.

Kyle followed her gaze. "Not home yet, huh?"

She shook her head. "Nope."

"He ever coming back?"

She didn't know. The last postcard she had received from Mr. Bannock was a week ago. From New Orleans. No mention of him ever coming back to Vallor at all.

"Wife never came back either, huh?"

"No." She didn't like to talk about Patty Bannock. The separation and swift divorce had shocked her, and leaving town with Joey had stunned her.

"Oh, well," he said. "That's the breaks, I guess."

That he didn't sound sympathetic didn't surprise her. His mother had left Vallor when he was only four, and he had had something like four step-mothers since. The first three hadn't lasted very long, and there were already rumors flying about the fourth.

He shifted his jacket and looked back toward the tracks. The gentle rise and fall of the road made the going appear more difficult than it was. "You remember," he said, scratching an ear, "that party that summer?" He smiled. "Seemed like the whole world was here, remember?"

She did.

Patty and John had thrown a seventh-birthday party for Joey, and not only did it seem like half the town had shown up at one point or another, but a ton of relatives from all over the country, too. Not Mr. Bannock's; his people were all dead. They were Patty's, and spent every second fussing over the kid. Mr. Burgoyne had brought over a couple of his smaller, tamer horses for the kids to ride; Chief Baer, in a rare decent mood, had parked a patrol car on the road and let the kids turn on the spinning lights, use the siren, a couple of times call in to the station on the radio; Kyle's Step-mother-of-the-Day had too much to drink and nearly stripped naked; even Mr. Trout had wandered down from his place at road's end, his white beard and long white hair making the kids think Santa Claus had come early; she and Mag had snuck glasses of wine from the grown-ups' table and chugged it behind the house—Mag had thrown up, and she had had a splitting headache for the rest of the day.

Not to mention some old guy, one of Patty's people, who kept hitting on her all the time, thinking, because of her height, she was a lot older than she was.

Actually, now that she thought about it, it was kind of cute. In a sick sort of way.

Kyle cleared his throat. "Going back, I guess," he said, taking a step in that direction.

"Oh. Well. Thanks."

"No sweat."

Good Lord, he wanted to kiss her. She knew it; she just knew it.

He took another step. "School, right?"

"Right."

"Okay." He nodded and walked away, stopped at the end of the bridge and said, "You weren't kidding about Saturday, were you?"

"What about it?"

"The game."

"Oh. No." She grinned. "Wear your boots."

It took him a second to get it; when he did, he laughed, waved, and walked off. Faking a limp for a few steps just to show her the sacrifice he had made. Turned, waved again, and moved on.

Without really knowing why, she watched until he began to sink beyond the first low rise. When she turned away and looked down at the creek, she felt . . . not sad, not really empty, just not . . . right.

She thought she heard Grandma laughing.

"Knock it off," she muttered. "It isn't funny."

Still, all in all, she felt kind of strange and nice inside, and more than a little nervous. Mag, of course, would think it was great and would probably insist this was a great excuse to head down to Dove's and empty their bank accounts. That was always her response to most good news—head for the nearest clothing department and raid her purse.

Sharon giggled, made a face, and waggled her fingers at Mr. Bannock's house as she went by. Home soon, she thought; soon and safe.

Maybe she ought to get her brother to—

The long rolling explosion startled her so much she dropped her books.

Automatically she looked up, through the thin and thick branches looking like cracks in blue ice.

No clouds.

No wind.

She could have sworn it was thunder.

She knew it had to be thunder when the wind squall came up. Sharp. Cold. Scattering her papers across the road. Forcing her to turn around and hunch her shoulders, cover her eyes, close her mouth.

The force of it shoved her a few paces toward the bridge.

Dust slapped the back of her jacket and jeans.

She was ready to go to her knees, when abruptly it stopped.

The first thing she thought was: Great, now I'll have to take a shower.

The second thing was: It didn't make any noise.

The wind didn't make any noise.

Deputy Schmidt squinted knowledgeably at the sky through his sunglasses. "Sonic boom," he declared with assurance.

Chief Baer watched the attendants wheel a humming Mrs. Grauer into the ambulance. "Thunder," he said.

"No clouds."

Baer looked up and frowned. "Oh."

"Sonic boom."

No contrails, no silver speck, nothing up there but nothing.

When the squall hit, it took his hat from his head and pinwheeled it across the old lady's lawn. He chased after it, shading his eyes with one hand, cursing when he slipped on the grass and fell on his rump.

He heard the frantic creak of a shutter.

He heard Schmidt yelp in pain.

He heard Mrs. Grauer's slow rising scream.

What he didn't hear was the wind.

* * *

IN THE MOOD

Kyle rolled his eyes when the thunder broke, thinking that today of all days it was finally going to rain, he was going to get drenched, catch triple pneumonia, spend the rest of his life in a hospital, and never get to go out with Sharon.

When the wind slammed him to his knees, he cried out in startled pain and ducked his head, feeling the grit scour the back of his neck while his teeth chattered in the knife-edge cold.

When the wind stopped, he thought he had gone deaf because, except for the thunder, he hadn't heard a thing.

Mag stood at the kitchen door and hugged herself while she searched for the clouds the thunder told her had to up there.

When the squall hit the back porch and knocked all her mother's plants off the railing, she tried to open the door and save them, but the wind wouldn't let her.

It blasted through every crack and window in the old house.

The furnace roared on.

Napkins fluttered helplessly off the kitchen table.

In the yard the umbrella clothesline spun like a carousel.

She reached for the door again, and the wind stopped.

Everything stopped but the clothesline.

Les stood in the stable doorway, holding on hard to his hat, and watched the horses, afraid they would bolt the way they had been acting, counting himself lucky he had kept them in the large paddock instead of the pasture.

The thunder had frozen them.

The wind made them turn their backs, lower their heads. Even from here, he could see their flanks quivering, their nostrils flaring.

They're going to bolt, he thought; they're going to bolt.

A few yards away from the herd, Royal stood alone. Ignoring the wind. His head up and slightly tilted. His ears pricked and turning.

What do you hear, boy? he thought; what do you hear?

It must be something, because he couldn't hear a damn thing.

3

In southern Indiana, the trees have already lost most of their leaves, and those that remain have barely any color. The dry summer has given autumn dust instead, spinning along the highway, every few days lifting like smoke to blur the sun and sky.

When the wind blows, the dust sounds like hail on the windows.

The bus pulls into Evansville depot just a few minutes past noon, brakes hissing, passengers lurching slightly. The schedule claims a forty-minute layover, and half the people aboard make directly for the restrooms, the snack bar, or the fresh air to stretch their legs, turning their backs to the easy wind and blowing dust.

The others just sit, dozing or staring out the tinted windows, hoping without much hope that the weather will be better once they get home.

The little cowboy, hat dangling on its beaded strap down his back, squeezes into the aisle past his mother, excusing himself when he accidentally steps on her foot.

"Where are you going, honey?"

"I have to pee."

"I'll come with you."

"No," he says with a soft smile. "It's okay, Mommy. You can see the door from here." He points out the window, just in case she's missed it.

Reluctantly: "All right. But you know the rules."

"Yes, Mother."

She giggles. When he nods like that and calls her "mother," she knows she's stated the obvious again. She slaps him lightly on the rump. "Just be careful."

He nods, closes his eyes, opens them quickly as a long peal of thunder startles him, tumbling, crackling, rising and fading like a train growling through the night. Outside, passengers look up hopefully; inside, two more hurry from their seats to the exit, muttering that it was about time.

The little cowboy looks up the aisle after them.

"Joey?"

"Huh?"

"Are you all right?"

He nods, a little shakily.

"It's just thunder, honey. I know you don't like it, but it's only thunder." She leans toward the window, the better to check the sky. "Rain, maybe, huh?"

"I don't . . ." Suddenly he smiles. "Can I have some change?"

"Why?"

He leans across her and points again. "When I'm done, I want to make a call."

"Honey, I don't know."

"Please, Mom? Huh? Please?"

She looks at the telephone fixed to the depot's outside wall, and shakes her head. "You'll never reach it, sweetheart. It's too high, see?"

"Then you can dial for me, okay? Okay?"

She sighs so he knows she knows she's being overindulgent and regretting it. Then she grabs her purse and pulls herself to her feet. "All right, kiddo, all right."

As they make their way up the aisle, the bus rocks against an abrupt blast of wind. She grabs the back of a seat and waits until it passes, then leans over and whispers, "So who are you going to call?"

He doesn't look back. "Guess."

4

1

It wasn't hard to picture Mag: in the kitchen, one of the chairs dragged under the wall phone, feet up on the seat, one arm wrapped around her shins, the receiver constantly shifting from ear to ear, the coiled cord forever threatening to strangle her. Sharon had seen it often enough; there were times when she seemed to spend as much time at the Baers as she did at home.

"I'm telling you," Mag said, her voice in a whisper as if fearing to be overheard, "it spun for about five minutes."

"Sure." Sharon sprawled on the living room couch, head propped on one armrest, feet dangling over the other, her favorite phoning position.

"Weird."

"Now that's true. It took me forever to get all my papers."

"I almost freaked. Maybe it's the end of the world, you know?"

Sharon laughed. "Yeah, right. One lousy thunder thing, it's the end of the world?"

"There weren't any clouds, Sharon. No clouds."

"So?"

"So you can't have thunder without any clouds."

"How do you know that?"

A long patient sigh. "Science, you dork. Don't you ever pay attention?"

Sharon didn't answer that one. Her grades were significantly better than

Mag's, a fact she never, but never, brought up. Instead, she said, "You've been listening to that guy too much."

She winced.

Mistake. Bad mistake.

"Reverend Trask isn't a 'guy,' Sharon," Mag said stiffly.

"Okay, okay, I'm sorry."

"He knows what he's talking about."

"Okay, already, I said I'm sorry."

Considering where they lived, cable was a godsend. Brother Phil always said that all they ever got with an antenna was the mooing of the damn cows. He had been saying that, she thought, since the day she was born, and it still, once in a while, made her laugh.

But it had brought them some of the most bizarre programs, too. One of them, in her mind, was the "Lord's Gospel News," a church thing from someplace down South that had hooked Mag big time. No one knew why; no one could explain it. And she was so defensive about it, no one had the nerve to put her on the spot.

"Just so you know," Mag said, pouting.

Sharon looked at the ceiling for help. For all Mag's language—which Mom called "earthy" and Brother Phil called "longshoreman"—for all the way she dressed sometimes, for the trouble she got into and the not-always-undeserved reputation she had around school, she still took her belief in God seriously.

Okay, Reverend Trask's God.

"No bread today," her friend persisted. "Mom called from the bookstore. She couldn't get any bread."

"I know."

"So . . . ?"

This one was too dangerous. She lifted her head and looked out the window. "Hey, there's Fish Man," she lied.

"Really? No kidding?"

"Nope."

Now there was excitement, the prospect of gossip. "What's he doing?"

"Hard to say. It looks like . . . oh my God."

"What? What?"

"He just ate a frog."

She bit her lips and closed her eyes.

When Mag finally shrieked her name in the midst of laughter, she relaxed. A close one. But leave it to icky George Trout to provide the way out of a sticky situation. Neither of them liked him very much. He was nice enough, she supposed, but he lectured all the time, and all the time talked about nothing but the crimes he had written about, the crime scenes he had been to, all the famous cops and FBI guys he knew and had known. It was like he was the world's expert on people cutting and shooting and slicing other people up, even though he had never once been on TV, and he wanted everyone else to know it. She figured you had to be sick in the head to like stuff like that. There had to be something wrong with you to actually enjoy stuff like that. And somehow he had sucked Mr. Bannock into it, too. Now Mr. Bannock was gone, and Joey and Patty were gone, and the Fish Man refused to talk about it. None of his business, he had told her once when she'd had the nerve to ask; none of his business, none of hers, and besides, John Bannock was only following his dream.

When Mag finally sobered, she said, "So what about Saturday? You going or what?"

Sure enough, when Sharon told her about Kyle, she insisted they head for Dove's after school the next day. This would require major planning if Sharon didn't want this one to get away.

"This one? What do you mean, this one?"

"Figure of speech, girl, now pay attention."

"Can't go tomorrow anyway. Mom's working late, Phil's going to Cairo to chew out some supplier, so I gotta make supper."

"No sweat. Wednesday, then."

"Maybe."

"No maybe. Yes. Always yes. Besides, those jeans are getting a little rank, if you know what I mean."

Sharon blinked. "What?"

"Horses, dust, personal perspiration excretion. You need something fresh, girl, something . . ." Mag's familiar wicked smile was clear. "Tight."

Sharon sat up. "You're disgusting."

"I work with what I have."

"Even worse." She stared out the window. "And how do you know he'll even notice."

"He's a man. He'll notice."

"It's a football game, for God's sake."

"So you think he'll be looking at the players' tight pants?" Mag laughed. "You, my dear, have a lot to learn."

"And you have so much to teach me," she mock sneered.

"You know it. Now go away, I have to clean this place before Momma Baer gets home and has a cow."

Mag hung up without another word, and Sharon let the receiver drop onto its cradle. She hung her head, hands draped between her knees. Tight jeans. Kyle. Mag as her mentor. The next thing she knew, Mag would have her trying on one of those new bras, the kind that squeezed and pushed, trying to give her a figure where not much of one existed. Tight jeans. Kyle.

She massaged her temples to forestall a headache, sighed, and decided she might as well sweep off the front porch. She had already run the vacuum over the rugs to pick up the dust the wind had forced inside; she had checked the refrigerator for the evening's supper menu and made sure all the ingredients were there; she had called Phil to be sure he'd be home for supper, called her mother at the insurance office for last-minute instructions; she had done everything that was expected of her.

Every day.

Every time.

Tight jeans.

Maybe that wasn't such a bad idea after all.

It would sure give Phil fits, and that just might be worth it. She loved her big brother, she'd clobber anyone who said different, but the older he got the harder he tried to be the father, the more he got on her and her mother's nerves.

Tight jeans.

A slow and wicked smile, just like Mag's.

2

Cornman Center wasn't the largest or most prestigious hospital in the county, but it was adequate enough to serve Vallor and the area immediately surrounding it. Originally a long two-story brick building, additional single-story wings on either side in the sixties had given it a squared **U**-shape and made it look far larger than it was.

Chief Baer stood under the east wing entrance portico, a cigarette in one hand, not so glad that he was finally able to smoke as he was grateful to be outside. The psychiatric unit had never been his favorite place. Blank eyes, blank stares, mutterings and murmurings; the patients who stayed here were, for the most part, only in transit. Evaluation, interim treatment, then on to someplace where the facilities for longer-term treatments, or permanent residence, were more readily available.

Mrs. Grauer, like those dancers before her, would not be leaving.

The glass doors behind him slid open, and a paunchy man, whose wire-rim glasses and severe tonsure made him look more like a monk than a doctor, joined him, shivering a little in the portico's shade.

"She be all right?" Arn asked.

Carl Bergman shrugged. "I guess so." A stethoscope dangled around his neck; his hands were tucked into the pockets of his long white coat. "She's sedated. We'll do the tests. We won't find Alzheimer's or a stroke or drugs, prescription or otherwise, and we'll wait for the family to blow its stack and somehow blame us for whatever just happened."

"I wish I were twenty years older," the chief said miserably. "Then I could truthfully say I was getting too old for this damn job."

Bergman chuckled. "You hate puzzles."

"Damn right."

"Always have."

"Damn right."

"So, you want one anyway?"

Arn groaned loud enough to make the psychologist laugh again, then nodded as if this were his lot and no miracles in sight to protect him from it.

"One of my boys went inside," Bergman said, referring to the ambulance attendants he had trained himself. "Guess what they found?"

"Don't tell me."

"The TV was on."

"Carl, I'm begging you."

"Guess who was on?"

Arn slumped against a portico post and flicked his unfinished cigarette onto the tarmac. "The preacher."

"Reverend Lanyon Trask his own self."

"You know, that guy must own that damn station. It's like he's on every time you look."

"It just seems that way, Arn," Bergman said sympathetically. "It just seems that way."

"Well, if it seems that way," he answered angrily, "why the hell was he on for all those poor souls?" He gestured angrily at the building. "Every damn one of them."

"That we know about," Bergman corrected gently. "We didn't check inside every time, and they didn't always remember."

"You want to take a bet?"

"Nope."

Arn took off his cap and rubbed his face, hard. "Some kind of mass hypnosis."

"A secret electronic transmitting signal."

"Unimaginable charisma."

"The power of prayer."

They looked at each other and laughed, Bergman so hard he had to take off his glasses to wipe his eyes, Arn so hard he began to cough. When the spasm passed and they had sobered, he replaced his hat and hitched up his belt. Rubbed a finger under his nose. Touched the handle of his side-holstered gun as if for luck.

"You know, Carl," he said quietly, as he looked at the dust the wind had left behind, "sometimes I think that guy is right, you know?"

"About what?"

"The end of the world."

"Arn, look—"

"I mean, Jesus," he said, shaking his head, stepping to the curb, into the sun. "We've got people flipping out because of some TV preacher, we got people robbing grocery stores instead of banks, we got winter coming up and there'll probably be rationing and we don't even got a war on, we got this guy over on Polk who shotgunned his neighbor because the poor sap didn't want to invade Canada to hijack some wheat, we got . . . we got . . ." He clamped his mouth shut and stuck out his chin, defiant and trembling. "Mag watches this Trask guy, you know. She does. Really. She goes to church with her mother, and she watches this guy when she thinks I don't know it. My own daughter, Carl. My own daughter."

Bergman gripped his shoulder. "Religion's not a bad thing, Arn. You know that. God isn't a bad thing."

Arn didn't answer. He knew Carl was right. At least about God; he wasn't so sure about the other. But he couldn't help feeling a little lost these days, a little helpless. And if Mrs. Grauer and the others all felt the same way, no wonder they flipped. The pressure was too great.

The doors opened and a nurse hurried out. "Dr. Bergman?"

"Yes?"

"It's Mrs. Grauer. She's singing again."

Arn smiled, nodded to Carl that he should go ahead, go on in, I'll be okay, and took a step toward his patrol car. Then he turned and said, "Hey, Carl."

Bergman looked over his shoulder, an eyebrow raised.

"It can't be all that bad."

Bergman smiled tentatively, waiting.

"At least she knows the words."

3

Les started for the house, thinking he had had enough of thunder and wind and horses for one day. If Fran wasn't busy, he would pack them into the Jeep and head for town. Dinner, a movie, a bar, get home and rip off their clothes and roll around in the living room. He may not be a kid anymore, but the day he got too old for that was the day he'd stick his head in the chipper and let his brains mulch the garden.

He was halfway there when he heard the noise.

A frown, a tilt of his head, and he turned.

It was Royal, and the other horses milled around him, butting each other lightly, nipping harmlessly at the nearest flank, the nearest neck.

"Now what the hell are you up to?" he said.

Royal pushed out of the herd, head bobbing, tail slapping.

Les grinned and pointed. "Hey, are *you* looking at *me?* Are you looking at *me?* Are you *looking*—"

Royal snorted and began to run at the fence.

Les's grin faded as soon as he realized how wrong he was.

IN THE MOOD

It wasn't a run.
It was a charge.

4

Kyle didn't know if he was in love or not, but he sure hoped he was. Otherwise, all this misery would just go to waste.

By the time he spotted the tracks, his legs ached, there was a definite blister rising on his left ankle, the jacket hanging over his shoulder had gained a hundred pounds, and all the sweat had apparently turned the dust beneath his clothes to clammy mud.

He had half a mind to stop at Hummaker's and use the old man's phone, call home and . . . he shuddered.

No. Not even if he lost his leg or got run down by a car would he call Isolde for a ride. Jesus, what kind of name was that, anyway? His father called her Solda, but Kyle refused to. "Solda" was familiar; there was no way he wanted her to think he was getting familiar.

Bitch.

Bleach blonde, no hips, chest out to Kentucky, and a fast hand with the checkbook. Ignoring him as if he didn't exist, smiling at him only when his father was in the house. Just like all the others.

He wished life was like TV sometimes, so he could sit down with his father and tell him man-to-man what he felt, what he saw. Without getting his head knocked off. Which the old man had tended to try now and again. Not so much these days, though. Kyle was taller than him now, and out-weighed him by forty, fifty pounds.

Now all he did was threaten to cut him out of the will, not send him to college . . . worse, make him work in the store.

He shuddered again and trudged on. It could be worse, though. His father could be like Sharon's. Before the freak went to jail.

Maybe that last part wouldn't be so bad, actually. At least the son of a bitch would be out of his life.

He grunted and walked on, limping deliberately to keep as much weight off his ankle as he could, feeling the blister rub against the leather, feeling the pain and hoping he wouldn't be crippled for life. He grunted. He would make it okay. Only a half dozen blocks up, a couple over, and he'd be home. He could do it. No sweat. And it'd be worth it, being a gimp for the rest of his life, because Saturday he was going to the game with Sharon.

5

Les tripped over an exposed pine root, spun, and fell back against the side of the house, arms out to either side, hat long since fallen to the ground.

"Les?"

He blinked sweat from his eyes and tilted his head back.

Fran had her head out the kitchen window, concern in her eyes, a smile on her lips. "What *are* you doing?"

"Royal," he gasped, and saw her look up.

"What about him? Is he all right?"

Les couldn't speak. His throat was too dry, his lips felt cracked, and his lungs simply wouldn't give him enough air. He could only let himself slide to the ground and search for the palomino.

"Les?"

Royal stood at the paddock fence, reaching over, nibbling at the top of a tall weed.

Les didn't get it. The horse had charged him, no question about it. Jumping the fence shouldn't have been a problem.

"Les?"

Why had he stopped?

"Les, damnit, if you're having a heart attack, I am really going to be pissed."

He waved a heavy hand—*I'm okay, just winded*—and dried his face with a sleeve. But when he tried to push himself up, he discovered his legs wouldn't work, shifting around but not supporting.

While Royal ate the weed, and watched him.

6

1

George Trout was tired of rapists, serial killers, mass murderers, child beaters, wife beaters, killer hookers, love-triangle murders, freak-show killers, killers for God and country and the Almighty Dollar, lynchings, muggings that ended in someone's cut throat, police killers, priest killers, mother killers, nun killers, gangs and hitmen and vigilantes and postal workers who decide to wipe out whole zip codes.

He was also tired of being called the "Fish Man" by half the ignorant teenagers in town, whose cumulative brain power didn't even approach that of his terpsichorean namesake; or "Santa" by just about every child under nine who wasn't Jewish; or "St. Nick" or "Saint" by adults who ought to know better but thought they were being clever or original; or the name of just about any actor, the more obscure the better, who happened to match his physique and facial and cranial hairstyle.

That he kept his thick wavy hair to his shoulders was pure vanity.

That he didn't shave off his beard was pure superstition.

He had done it one summer when he couldn't stand the itching, and his life had taken a nosedive straight into the toilet. By the time it had grown back, pure white and thicker than it had even been before, his new career had taken off, and try as he might to prove himself a rational man, he couldn't bring himself to pick up the razor again.

That he didn't exercise more to lose a few pounds and inches was simple laziness. He was not a gourmand; he just liked to eat. He wasn't obese because, he sincerely believed, he also liked to walk, a couple three miles pretty much every day when the weather was halfway decent, and he would not stoop to having junk food meals just because he didn't feel like leaving the house for a meal.

Walking calmed him.

Walking helped him decide what to do next.

Walking got him out of the house when the house felt as if it were going to crush the life out of him.

And walking this afternoon was a way of trying to figure out what had caused that almighty thunder and very peculiar wind.

Just past the Gillespie house, the road swept south around a moderately sharp bend, straightened when it reached his home, and passed through what in better times would have been fields thick and high with corn. Halfway along, it became Madison Street, curved again, and darted back into town to eventually become its main shopping district. A single black loop with an occasional break for a dirt road for the farmers.

By the time he had reached the small county sign that marked the change in names, he knew he had made a mistake.

The fields were nearly bare, what little crop there had been this year already harvested. To his left stubble and dry dirt until they met Oakbend Creek; to his right, stubble and dry dirt until the land humped in abrupt, low wooded hills. Climb those hills and he supposed it wouldn't be long before he fell into the Mississippi.

Depressing; the landscape was depressing, and he turned around immediately, angry with himself because he knew, finally admitted, he just did not want to work.

He didn't care about the thunder, he didn't give a damn about the wind—he just needed some fresh air. He needed to clear his head of its current project so he could concentrate on the increasingly unpleasant feeling that he had made a huge, potentially disastrous mistake.

John Bannock was a good man, had indeed saved him thousands over the years in taxes and avoided bad investments, but he was not now, and probably never would be, a nonfiction writer. The sold articles were blips in an otherwise steady line, more to do with George's influence with editors than anything John had ever put on paper.

The material he had gone over that morning proved it.

Although the man had proved to be a natural interviewer, the kind of guy you talked to without feeling you were being interrogated, what he had come up with was . . . nothing new.

Men and women on death row were hardly original thinkers.

Death, family, the afterlife or not, remorse or not, bitterness or not, legacies, the crimes themselves over and over and over again . . . whatever George had thought Bannock would uncover amid all that misery and self-examination wasn't there.

A lot of words on a lot of paper, full of sound and not a whole hell of a lot of fury.

He shook his head and prayed he wouldn't have to do the rest of the work himself. That rather defeated the purpose of collecting a few bucks without having to lift more than a finger or two. Unfortunately it didn't look good. Not good at all.

He patted his flushed face with a tartan handkerchief, glanced at the damp cloth with distaste, and jammed it back into his hip pocket. The only time he didn't mind sweat was when he shared it with a woman, so why, he wondered, had he fallen into the preposterous habit of wearing a white suit all the time? With, mind you, a gold-thread waistcoat and matching tie. Not to mention the embroidered suspenders. When the hell had that non-sense started?

It seemed particularly ludicrous these days, when merely stepping off the porch attracted half the county's dust to the tailored Italian linen.

To take a stroll in it on a day like this was insane.

The obvious thing to so, the only sensible thing to do, was to go on home.

He didn't.

He couldn't.

He mopped his face again.

He couldn't face one more photograph of a corpse, one more high school yearbook picture of a pretty young thing who ended up on a morgue slab, one more wedding portrait of a young man who subsequently burned his whole family to death.

One more picture of a dead baby.

He lived in a dark-brick-with-white-trim graveyard, and he couldn't stand it anymore.

2

Being chief of police was too often too political for Arn's taste, and one of the ways he fought it was to keep his office on the first floor with the rest of the department, instead of on the more fancy second or third with the department heads and the mayor. Some of the force didn't much care for it, having the bossman around all the time; others found it a lot easier to suck up when they didn't have to walk so far.

Arn paid neither group much attention—he had worked his way rapidly up through the ranks, patrolman to detective to here, and he wasn't about to let ass kissers and grumps spoil the love he had for the job.

Except the paperwork.

He hated the paperwork.

He sat at his desk and glared at the reports his lieutenants had passed on, waiting to be read and signed. His bright idea. Being chief also didn't mean he should be kept out of the loop. But on days like this, when the bad guys were at a minimum and everyone on every shift had decided to catch up, he almost wished he were walking a beat again.

His smile, therefore, was genuine when Rafe stepped into the office.

"Chief?"

Arn sighed.

It was *that* tone.

"We got another one, right?"

Schmidt shook his head. "Worse."

3

Sharon sat on the porch steps and stared at the clump of trees across the road. She had changed into a T-shirt, shorts, and tennis shoes to sweep off the porch, and now the chill that underlay the afternoon's warmth felt good on her skin. She had begun to feel a little stupid for walking out of school like that, and didn't want to be inside when the telephone rang.

The school, Mom? No, they didn't call. I was probably outside. Why?

They had probably already called her, but every ounce of innocence she could muster would come in handy for the explosion sure to come.

She looked up the road, following it as far around the bend as she could. Trout's house was hidden, even in winter, because the trees up there were mostly pine, with a few oak thrown in for autumn color. In fact, most people thought her house was the last on the street, and she knew Fish Man did little to correct the impression.

Queer; weird; the man was bizarre.

Down the road about a hundred yards, on the other side, was the Yermans' place, empty now because they had gone to Florida for some family thing or other. Nice people, but forever trying to convert people into eating carrots instead of steak. Which, considering the area they lived in, was kind of like trying to convince Mag that worshiping the Devil was more fun than watching that Trask guy on TV.

But their money was good.

She got ten bucks a day for walking around the house, making sure no windows were broken or doors were open, picking up fallen branches, stuff like that. Sweep the porch like she did for Mr. Bannock—only that was for free, and he didn't know about it—and lug home any deliveries that might be made.

She looked back at the trees.

Checkerboard, she thought then; the street's set up like a checkerboard. No house faces another, and there's at least a hundred yards between them. House square; tree or piece of field square.

So which, she wondered, was red, and which was black.

4

Arn stared at the fax Rafe handed him, fully aware the man was at attention. He was always at attention. Even when he was walking. Even when he chewed that godawful smelling, godawful blueberry-flavored gum.

"I don't believe it," he said hoarsely.

"I called, just to be sure, Chief," the younger man said.

"You tell anyone else yet?"

"No one's seen it but me."

"Thank God for small favors."

Rafe snapped his gum.

Arn glared, but the man only stared back blankly, not realizing how annoying the habit was. Then he reached into a bottom drawer and pulled out an old pint bottle of Wild Turkey.

"Chief." Schmidt was horrified. "You quit. You promised."

Arn tapped the fax with a stiff finger. "And this says I got a right to start again."

5

George yanked off his jacket and did the unthinkable: He grabbed it in one fist without caring about wrinkles and let it dangle at his side. Then he unbuttoned his waistcoat. Loosened his tie. Wished to hell he had foregone the damn suspenders. It was the middle of October, for God's sake; he wasn't supposed to be this damn hot.

Just ahead, the fields ended on both sides of the road. On the left the woodland was thin, many of the trees lightning-struck, half-fallen, and bare. The land was lower there than the roadbed, and after a good rain, the whole area turned into a standing marsh. On the right were his beloved pines, guardians of his privacy, many of them planted himself and force-fed to get within at least poking distance of full height before he grew too old to enjoy them.

The house, set back from the yard, was there only if you knew where to look.

I will go in the kitchen, he decided, and get a drink, something to eat, then sit on the porch and wait for the sunset. I will not answer the phone, I will not think about work, I will not worry about that over which I have no control.

Like, he added with a disgusted look, those crows.

A flock of them, at least twenty that he could count, picked their way across the field on the right. This section had been left fallow, and there was, surprisingly, grass and weeds still growing. The only color, save for the pines, that he could see.

He hated them.

Instead of heading for the highways and interstates to pick at roadkill like normal disgusting carrion eaters should, they stuck around here. Loud. Argumentative. As if this was their territory and he the intruder.

Too often, when a few made it a point to hunt through his backyard—just to annoy him, he was sure—he would stomp onto the back stoop, waving whatever had come to hand. All they did was hop a little, look at him, and not take wing until he actually stepped onto the grass. Then they sat in the branches and mocked him.

For no reason he could think of they weren't afraid of him at all.

He watched them strutting along the rows, pecking, upright and arrogant, bend over and menacing. Muttering to themselves. Glancing toward him once in a while.

Can they see me? he wondered. How good was their vision?

He waved the jacket.

They didn't budge.

"Bastards," he muttered, and walked on.

On impulse he reached down and snatched up a stone with his left hand, and threw it awkwardly.

It didn't go very far, but it went far enough.

The flock rose into the air, plumes of dust rising with them, and flew straight at him.

6

"Chief."

"I put it away, okay? It's gone. Forget it."

"So maybe I should, you know, take it."

"Rafe, you are, I swear, worse than my wife sometimes."

"But—"

"Rafe, knock it off. It's a test. I keep it there for a test. Just to keep me honest."

"Okay. Sure."

"And we have more important things to worry about than my drinking on the job. That's history. This is the present."

"So what are we going to do?"

"You get hold of the others, get them in here right away. If they're on the road, call them in. This isn't going out over the radio, and I'm not going to wait for shift change. And while you're doing that, I'm . . . oh hell, I'm going to have to make a couple of calls."

Arn folded his hands on his desk and rested his forehead on them. "Tell me something, Rafe. Why me? Why now?"

Rafe laughed. "It's the end of the world, Chief."

"Not funny, Rafe. Not funny."

7

Straight at him.

Slowly.

He could see each wing, up and down.

He could see their eyes, dead and watching.

He could hear them calling, harsh and raucous.

He could see their beaks.

Sharon nearly fell off the steps in her haste to get up, frowning as she searched the sky for the source of all the commotion.

It sounded like every crow in the state was being attacked. They screamed, they called each other, and she knew that whatever had disturbed or attacked them was in serious trouble. She had seen what crows and jays could do to a nosy dog or cat, but this sounded a lot worse.

She trotted down the walk to the street, left hand on her hip, shading her eyes and squinting, swiveling her head slowly to pinpoint the direction.

Her eyes widened.

The Fish Man; they were over by the Fish Man.

"Damn," Les said. "What now?"

Fran was at the kitchen window, head slightly forward, fingers on the sill. "Birds," she said.

He stood behind her. From the open side window he could see past the trees and outbuildings to the paddock. A half dozen dark shapes swooped over the horses' heads, and they had scattered, most of them already out of sight behind the barn.

"What the hell's the matter with them?" he said.

Fran shrugged.

And gasped.

One, a bay, swung its head sharply and struck one of the diving birds. Stunned, it hit the ground and tried to stand.

"Les . . ."

The bay stepped on it.

It didn't rear, or kick, or charge it.

The bay walked over to the struggling bird and stepped on it.

And looked straight at the house.

Sharon ran back to the porch and grabbed the broom.

Arn slapped helplessly through the thick sheaf of papers in the open folder on his desk, groaning when he couldn't find what he wanted.

"Rafe!" he bellowed. "Rafe, get in here!"

Detective Zayle came to the door instead. "He's on the horn, Chief. What's up?"

"I can't find the damned number!"

"What number?" Zayle wandered in a little fearfully, one hand instinctively moving to be sure his tie was straight. Then he glanced at the folder and said, "Oh."

Arn ordered himself to be calm. "You heard."

Zayle nodded.

"I can't find the . . ." He blinked when the detective lifted the telephone book from a small table near the window and held it up. "Oh. Yeah." He grabbed it and flipped open the Yellow Pages.

Froze.

"Entelong Insurance," Zayle said timidly. "On Madison, near Twentieth."

"I know, I know," Arn snapped. "I was just thinking."

Zayle nodded and backed out of the room.

Arn found the company's number, hesitated, whispered, "Why me?" and punched for an outside line before he lost his nerve.

George couldn't run. He hadn't run in years, and the best he could do was an ungainly lumbering trot.

The crows circled him, and for a hysterical moment he felt like a lone covered wagon under attack. He had had the sense to hold his jacket over his head, one hand keeping the collar up so he could see, while the other batted at the birds when they came too close.

Peck his eyes out.

Eat his tongue.

Long sharp beaks penetrating his ears.

That's what kept him running, even though he could barely breathe, even though he felt as if someone were stabbing tiny needles into his side, even though his vision had begun to darken at the edges.

They cawed at him.

They beat at the jacket with their wings, much more powerful than he ever believed they would be.

He stumbled, went down on one knee, and rose again, this time thinking this was of course a dream and he had put himself into *The Birds*, and as he rather pathetically fled for his own life, downtown was under attack by rampaging gulls while robins and jays massed at the schools and waited patiently, silently, for the last bell.

When he came abreast of his fence, he angled toward it and used it to pull himself along one-handed. Walking now. Shambling. Gulping for air, licking his lips, tasting salt and grit.

His arm grew tired and dropped to his side, letting the white jacket fall over his head like a cowl.

He grabbed the fence with both hands and pulled. Yanked. One foot at a time.

While they circled and screamed and something stabbed him behind the knee and something stabbed him on the ankle and something beat at his head and all he could see was the withered ground and his shoes no longer white and the fenceposts as he passed them and the flick of a dark body he slammed away with the back of his hand.

He reached the open gate and fell to his hands and knees.

I will crawl, he commanded; I will crawl, goddamnit.

He couldn't.

He just . . . couldn't.

Arn stared at the plaster ceiling and prayed for strength.

IN THE MOOD

*   *   *

Sharon sprinted around the bend and cried out when she saw the Fish Man on the ground, rocking back and forth while a cloud of crows dove and swooped over him. Broom high, she charged, screaming, and several of them left the flock and flew toward her.

Slowly.

Not a sound.

Not a sound.

"Les?"

"Honey, if you think I'm going out there, you're out of your mind."

Panting made him dizzy, and he felt himself ready to topple.

No, he commanded; goddamnit, no.

When he heard the scream, he thought it was one of the birds; when he heard it again, he shifted his unsteady weight and lifted a corner of the jacket, just as Sharon Gillespie, at a dead run and swinging a long broom like a club, swatted two crows out of the air.

"Mr. Trout!" she called, and swung at another one. "Mr. Trout!"

Not on my knees, he thought; please, God, not on my knees.

He grabbed the nearest gatepost and hauled himself to his feet, swaying, using his other hand to swing the jacket as if he were merely shooing away flies or a couple of pesky bees.

Swinging as hard as he could, as often as he could, until a hand gripped his shoulder.

"It's okay, Mr. Trout," she said. "It's okay, they're gone."

He couldn't speak. His lips moved, his tongue moved, but he couldn't speak. His eyes stung, his chest hurt, and there was a buzzing in his ears.

"Come on," she urged softly.

She pulled at him gently until he moved; she guided him as best she could while she watched the sky until they were on the porch; she led him to his favorite chair, an old cane rocker, and helped him sit.

She did not let go of the broom for a second.

"My God," he said, eyes closed, ready to weep. "My God."

"I'm going to get you something to drink." She hesitated. "Is that all right?"

He nodded weakly, not giving a damn if the entire town traipsed through his house. "Ice," he managed as he heard the screen door slam shut. "Ice," he whispered. "Ice."

"Annette," Arn said. "How are you? This is Chief Baer."

"Arn! Well, I'll be. How are you doing?" She laughed. "You finally thinking about increasing that life to a flat million?"

He couldn't smile. "Annette," he said, "I have news."

"Oh God," she said, "has something happened to Sharon? Phil? Are they all right? Was there an accident? Was—"

"No, Annette," he said. "Far as I know, Sharon is in school. And I've heard nothing about Phil."

"Then what . . . ?"

He couldn't do it.

He couldn't bring himself to do it.

Then he heard what might have been a moan deep in her throat. "Tell me," she said flatly.

"It's Rod," he said.

"Tell me he's dead, Arn." She laughed bitterly. "Make my day and tell me the bastard's dead."

It took a few seconds to find the glasses, a few seconds more to realize his huge refrigerator had an ice maker in the door. She filled two tumblers and rushed them back to the porch, handed him one, and said, "If it's all right, Mr. Trout, I'm going to find a cloth or something and wet it. You need to—"

"There," he interrupted, pointing. "Look there."

The crows had started to fly past the house, one by one, at eye level. Unless, she thought, it was the same bird.

"I don't get it."

She wasn't scared now, not like she'd been before. Or maybe she was, but she was still too pumped to realize it.

"Watch," he said numbly. "Watch."

*   *   *

Arn felt gas and bile churn in his stomach.

"Tell me, Arn."

"I . . ." He swallowed, and wished someone out there could read his mind and bring him a glass of water. "I've gotten word from Denver."

He remembered the pint.

Without an ounce of shame, he yanked open the drawer and grabbed the bottle. There wasn't much left inside, but it was enough.

"Arn, damnit, you telling me they let him go?"

He drank, coughed as discreetly as he could, and tossed the empty bottle into the wastebasket.

Her voice began to rise, rage and panic. "How the hell could they let him go? Why didn't they warn me? I'm supposed to be told when there's a parole hearing, Arn, and nobody told me a—"

"He wasn't paroled, Annette," he said.

"—a damn thing about it. I . . . I . . . my lawyer. Arn, I have to call my lawyer. I have to call Sharon. I—"

"Annette!"

"What?"

"He wasn't paroled, Annette. He escaped."

8

George kept his finger up. "Watch."

The girl did, shaking her head that she didn't understand.

"Watch."

"Mr. Trout, I don't—"

"Look at him, girl, damnit, look at him!"

She went to the railing despite his warning grunt and leaned out as far as she could when the crow passed again.

She dropped the tumbler into the flower bed below.

George closed his eyes.

"Blue," she said. "Mr. Trout, its eyes are blue."

Part 3

1

1

One of those special days, the kind of autumn afternoon when no one minds being in Manhattan, or even that it's Monday.

A chill in the side streets where the sun keeps its shadows, a warmth on the avenues where the skyscrapers let the sun brush pocket parks and sidewalks. Suit jackets but not overcoats. Sweaters but not windbreakers. One last chance to sit by the fountain across from the Warwick and eat a hot dog from a vendor; one last chance to walk through Times Square before the wind grows winter's teeth; one last chance to lie in the Sheep's Meadow and pray for one more layer of tan.

The sky is sharp, the buildings have edges, and if the Halloween decorations were up two weeks early, it wasn't as bad as the idiot on Fifth Avenue who had put a white plastic Christmas tree in his display window.

One of those special days.

2

Tony Garza sat on the edge of his bed, head low, legs and feet bare, staring at the carpet whose faded design he had memorized a score of years ago, so familiar now he could shift the lines to make faces and continents without losing the original. Absently he scratched his stomach. Thinking he ought to clip his toenails again. Any longer they'd start shredding his socks. A hell of a thing, a man his age in his condition, walking around with holes in his socks.

A hell of a thing.

"Huh."

He looked at his hands, then. Turned them over and checked the palms. He looked between them at the way his boxers were snug around his thighs and still no flab. He straightened. He pushed himself up and walked down the long hall of the Pullman apartment to the living room, stood at the window, and looked down at the street. The Monday morning rush was over, but they still cut through, thinking they'll save time. He often day-dreamed about unloading a box of huge tacks down there, just to see how many tires would blow before the idiots caught on.

Ari claimed it was just life in the city, nothing to raise your blood pressure about.

Maybe so, but it was still a pain in the butt.

He leaned closer to the pane, looking down the block. No police today. Only a small piece of yellow crime scene ribbon left, flapping in the wind. All that was left of cop cars and TV vans that had packed the street Saturday morning, cops and newsmen talking to everyone who ever took a breath around here.

They hadn't paid much attention to him, standing on the stoop the next morning, a stooped old man with half a roast beef sandwich in one hand, horseradish stains on his shirt. A few questions, a take it easy old fella pat on the back, and they moved on to someone else.

The building's super, Manny Pulero, low-slung jeans and grimy T-shirt, had popped out of his hole just long enough to ask what the hell was going on.

"Guy murdered," Tony had answered.

"So what else is new?"

"My bedroom radiator's still busted."

Pulero, squat and dark, with a scrawny Zapata mustache, shrugged expansively. "So what else is new?"

And popped back into his hole.

Tony swore that was the only English the little bastard knew.

Yellow ribbon flapping in the wind.

Leaves dancing in the gutter.

He sniffed and faced the room, hands trying to find his pockets until he remembered he wasn't dressed.

"I," he announced to the old chairs, the old tables, the old wallpaper, the old rug, "am bored."

Maybe it was time he visited some of the family.

Maybe not.

What the hell.

But as his left hand brushed over his cheek, he knew it was definitely time to give himself a shave.

3

Ari Lowe sat in his kitchen, pushing a spoon through a cooling bowl of oatmeal, waiting until he could catch his breath. He had damn near coughed his lungs out a few seconds ago, and for those few seconds he was afraid the pressure in his head would explode something in his brain and leave him on the cracked linoleum floor, unable to call for help. Helpless as a baby fallen from its crib.

Dying.

He puffed his cheeks and blew out a long sigh, finished the oatmeal without tasting it, and sat back, hands still on the table.

He studied his fingers, more bone than flesh, and wondered what it would be like to be like Tony, still living as if he had another century ahead of him, still charming the ladies out of their drawers, still leaving parts of himself with women who didn't seem to mind the disparity in age. Eating a decent breakfast, not this damn gruel. Eating roast beef and horseradish in the middle of the night, knowing he wouldn't wake up before dawn with acid crawling through his system.

Jealous? No.

Envious? Yes.

But what is, is. If he kept this up, these daily comparisons, he'd end up sticking his head in the oven. Hell of a way to die, his ass in the air.

His daughter would have a fit.

He grinned, stood, washed the bowl, and the glass that had held his orange juice, and went into the bedroom where he made the bed, fluffed the pillows, picked up the dirty clothes from the day before and stuffed them into the bathroom hamper. Then he went into the living room and wondered if the rug needed vacuuming today. He had done it two days ago, but even closed windows let the city grit in.

Might as well.

It'll kill time.

Then he'll walk down to the Korean's to get the paper, see if there was anything new on the murder. Which there wouldn't be. Same old thing—another dead body, no witnesses, no clues, police expecting a break any day now.

And Ari Lowe had slept through it all, had to wait until his friend told him all about it the next morning.

The way Tony had told it, it was actually kind of funny, but it didn't stop him from feeling a little queasy.

Murder. Right here on the block. First one that he could remember. People beat each other up, had screaming fights after midnight, broke in now and then to swipe TVs and VCRs, whatever loose change they could find.

But murder?

And he missed most of the excitement?

Something, he thought, is missing here.

Yeah, he answered sourly; your goddamn life.

Which reminded him, as he laughed, that he'd better check the cupboards and refrigerator. Tomorrow the guys were coming over here for a change, and he had to make sure there was enough to feed them. Tuesday night at the trough. Then he had to check the cards, the chips, deal himself a few hands to be sure he hadn't lost the touch, see to it that Tony didn't forget to get the beer.

Not so bad when you thought about it.

Not so bad at all.

4

"Nobody answers, Mom."

"That's okay," she says as she replaces the receiver.

"But why not?"

She laughs and gives the little cowboy a gentle shove. "Out to lunch, shopping, going for a walk . . . lots of reasons. It's the middle of the day."

He pouts and says, "I want to go."

"I don't think so, hon."

"Why not?"

She points at the driver, who's standing near the back of the bus, one of the shiny panels cocked open. His hat is in his hand, his hand is on his hip, and he's shaking his head angrily at another man beside him. The second man wears coveralls liberally smeared with dirt and grease.

"I think we've got engine trouble," she says.

"Does that mean we have to stay?"

"Joey," she says sharply. "Stop whining. We can't do anything about it, so there's no sense getting upset."

"You always say that."

"Because it's always true."

He glares at the two men. "So what do we do until they're all done, Mommy?"

"Well . . ." She looks around, every so often exchanging what-can-you-do glances with other disappointed passengers. Then she says, "We can always have some ice cream," and points at the snack bar.

"Chocolate?"

"Whatever you want."

The little cowboy puts a finger to his chin and pretends to think about it. "Okay," he says at last. "But I want to try another number first."

5

Dory Castro woke with a splitting headache, groaned aloud to be sure the world knew of her suffering, and sat up as slowly as she could to keep her head from rolling off her neck.

Brittle sunlight filled her bedroom.

Outside the window she could hear the grumble of an idling truck, the yapping of her neighbor's dog, the near-hysterical shouts of her neighbor trying to shut the damn dog up. A couple of preschool kids shrieking as they played.

An ordinary day in suburban Philadelphia.

Thank God, she had taken the day off. Early on, she had learned that returning to work the Monday after a conference was about as productive as trying to roll grease up a hill. Now she would be able to grind the liquor and boredom out of her system before she set foot in the office. Where, no doubt, there'd be a million questions about Rainer's death. Possible suicide, or so claimed the local news programs; word had gotten out that he was on the shortlist for a pink slip.

Not that she would have anything to tell them—she had been in the shower at the time the creep had taken his dive, and didn't even know what had happened until she showed up at the meeting, properly apologetic for her tardiness, ready to go.

Naturally, the day's schedule had been canceled once the word got out, and some jackass from Colorado even wanted to put together an impromptu memorial service. For the company's image.

Yeah. Right.

The people from the Atlanta office had pretty much left before lunch. For her and some of the others, however, it was sightseeing in the afternoon, the executive suite thrown open that night for what was supposed to be a respectful gathering, for what turned out to be a hell of a party that introduced her to a guy from Wisconsin. Damn good looking. Buns to die for. An ego in bed that sorely tempted her to break the rules, do two in a single day.

Temptation, however, wasn't strong enough for such drastic action.

Besides, when all was said and done, she hadn't felt like it.

"Bad, girl," she said, giggling, as she wandered through the townhouse, T-shirt and panties, searching for a reason not to go back to bed. "You are just plain bad."

She found it downstairs, in a framed picture on the mantel of her gas-log fireplace. There she was, and there they were, all of them grinning like idiots at the camera.

"You guys," she said fondly.

She wondered if it would be appropriate for a couple of tears now, to prove how she missed them.

She could feel them at the corners of her eyes, ready to fall, but with no one watching, there wasn't much point.

Maybe she would give them a call. It had been a while. And she really did miss them, in a bizarre kind of familial way. While she was at it, maybe she'd even give Pop a ring. At least he hadn't condemned her after Arturo had walked out; at least he hadn't implied, or said outright, that it was all her fault. At least Pop didn't sing the same damn song—no children to hold the family together, married to your job, what did you expect, Dory? You want Artie to do the housework in addition to his own work? What kind of woman are you? Is this the way you were raised?

She closed her eyes quickly, turned away from the fireplace, and willed her fists to open.

It took a while.

It took a long while.

Once she thought she was ready, she went into the kitchen, made herself some toast and coffee, and brought the plate into the back room.

"Hi," she said.

The sunlight didn't seem quite so brittle anymore, not the way it lay across the wood, making it shine in spite of its age, in spite of its condition.

She sat on the bench, put the plate beside her, and let her fingers hover over the keys. Sensing. Almost dowsing. Until they flexed once, ready, and she scarcely felt the ivory as she swayed in time to a torchlike, Memphis-inspired, only lacking a hard bass "String of Pearls."

Glenn Miller wouldn't approve, but she didn't give a damn.

He was dead.

She wasn't.

Not yet.

With any luck, Greta Holtz, the neighbor with the dog, would complain to the police about the music. The police would show up sooner or later, Dory would smile and apologize and suggest that Greta cut her damn dog's tongue out. An old routine. The cops didn't care. They hated that dog, anyway, and they didn't much care for Greta, either. Always bitching about the neighborhood kids, the cars not parked in their appropriate spots, supposed prowlers in the middle of the night . . .

Dory had a feeling rookies were specifically assigned to this area, to break them in, to give them a taste of Greta to prepare them for their destiny.

Maybe she should help them out.

Two in one day was always out of the question.

Two in one week, though, was something else again.

She played on.

Just a little louder.

6

Ida Lefcowitz dithered at the front door. She had to go out. Prescott needed his food and got awfully testy when he wasn't fed on time. Just like her late husband, and wasn't she sorry now that she had named that fool animal after him. Still, she loved the hairy little thing, and he needed his food.

But she was afraid.

The nearest store was the Korean's, and while she didn't mind talking to him even if he didn't have the sense to learn decent English, it meant going by that other place.

It meant maybe seeing *him.*

Even crossing the street and going down the other side, she still might see him.

She didn't think she could stand it.

All weekend she had stayed home, huddled in her chair, the TV on but unwatched, waiting for him to come to her door, smash it down, and murder her. Sneaking Prescott out only after dark, hushing him, praying that he wouldn't take very long. Like some kind of criminal, she was. Like some kind of prisoner.

It wasn't meant to be that way.

All she had done the other night was get back home, had her coat and gloves off, realized she had forgotten the skim milk, and went out again. Stood on the sidewalk, one finger on her chin, trying to convince herself she really needed that milk, but she hated walking without Prescott to guard her, and he had already fallen asleep in his bed.

That's when she had seen the shadows on the sidewalk.

Two of them, although she honestly couldn't be sure. Her eyes weren't bad, but at night they weren't as good.

Two of them, looking as if they were dancing down there; then suddenly, only one of them, walking away, the other vanished. Gone. Without a sound. Making her wonder if she had actually seen it at all.

But it had been unnerving enough to send her straight back inside, explaining to a grumpy Prescott that she would wait until morning to get the milk, she didn't need it to get to sleep.

That other shadow had to be that awful Mr. Garza. Who else on the block was that big?

Then the police came—*did you see anything last night, ma'am, anything strange?*—and she found out.

She found out.

And she couldn't stop thinking that maybe that awful Mr. Garza had seen her, too.

In that one horrific moment, she had told the police she hadn't seen a thing, had been inside all night, watching the TV and reading the paper. She had lied, and they had gone away—*if you think of anything, ma'am, just give us a call*—and for the first time in years she regretted living on the first floor.

He was big enough to look right in. She was positive of that; he could stand on the sidewalk and look right in and see her and let her know that she was next.

Because he knew.

Several times she considered calling her son on Long Island, but she already knew what he would say.

"Mother, don't get involved." Or, "Mother, it was dark, and you know full well that Mr. Garza is over eighty. You really think he could do something like that?" Or, "Mother, do you know how late it is? Can't we talk about this in the morning?"

Mother.

She clasped her hands at her bosom.

Mother.

He had never called her "Mother" before. It was always "Ma," or "Mom." Never "Mother." Not until he had married that woman, who took him out of the city.

She shuddered at the memory of the day he had left, kissing her, hugging her, inviting her again to come live with them where it was safe. All the while, that woman standing behind him, smile as false as the eyelashes and the fancy fur and the teeth, my God, the teeth so perfect you could tell they'd been capped a mile away, for crying out loud.

Then Prescott barked behind the closed door. Just once. To let her know he knew she was still out here. Dithering like an old maid.

"All right, darling," she whispered. "All right, all right, I'll be back soon."

If, she thought as she adjusted her gloves and stepped outside, she wasn't murdered first.

She hadn't taken two steps before she realized she was crying.

7

"Is everybody in the world out shopping, Mom?"

"Joey, I told you to stop it."

"I want to try another number."

"And I'm hungry, kiddo, so how about we have the ice cream first?"

"Can I call after?"

"Yes, you can call after."

"Chocolate?"

"Yes."

"Then will they be done?"

She looks at the mechanic, at the driver smoking beside him, and shrugs. The only announcement she's heard said the company was doing its best to get this vehicle back on the road, but meanwhile, they were bringing another one down from Staser, just in case.

"I hope so," she says. "I really hope so."

8

Tony took his time getting dressed, scowling at his stomach when it rumbled, scowling at the kitchen when he couldn't find anything that appealed to him.

So, big deal. A trip to the Korean's, what's the problem? It's a beautiful fall day, get what you want, come home, eat, roust Ari, and . . . do something.

Call the kids.

What the hell.

He pulled on a new cardigan, rolled his eyes when the buttons strained at their holes, and hoped Ari wouldn't fuss about his weight. Always fussing, that man. Always worried about something or other.

He made sure he had his wallet. He made sure in the mirror by the door that he looked okay. He made sure he had his keys, and then he went out onto the stoop, enjoying the chill the wind cast across the street.

Finally, it felt like October.

It was about time.

"Good morning, Mrs. Lefcowitz," he said to the little woman just passing the steps.

She froze, trembling like a wet dog.

Tony frowned. "Mrs. Lefcowitz, you okay?"

Her head swiveled slowly toward him, and he couldn't help but gape at the tears he saw making tracks on her cheeks, in her makeup, the way she clutched her bag as if he were going to steal it.

"Mrs. Lefcowitz, what's wrong?"

Bad news, he guessed; the poor old woman's had bad news. That damn kid of hers, out on the Island. What the hell has he done now?

He took a step down, smiling sympathetically, one hand out as if to offer comfort.

Ida's mouth opened.

Wide.

Mewling, whimpering.

"Oh, my God, Ida." He was afraid now she was having an attack of some kind. "Oh my God."

He hurried down to the sidewalk, checking the street for someone who might help, then reached out to take her elbow. "Let me take you back home, Ida, okay?" He leaned down. "Let me help. You need medicine or something?"

"You," was all she said, her eyes wide, not blinking in the wind.

Startled, he let his hand drop. "I . . . what?"

She backed away, still trembling, still crying, one white-gloved finger trying to point. "You."

Oh hell, he thought, and looked to the doorway, hoping by some miracle that Ari would be there. He knew how to handle situations like this; he would know what to do. Hysterical women were not Tony's forte.

Then she said something else, and he jerked his head around. "What, Ida? What did you say?"

"You," she whispered harshly, lips twisting, hands flailing at her chest, at the air. "I saw you."

He didn't know what to say. The old woman kept backing off, nearly tripping over herself, head shaking violently, those hands still batting at the air. His smile flicked on and off, on and off, as he searched the street for a cop, for Ari, for any damn somebody to take care of this woman before she dropped dead where she stood.

Suddenly she bolted. Just turned and ran. Scurried away, looking over her shoulder, eyes gleaming with tears, mouthing things at him, whimpering.

He didn't move.

That night.

He took a deep breath.

I saw you that night.

2

He stands on the side of the two-lane highway, in a baggy denim shirt with the sleeves rolled down, baggy jeans almost new. A duffel bag lies at his booted feet. He is tall and seems lean despite the looseness of his clothes. His hair is cropped short, speckled through with iron gray, too short to be touched by the slow steady wind that blows across the empty prairie.

Five cars have passed him in the last three hours. Not one of them slowed down.

He doesn't mind.

He has learned there is no sense railing or even swearing at things you can't control. A waste of good energy. A waste of valuable time.

Besides, he knew all along that this road would be less traveled than the interstate not twenty-some miles away. Fewer opportunities to keep his feet from aching, fewer chances to rest, less people to have to talk to.

That suits him just fine.

Ten minutes later he hoists the bag to his shoulder and begins to walk. On the road; no sense using the sloping shoulder where he might turn an ankle, hobble him, slow him down. The land is flat here, the mountains so far in the distance they were little more than haze. There'll be plenty of warning when the next chance comes along.

An hour later, the sun just past noon, he hears the engine behind him and stops, drops his bag, looks west, and sticks out his thumb.

He's not worried.

A sound like that is no high-powered machine. He guesses a pickup long past its prime, and grins when he sees he's right. Turns the grin to a polite smile as the pickup draws nearer, his shoulders slumping just a little, his knees sagging just right. Look too strong, too able, the driver might think you can walk all the way to Kansas without breaking a sweat.

The truck slows.

Stops.

The driver leans over and says, "Hey."

He nods. "Hey, yourself. Lift?"

"Where you headed?"

He nods east, wearily. "Don't matter, really. Place where there's work."

The driver, young and trying to grow a beard, shrugs. "Tell me about it." He shrugs again. "Stow your stuff and hop in. Could use the company."

The duffel bag goes into the bed, beside a ripped tarp that doesn't really cover a worn saddle and whatever else was beside it. The hitcher climbs in, groans his pleasure and grins, and thanks the driver for the lift.

"No sweat. Like I said, I could use the company."

An out-of-work cowboy, the hitcher learns, wandering from ranch to ranch without a hell of a lot of luck. Tried rodeo for a while but that didn't work out. Tried piecework in a factory outside Boulder, but that didn't work, either. Tried a lot of things.

The hitcher nods how well he knows that song, but doesn't offer a verse of his own. A few grunts, some meaningless crap about jobs for men his age being too few and far between, and the out-of-work cowboy is pleased to pick up the slack. He's not as young as he looks, but the roads he's been on don't show in his face.

He has stories.

He tells a few.

Finally he says, "Man, I gotta take a leak," and pulls over, nothing but prairie and sky and a long straight road, and the hitcher climbs out to stretch his legs, leans into the bed and opens his bag.

The driver comes back, grinning.

The hitcher grins in return. "You okay?"

"Never better."

"Stupid son of a bitch."

The hitcher lashes his right arm out and catches the cowboy square across the face with the claws of a hammer.

The cowboy shrieks and stumbles back, hands clamped to the hole that was his cheek, trips as he steps onto the shoulder, and falls onto his side.

IN THE MOOD

The hitcher straddles him, no jokes, no laughter, and uses the hammer again.

And again.

Carefully leaning away from the spray and spray of bone and hair.

Then he grabs the cowboy's ankles and drags him into the prairie, far enough from the road that even a high-riding trucker couldn't spot him. Money from the pockets, eighty dollars, a few quarters. Nothing more. He leaves the wallet, isn't so dumb that the credit card tempts him.

As he returns to the pickup he makes sure there's no blood on his jeans, on his shirt, wipes the hammer clean on the buffalo grass and puts it back into his bag, slides in behind the wheel, checks his face in the rearview mirror, and drives on.

Five minutes later he begins to laugh.

He has forgotten how good it feels, the rush, the tingling; almost as good as the loving of a good whore. And here it was only Monday. He patted the front of his left shoulder with his right hand, a sign to keep his good luck intact.

It won't last.

He isn't stupid.

But he is determined that it will last just long enough.

3

1

Clouds move over the Gulf toward the delta, high and thin, streaming from a dark band that bulges on the southern horizon. Gulls make their way inland, not hurrying. Not yet. And the water is marked by only a handful of whitecaps.

Around the city, flags and pennants begin to stir.

The tourists are grateful the air has begun to cool; the locals begin to check their shutters and candles.

2

Lisse Montgomery didn't believe in astrology, but her mother had always told her, only half joking, that she must have been born under a bad sign for all the trouble she used to get into when she was a kid.

Not that anything has changed, she thought glumly.

Here she was, sitting in her dreary kitchenette bright and early Monday morning, her car half dead in the apartment parking lot, some kind of maybe big old storm making its way in off the Gulf, hardly any sleep the night before, and no job to go to. It was enough to make her cry, but she had already done that last night until her throat was raw and her eyes puffed up and she had come that close to deciding to swim the river with an anvil tied around her neck.

Foolish, of course, it wasn't all that bad, but she figured she was entitled to a little self-pity.

Later, or after the storm passed, whenever the energy struck her and she got tired of this place, she would haul her sorry butt downtown, work on her smile, and start making the rounds. Hotels, cafés, casinos, restaurants . . . there were scores of places that could use her particular service industry skills. Scores of them.

But damnit, she had liked the Royal Cajun. Slow and easy, a few perks here and there, nice people to talk to, to work with, no pressure to speak of.

John Bannock.

She made a face.

Sometimes, swear to God, no matter how hard she tried, she still acted like a moony teenager, forgetting everything she had learned about men over the years, everything she had learned about herself. It was like a switch gets thrown and her brain turns off. No more sense than a log and twice as thick.

She had long decided that her sign was the black cat.

John Bannock.

He was different, though, nobody could argue with that, and she certainly couldn't claim that he hadn't shown her an interesting time. That he hadn't been a gentleman. That he hadn't been honest with her from the first time they'd met.

And he sure had a way with words. Never once talking down to her. Never treating her like a waitress, someone to serve him, then wave away.

Angel, he had called her; she was his angel.

Of course he'd been dead drunk at the time.

Still, he had called her his angel.

She giggled.

Angel.

Yeah. Right.

Still . . .

"Imagine it, Momma," she said to the chipped coffee cup she held in her left hand. "I slept with a drunk, and he didn't even touch me."

No, he gave her dreams instead.

No, he had done something to a punk kid neither of them could explain.

No, he . . .

. . . looked so hurt, so darned *hurt* when she'd walked away from him yesterday afternoon, and every time she remembered, the tears cranked up again.

Except now.

She pushed away from the table only big enough for two, and wandered into the front room. Nothing fancy here, definitely nothing expensive, but it was as comfortable as her tips and meager salary had been able to make it. A couple of chairs, a couch, a flea market end table, a coffee table, travel poster prints on the walls with strings of Krew beads draped over the frames, a TV, and an air conditioner in the window that was a genuine miracle—it worked, and it was, most of the time, practically silent.

Decent, she thought, not exotic.

Today it felt hollow.

John Bannock was missing.

"Oh, please," she muttered, and decided to get dressed, get moving, get a job.

After all, what had he really done for her? Gave her a little work for which he had paid too much and they both knew it. Had her read about people who were going to die. Saved her butt from that lech who had turned out to be that preacher on TV. Made her laugh. Took her on a ferryboat picnic where she had seen a dreamcrow's blue eyes in the blue eyes of a boy. Had her spend a couple of hours in a police station.

Scared her half to death, for crying out loud.

And she had left him alone.

"You," she said to the bathroom mirror, "are a piece of work, Lisse Gayle. Ain't you got any shame?"

The trouble was, she did.

She saw it in the way she fussed with her hair, keeping it down on her shoulders, letting the curls do their work; the way she fussed with her blouse—how many buttons to keep open?; the way she wished she had more clothes to try on.

There was no fooling herself.

She had to go.

If nothing else, she had to apologize for the way she had behaved. If she didn't, it would eat at her something awful, and then it would be too late because he'd be gone.

Stands to reason she was about to make a great fool of herself, and the only thing that could save her would be that damn fool car giving up the ghost to protect her from doing something she couldn't understand.

It didn't.

3

Ace, what do you think you're doing?

"Packing."

Why? Are you finished?

"What difference does it make? I'm getting out. Haven't you heard? There's a storm coming."

That's not why you're leaving.

"You know so much, why bother to ask?"

I know what I know, Ace, I know what I know. So where are you going?

"You have to ask?"

You know the rules, John. You have to say it.

"Home, Patty, okay? I'm going home. I've had it. I quit. No more. You were right all along. I'm not a writer, I'm what they used to call a pencil pusher, except now I use a computer and some fancy programs to do most of the work. The only reason those articles sold was because of George, not because of anything I did."

You're selling yourself short, honey, and you know it.

"All I know is, I'm going home."

Okay. Then what?

"You know damn well what. I'm going to find you and Joey, and we're going to try to work things out. You win, remember? You win."

What about that preacher?

"He's nuts. Where the hell did I put that damn pen?"

It's under the bed. And Casey? What about him?

"Out of his mind with painkillers. Maybe just out of his mind. I mean, his whole town . . . I'd be a basket case myself. Now where is that stupid . . . I see it. How did you know it was there?"

Figure it out. And the girl?

"Lisse?"

You're quick, Ace. Don't forget the stuff in the bottom drawer. You always forget the stuff in the bottom drawer.

"I got it, I got it, okay?"

Lisse, Ace.

"She's gone. Scared off. Has more brains than I do, that's for sure. At least she knows when to cut her losses. I should have cut mine a year ago. More. I never should have started this thing in the first place. Patty, you can't know how sorry I am. You can't know, but by God, I'm going to tell you to your face, anyway. I swear it. I really swear it."

What are you going to tell George?

"I'll work on it on the way home."

Ace.

"What?"

Suppose you do go home.

"No supposing about it."

You think all this is going away? You think what's in that computer, what's on all those pages is going to disappear? You think what you saw never happened? You think—

"Shut up, Patty, okay? Let me finish this."

Ace, do me a favor and stop that damn whistling.

"What?"

You always whistle when you don't want to listen to me. You always did. What is that, anyway?

"For your information, it's 'So Rare.' Tommy Dorsey. Jimmy Dorsey. One of those."

It's awful.

"Hey, it's a classic."

The whistling, Ace, the whistling. You never could carry a tune in a bucket.

"Well, I like it."

And I won't go away, you know. That won't make me.

"What did I do with the—"

The bathroom. On the floor by the toilet. Where you always leave it.

"Thanks. For nothing."

Ace.

"Now what?"

You never answered my questions.

"Go away."

IN THE MOOD

Sure. But first work on this: All that stuff will still be there, at home, no matter what you do. It ain't going away.

"How the hell can you know that?"

Figure it out, Ace. Figure it out.

4

Although the electric candles were lit in their brass sconces, they weren't strong enough to dispel the gloom that slipped through the arched windows at each end of the hall. Sound seemed muffled. Air had weight.

Giselle Grudeau pushed her housekeeping cart out of the service elevator on the sixth floor, stopped, and waited for her heart to catch up. Too fast; she had been working too fast, trying to get done quickly so she could get home early.

As she stood in the secluded alcove, out of sight of the guest rooms, she decided once and for all that she was going to change her name. Giselle had been just fine when she was a girl; she had had the shape for it, kind of like that Lisse girl, only much more in the chest, more round at the hips. Now she was round everywhere, just like her sister, and Giselle was all wrong. Bertha, she figured, was probably more like it. Something to go along with all the weight, all the pounds that had crept up on her ever since that no good bum of a husband had left her, to go to California and be a star in the movies.

She grunted a bitter laugh.

Hadn't seen him in any movies, hadn't seen him on TV, and the next time she saw him, which would be too soon for her, she would take a brick to his head.

"Lord," she whispered, "forgive me."

But she'd still use that brick.

A sigh, a check to be sure her hair wasn't flying out of the net that covered it, and she pushed the cart into the hallway, wincing at the creak one of the wheels made.

She wanted to be quiet.

She didn't want anyone to know she was coming.

Especially she didn't want *him* to know she was around.

Six-seventeen had spooked her mightily. Seeing him like that, on the ferry, doing that punk like that. Hearing that punk scream, seeing him fall

165

like he was flat-out dead. Something not right about it, when she thought about it later. Something definitely not right.

She had told Reverend Trask that, first time the reverend had asked her, in private, to do some of the Lord's work for him. And Him.

"Nice man," she had said, not nervous at all being in the reverend's presence, "but I get this feeling about him, Reverend. A strong feeling. Powerful."

The reverend hadn't blinked. "Like . . . ?"

Giselle wasn't good at words, barely got herself out of school, never did get to high school, but this time what she wanted to say came easily:

"Haunted. Like he's haunted."

But he definitely was nice. Said a hello every time they passed in the hall, never asked her for special stuff, man even made his bed every morning, no mind that she had to tear it apart to change the linens. Made his bed. Kept the bathroom clean. Made her feel a little guilty, snooping around, looking for stuff and telling the reverend what she found. Which wasn't much. Some papers, that's all. Couldn't work that tiny computer, and didn't dare take any of the tapes, even though the reverend offered her a bonus. Didn't dare. He would have known. She didn't know how, but Mr. Bannock would have known.

Weren't for the fact she was doing the Lord's work, she'd never even think about snooping a room. That was more her sister's line, always giggling and hooting about what she found in drawers and under beds, never once thinking what she was doing was wrong.

She checked the watch pinned to her uniform breast, rolled her eyes, and hustled. Vacuum, dust, straighten, change, singing hymns under her breath to pass the time. Thinking a few prayers now and then that the storm wouldn't get here before she was done. Not a hurricane, the radio said, but a good blow just the same. That ferry wasn't never in any danger of sinking, but it sure didn't take the wind very well.

When she reached 617, she hesitated.

Miz Grudeau, Reverend Trask had told her last night, I don't like to do it, you know I don't, but I must ask you to poke around a little harder tomorrow. Mr. Bannock doesn't know it yet, but he's doing the Lord's bidding, and the only way we—you and I—can help him, can give ourselves to the Lord and His mission in these terrible days, is by knowing exactly what it is Mr. Bannock is up to. I wouldn't ask you, Miz Grudeau, I wouldn't ask you if it weren't so terribly important.

Giselle took out her master key and knocked on the door. "Housekeeping," she called brightly, counted to ten, knocked again, called again, counted to ten again, and when she heard no response, she opened the door.

"Morning, Mr. Bannock," she said gaily, backing in with the vacuum cleaner. "How you doing today?"

She turned, smiling broadly, her very best smile, and stood for a long time before she said, "Oh . . . Lord."

5

The house had no age. Old, young, it didn't matter because the climate took care of the cosmetics and let the passersby draw their own conclusions.

Mostly white, where it wasn't peeling; bougainvillea and magnolia, live oak, and a trellis at the portico that failed to contain a rambling rose; a neat but far from perfect small front yard; an eight-foot wall along the sidewalk and down the sides, whitewashed once, bleeding dark brick now. Just west of Tulane.

Any number of visitors couldn't help wondering why Lanyon Trask didn't take some of the money his church gave him and fix the place up. Make it a showcase. Make it worthy of the man who lived in it all alone.

But Trask liked it just fine, just the way it was. Old and comfortable and . . . fitting.

His office was at the back, high ceiling and built-in bookcases, a small teak desk an Alabama aunt had left him in her will, an armchair, a standing globe. A simple wood cross over the sliding doors that led into the parlor. If you didn't look up, you'd never know it was there.

He did.

He faced it from his desk every day.

He glanced at it now as he replaced the receiver and leaned back in his chair, folding his hands across his stomach. Behind him were French doors that opened onto a patio where he wrote most of his sermons; to his right a door that led to an office that had once been a sewing room. It was the same size as his, with a computer, copier, fax machine, and things he didn't know about but were necessary for his secretary in order to keep the church moving. Living.

"Mrs. Cawley," he called.

No intercom; he hated the infernal things. They had no faces, and faces were what he insisted on talking to whenever he could.

Faces, like John Bannock's.

A woman came to the doorway, plump and floral-dressed, her pure white hair in a complicated twist that never seemed to stay where she wanted it. Reading glasses on a black ribbon, resting on her bosom.

"Yes, Reverend?"

He glanced at the cross again before swiveling around to face her. "He's gone, Emma."

"Oh, dear."

"I may . . ." He squinted. "I may have to take a trip."

Emma Cawley took one step into the room, one hand fussing with her glasses. "The governor," she said. "Wednesday."

He smiled, and waved the politician away as if he were shooing a pesky fly. "He needs my contribution, not my blessing, Mrs. Cawley. And I'm sure, somehow, he'll survive without either."

Mrs. Cawley ducked her head, a gesture he knew all too well. It wasn't her place to criticize, it said. Which she did. Often. Twenty-four years apparently gave her that right.

Then she clasped her hands at the white belt around her waist. "Are you sure, Reverend?"

"Yes, Mrs. Cawley, I'm sure."

They had only spoken of him once, the morning after he had had the dream.

floating

blue eyes

a never-ending sunset

It had terrified him.

"Will you need help?"

Ordinarily he would have said no; ordinarily he would have relied on the plain silver cross that hung around his neck, inside his shirt, and the plain small Bible he kept in his briefcase. A prayer, perhaps. And a walk in the garden beyond the patio, not searching for signs, just a little solitude.

Ordinarily he would have relied on faith.

"Yes," he said at last. Wearily. Sadly. "Yes, Mrs. Cawley, I believe I will."

And whispered, after she had left, "God, forgive me."

4

"All I want to do," said John to the desk clerk, "is get out of this city. "Is that so hard?"

He winced; he was whining. He could hear it, but instead of making him ashamed, it only added to his exasperation.

"Not long," the young man assured him patiently. "Really, Mr. Bannock. Not long."

And what, John wondered, is not long in New Orleans time? An hour? Two? Tonight? Next goddamn month?

Hands in his pockets, he paced away from the counter, to a narrow corridor at the juncture and back and side walls. At the end of that corridor was a single glass door. Past the door was the parking lot. In the parking lot was supposed to be his rental car. It wasn't. One had been, over an hour ago, but it had sputtered and died before he'd reached the exit. The company had been most apologetic, understood his concerns and needs, and promised rapid replacement.

He paced to the staircase and looked up.

Of course he could have taken a plane out. That had been his initial plan. The problem was seats. There were none, not until first thing in the morning. He had almost shouted, "Jesus, lady, they can do it in the movies, why the hell can't I do it, too?"

He felt the clerk staring at him.

He didn't care.

He was scared.

*   *   *

The first telephone call, not forty-five minutes ago:

"Mr. Bannock, glad I could reach you. This is Detective Xavier, New Orleans Police? We spoke yesterday? The young man who attacked you and your lady on the Algiers ferry? Pete Hundrel? I thought you might like to know that, well, simplest is best, I suppose—he's dead."

Hundrel woke before dawn and snuck out of his hospital room. The odd thing was, he stole a broom from a supply closet, then made his way to the roof. An orderly and a nurse spotted him and chased him, but they were too late.

"Damn fool rode that handle, you know? Like kids do, pretending to be witches and stuff? Got on that damn broom, shouted something, the witnesses aren't clear exactly what, and ran right off the edge. Didn't stop, didn't hesitate. One arm over his head, waving to beat the band. Didn't scream on the way down, either. Just thought you'd like to know, Mr. Bannock. Just thought you'd like to know."

Shaken, John told the desk clerk to tell anyone else after him that he'd already checked out and was halfway to Hawaii.

The second call came not ten minutes later.

The clerk took a message with John standing right there, rolling his eyes as he mouthed, *it's Reverend Trask.* John shook his head vigorously, the clerk approved, and gave Trask the Hawaii story word-for-word.

"Not happy," the clerk said when he hung up. Grinning.

John gave him ten dollars, and another ten for whoever called next.

And paced.

Waiting.

Trying not to think about Levee Pete, and failing miserably.

Pacing, checking the parking lot every ten minutes, glaring at his luggage stacked by the rear exit, trying to figure out a way to make the rental company get a move on. You get in the shower, the telephone rings; you light a cigarette, the waiter comes with your meal.

He was driving himself crazy, and he knew it, and couldn't stop it.

Levee Pete, and Joey's eyes.

He stopped in front of a bank of telephones next to the elevators. Two were house phones, three were pay phones, each separated from the other by partitions of stained wood. He could call the rental company again, but all they'd do is assure him his car would be there any second now, don't worry about a thing. He could try the airlines again, but short of a miracle or spending all day at the airport hoping for a standby seat, there was nothing to be gained there but more frustration.

Using George's phone card, he called New Jersey.

Casey Chisholm was gone.

According to a much aggrieved nurse, Casey had insisted on being sent home for the rest of his therapy. His doctor had signed him out. Highly irregular, the nurse complained. Reverend Chisholm was really in no condition to be moved. Highly irregular, and no, he had left no messages for a man named John Bannock.

John replaced the receiver and stared down the corridor toward his bags. His phone book was in there somewhere, and with it, Casey's home number. Was it worth digging through to find it and try a call?

The clerk called his name softly.

John rolled his eyes—*now what?*—and turned, scowling, and brightened when he saw a man in blue coveralls at the desk, holding up a set of car keys.

Later, he promised himself; on the road, later, he'd give Casey a call.

The forms were completed, the deposit made, the clerk given another ten, the man in coveralls a twenty, and John waved away the offer to carry his bags to the car. He shook hands with the clerk, tossed the keys up, caught them, and saw Lisse Montgomery come through the front door.

She said, "Look, I just wanted to apologize. I behaved like a jerk, and I'm sorry."

He answered, without thinking, "No sweat. You ever been to Illinois?"

5

1

Ari opened the door before Tony pounded it off the hinges, and backed away hastily when the larger man stomped into the living room.

"What?" he said anxiously, peering into the hall before closing the door and locking it. "We on fire? What?"

With a studied sigh, Tony lowered himself onto the couch and clamped his knees with his huge hands. "I've been thinking," he said, nodding Ari to the easy chair by the window. "I've been thinking."

Ari sat, staring at his friend for signs of stroke, drugs, liquor, dope, recent God forbid sex. It was barely noon, and the man was whatever it was the kids on the TV said these days. Stroked? Stoked? Hyper? Whatever. He didn't care; it just made him nervous.

"So," he said carefully, trying to read the man's eyes, "what are you thinking about?"

Garza leaned back without releasing the grip on his knees, examining at the ceiling, licking his lips, pursing them, sucking them in.

Oh God, Ari thought, it's Miriam again.

"I've been thinking about that guy," Tony said at last, keeping his gaze on the plaster Ari had been meaning to fix for years, there were so many cracks it looked like a road map. "The one that got killed."

Ari shrugged. "What about him? They won't catch the guy, they never do. So . . . what?"

IN THE MOOD

Tony sat up, the forefinger of each hand tapping his knee. "So I'm thinking it's kind of too close to home, you know what I mean? Creepy."

Ari agreed.

"So I'm thinking, maybe it's time for another trip, you know? Get the hell out of the city for a while. Stretch my legs. Breathe different air. Meet new people." He grinned and winked. "Get laid."

Ari rolled his eyes. "You can't go anywhere without you have to think about sex, right?"

"Of course not! It's—"

"Enough already." Ari looked to the window, reached out a hand, and straightened the curtains that didn't need straightening. "I don't want to hear it. You have a good time."

Which Tony would. He always did. Packed up, left, came back a week, a month later, sometimes with a new wife, sometimes with just a woman, all the time with unbelievable stories that kept them up long after midnight, him laughing so hard he was afraid for his heart.

Just once, he wished, reaching for the curtains again; just once.

"Will you stop that?" Tony yelled with a laugh that rattled the panes.

Ari yanked his hand back and smiled sheepishly. "Habit."

Tony pointed at him. "New habits, my friend. You need new habits."

"Sure. Like what?"

Tony rocked forward, lowered his voice. "Like going with me this time."

Ari started to laugh, had some of it out before he realized his friend wasn't kidding. He shook his head before giving the idea a chance. "Can't. You know I can't."

"Why not?"

Ari looked around his living room as if that was answer enough—does this look like the place of a man who has so much money he can pick up and leave without thinking about it?

But he said, "The game. Tomorrow's Tuesday. I've got the game, Tony."

"Screw the game."

Ari rocked back in his chair, shocked, disbelieving. Screw the game? Screw the only thing in his life that he could count on, except for Tony? Screw his major supplemental source of income? Screw the fun and the bad jokes and the beer and the gossip and the stories and the excuses and the sound of living people right here in his own house?

173

"You are out of your mind," he said calmly.

"Nope." Tony shook his head. "It's a perfect day, it's a great life, it's a lousy city, let's get the hell out of here for a while before that son of a bitch decides to slice one of us open."

"I can't."

"You won't, you mean."

Ari gestured. "Whatever. I'm not going."

He lay a hand on his stomach, feeling the fluttering in there. Part of it was because it was almost tempting, part of it because Tony had never, seriously, asked him before.

"I'm paying," Tony said.

"The hell you are."

Tony rocked back, then forward again. "Listen to me, Ari. We know each other too long, okay? for this kind of game. I ask you on a trip I know you can't afford, you think I'd do that without paying the expense?" He clapped a hand dramatically against his breast. "You insult me, you little fart. You cut me."

"Tony—"

"I'm thinking of your health, you dope. You only go to New Jersey when that . . . when *she* remembers to invite you. Where else do you go? Florida once every three years? Bunch of old people wrinkling in the sun, waiting to die? What the hell kind of fun is that?"

"I like it," he answered primly.

"Good. I'm glad for you. So come with me, there aren't any old people, at least none that matter, and it'll be great. We'll drink, okay? Get drunk, get laid, get rested, come back and brag to the Korean that we ate better food than he's ever had in that damn store of his."

"The game," he said again, weakly.

"Screw the game," Tony said again, loudly. "The boys will still be here when we get back. They won't hate you, they'll envy you. You'll be a hero, old dope. They'll kiss your scrawny feet."

Ari couldn't help it; he giggled.

Garza nodded emphatically. "I'll slip that idiot Pulero a few bucks to watch our places. He does it for me, hasn't stolen anything yet." He grinned. "We come back, you'll have a month's worth of cleaning to do to get rid of all the dust. You'll be in heaven."

Ari couldn't resist a quick smile.

Maybe it would be fun.

Maybe it would be worth it.

"I'll have to tell my daughter."

"Why?"

"If she calls, she'll worry if I don't answer."

Tony just looked at him, expressionless.

Ari didn't like the look, didn't like the feeling, and shifted his gaze to the window, to the buildings across the street. Not dirty, pretty nice all in all, but still, it was the same view. Always the same view. He never had a view in Jersey; she never let him stay long enough to have one.

Maybe it'd do her what do you call it, her karma, some good to worry a little.

"I'm not saying I'm going."

"Of course not."

"But if I did, where would we go?"

Garza shrugged elaborately. "California. Arizona. Paris. London. Athens. What difference does it make?"

"I don't have a passport."

"Jesus." Tony shook his head in mock despair. "So we forget London, let them suffer without us." He leaned forward, resting his forearms on his thighs. "You know, for a man who can deal himself a full house without blinking, you act like an old woman sometimes."

"Cheat?" Ari's voice rose. "You call me a cheater?"

Garza just grinned.

"He called me a cheat," he said to the window. "A card shark. A thief. Then he wants me to go off on some trip I don't even know where the hell it is."

Tony grinned. "So . . . you going?"

Ari shrugged, but the smile felt good. "When?"

Garza shrugged back. "Tomorrow."

"What?"

"First thing."

"You want me dead, don't you," he said. "You're trying to kill me."

"No," Tony said. "Believe me, no."

2

Dory set the receiver on its cradle and stared at the kitchen wall for a very long time.

Thinking nothing.

Seeing nothing.

Focusing finally on her hand still gripping the receiver. A few lines across the knuckles, no color on the nails. Then the wall phone. Then the wall.

The call had been unexpected. Absolutely. But not unpleasant. Far from it.

Very far from it.

She nodded, smiled briefly, and decided to go treat herself to a dinner out. When she got back, she would pack. When she woke up, she would call the office and give her best imitation of someone dying of whatever they used to call it in the old days. Consumption. Something like that. Take another couple of days off, they would say, solicitous on the phone while in the office they would look for ways to booby-trap her career. Again.

It might be fun.

Stay away, come back, watch their faces as she hauled their corporate asses over the coals.

She returned to the piano and tried a little New Orleans blues. Smoky rooms and ceiling fans and people slumped over their drinks, listening to the confirmation that all their dreams were dead, no chance in hell they were ever coming back, this, my friend, was as good as it gets.

It made her smile.

Dory "Slick Mama" Castro they would call her.

It made her laugh so hard tears soon fell on the keys.

Maybe . . . damn, maybe she would call Jerry. She hadn't seen him in a long time, and the way he kept leaving messages on her machine, he sounded just like what the doctor ordered. Take him to dinner. Flirt a little. Promise him everything, give him . . . whatever.

No.

She smiled.

No dinner.

Something better.

A lot better.

3

"The problem is," Garza said, "I'm a little worried about Ida."

"Ida Lefcowitz?" Ari frowned from his chair. "What's to worry?"

"I saw her today. She seemed . . . hell, she *was* upset. Just burst into tears when I said hello."

"Her son, I'll bet. Damn kid. You know, the last time I saw him was when? Last spring?"

"She looked sick."

"She is sick, Tony. Got a heart wouldn't keep a bird alive."

"Maybe I'll look in on her before we go."

4

The best thing about Jerome Nash was his willingness to try pretty much anything once, as long as she asked him in what he called her special way—a little pout, a little chest thrust, a little hint of reward she never failed to deliver. That she didn't see him all that often kept the requests from getting stale, kept him from thinking that maybe he ought to just stay away, kept him wondering what she'd come up with next that would warrant the Reward.

So when she suggested they combine a little fun with an old-fashioned Amish family restaurant meal out in Lancaster County, he was slightly puzzled. The Amish weren't exactly high on her list of fun people; and tossing apples down on trains passing under the trestle wasn't exactly the kind of half-baked excitement she usually devised in preparation for the Reward. Still, the pout and the chest thrust was sufficient to keep him grinning like a jackass during the ride out, and climbing the girder trestle was tricky enough for him to show off a little, play the macho stud, help her up, while lugging a full sack of apples she'd brought with her.

There was wind, too, with a bite, and stars that slowly faded as the leading edge of a forecast storm made its way across the state. There was darkness as well, as the surrounding farmland provided little illumination save for an infrequent island of house light too distant to be a threat.

The walkway on top was narrow, barely wide enough for two, with rough wood planking that creaked, and a rusted iron railing on both sides only a couple of inches wide; the trestle itself trembled slightly in the wind, the tracks below visible only as an occasional glint in the fading moonlight.

He giggled a lot and warmed up his arm by tossing a couple of apples into the dark, then listening for their landing.

She kissed him hungrily.

He kept his hands to himself.

He knew the routine, and even though she could tell he was freezing up here, she also could tell he was getting into it big time. The train thundering beneath them, shaking the trestle, a zillion tons of power rising through his soles. She had a feeling he would want her, right then, right here.

It was tempting.

A zillion tons of power rising through her back.

She had checked the timetable, and when she saw it, saw the light diamond hard in the west, she swallowed hard and told him to get ready, handed him an apple and said the one who made the loudest splat would be the winner.

He told her she was nuts.

She shrugged the truth of it and watched the train's approach. Freight train. No great speed. Just unstoppable power.

Half a mile, and the whistle sounded for a crossing, and Jerry began to mime pulling the pin from a grenade, looking to her for approval even though he could barely see her face, worrying suddenly that the engineer might see them when the headlamp's glow reached them.

She kissed him hungrily.

He kept his hands to himself.

She had an idea, she told him, and asked him to sit on the railing. He laughed, told her she was nuts, he wasn't about to do something like that, until she brushed a palm across his groin and wondered aloud what it would be like, him on the railing, without his pants, she on the walkway, kneeling at his feet, all that power beneath them.

All that power.

Her back was to the train when the glow reached them, but he saw just enough, and he laughed, and he nodded, and he unbuckled his belt and pulled down his zipper and unbuttoned his pants and hoisted himself onto the railing, hands on her shoulders for balance, giggling nervously as the trestle began to vibrate and the engine passed beneath them and she stroked his thighs and lowered her head and promised him loudly he'd never feel a thing.

She lied, of course.

Bend over, straighten up, and he was gone with a startled yell, and she leaned over and shook her head. Not like the movies. He hit the top of a boxcar, and rolled helplessly toward her while the train kept moving.

He disappeared between two cars.

And the train kept moving.

Whatever was left wouldn't be found for hours, maybe days.

Interesting, she thought as she made her way toward the trestle ladder; interesting.

Not two minutes gone, and she couldn't remember his face, couldn't remember his voice.

Except for the scream, of course.

Except for the scream.

5

How much luck left for the dance, Garza wondered; how many steps would it take to get it done.

A few more than four this time; definitely a few more than four.

He passed a knuckle over his eye, took a breath, and stepped outside. Past midnight, and the street was deserted, not much traffic anywhere as far as he could tell. Monday nights, not Wednesdays, were the quietest of the week.

He hurried down to the sidewalk, then strolled up the sidewalk. Anyone watching would see an old man too old to sleep, needing night air, nothing more, and probably thinking he was out of his mind.

The light over Ida's building's entrance was out, the vestibule lit only by a bulb burning in the hall on the other side.

A sign.

No sense walking up and down, checking for witnesses. Either they were there, or they weren't. Nothing he could do about it.

What the hell.

He climbed the steps heavily, pulling at the iron railing, pushing in the door, pausing in the vestibule. No intercoms here. Just scarred and tarnished mailboxes set into the wall.

The inner door was unlocked.

Another sign.

Her apartment was first on the left, and he stood there for a moment, wondering. Knock, and that damn excuse for a dog would bark its head off. Ring the bell, he'd get the same. She wouldn't open it, anyway. As soon as she saw his face, she'd start screaming or something.

What the hell.

He knocked softly, and sure enough, that dog-thing began to bark, high and muffled.

He knocked again, and leaned against the door, his left palm braced over the peephole.

Waiting.

Listening to the barking, listening to the hush of the building.

When he heard her voice say, "Who is it? It's late," he waited, and knocked again.

"Move your . . . I can't see . . . hush, Prescott, I can't hear."

"Mom," Tony whispered. Hiccupped loudly. Hiccupped again. "Mom?"

"Sam?" Fear, and hope. "Sam?"

"Mom? I'm . . . sorry, I'm a little drunk." A giggle. A belch. "Mom?"

The sound of bolts and chains, and Tony shook his head vigorously, made a guess, and shoved just as the door began to open.

The barking suddenly louder, and Ida crying out in surprise.

He stepped in and closed the door behind him. Prescott was at his feet, and he lashed out, catching the dog in the ribs, punting it across the room where it struck a wall, a piece of furniture, he couldn't tell, it was too dark.

It didn't matter; the dog was quiet.

"You," Ida gasped. "You go away."

He sighed and flexed his fingers. No razor tonight. That was for outside.

"You go, or I scream." Bundled in a tufted robe, hair in a net, face as pale as the wall beside the door. Backing away. Hands fluttering. "Please."

He grabbed her by the throat with one hand, lifted her effortlessly off her feet, and carried her down a short hallway, looking for the bedroom, while she tried to claw at his fingers, kicking feebly. When he found it, he dropped her onto the bed without releasing the choke; he sighed, and he squeezed, and it didn't take very long.

Then he took off the robe and put her back in bed, pulling the covers to her chin. It was silly. Someone would see the bruises right away, but he didn't want the old cow found on the floor, or seen in her too-thin night-gown.

If that damn dog was dead, she wouldn't be found for days.

He decided, all in all, it would be better to make sure.

6

"To the airport," Tony announced grandly to the cab driver. "And don't spare the horses."

Ari laughed as the taxi pulled away from the curb. Nervous. Excited. The first crazy thing he had ever done in his life. "I don't get it."

Garza settled in his corner, grinning broadly. "What's to get? We're away, my friend. We are away!"

"But who the hell do you know in . . . what's that place again?"

Tony smiled at him, reached over and patted his knee. "Vallor, Ari. Vallor, Illinois. And who I know there is someone very special, my very special friend. We, you and I, are going to see my daughter."

The pickup finally gives out seventy-some miles west of Des Moines.

He doesn't care. It got him this far without much trouble, and he figures that's good enough.

He stands on the shoulder of the highway and shivers a little. It's late, not much traffic, but he doesn't care about that, either. Someone will drive by, see him with a saddle at his feet, get all misty about cowboys, and pick him up.

One day, maybe two, and then he's home.

The bastards won't know what hit them.

Especially Annette and Sharon.

Loving wife, loving daughter.

Headlights, so he smiles and holds out his thumb, using his left boot to nudge the saddle closer to the road.

The car stops right on the highway, directly in front of him, so all he has to do is lean over when the passenger window slides down.

"Hey, cowboy," the driver says, "need a ride?"

Five minutes later the saddle is in the trunk and they're heading east at speed.

"So," the driver says, "you do the rodeo circuit, stuff like that? Broncs and bulls and sixguns and shit?"

And Rod Gillespie takes a moment before he says, "Yeah, something like that."

"So," the driver said, checking her out in the rearview mirror. "Business? Pleasure?"

"Yes," Dory answered with a coy smile.

He nodded. "Good. Mix one with the other, you don't ever get bored."

"That's right."

"You know people out there?"

"Yes."

"Good. Doesn't pay to go places where you don't know anyone. No fun, otherwise."

Dory watched the interstate, watched the airport grow just ahead. "You don't travel much, do you?"

"Not me, ma'am. Too busy. I drive all day, all night, I just don't want to go anywhere but my own place, know what I mean?"

The car swung onto the off-ramp without losing speed.

"What does your family think?" she asked.

He shrugged as he leaned forward, squinting to read the airport signs. "Only have a brother, he doesn't give a you know what."

"Too bad. Brothers are—right up there, slow down, you'll miss it."

"Sorry." He pulled over, braking so hard she had to brace herself against the seat back. "You got a brother?"

"A few."

He laughed. "That who you're going to see? Out there in Illinois? One of your brothers?"

"No," she said, grabbing her small carry-on, opening the door. "My sister."

"Chicago?"

"Vallor," she answered as she handed him his tip, thinking it was too much but not giving a damn.

"Never heard of it."

7

1

The parking lot didn't hold more than a few dozen cars in one single and one double row, the single row closest to the hotel's modest rear entrance. It was surrounded by a high cyclone fence crawling with wilted vines; a narrow gateless gap opened onto the street. Sunlight broke into knives where it touched windows and chrome, aiming for John's eyes, giving him, with the heat, an instant headache. The rental car was at the back, and despite the lot's size, he was already sweating by the time he'd loaded his suitcase into the trunk, his briefcase and carton of papers into the backseat.

Lisse had helped, smiling nervously whenever he looked her way. Which was as little as possible once he had realized what he had done. Speaking softly. Awkwardly. Not at all sure he knew what the hell he was doing, and not knowing how to take it back. Hoping she would take the first step.

"This is nuts," she said when the car was loaded and they stood at the trunk, squinting up at the back of the Royal Cajun, examining the diamond shapes in the fence, staring at the blacktop that felt soft underfoot.

"Yeah," he answered, swiping at the damp hair that wanted to mat to his forehead.

"I mean, no offense, but I don't even know you."

He shrugged. What could he say? She was right, and searching for an out.

But, he noticed, partly disappointed and partly pleased, not very hard. He jiggled the keys in his left hand, looked at the hotel again, and felt his mouth work at a lopsided grin—if this kept up, he'd be counting the windows next, just to avoid looking at her eyes.

"Listen, Lisse," he began.

"The trouble is," she interrupted, one hand tucked into a hip pocket, the other shading her eyes, "I kept thinking about you, you know? What I did? Guilt, I guess. I was brought up better, I know that."

"Don't worry about it. I didn't blame you at all."

"You sure?"

"Sure."

The end, then. He could feel it coming, could feel her turning away without having moved a muscle.

"Wow," she said, lifting her chin to point. "You think if you get rich with your book, you'll live like that?"

Over the tops of the cars between him and the exit he saw a long limousine pull into the lot. So soft a gray it seemed insubstantial, its windows so heavily tinted they looked solid black. It paused at the hotel's back entrance before sliding past, hood facing the fence.

"No way he can turn around," John said. "He'll have to back out." His own car was in the middle of the back row, and he checked automatically to be sure there was enough room between him and the fence there so he could just turn left out of the slot without a lot of backing up and inching forward. "Wonder who it is?"

The rear door had opened and a giant stepped out on the other side.

"Well," she said. "My, my."

He wore a suit a few shades darker than the limousine, obviously tailored for his size but unable to hide the breadth of his chest, the thickness of his arms. His face, John thought as the man glanced in their direction, should have been rugged and harsh, but it was round and pleasant, and made softer by the thick dark hair brushed straight back from his narrow brow to curl gently at his shoulders. Eyes behind gold wire-rim sunglasses. Skin vaguely, naturally, dark. He walked to the limousine's trunk, heading for the hotel door, when he stopped abruptly and leaned down, one hand braced on the roof.

"Movie star?" John wondered.

"Singer, probably" Lisse told him. To his look she added, "They stay here sometimes. Casinos and clubs, you know? The ones who don't want all the fancy crap. They like to hide out." She made a face. "Lousy tippers, too."

The giant straightened and stared at them.

"Uh-oh," she whispered.

"Well, I don't want his autograph, no matter who he is," John said, turning away, shaking the car keys, this time in agitation. "Gotta hit the road."

"John," she said softly.

He looked at her, looked across the lot and saw the giant moving toward them, sideways between the cars. When he reached the lane between the rows, he stopped, and smiled.

"Mr. Bannock? John Bannock?" A quiet voice, husky, with a faint accent John couldn't place.

He frowned. "Yes?"

The giant nodded a greeting. "Alonse Paytrice, sir." He gestured toward the limo. "A moment of your time, sir."

"Sorry," John said pleasantly. "I'm on my way out."

Paytrice took a step toward them, and John felt Lisse backing away, rounding the trunk toward the passenger door.

"Wish you would reconsider, sir," Paytrice said, still smiling. Another gesture toward the limo. "Just a short conversation."

"Look," John told him, trying to be reasonable, "I don't know you, I'm sorry, and I don't know your boss. I'm in a hurry, all right? Maybe another time."

"Reverend Trask," the giant said.

John stopped. "What?"

"Reverend Trask." The gesture again. "Just a moment of your time, sir, that's all he requests."

John stared at the limousine. What the hell is this, muscle for a minister?

"No. I've said all I have to say to your boss, Mr. Paytrice, and he knows it. Sorry." He opened the car door, nodded to Lisse to get in. "I'll drive you home," and she nodded gratefully as she slid in.

"Mr. Bannock."

John ignored him.

"Mr. Bannock, please, sir."

He checked back as he crouched to get in behind the wheel and saw the giant moving toward him, hands out as if to apologize for what would come next if he didn't listen.

Crazy, he thought; this is nuts.

"Mr. Bannock!"

John slammed the door, hissed at the heat packed inside, and rolled his window down as he slid the key into the ignition.

Lisse said nothing, her hands clasped tightly in her lap.

"Who the hell does he think he is?" he muttered, and jumped when something slammed against the hood.

The giant stood in front of the car, still smiling, palms pressed against the hood.

"Move, please," John called, and turned on the ignition.

Paytrice shook his head.

"You can't run him over," Lisse said, as if he might try.

"A bulldozer couldn't," he said angrily, and called, "Get out of the way!"

"John, maybe you ought to—"

He hushed her with a sharp gesture, and glared at the giant for several seconds before getting out again.

The giant straightened, hands floating to his sides.

"I'm not going," John told him, a glance back at the limousine. "Get it through your head, all right? I'm not going. So please move."

"Sorry, sir," Paytrice said, "but you are."

He came around the car, and John backed away. Not seven feet tall, but at least halfway there, forcing John to look up. His hip bumped into the front of the car parked directly behind his, and he winced, still backing, looking around for someone to help, a policeman or hotel worker, someone, anyone.

In the lane he stopped.

He could run, hit the street, find a cop; he could run, duck inside, get the clerk to call a cop; he could run, but why should he, damnit?

"This is stupid," he said, panting a little in the heat.

Paytrice nodded agreement as he squeezed between the last two cars. "Yes, sir. Just move on, sir, and it'll only be a moment."

"No."

The giant stopped, surprised. "Sir?"

"Look, Mr. Paytrice, your boss and I have already spoken, and there's nothing more I want to say to him. I don't appreciate the intimidation, and you've scared my lady friend half to death." He almost smiled. "Hardly the way a good Christian should behave."

Paytrice frowned. "No call for that kind of talk, sir. Now move, please." The husky voice deepened. "I will carry you if I have to."

"In Hell," John said, suddenly too angry to think straight, see straight.

Paytrice reached for his arm; John moved to one side.

The giant reached again, quickly, and caught him, and John gasped at the pain.

"Move, sir," Paytrice ordered.

John took one submissive step, twisted, and broke free again, and watched his rental car slide out of its slot, Lisse pointing frantically at the end of the lane as she made the turn.

Paytrice clamped his left shoulder. "Not a good idea, sir, I run pretty fast for a man my size."

Movement to his left made him look, and another man eased out of the limousine. "My God," he said.

"My brother Sebastian," Paytrice said. "We're twins." He grinned. "I'm the little one." He leaned down and the smile broadened. "The nice one."

John looked up into the giant's face and was terrified, and was furious. Broad daylight, big city, and a damn clergyman's bodyguard is kidnapping him, for crying out loud.

Without thinking he reached over and grabbed the man's wrist with his right hand, realized his fingers wouldn't go all the way around. "Don't do this," he warned, almost pleaded. "Alonse, don't do this."

Paytrice cocked his head at the unexpected threat, squeezed a little harder. "Just walk, sir."

John dropped his hand and ducked under the giant's arm, breaking the hold but not quickly enough. A fist swatted his back, slamming him into the grille of the nearest car, doubling him over the hood. He couldn't breathe. He began to slide to the tarmac, sun-hot chrome and metal burning his palms and chest. No one helped him until he reached his knees, then a hand bunched the back of his shirt and yanked him to his feet, held him until he could stand, and spun him around.

Paytrice wasn't smiling.

John, one hand clutched to his chest, gulped for air, wanted to throw up, could hear Lisse banging a fist on the car horn.

"Now?" the giant said.

John sagged against the grille, blinked sweat from his eyes, and looked up.

It was the heat; it was the dark smudge of a cloud sliding over the hotel roof; it was that incessant damnable horn; it was that expression on the giant's face, impatient and smug; it was pain in his chest and on his palms and in his shoulder and in his arm.

floating.

he was floating.

He grabbed the giant's hands, and Paytrice chuckled and closed his fingers around John's. And squeezed.

Nothing happened.

John stared at the sunglasses as the man's eyebrows rose in surprise.

"No," he said.

And squeezed back.

Paytrice gasped immediately, whimpered, and dropped hard to his knees, sunglasses askew, eyes wide and not understanding. Swallowing hard. Sweating hard.

"Sir," he said, voice unnaturally high. In pain. In fear. "Please."

"You tell him."

Paytrice nodded quickly, struggling not to bend over. To bow.

A shout, maybe not the first one. John saw the brother sidling as fast as he could between the parked cars, brandishing a fist.

"You tell him," John told Alonse. "Tell Trask to leave me alone."

A single tear on Paytrice's cheek as he nodded, just once.

John released him and ran down the lane, waving at Lisse to get moving. She did, at a crawl, until he swerved around the trunk, yanked open the passenger door, and threw himself inside.

"Go!" he cried.

"Where?" she said as she maneuvered through the gap and turned right.

"Anywhere," he said. "Anywhere."

2

Alonse Paytrice knelt in the parking lot and sobbed, hands useless on his thighs.

His brother towered over him, not knowing what to do, what to say. "How he do that?" he asked finally, fingers brushing his brother's shoulder.

"I don't know." Alonse didn't wipe his eyes, didn't wipe his nose. "I don't know." When he finally looked up, when he could finally see, he said, "That man ain't right, Seb, that man ain't right."

"Stronger than he look."

"No." He accepted Sebastian's help to his feet, but shook the hands off once they started back to the limo. "That ain't it, Seb. Something else. Something else."

3

John switched places with Lisse the first chance they had to pull over. Twenty minutes later they were on the interstate, headed for Baton Rouge. His original plan was to simply ride up the Mississippi on I-51 all the way to Illinois, cut east, and run straight for home. Now he wasn't so sure.

Neither was Lisse.

"He'll find me," she said for the fifth, maybe sixth time. She barely looked at him. "A man like that, he'll know how to find me. Those men . . ." She shuddered. For the fifth, maybe sixth time.

He didn't speak.

He couldn't speak.

Levee Pete and Alonse Paytrice.

What the hell was going on?

He was about as unathletic as they come. Walking was the most exercise he got, and that, not every often. When he was a kid his height had protected him from bullies; when he became an adult, his height was still somewhat intimidating—that, he thought with a grin—and that damn presidential resemblance. But against a giant like Paytrice?

The sensation, the floating, had ended as soon as he'd grabbed those monster hands, nothing left but anger.

No, he corrected; not anger . . . purpose.

Whatever that meant.

The leading edge of the Gulf storm continued to catch up with them, muting the sunlight now, softening the shadows.

"Do you have relatives?" he asked at last. "I mean, someplace I can drop you? Friends, maybe?"

"No," she said. "They'll find me."

"Then maybe you should . . . uh . . ."

"Stick with you?" She laughed, not quite strained. "I don't think you're very safe, you know. You got that lightning thing, bad news stuff, it comes to you out of clear blue, you know what I mean?"

"I didn't used to," he answered sourly.

"Nothing better to do, though," she said, looking out her window.

"Thanks." But he smiled.

A mile, and he saw nothing. Nothing registered but the cars ahead of him, the semis jetting past him, the way the afternoon grew slowly darker.

"John?"

"Yes?"

"How'd you do that? That man?"

"I don't know, Lisse. I swear to you, I don't know."

She grunted. "Tell you the truth, I ain't surprised." She sighed. "He didn't scream, like that kid, but it was close enough, the look on his face."

He knew.

"I don't get it. What does he want? The reverend."

He shook his head, raised an I-don't-know hand, and told her about the conversation he'd had with the minister after she'd left. Her eyes widened in disbelief.

"The Antichrist? You're kidding."

"That's what he said." He wanted to laugh; he couldn't.

"You have a kid, right?"

"Yes, right."

"What's his name, Damien?"

He did laugh then. "No. Joey. His name is Joey."

"Watch that rig, John, he's drifting."

The eighteen-wheeler had slowed for an exit, signal light blinking, sliding over into their lane. John slowed to let him in.

"Joey," she said quietly. "Sorry, but that's no name for the Antichrist. He do sacrifices and stuff? You know, slice up the neighbor's puppies and kittens?"

He laughed again. "Not hardly. He . . . he loves animals. Especially horses."

"Cowboy, huh?"

"Twenty-four hours a day. Hat, shirt, gunbelt, the works." He smiled. "We have this cable channel, it shows westerns all day, and old cowboy shows. It took a crowbar to get him outside when Roy Rogers or Gene Autry were on." The smile wavered. "I wonder if she still lets him watch them."

"If he's the Antichrist, he can probably watch any damn thing he wants."

He looked over, saw the grin and felt the melancholy drain. "He can't think that, can he? Trask, I mean. That I'm looking for the Antichrist, and my son is it?" He shook his head quickly, and looked back to the highway when Lisse pointed. "Nah."

"Then that quest thing he said, what is it?"

"He's crazy, Lisse, that's all."

"Like a fox," she answered, squirmed in her seat and looked into the back. "That box, those the papers you were so hot to print out?"

He nodded, braking as a van cut in front of him to take the next exit. Barely breathing until the van actually left the highway.

"Maybe it's in there," she said thoughtfully. "The answer."

"I know it is."

"You know what it is?"

"Not positive. It's something, though."

"What got you all excited before?"

"Yeah."

"You gonna tell me?"

He hadn't planned on it, but as soon as she said it, he answered, "Yes. Maybe if I tell you, you can tell me if I'm nuts or not."

"Oh, you're nuts, all right. No question. Question is, why?"

Because I'm scared, he thought; because I'm scared out of my mind, and I don't know why.

Then she said, "John, we going right up the river?"

"That's the plan. We'll probably hit traffic by Baton Rouge and Memphis, but we should—" He looked over and saw her staring out the back window. He shifted his gaze to the rearview mirror, saw nothing out of the ordinary until the car behind him shifted into the next lane.

The gray limousine was back there, one lane over and a dozen lengths back.

"Oh . . . shit."

Lisse faced front, the fingers of her left hand plucking at her shirt. "Hanging back there."

He sped up, but not much, shifted lanes once before moving back into the right-hand lane behind an old station wagon packed with kids, a pair of mattresses strapped to the roof.

"Still there," she said.

He knew; he saw.

"Following."

She nodded. "He probably knows you're heading back home. I don't get it. Why not try to pull us over, or get there before you do?"

"I don't know." He lost its image for a few moments, found it again, smooth and gliding in the next lane over. "I don't know."

She snapped her fingers softly. "Or he's waiting for us to pull over. Gas, or something." She nodded to the dashboard. "You don't got but half a tank. You'll have to stop."

Another mile, while the traffic thickened.

"I need a hero," he said with a forced laugh. "Some guy who knows what the hell he's doing."

"You got a gun somewhere?" she said, only half joking.

He didn't have to answer, but he moved a little faster.

"Tell me something," he said. "You any good at navigating without a map?"

"Do I have a good sense of direction? Yeah, I guess so. Never got lost as far as I can remember. Why?"

"I have another plan."

He drove for another forty-five minutes, keeping to the speed limit while most of the rest of the traffic barreled by. Trying to beat the storm, he figured, nodding when she turned on the radio just in time to hear a newsman tell his listeners about the rain in New Orleans, the gusts of high wind.

The limousine hung back, evidently content to play shadow for a while. He had stopped checking on it twenty miles ago; it was there and, for now, there wasn't much he could do about it.

When the first drop hit the windshield, smeared the dust, he wondered if he really was nuts, thinking what he was thinking. He wasn't a hero—movie, real life, or otherwise—and the smartest thing would be just to pull over and let the man have his say. A rational thought for a rational man, but Paytrice had changed that. His dander was up, as George Trout would say, and when that happened, mules no longer had the corner on stubborn.

The wind picked up, swirling dust across the highway.

The temperature began to drop.

When the rain finally struck it was fast and hard, the wipers on full speed barely keeping up with the torrent. Cars pulled to the shoulder to wait it out. Trucks didn't bother. The station wagon veered sharply toward an exit, the kids at the back window ghosts in the rain.

"Won't last," Lisse said, her voice startling him. "Too hard, it won't last."

"In that case," he said, and at the last possible moment cut toward the exit, swept down the ramp without slowing down. Lisse yelped in surprise and grabbed for the dashboard when he ran a red light at the bottom, praying there were no cops nearby. He braked only when he reached the next corner, swung right into a small shopping district, most stores dark, many boarded up, cars at the curbs old and bleak.

The rearview mirror was empty of everything but the rain.

"East and north," he said when Lisse looked at him for an explanation. "Just head us east and north."

"John, we're lost."

"That's the point, isn't it? Where are we?"

"I said we're lost. If I knew where we were, then we wouldn't be lost." She giggled. "Mississippi, I think."

"Good."

The gray limousine was gone.

"We'll stop in a couple of hours, get a room, get some sleep."

"Two rooms," she said primly.

"If you say so, it's George's money."

"And food. I'm starving. I ain't hardly eaten all day, them drive-thru burgers don't count."

He looked at her, barely seen in the dark, the sun long gone. "Funny about your English."

"Hey."

"That accent, I could listen to it all day. But your English comes and goes, have you noticed?"

"My English is good enough for me, Yank. Nobody ever complained about it before."

"I'm not complaining. Just something I noticed."

"So it slips when I get nervous. You wanna make something of it?"

"You're nervous?"

"Shit, no, I'm scared half to death."

The room was small, musty, at the back of a motel near the Tombigbee River. Thin walls, stains in the bathroom sink, water dripping constantly from the pines that overwhelmed it. The window air conditioner didn't work, and the television bolted to the chipped chest of drawers had only two stations—one from Memphis, one from Birmingham. Once in a while.

He had tried to call Casey but there was no answer at the rectory, none at the church. Information gave him a number for the doctor, Mel Farber, but no one answered there, either.

Fingers crossed, but no hope at all, he tried calling home.

His answering machine didn't pick up; Sharon must have turned it off.

When he failed to get hold of George, he wanted to tear the phone from the wall.

They lay in their own beds, not really sleeping.

Crickets and tree frogs.

"John?"

"Hmmmm?"

"What if he's there when we get there?"

"My turf." He chuckled. "My turf, my friends, my town."

"They'll protect you?"

"Us. Yeah. I hope so."

"I sure wish that made me feel better than I do."

Crickets and tree frogs, a passing car that sat them up until the headlights moved on.

"Those papers, John. What's in those papers got you all up like that?"

"You heard some of the tapes, right?"

"Sure. A couple."

"You notice anything in common?"

"You mean, aside from they killed a whole mess of people?"

"Think about it."

"I'm too hot to think, I'm too tired to breathe. Don't play me games, John, this ain't the time."

"They didn't care, Lisse. Except for a couple, like that guy in Rahway, they didn't care about anyone they killed. Not even family members. They did it because they felt like it. Because they were in the mood do to it. When they weren't in the mood, they didn't do it. A score of them, Lisse. More than that. And I know, I *know,* that if I talked to more, it would only be the same."

A night bird, calling.

"That means . . . you saying that means there are people out there, a ton of them maybe, doing the same thing?"

"Exactly what I mean."

"They kill because they want to."

"No. They just kill. There's . . . I don't know . . . there's nothing inside anymore, I think."

"No, that can't be."

"I hope you're right, Lisse. I really hope you're right."

Another car, speeding, trailing voices whooping.

"Your friend, the minister?"

"Priest."

"Whatever. He said you were marked. This what he meant? That you should find this out?"

"I don't know. I don't know what he meant."

"Scary thought."

"Tell me about it."

"End of the world."

"A year ago, I would have laughed. I still doubt it, but you'll notice I'm not laughing."

A mattress creaked.

"John?"

"Yeah?"

"No offense, you know, but . . . who are you?"

The crickets stopped.

8

The bus is on a wide, hard-packed shoulder, interior lights off, flares stabbed into the ground ahead and behind. There are no streetlamps. There are no nearby buildings. There may be moonlight, but it isn't strong enough. There may be night noises, but all Patty can hear are soft snores and soft whispers and once in a while, an angry slap to someone's thigh, followed by a curse of supreme exasperation.

She sits by the window, but there's not much to see, only the darkness. Joey is curled on the seat beside her, his head in her lap, hands tucked under his chin, eyes closed. Her left hand strokes his hair absently while she tries to make sense of this run of bad luck.

There had been no bus from Staser, but a smaller company, local and struggling, had stepped in with an offer, and by that time the passengers were too angry, too tired, too anxious to get home to refuse.

Joey had been upset. Not with the bus; even he understood this was something she couldn't control. It had been the ice cream—it had run out. Try as she might, she could not get him to understand that they had been lucky to get any ice cream at all. Cows, she'd said, were dying. Babies needed the milk more than he needed his chocolate cone.

His face had reddened; his eyes had darkened; she had braced herself for a tantrum, suddenly and deeply afraid. Not for herself. For the others.

Then he had smiled, a lovely, beatific, terrible smile.

"That's all right, Mommy. I'll wait 'til we get home."

Three breakdowns later he had fallen asleep.

Four rows up, on the other side of the aisle, a match flares, and Patty watches it, smells the sulfur and the tobacco. A heavyset woman blows smoke out her open window, calling to someone passing by below. Flashlight beams turn the windows up there nearly white, the passengers fleeting silhouettes. The windshield and rear window are dancing fire, from the flares.

"For crying out loud, how much longer?" the woman demands hoarsely.

A muffled voice in return.

"Yeah, right," she says. "That's what you said an hour ago."

No one else speaks.

Over the next hour, several people leave to stretch their legs and watch the repair work; over the next hour, Patty dozes, wakes, dozes again; over the next hour, not a single car or truck passes them on the road.

Patty shifts, her back sore, her left leg numb. She would love to get up, walk around a little, but that would mean waking Joey; she would love to get her jacket, up there on the wire shelf, it was cold in here, but that would mean waking Joey.

White lights slash through the interior, jerky, too bright.

Then she hears a smattering of applause and sits up.

"You're kidding," the smoking woman says through the window. "You shitting me, kid?" At the answer, she laughs. "Hot damn."

They stir, then, all who had been sleeping, and Patty smiles wearily, gratefully.

Joey sighs loudly.

When she looks down she can't really see his face. Only the one vivid eye when he looks up at her and says, "Are we home yet, Mom?"

"Soon, honey. The bus is fixed, I think."

He giggles. "You wanna bet?"

Her hand squeezes his head in mock scolding. "Don't say that. It's bad luck."

The eye closes. "Not really."

"Yes, really."

He giggles again. "Not."

"Yes."

"Not yes."

"Not no."

His head pushes closer to her stomach. "Okay."

Passengers hurry back on board, yawning extravagantly, laughing, rubbing hands and nodding to strangers, top-of-the-voice anxious to get on their way. The driver is the last to board, and takes his seat, grabs the wheel with one hand.

"Screw up and you're a dead man," the smoking woman warns.

Everyone laughs, even Joey.

And quiets, until the engine catches and sputters and rumbles, and the bus shakes itself awake.

The applause is loud and only half mocking as the bus pulls onto the road, headlights boring white tunnels in the black.

"Mom?" Sleepily, through a yawn.

"Hush, dear, it's after midnight, Tuesday already. Get some sleep. We'll be there by morning."

"Mom?"

She looks down.

Sees the eye.

Nothing else; just the eye.

"We're gonna have a party."

She says nothing; she dares not.

He shifts again, snuggling. "Grampa's coming."

She can't help it: "What? How do you know? You didn't talk to him, right?"

Small hand on her hip. "Aunt Dory, too."

The heater is on, the blower dragon-loud, but she can't shed the cold. "Joey—"

"Daddy." His voice is flat. "Daddy's coming home."

And she thinks, oh my God, Ace, what the hell are you doing?

The bus grumbles, and morning is no closer. The driver announces through the faulty intercom that moving faster might mean another breakdown. Something about transmissions. Something about hills and speed. He apologizes, swears they will arrive before noon, swears again when something grinds, deep in the vehicle's bowels below the floorboard.

Patty holds her breath, but the bus doesn't stop.

The woman near the front, still blowing smoke out her partially open window, demands champagne on arrival, and a few people laugh.

Another suggestion from a man in back—caviar and Jim Beam—and it isn't long before a menu is proposed. Thirty-four people on the bus, a party being planned, survivors already preparing for a reunion.

Deep in the early morning, and very few can sleep.

Patty's thighs are numb from the weight of Joey's head, and when she tries to shift, he groans, rubs his eyes, and sits up, disoriented, blinking, trying to look through the window and seeing nothing but the dark.

"Sleep, hon," she says, rubbing her legs.

"Can't." He looks around, puzzled at the laughter, the talk. His expression wants to know why they aren't fast asleep. "What are they doing?"

"Coping," she answers with a quiet laugh. "The Ride from Hell."

The couple in the seats in front of them want to know where they're going to get all this party stuff, what with the shortages and all. Don't they realize people are going hungry, people are actually starving to death?

No one cares.

The woman with the cigarette turns around and says, "Lady, don't worry, the Lord and the bus company shall provide and succor. And give me a damn refund."

The laughter is loud and long.

Joey lays back down, Patty's arm light across his stomach. She can see his eyes, a bit of his mouth, can feel the night's chill although the bus has grown too warm. She wants to ask him how he knew his grandfather and aunt were coming for a visit, how he knew about Ace, but she has learned there are some things it doesn't pay to question.

Still . . .

"Joey?"

His gaze shifts as she looks down.

"Can you . . ." She looks away, trying to find the words even though she knows them. "Why, Joey?" she asks instead.

He stares unblinking.

The bus thuds over a series of potholes, rocking hard.

"There's a man, Mom," he says. Staring. Unblinking. "He's coming, too. He acts old, but he really isn't. That's silly, don't you think? He's silly."

She swallows, says nothing. Another question best left unasked.

He closes his eyes. "Mom? What's the Antichrist?"

Streetlights now, the glow sweeping through the bus, sweeping shadows across the ceiling, making things move that weren't moving at all.

White and dark.

"Mom."

White and dark.

His eyes open.

He smiles.

"Give me your hand, Mom."

Patty stiffens. "No, Joey, please."

"Mom. Hand."

White and dark.

"Please, Joey, please, I . . ." She shakes her head. "I don't want to. Please."

His fingers find the hand that lies on his stomach, and when she tries to pull away, the smile fades.

"Mom."

She feels the tears, trembling lips.

"He's wrong, Mommy," Joey says quietly, taking her hand in both of his, pulling it up, snuggling it under his chin. "The funny old man who isn't really old? He's wrong."

Part 4

1

1

A two-lane blacktop, swirled with dust. On the north side an open field, brittle cornstalks sagging under their own weight, a stand of trees in the middle distance, and nothing more. On the south the view of another empty field partially blocked by a line of trees that hug the bowed fence on the other side of the shoulder.

Straight ahead, trees and hints of rooftops and a silver water tower that rises above them like a Welles Martian machine.

"It's changed," John said, squinting into the setting sun despite the sunglasses Lisse had insisted he wear.

"How can you tell? We're not even there yet."

"Believe me, I can tell."

She reached over to touch his arm. "You've been gone for over a year. Bound to be something different." She poked the arm, withdrew her hand. "You've changed, for one thing."

"Can't argue with that."

He pulled over, the engine idling, and pushed a finger across his cheek, not quite scratching. They hadn't bothered to keep watch for the gray limousine since leaving the motel shortly after dawn. Either Trask would find and follow them, or he wouldn't; either he'd be here already, or he wouldn't. Neither of them thought the preacher had given up and gone home.

"Stalling, Yank," she said lightly.

"Yeah," and he pulled back onto the road. "What we'll do is, we'll go to my place, okay? Freshen up, see what's going on."

"Then what?"

He shrugged. Probably, get hold of George and tell him what they had discovered in the inmate tapes. Maybe it was nothing, maybe it was something, he didn't know. He still wasn't sure if he wanted to tell Trout about Levee Pete and Paytrice. Aside from the fact that he might be laughed at, he needed more information himself.

Lisse rubbed her arms. "Chilly up here."

"It's October," he reminded her with a smile. "Halloween just around the corner." A glance over. "Just how far north have you been?"

She pointed at Vallor. "This is it."

"God, you're going to freeze, poor thing."

A quick laugh as the farmland ended, replaced by a high school and its fields, car dealerships and strip malls, a park, a Holiday Inn, then houses and streets and corner stores.

"The main drag," he announced when the stores and streetlights and traffic lights began. "Madison." A few blocks later he pointed. "Town Hall."

"Ugly," she said. "Lord, that's ugly."

"It's supposed to be impressive."

"Okay, it's impressively ugly." When he turned at the next traffic light, she hugged herself. "Bigger than I thought."

"Well, it's not New Orleans," he said, feeling oddly defensive, "but it's big enough, I guess."

He turned left on Jackson Street, slowing so he could lean over as they passed Vallor High West. A large banner had been strung over the main entrance, exhorting the football team to victory in Kentucky.

"Kentucky? What the hell are they doing in Kentucky?"

At the railroad tracks he stopped again, sliding his palms over the steering wheel, back and forth, up and down.

"I take it we're kind of close?" she asked.

He nodded. "A couple miles up the road." He inhaled slowly, blew the breath out. "It's been a long time." A brief smile when she patted his arm, and for a moment, just a moment, he covered her hand with his without looking over. When her fingers slid away, he squared his shoulders, muttered, "Into the breech, you jerk," and pressed the accelerator.

Lisse kept silent until they reached the Burgoyne ranch. "You ride?"

IN THE MOOD

"Nope. Those things scare the hell out of me."

"Me, too."

He stopped just before the bridge, leaning forward, gripping the steering wheel tightly. "Son of a bitch."

"What?"

He nodded toward a low house on the other side of the street, beyond the creek. The trunk of a small car was visible in the driveway through the trees and shrubs. He wasn't sure, but he thought he saw another one in front of it.

"Company," he said.

"Your house?"

He nodded.

"Maybe . . . maybe your wife's come back."

Maybe, he thought, but he didn't like it.

He inched the car forward, ignoring her puzzled look, stopping again when he could see the front of the house, the porch, and a man sprawled in a lawn chair by the front walk, legs outstretched, hands clasped across his stomach, eyes closed in the fading sunlight.

"God damn."

"What?" she whispered.

"Anthony Garza," he told her. "Patty's father. He—Jesus, what the hell is *she* doing here?"

A woman stepped onto the porch from inside, short and slender, wearing a sweater that reached halfway down her thighs, jeans and sandals.

"Patty's sister," he explained, confused and angry. "Dorina Castro. Christ, she lives in Philadelphia, for God's sake." He frowned as Dory hurried down the steps and leaned over her father, hands on his shoulders, whispering something in his ear.

"Family reunion?" Lisse guessed.

He shook his head, trying to think, trying to decide. "Sharon must have let them in. The girl, she lives up the street, who's supposed to be watching the house for me. Her and her brother, Phil. God almighty, how long have they been here?"

"Well . . . why don't you ask them?"

He watched Garza open his eyes, grin up at his daughter, cover her hands with his before shaking his head and pushing himself to his feet. Stretch his arms overhead. Peer up and down the street.

"No," John decided suddenly, twisted around until he could see through the rear window, and backed up hastily. He swung into the Burgoyne driveway and sat for a moment. "Plan B," he said then, and drove back across the tracks, took his first right and sped down the street until he reached Madison again. Another right, and west a second time.

"Where are we going?"

"A friend."

They thumped over the tracks again, fields on both sides now.

"I don't understand," Lisse said nervously.

"Tony Garza hates my guts," John said tightly, the rasp more pronounced. "I never did know why, but he cannot stand me. Even before Patty left, he made it clear I was tolerated only because I was his daughter's husband. And because of Joey. He never comes out here to visit unannounced. Never. Last time was a couple of years ago, for Joey's seventh birthday. Patty wanted a big party, we were not having a good time of it, and I hoped it would make things better."

It hadn't.

"But if he's here," she said, "doesn't that mean Patty is, too?"

"Could be," he admitted. "But I'm not going there until I find out."

"But it's your house," she protested. "You have a right."

"He thinks he has a bigger right," John said bitterly. "After all, he paid for the damn divorce."

2

They sped through empty fields spotted with crows and what remained of a corn harvest. When the road swept north in a sharp bend, he followed it too fast, and they nearly ended up in a ditch on the other side. That slowed him down; that, and the whimper Lisse made.

"I'm sorry," he said, wiping his face with one hand.

"Don't be. Just don't kill me before we get where we're going."

He pointed. "There."

She saw a small dark-brick house set back in a clump of trees, facing the road and what looked to be a dry marsh on the other side. John pulled into the driveway, turned off the engine, and leaned his head back, closed his eyes.

She opened the door right away and stepped out, shivering in the cool air. This was without a doubt the most stupid, flat-out out of her mind thing she had ever done in her life, and there wasn't a damn reason in the world she could give for it, either. A few slow breaths while the car creaked and cooled behind her, a push of her fingers through her tangled hair. Lord, I would kill for a shower, she thought, looked down, and abruptly realized that the only clothes she had were the clothes that she wore.

"I don't know you, do I?" a man's voice said.

She shaded her eyes, frowning until she saw him—on the porch, in a high-back bentwood chair, wearing a rumpled white suit and gold vest. His hair was sinfully thick and wavy, sinfully white and long, a perfect match for his beard.

"You're not one of my ex-girlfriends, are you?"

She smiled and shook her head, walking across the dry lawn as she gestured at the car. "That there's John Bannock. He says you're a friend of his?"

The man sat up. "John? He's back? Who the hell are you?"

"Lisse Gayle Montgomery," she said stiffly. "You're George Trout, ain't you?"

"Damned either way," he said, bowing without standing. "He dead in there or what?"

She stopped at the foot of the steps. "Tired. Exhausted, more likely. We've been kind of on the run."

Trout sagged back, and she saw the lines around his eyes, his mouth, saw the way he wouldn't meet her gaze. It wasn't her, she knew she didn't look that damn bad, but before she had a chance to say anything, she heard a car door slam, and John rose over the roof.

"Damnit, John," Trout yelled.

"Damnit yourself, George," he said amiably. "How about getting off your butt and helping me with my things."

"No."

Lisse blinked.

"No?" John pretended to clean out an ear with his finger. "What do you mean, no?"

"I mean I am not setting foot off this porch, that's what I mean. I mean I am never leaving this house again, that's what I mean. I mean if you want help carrying whatever the hell you think you can't carry on your own, wish for it, son, because I'm not moving."

John looked almost comical, gaping the way he did, and Lisse felt sorry for him, returned to the car and muttered, "I'll get the carton, you get the suitcase, okay?" When he stared stupidly at her, she added, "Close your mouth, you'll catch flies."

She opened the passenger door and yanked the seatback forward, had the carton in her arms when he opened the trunk and said, "I don't get it, Lisse. He's acting weird, I don't get it."

"You . . ." She felt something in her chest, something breaking apart. *"You* don't get it? *He's* acting weird?" And she began to laugh. Silently, and hard, until the carton fell from her grip and she sat sideways on the front seat, shaking her head because she didn't want to laugh, it really wasn't all that funny, but she couldn't resist it. Dear Lord, she couldn't resist and she just wanted it to stop.

She closed her eyes tightly, opened them, and he was on his knees in front of her, holding her hands, whispering something, she couldn't tell what, but the earnest, fearful look on his face quickly stopped the laughter.

"Don't you feel it?" she asked, pleading.

"Feel what, Lisse?"

"Like it's Alice time, you know? Like we've run off the road and dropped right into a rabbit hole, you know what I mean?"

The look on his face then was as good as a slap.

"Don't you dare," she said, snapping her hands away. "Don't you dare, John Bannock."

"Lisse, it's been a long trip and—"

She felt her skin tighten, felt the sandpaper in her eyes. "You think I can't know about *Alice in Wonderland*? You thinking again I ain't nothing but a dirt-poor waitress got caught in your damn nightmares, that I don't know about things? Book things? Learning things? Don't look so surprised, it's all over your face. You think—"

"John," Trout called. "Is everything all right?"

"Don't," she snapped when he turned his head. "I ain't done yet." She lifted a finger, held it in front of his face, forcing him to stare at it, to pay attention. "Two nights I slept with you, John Bannock, and you ain't touched me once. I cleaned you up when you was drunk and scared out of your mind. I lost a job on account of you. I—not a word, John, not a word—I come all the way up here because you needed me and . . . and because maybe I guess I needed you, too, though the Lord knows I surely don't know why. So do not . . . do not *ever again* think that I am stupid. Do not ever again treat me like I am not a person, like I do not exist, you hear me?"

She glared, and the finger began to tremble, and when he curled his right hand around it gently, she swallowed, and nodded once, and said, "Good."

And smiled.

"Goddamnit, John," Trout yelled, "I want an explanation!"

"When he hears it," John said quietly, "I don't think he's going to want it."

"I think he will," she told him. "You haven't seen him yet. He's scared. Maybe . . . maybe more than you."

But not, she thought later, more than her.

Blue eyes in a crow.

Floating dreams.

They sat in the overstuffed living room, low flames in the fireplace reflected in the dark television screen to the right of the hearth. She had taken a shower and, at Trout's insistence, checked through the closets of his spare room, not surprised, really, at finding women's clothes there and in one drawer of the dresser. She picked a dark shirt a size too large, and jeans that fit just about right. No makeup, though, but she figured, hell, she looked a sight better than she had.

She couldn't help noticing the room had only one bed, though, queen size and buried under a trio of thick quilts.

While John was in the shower, she sat in the large kitchen watching as Trout put together a hasty sandwich meal, answering his questions about New Orleans, nodding, muttering, stopping only when she told him about the kid, Levee Pete, and how he had died. Reverend Trask he dismissed with a disdainful wave and a curse.

TV trays in the living room, condiments and bottles of beer on the glass-top coffee table.

After starting the fire, complaining about the night's chill, he dropped into an armchair, its back to the large front window blocked with heavy, floral drapes. She took the two-cushion sofa, and when John came downstairs, pushing at his damp hair, she found herself holding her breath until he shook off the offer of the room's only other chair and sat beside her.

Dumb, Lisse, she thought, trying not to grin; you're dumb.

They talked while they ate, talked after the meal was done. Explaining, speculating, arguing, cross-talking, wearing themselves out until Trout finally held up one hand.

"So what we have here is . . . what? Signs and portents, that kind of thing?"

"I don't know," John said wearily.

"He says that all the time, but he knows better," she contradicted.

Trout looked at her steadily, eyelids nearly closed. "And what does he know?"

She waited.

John said nothing.

She curled into the sofa's corner, bare feet tucked under, leaning her elbow on the armrest. Watching the flames and the sparks. "I've been thinking . . . those people he talked to, there has to be more of them. All over. I've been thinking maybe something made them that way. I . . . John's friend, that priest? he said John is marked, and believe me, I believe it now. Maybe to find out why those people are the way they are, maybe to stop more people from getting that way." She shrugged and looked to John, who only stared at his shoes. "I guess, anyway."

Trout reached into his jacket pocket and pulled out a pack of cigarettes. He lit one from a silver lighter and blew smoke toward the ceiling.

"If it's true," John said softly, "why me?"

"If it's true," Trout told him, "the why you isn't as important as the what next."

"George, I have to tell you . . . I'm getting a little angry here."

Trout smiled crookedly, cocked his head, and sighed. "Damn, you hear that?"

Lisse listened, and nodded.

Hoofbeats on the road.

Trout heaved himself from his chair and went to the window, pulled aside the drapes from the center, and cursed. "Black as pitch, are they nuts?"

When John didn't move, she uncurled herself and stood beside Trout.

White darts from flashlights and electric lanterns danced over the road, over the lawn, and she could see the shapes of a half dozen horses and riders as they moved left to right and out of sight past the trees.

She could still hear the horses.

"That ranch place?" she asked, turning around.

John nodded. "Les, Les Burgoyne, he and Fran, his wife, like to take people out just after nightfall. They claim it's almost as good as a haunted house ride."

She believed it. Up off the ground, nothing but horses' hooves for sound, seeing only what the flashlights allowed, seeing stuff where the flashlights used to be . . . she believed it.

Trout returned to his chair, picked up a bottle of beer and turned it slowly in one hand. "There're a couple of things you'd better know, John."

"If you mean the house, I already saw them."

"Ah."

Lisse stayed behind him, glancing out at the night, glancing at John looking old and weary.

"If you don't mind," John said, "I'd rather not deal with them until morning."

A hand waved expansively. "You're welcome to bunk, you know that."

"Thanks. I appreciate it." He coughed quickly. "We appreciate it."

She couldn't see the older man's face, but she sensed a smile, probably thinking he knew something.

"There's something else, though," George said, finally drinking from the bottle, wiping his chin although he hadn't spilled a drop. "Rod Gillespie escaped from Denver the other day."

John looked to the ceiling. "Jesus, you're kidding."

"No sir, I am not kidding. Apparently, despite law enforcement's best efforts, he's still loose and probably heading this way. There are a couple of bodies between Colorado and here they think are his doing."

Lisse let the drapes close. "Who's Rod Gillespie?"

Neither man answered for a moment; then John said, "Seven or eight years ago—"

"Eight, I think," Trask said.

"—he was working for Les Burgoyne, not a lot of money but he couldn't hold a job anyplace else. On a Saturday night, I think it was, he got home late, drank too much, and beat the hell out of his wife, Annette, locked his

213

son in a closet, and beat the hell out of his daughters, Sharon and Kim. Kim . . ." He shook his head. "Kim was only six at the time. He raped her, strangled her, then took his car and drove to the other side of town, to one of those shopping centers we saw. He robbed a liquor store, gunned the clerk down, drove home with a case of whiskey and sat on the front porch, drinking straight from the bottles. When the cops finally got there, he had gotten his rifle out."

"The son of a bitch," said Trout, "with more whiskey in him than blood, shot up two policemen, got in his car, and . . . the luck of the damned and the drunk, got away."

"You're kidding." Lisse returned to the couch and curled up again.

"Seven months later, he turns up in Colorado Springs, gunning down a couple of college kids in a bar. This time he didn't get away. Lots of legal wrangling, people screaming for his head in two states, and Colorado got him. Consecutive life sentences. After which," he added wryly, "he was supposed to come back here so we could fry his little ass."

"And he's out?"

"Yes, my dear, he is out."

There was nothing she could say. Maybe there were a few questions, but by the expressions on their faces, she knew they didn't want to talk about it. It was bad enough the man was free.

A faint rumble outside, and John looked up, surprised. "Rain?"

Trout rolled his eyes. "If you can call it that. Last couple of nights, we've had some thunder, some lightning, just enough rain to settle the dust. It's all gone by morning."

Lisse started to say, "That's better than nothing," but a huge yawn cut her off, and she smiled sheepishly at the others. "Not the company," she apologized.

John yawned as well, they laughed awkwardly, and after some fumbling and mumbling, Trout hustled them off to bed, claiming none of them were in any shape to think straight, much less make any sense.

Half an hour later she was under the sheet and quilts, watching as the ceiling was washed with lightning white. There was as much distance as possible between her and John, yet she couldn't help feeling he was only a finger touch away.

Finally she rolled onto her right side, tucked her hands under her chin, and listened to the storm that didn't bring any rain.

IN THE MOOD

* * *

"You awake?" he asked quietly.

"Yes."

"You hear that?"

"The thunder?"

"No. Listen harder."

She did, and frowned until she understood what he meant. Without thinking she swept the covers aside and hurried over to the small window that looked over the porch roof to the road. A distant lightning flare showed her nothing.

"You know," he said, "you are not entirely invisible."

She whirled, glared, and hurried back to bed.

A finger touch away.

"It was a horse, wasn't it," he said as she lay there, shivering a little, not all because of the chill.

That's what she heard, or thought she heard, but she couldn't bring herself to tell him. Nobody, not even his rancher friend, would ride a horse this late at night in weather like that. Hell, even in westerns they tucked the damn things in for the night.

She rolled onto her back, left arm at her side.

Very softly: "Lisse?"

Very softly: "Yeah. I think so."

She felt movement then, a sliding across the sheet. Her hand shifted, and bumped into his, and before she could move it away, his fingers covered hers.

Holding her breath.

Closing her eyes.

"I just want you to know," he whispered, "I'm falling asleep. I don't want to, but I am."

Breathing again, and smiling at the ceiling.

He squeezed her hand once, and she squeezed it back. Once.

He sighed so softly she wasn't sure she heard it.

He sighed again and said, "Trask is wrong."

Or maybe he didn't.

She wasn't sure.

She was floating.

2

1

The smells woke him up.

Subtle things, signals that he wasn't in a hotel room anymore, that he wasn't in Louisiana or Texas or New Jersey or Maryland. Even inside there was autumn in the air. In the few seconds before he sat up, he smiled lazily and stretched. Grateful he didn't have to travel anymore. Grateful he didn't have to talk to people who looked back at him with not a whole lot inside.

He stumbled through the rituals of waking, stared at his reflection in the bathroom mirror and said, with a grin, "Prez, you look about as stupid as you feel."

He moved down the carpeted stairs, smelling coffee and toast, hearing voices in the kitchen. He stopped in the hall when he heard his name:

"John works with numbers, my dear. Perhaps he thought there was something to it last night, but he won't this morning."

"He saw what he saw, Mr. Trout."

"George. Please."

"Thank you. But he still saw what he saw. And did what he did."

"There are, as they say, rational explanations for everything. Even what I saw."

"All those people you write about, they always do things sane?"

He stepped through the doorway and said, "I'm hungry and I want to go home. What's for breakfast?"

"Brunch, you mean," George said sourly. "It's practically noon."

John shrugged. He felt better than he had in a long time, had obviously needed the extra hours of sleep, and despite the looks he got, didn't feel the slightest bit guilty. He made a sandwich, poured some juice, and ate while George flipped through the morning paper, pointing out stories that proved beyond a doubt that the world was going to hell in a handmade basket.

"Slasher in New York, that strangler Sandman in Phoenix, some idiot calls himself a reincarnated Jack the Ripper over in Idaho. Can't be a serial killer or mass murderer these days unless you give yourself a name." He folded the paper and tossed it contemptuously into the sink. "Sick of it. I'm sick of it."

John was astonished. Usually Trout reveled in such stories, spinning elaborate schemes to get these killers' stories for another book. He wondered if his own work had anything to do with this about-face, or if something had happened he didn't know about yet while he'd been gone.

"TV," Lisse said, hands around a cup of coffee. "You don't give them a name, they're just like a bunch of others."

"It's still sick," George told her. "More, because I think you might be right."

No one mentioned the dreams, the crows, the blue eyes, Levee Pete.

"It's not like we're all that sane around here, either," the old man continued, leaning back, dangling his arms at his sides. "We got that Gillespie scum they think's on his way. We got more than a dozen people going off the deep end, dancing naked in their yards, getting hauled off to the Psych Ward at Cornman—"

"What?"

George laughed, and explained about the epidemic of what he called the world enders, all ages, who've been driving the police up the walls. "Arn— that's Chief Baer, my dear—told me something else, too. They go into the house, see if there's drugs or whatnot, which there aren't, and every one of them's got that Bible thumper on TV when it happened." He scowled, one eye closed. "Can't think of his name."

"Lanyon Trask," John said quietly.

George blinked. "Right. That's—Jesus, John, that's the same guy that chased you up here, right?"

"Me or the Antichrist," he answered with a false smile.

"So," said Lisse to him quickly, "what's the plan? You going home?"

He stared at what remained of his sandwich, swiped at his forelock, reached for the orange juice. "If they're there," he said, "it can only mean one thing."

"Your boy is back?"

He nodded. "No one else knows them around here. Someone had to let them in. That could only be Patty."

"Gathering the family around her," George guessed. "Strength in numbers. But hell, John, no offense, but she's already taken you for everything you got. Including the boy. What the hell else can she want?"

"Reconciliation," he answered, looked up suddenly as he realized there was no hope for him in that word. Only a week ago he would have killed for it; now, back here, all he wanted was to see his son again. His voice was tight: "She's out of money or something. She's got no place to go."

"She's got her family," Lisse said without looking at him. "She don't need you, John." She sipped at her coffee, grimaced, and set the cup down. "And what did you mean, took him?" she asked George. "He still has—"

Ace?

Startled, John looked behind him.

Trout pushed away from the table but didn't rise. He looked around thoughtfully as one thumb hooked itself around one suspender strap. "I don't know if it's my place," he said.

Ace, don't let him.

He stood so quickly he almost knocked the chair over. "I have an idea."

George looked at him oddly. "Are you all right?"

A shadow in the hall; John nodded that he was fine.

"Couple of years, maybe she does want to come home, you know?" Her face tightened. "Not that she deserves it. From what I've heard, that is."

"A couple of years?" George's head turned slowly. "My God, John, what did you tell her?"

Ace, please!

John started for the stairs, intending to fetch his windbreaker from the suitcase in the bedroom. "I've got to get home," he called over his shoulder. "Lisse, you want to come?"

He stopped when he heard Trout clear his throat. He knew that sound, what it meant, and he grabbed for the newel post and hung on.

Ace, don't you dare. Don't you dare let him!

"Patty," he whispered desperately to the shadows at the head of the stairs. "Patty."

"After all you two have been through," George said, sounding disappointed, sounding sad.

"You gonna hint around all day or are you gonna tell me?"

Ace, if you let him do this . . .

John didn't move.

"Their marriage was over a long time ago," George said. "There was a party for Joey, big one, everybody came. Half the town, mostly her relatives. John doesn't have anybody left, so we, his friends here, were pretty much it. It was supposed to be an attempt to keep things together. Obviously it didn't work. Next day—"

Ace!

"—she gets a hotshot lawyer from Chicago, paid for by her father, and raked John over the coals. He—"

Oh . . . Ace.

"—lost everything. The house, his money . . . you name it, she took it. At the end, when everything was signed, she let him rent the house so he could keep working. Can't get alimony or child support if the husband doesn't work, and he had a pretty good business going here. I told him, rent an office downtown, don't be beholden to her, but he wouldn't listen. Then . . . then she left town with Joey, and they haven't been back since."

"I don't get it," Lisse said. "I mean—"

"That was almost four years ago, my dear. Two years ago, she pulled that particular rug from under him, too. Evicted him just about the time he started writing those articles, then gathering material for that book. He couldn't go home, Lisse. He doesn't have one."

Ace. You bastard.

Still griping the polished wood, John swung around until he sat on the steps, legs stretched into the hall. He heard Lisse's questions, heard George's soft answers, but he didn't listen to the words. He wanted to think of a way to reconcile George's story with the one he'd been telling himself for nearly half a decade, and when he failed, miserably, he shuddered in a deep breath and looked at the ceiling.

See you around, Ace, you stupid son of a bitch.

Lisse called him; he didn't move except to turn his head and look down the hall, into the kitchen. She was no doubt angry, but it didn't show on her face. No pity, either, and that made him smile. Not much, but he smiled.

"John, get in here," George said with a brusque wave.

Slowly, his muscles and joints aged a hundred years, he pulled himself to his feet, rubbed the back of his head, and returned to the kitchen, where he leaned against the door jamb, one hand in his pocket.

"You didn't tell her everything," he said. And waited for Patty's ghost to say something, to interrupt.

"John, you all right?" Lisse started to rise, but he gestured her back down.

Waiting for the ghost until he realized it was gone.

"So . . . what else is there?" she said, trying to be serious and light at the same time. "What are you hiding from me, Yank?"

When the wall phone rang not far from John's head, they all jumped so hard the dishes and cups rattled on the table, and John nearly slid off his feet.

"Jesus," he said, one hand dramatically patting his chest over his heart.

Lisse laughed nervously; George scowled and mimed that he was the closest so answer the damn thing.

John shrugged and picked up the receiver.

"Hello?"

"Hi, Daddy," said Joey with a giggle. "Welcome home."

The phone went dead.

2

The roan snorted its impatience; there was still green grass out there in the vast back pasture and she wanted some. Les, however, wouldn't give her her head. The leg seemed all right, but he didn't want to take any chances.

"Walk," he told her. "It'll do you good."

The horse tossed its mane, snorted, but didn't test him.

Fran rode beside him on a gray with as many years as the roan, enjoying the warm sun and the cool touch of the air. "It'll be just fine," she said as they made their way north across the pasture. "A little tight, but we aren't broke yet."

Les supposed she was right, but he sure wished they had more horses to board, or riders to teach or take along the trails he had made around Vallor. Reassuring words and bright smiles worked on him just fine, but the bank account was deaf and blind.

He checked back toward the outbuildings, frowning concern.

"They'll be okay," his wife assured him. "Rafe's a good man."

He knew that. He just didn't like the idea of Sharon and her boyfriend on his property while that killer of a father was still loose. Suppose he came here? Suppose he—

"Les, stop it," she scolded gently, with a smile. "Let's just do the check and get back, okay?"

Midway across the pasture the ground dipped into a long, steep grade. Coming up to it, the land beyond was cut short, and more often than not, like now, you couldn't see the other horses grazing out there. As a kid he'd always thought it a little spooky—seeing nothing for the longest time, then suddenly seeing a head pop up over the edge as a horse or, in his father's day, a cow made its way up the slope.

Spooky.

When they reached the end of level land, the first thing he did was make a swift headcount. Ten, and Royal. No one missing. Most of them were in the center of the lower pasture, using the trees that lined Oakbend Creek for shade while they drank or ate. The others were scattered, but nothing out of the ordinary.

Then Royal raised his head, shook his mane, and turned to face the slope.

The roan backed up a step and pawed at the ground.

"Hey," Les said quietly, patting the horse's neck. "Hey, it's all right."

"What is with that damn thing?" Fran said, staring angrily at the palomino.

"Beats me." He jerked his head. "Let's go on in."

She didn't argue, and the roan seemed more than eager to obey. When they reached the fence, Les took bridle and saddle and set the horse loose in the paddock, along with Fran's mount. As they lugged the equipment back to the tack room, he heard Royal out in the pasture.

Calling.

3

John dropped onto the porch's top step as he struggled into his windbreaker. Lisse had taken one of the pullovers she had found in a dresser, too large but comfortable enough. She paced up and down the walk, the breeze taking her hair and veiling across her eyes. George sat in his chair, legs crossed, pushing back every so often as if it were a rocker.

"How did he know?" she asked, not really expecting an answer. A gesture toward the car. "I mean, how could he know?"

His right hand trembled, and he grabbed his knee with it.

The voice. That voice.

welcome home, daddy.

"I got another one for you," he said.

She stopped on her way to gate, turned, and waited, arms folded under her breasts.

"She called me once. In New Orleans." He looked over his shoulder and George raised his eyebrows. "I was in the lobby, the phone rang, there was no one around, so I picked it up, and it was her. I didn't say a word, and she knew it was me. She said give it up, it was too late. Then she hung up."

George stared at him; Lisse's cheeks colored.

"No," he told them irritably, "I wasn't drunk. I hadn't had my first drink yet."

Lisse swiped at her hair. "Then how did she know?"

"Too late for what?" George wanted to know.

"How did Joey know?" John countered. He scrubbed his face, blinked rapidly several times, and wished he could find Casey. He would know what was going on. He would have the explanation, would know what to do. How he knew that he wasn't sure, but he did.

A lie, Prez, he told himself then; that's a lie and you know it.

"ESP, something like that," said Lisse. When George snorted, she scowled. "You think that's funny?"

"I think," George answered, "that it's a beautiful afternoon, the sky is clear, the sun is bright, and talking about ESP is best reserved for campfires and dark nights."

"ESP," she retorted, "doesn't just work in the dark."

John stood, took a deep breath, and stretched his arms out to his sides.

George was at least partially right—it was indeed a beautiful day, Halloween was on its way, Thanksgiving just around the corner. And nothing, ever, would ever be the same again.

"Where are you going?" George asked suspiciously.

"For a ride." He dug the keys from the jacket pocket, asked Lisse if she wanted to come, and started for the car. "You're welcome to join us," he called to his friend.

"I told you, I'm not leaving this house again. This porch is as far as I go."

Lisse opened the passenger door and turned. "I thought you didn't believe in ESP?"

"It's more than that, my dear," he answered grimly. "A lot more than that."

John ignored the look she gave him, and when she was ready, he backed out of the drive and aimed the car for the bend. Moving not much faster than a walk.

"Where are we going?"

"You can't wear his girlfriends' clothes all the time. I thought we'd head into town, do the Dove's thing." An apologetic laugh. "Dove's, see, is the largest department store in town. When you go shopping, even if you're not going there, you do the Dove's."

"No money," she said, pushing the sweater's sleeves up to her elbows. "You, either."

"No, but I still have George's credit card."

A smile, a nod, and, "I suppose we'll just happen to pass your house on the way?"

He didn't answer right away.

"John."

"I want to know," he said quietly, "why that kid on the ferry had Joey's eyes. I want to know why I can make people so afraid of me they jump off buildings." He looked at her, hard. "We're going to find out what's going on, Lisse." He looked back at the road. "We're going to find out now."

As they approached the bend, he began to tap the steering wheel with one finger. "The first house you'll see will be down on the left. That's the

Gillespie place." He nodded to her unasked question. "Rod is Annette's husband. Used to be, that is, until she divorced him after . . . it happened."

"I would've killed him."

"Believe me, she wanted to. Still does, probably."

The road curved, and he held his breath for a moment when he saw a cruiser parked in front of the house, facing west, a deputy inside. The man looked up at the sound of John's car and opened his door.

"Oh my," Lisse said quietly.

"Someone's home," he guessed as they drove past. He didn't look at the cop, hadn't recognized him, but he didn't miss the way the man kept his hand on his holstered gun. "Annette's probably still at work. Used to run an insurance office. Phil is the son, about twenty-three, twenty-four, I don't know what he does. I'll bet it's Sharon. She'll be a senior now, I think, and stayed home from school."

Once the house was behind him, he exhaled loudly, but he didn't speed up, glancing in the rearview mirror to watch the cop watching him. A flicker of bright light made him blink back to the road ahead, the over-lacing branches cutting the sunlight into patches and bars, chilly one second, warm the next.

He pointed out the Yerman house, on the right, and a hundred yards later, a large clapboard house clearly deserted for quite some time, its hedge overgrown, the windows black where they didn't catch the light. He couldn't remember who used to live there; the place had been empty for at least a year before he left.

"Where's your—" She stopped, wincing.

"It's okay. Don't worry about it. Coming up on the right."

She reached over and touched his arm, squeezed it once, quickly. "Nobody's next to each other out here."

"Yeah. You probably didn't notice, but past the creek and that ranch you saw yesterday, they're a little closer together. Out here, they sometimes call it Football Road, because there's a football field's length, give or take, between each place."

Another house on the right, one more on the left, and he couldn't help it—he stopped.

"We don't live right," Lisse said, angrily, partly sadly.

The car they had seen the day before was still in the driveway, a second one in front of it facing the detached garage, both fairly new.

On the grassy shoulder, almost on the lawn, was the gray limousine.

4

Sharon helped Fran and Les with their gear, unable to hide a grin when Kyle nearly fell on his face trying to carry one of the saddles. He was doing his best, but it was clear that even with the stables empty, he was nervous. Like a horse was going to jump out of the shadows and bite off his butt.

Once everything was clean and in its place, she walked outside, hands in her hips pockets. A deep inhalation. "Boy," she said with mock enthusiasm as Kyle joined her, "don't you just love that smell?"

He gave her a disgusted look. "It's horsesh—manure, Shar, for crying out loud." He sniffed his sleeves and grimaced. "God, it'll take years to get this stink off me."

She walked toward the fence, angling toward the paddock on the left. "You get used to it."

"Never in a million years."

She did not look toward the house. She did not want to see Deputy Schmidt there, his patrol car at the top of the drive next to Les's battered Jeep. She did not want to be reminded. They had worked all morning, and he had been there the whole time. At least he hadn't tried to talk to them. Just chewed his gum and stayed by the door. When the Burgoynes returned, he headed for the house, told her not to stray, he was only going to check in.

Like she needed the reminder.

She leaned heavily against the chest-high fence and let her arms dangle over the top rail. "Now, they're not so bad, right?" she said, nodding to the two grazing horses when Kyle joined her.

The roan's ears twitched at the sound of her voice, but it didn't look up. The gray stayed near the gate, staring out at the pasture.

They could hear the palomino, sharp and distant.

"I was going to go shopping today," she said, folding her arms on the rail to provide a rest for her chin.

"Skip school? You?"

"For Saturday," she told him.

He looked down at his feet. "These boots are ruined. God, you'd think they were made of paper. What do you mean, for Saturday." He raised his eyebrows. "For me?" He laughed. "You wanted to impress me?"

She turned her head slowly and stared at him with narrowed eyes. "Dovinsky," she said, "you are a jerk. A total jerk."

He grinned back at her. "Me, too."

"You too, what?"

A one-shoulder shrug. Suddenly the horses were fascinating.

Her eyes widened. "New stuff?"

Another shrug.

"To impress me?"

"Hey, Shar, that horse is . . . holy shit, it's like a damn hose, for God's sake."

She smacked his arm with a palm. "Don't change the subject."

"Damn," he muttered, and aped her stance at the rail. "You know, we're the same size like this."

He grinned.

She grinned back. "In your dreams, Kyle, in your dreams."

But she was so glad he was around she wanted to hug him. He'd just shown up that morning, no invitation, said he heard the news and figured she wouldn't be in school and figured maybe she could use some company if her brother wasn't around. Which Phil wasn't. In fact, he and her mother were on their way to Chicago to see a lawyer Chief Baer had told them about. She had refused to go, and only the chief's solemn promise that she wouldn't be alone for a second had convinced her mother it was all right to leave her behind.

In a way she had been awfully disappointed that Phil hadn't argued harder; in a way she was glad, because her mother was in the middle of a hysterical temper that would have made the trip hell; and when Kyle had asked if she was scared, she was amazed to realize that the terror she had felt when her mother told her what had happened had been replaced by something more. Something darker. Something that scared her more than her father ever could.

Kyle straightened and walked slowly along the fence. "What's the matter with that horse? Is it crazy or something?"

She followed, listening to Royal.

What made the sound worse was that they couldn't see him.

"I don't know," she said. "I guess he's—"

She stopped when she felt the breeze at her back. Pushing her gently. Getting stronger.

Kyle turned into it, squinting, then taking her hand. "Hey, Shar, I think maybe we ought to get inside."

5

Ari Lowe stepped onto the porch, grinning, thinking this was the best thing he'd done in years, crazy but nice. He had new clothes courtesy of Tony, clothes that didn't sag or bag—"Jeans? You want me to wear jeans? You outta your mind?"—a bed he could die in it was so comfortable, and more people around him that he'd had in . . . well, years.

He moved to the head of the steps and leaned a shoulder against the post. Lunch had been huge. That girl, Dory, had made stuff he'd never heard of, made him eat every bite and then some, flirting with him the whole time and taking decades off his life. All the time, Tony laughed and told stories and made it seem like this was his real home, not the apartment back in the city.

What amazed him, though, was the difference in the daughters. Dory was kind of dark, he didn't know what they called them these days—Latin? Hispanic?—but she was gorgeous. Slight, busty, and gorgeous. Made him start thinking about things he hadn't thought of since forever, even with Tony trying to drag him to Miriam or Mabel or whatever the hell she was called.

Patty, on the other hand, was pale. Like porcelain. Dark hair, like Dory, but slender. Kind of like a boy, only no boy he ever saw looked like that. She was quieter, too, a little maybe angry at something. When she joked, which was all the time, there was an edge there he couldn't quite put a finger on. Funny, though. He laughed so often, so hard, he just knew that before he had to go back, he was going to explode.

And the boy. Such a boy. Such a beautiful little boy, so damn cute in his cowboy suit, that Ari knew he'd have trouble growing up. Lots of girls, that's for sure, but the other boys were going to make his life hell until they figured out he could get them girls, too.

The only one he wasn't sure about was that minister. Not nearly as old as he pretended to be, joking with the rest of them but only out of politeness. Just showed up this morning out of the blue, looking for that crumb bum, Patty's ex-husband, and wouldn't you know it but Tony just grabbed him inside like he was one of his long-lost sons.

Tony was amazing.

The door opened behind him. "Ari, are you all right?"

"Just fine, Dory," he said. "Getting some air. We don't have air in New York." He grinned, glad there was at least one person here who was his size. "You know, I could get to like it. The air."

She smiled, bumped him with her shoulder. "You seen Joey?"

He shook his head. "Not since lunch. He went to play in the back, I think." He lowered his voice. "I don't think he likes that Trask." He lay a finger along the side of his nose. "But I think Trask likes him too much, if you know what I mean."

"Oh, come on."

"No. Really. You listen to me, Dory. I think there's something. I think there's something."

They gazed in silence at the limousine. He knew there were two men inside. Bodyguards. Tony and Patty had brought them heaping plates of food, but they never left the car, and Trask hadn't said a word.

"Maybe," he said, "he's not a real preacher."

"Oh, he is," she answered. "I've seen him on TV."

"Ah." That explained it. "He's not real, then."

A car drove by slowly, heading toward town. He couldn't see the driver, but a woman with touches of fire in her hair stared back at him until the car passed, only glimpses of it through the trees and shrubs.

"You have a secret lover, Ari?" Dory said, bumping him again.

"Only in my dreams," he answered.

Without warning she leaned over and kissed his cheek. "You're sweet, you know that?" Her arm slipped around his waist and gave him a quick hug.

Then the door slammed open, and Tony boomed, "Unhand my daughter, you wretch, before I challenge you to a duel!"

Dory rolled her eyes.

Ari grinned. For a woman like this, a duel would be worth it.

A breeze kicked up then, and he shaded his eyes against it. Sniffed, and took a step down to get a better look at the sky. Rain? He didn't think so; there weren't any clouds.

"What's the matter?" Dory asked.

"I don't know." His frown deepened, and he shrugged. "Guess I'm not used to all this air."

Then he saw the frown on Tony's face, and suddenly he wasn't so sure.

6

The yard is deep, the grass freshly mowed and still smelling of its cutting. Four trees at the back, thick and crowned high, the shade beneath cool and shifting as the last leaves tremble and prepare to fall. There are two gardens, one on each side, both in disrepair, only a few late blossoms, the rest nothing but weeds, the dirt hard where it isn't shifting dust. A simple granite birdbath half full in the center of the lawn. Just behind it is a swing set— three swings with canvas seats, the chains speckled with rust, the paint on the crossbar and legs peeling to expose rusted metal.

Joey sits on the center swing, legs tucked up and under, moving slowly back and forth. His hat is on, his eyes in shade. He stares at the unremarkable back of the house until his mother's face appears in the kitchen window. She waves, he waves back, and a few minutes later she comes out to join him.

"They're all here," he says.

She stands behind him, pushing him gently. "Not everyone, hon."

He squeals with delight as she shoves him hard, once, and sends him high. His legs kick out as he sails up the arc, tuck back under as he descends, and laughs when Patty hustles out of the way, sets herself in front and catches the chains as he comes down again. Her face is slightly flushed.

Joey grins and giggles. "Yes, everyone."

Once he's still, she backs away and mops her brow with a forearm. "Daddy?"

He nods.

"When?"

He shrugs. "I don't know. Yesterday sometime, I guess." He twists in the seat so the swing turns, chains creaking. "He's not alone."

"He's . . ." She frowns. "I don't understand."

Joey laughs, rocking his head side to side. "Daddy has a girlfriend, Mommy. Daddy has a girlfriend."

She looks away. "When did you see them?"

"Just now. They drove by the house. It's not his car, Mommy. How did he get the car?"

Patty looks at the house, turning her back to him as she does. "Joey, you can't see the road from here."

"You can't. I can."

A mild scolding: "Joey."

"I talked to him, too."

She turns quickly. "You did? When?"

He shrugs. "This morning. Lunchtime. Sometime." He tries to kick the ground with one boot, can't quite reach it and the movement swings him, twists him, chains creaking. "Mom?"

"Yes, honey?"

"Come here, please?"

She hesitates. His head is down, so she can't see his expression, and his voice gives nothing away.

"Mommy, please?"

"Sure, baby." She kneels in front of him so she can see his eyes. "What do you want?"

"I want to go riding."

She smiles. "At the stable? You?"

He pouts. "I can ride. I remember how. You showed me that time, remember?"

"That was a long time ago, sweetheart. You thought . . . I remember you thought the horses were giants."

"I was little then. I'm big now."

Not very, she thinks; in fact, you haven't grown an inch in years.

"I don't know," she says aloud.

"Grampa will go with us."

He would, too. He'd do anything for Joey, and Patty knew that if she refused, Joey would somehow get him to take him, anyway. It had never failed. Never.

"Well, we'll see. When? Tomorrow okay?"

He shakes his head. "Can't tomorrow."

"Oh? Why not?"

"We won't be here."

Slowly she straightens, right hand rubbing her hip unconsciously. "What are you talking about? We just got here."

A shrug. "Have to go today." He looks up and smiles brightly. "Here today, gone tomorrow."

"That's not funny, Joey. I don't get it. And I don't think riding is a good idea. If your father is here, there might be—"

"Today, Mommy," he says.

"Joey, no."

He says nothing. Kicks at the ground again, misses again, slides partway off the broad canvas strap, swings his legs once more and kicks up dust. Then he stands, one hand still holding the chain, the thumb of the other tilting his hat back.

"Well, ma'am," he says, trying to mimic a western drawl, "I guess we'll just have to see about that."

Her lips move, but no smile. "Joey."

He holds out his hand. "Mom, we have things to do, okay? I want to ride. I want to play with Grampa. I want to talk to that stupid old man." He wiggles his fingers. "I have to, Mom."

"Joey, this is—"

"Mom." He stares at her.

She doesn't move. A breeze kicks up, and she can smell dust and dying flowers and leaves already dead.

"Mom."

"Joey?" She can barely speak. "Joey, I don't understand."

He tilts his head, looking at her almost sideways, his hat slipping off and hanging by its beaded strap down his back. "Well, first thing is," and he points to the swing set's legs, "you'd better hold on."

7

George Trout sat on his porch, cut-glass tumbler in one hand, matching decanter in the other. Whiskey in both, and turning sour in his stomach. He hadn't tried to stop John from leaving, although he figured now that he probably should have. All the man would find was more grief, even if he didn't stop at the old house. He could understand now why people murdered other people. John couldn't do it, but he damn sure could. Take that woman's neck in his bare hands and twist it until her head faced wrong way around. She had a hell of a nerve coming back after all this time. And more than once since he had seen the cars parked in the drive he'd been tempted to march down there and give that scrawny bitch as scathing a piece of his mind as he could muster. And he would have, too, if he hadn't seen the crows. Gliding overhead. Waiting for him to leave. If they had lips, they'd probably be smacking them, thinking about the dinner they had missed the other day and how they were going to make up for it as soon as he left the porch. Little bastards. He grinned, then, and glanced at the loaded shotgun lying beside the chair. He wasn't all that good a shot, but he was good enough that he'd have feathers on the grass if one of those bastards tried spooking him again. Anyone asked, of course, like Mister High-and-Mighty-Ain't-I-Special Chief of Police Arnold Baer, he'd tell them it was for protection in case that other bastard came around. Blow his head off, too, and get a medal for it, by God. That'd teach them to call him Fish Man. That'd teach them to laugh at him behind his back, thinking he was a ghoul just because he wrote about what he wrote about. Teach them all, by Christ, and get him a fancy medal, to boot.

Then the air changed, he could feel it, and he didn't think he could move fast enough.

"Lord," he said, suddenly fearful, "not again."

8

Arn glared at the newspaper dispenser outside the luncheonette. The darn thing had taken his fifty cents and wouldn't open, even though he could see there were at least six copies left inside. The way things were going today, he might as well take out his gun and shoot the thing open. It couldn't get any worse.

First, he and Mag had had a hell of a row after her mother had left for work. He didn't want her anywhere around Sharon Gillespie until Rod was caught. Mag as much as told him to go to hell, Sharon was her best friend and she wasn't about to let her down at this awful time, and if he was so damn worried about her, why hadn't he made her go to Chicago with her mother? He had explained, she had sneered, the heat in the kitchen filled the air as if the oven had been on all night, and suddenly she had grabbed her jacket and books and marched out, slamming the door behind her.

Then, while his temper was still near to boiling, he had to stand in front of the mayor and listen while he was told how to do his job, protecting Vallor from the coming scourge and, at the same time, keeping anymore people from going absolutely nuts. Besides which, they had an important dignitary in town, Reverend Lanyon Trask, and there had better not be any trouble—protesters and the like—that would make the mayor, the police, or anyone else look like hicks and rubes.

By the time that was done, Arn was ready to quit, head out to Les's place, and muck out stables for the rest of his life.

Just before noon, he got a call from Carl Bergman, out at Cornman.

"Give me good news, Doc," he'd said. "I sure could use it."

"What I have for you, Chief, is chaos."

That's when he heard the noise in the background. "Jeez, Carl, what the hell's that? Mrs. Grauer gone off again?"

It had been meant as a joke.

What he was told was that they all had. Every single one of them still at the hospital. Screaming, singing, dancing, and more screaming. It had started the other day, just a stirring that had finally built up one beaut of a head of steam.

"So you sedate them, right?"

"Arn, if I give them any more, they'll be dead. Nothing's working. Nothing. Five have already broken their restraints, Mrs. Grauer among them."

"That old lady? Come on, Doc, she couldn't tear paper in half without someone giving her a head start."

"Twice," was all Bergman said.

Arn glanced at the drawer where the flask lay, waiting. "So why did you feel you had to tell me this, Carl?"

"Because three more have come in during the past hour, that's why."

"Well, why the hell wasn't I told?"

"Their families brought them in, that's why. I know you're keeping track, so . . ." He gave Arn the names, the ages ranging between twenty-eight and seventy-two. "And guess, Chief, what was on their TVs."

Arn thanked him, hung up, sat back, and stared at the ceiling for almost ten minutes before deciding it was time to get himself some lunch.

Which, he thought sourly as he tried to will the newspaper dispenser to give up the paper or give him back his four bits, was a joke because today, of all days, there was no bread, and the meat loaf was, of all things, mostly that soy stuff that didn't taste like anything God meant Man to put in his mouth.

Maybe Carl's right, he thought as he crossed the street; maybe it is the damn Millennium.

Why not?

It can't get any worse.

He was halfway to the door when he stopped, frowned, and looked up.

"Great," he muttered. "Just great."

9

Once over the bridge, John pulled onto the shoulder, knuckles white on the steering wheel, breath caught on barbs in his lungs. "My sister-in-law," he said when Lisse asked. "Former sister-in-law. Dorina Castro. I don't know who the little guy was. Probably a friend of Garza's."

He stared straight ahead. Wishing he had a drink. No water, no ice; straight from the bottle. His arms began to tremble with tension. He could feel himself swallowing, and couldn't stop.

"Well," he said. And swallowed. "I guess that's that." And swallowed. "So much for bearding the lion." And swallowed.

Two cool fingers drifted across his throat. "You'll strangle yourself," she said.

"Old wive's tale."

But he didn't swallow.

Lisse waved a hand in front of her face. "Wooo, mercy, what's that smell?"

He jerked his head to the left. "The ranch, remember?" He inhaled. "It's not bad."

"Not bad? Lord, it's worse than I don't know what."

One last swallow, and his hand over his eyes to clear them. Instead, he only blurred their vision, and the road and trees ahead lost their focus for a moment.

A breeze stirred off the road and into the car.

"Momma," Lisse said, "would switch me good if she knew I was thinking about confronting a preacher. Holy and all that, you know? That smell reminded me. Horses, see?" She laughed silently at his confusion and pointed at the ranch entrance. "Momma used to say, if I wasn't careful, one of them Horsemen guys from the Bible was going to ride straight into my bedroom one night, scoop me up, and wouldn't I be in a peck of trouble then, Lisse Gayle Montgomery."

Slowly, very slowly, he turned his head toward her.

"Even those guys on television, pompadours and slick-back, zillion-dollar suits . . ." A sigh. " 'Til the day she died, I couldn't say a word against them. She didn't go to church a whole lot, but those men were—what on earth are you looking at, John? I say something wrong?"

"There was a man," he said, raising a finger, focusing her attention. "One of those revivalists I told you about. My mother took to him because he was kinder than the others. Not a lot of fire and brimstone. But it was the same message—prepare to meet thy doom, the heavens were going to open, God was going to judge, and we're all damned unless we repent.

"It wasn't the message that kept people going to him, it was his manner. Quiet. Sorrowful, I guess. Some of those men, and a couple of women, as I remember, seemed glad it was going to happen. They were so convinced they wouldn't be damned because of who they were that they were actually glad. Their method was terror. Still is, I suppose. Scare the living hell, literally, out of their congregations.

"But this other man, he didn't want to scare us into heaven, he wanted us to be glad to be going. The others, they aimed for relief, you know? Relief you were the one chosen. This man, he didn't want us relieved, he wanted us happy.

"Mom eventually got tired of him, too, just like all the others. She wanted answers, see. She wanted to know why my father had walked out on us after they'd dumped him from the state police in Nebraska. She wanted to know why he'd been tempted by bribe money in spite of the good home we had. Look the other way, Officer, no one will know. He got caught in a sting, was fired, and five months later disappeared.

"That's when she started dragging me to the tents. The corner churches. The streetfronts. She didn't want to be happy, she wanted answers, and she never got them."

The finger curled into his palm, and he lowered the hand to the seat, stared at his knuckles as if seeing them for the first time.

"I work with numbers."

"Cold," she said. "No soul."

"Yeah." He smiled. "You could say that. A lot of things you can do with them, but they're not on the same level of imagination as, say, working with oils or sculptures."

"You've been trying to turn all this stuff into numbers."

He nodded, tentatively. "Two plus two. I accept they equal four. Screw around with them all you want, you still get four, one way or another." He looked back at the road, blew out a slow breath. "If I were an imaginative man . . . if I were to forget about numbers and look at . . ." His eyelids fluttered, and closed.

The breeze quickened.

"Chilly," Lisse said. "John, I don't see no clouds up there, but it feels like—"

Joey looks at his mother. "Hang on tight, Mommy."

"Honey, what—"

"Here we go," he sings. "Here we go."

With his eyes closed the rumbling sounded like the distant echo of cannon fire, moving toward him, keeping louder.

John's eyes snapped open.

Thunder exploded so loudly, so sharply, Lisse screamed and he gasped, and in the instant before the wind began, the rear window exploded inward, the windshield outward.

She screamed again, and he yelled, shoulders hunched as he threw himself at her, grabbing her arm and yanking her down while glass in fragments and beads and bee-stinger darts filled the car, swarming as the wind swept through, rocking the car, shifting it slightly forward. Grit struck the outside, hailstone loud. Dust made them choke as if it were smoke. A dead branch slammed onto the trunk. A dead leaf clawed at his cheek, drawing a drop of blood before he could dash it away.

Ten seconds, no more, and everything stopped.

* * *

He wanted to say something, but he couldn't. His head was pressed into Lisse's lap, and she lay awkwardly across his back, clutching his belt as if that would keep her from being blown away. When he grunted to let her know he was still alive, she pushed against him to sit up, took his shoulders and pushed gently until he was up as well.

They didn't bother to go through the questions, because there were no answers. All he could do was breathe heavily, almost panting, and wince at the tiny scratches he saw on her left cheek. Her hair was tangled, glints of glass caught inside. When she reached up to touch it, he said, "No, you'll cut yourself."

She stared, numb.

Once he was sure he could move without falling apart, he opened the door and stepped onto the road. Dust hung faintly in the air, but the sky was still clear, the road littered with leaves and twigs, with pebbles and stones blown off the shoulder.

"Come on," he said. "We'll get you to the ranch, take care of that glass."

It took her a long time before she moved, longer before she left the car, staring at it in amazement. She touched her cheek, and shuddered when the tips of her fingers came away speckled with blood.

"You're all right," he said, holding out his hand as she came around the front.

"Easy for you to say," she said, swaying, unsteady.

They walked hand-in-hand under the arch and up the drive, bumping into each other every few steps, not letting go even when they had to maneuver around a patrol car and Les's old Jeep at the top of the drive.

"I think I'm going deaf," she said shakily.

"Why?"

"I didn't hear the wind."

"Neither did I."

As they approached the main house, he saw beyond the pines at the side three people slowly rising from the crouch they'd obviously dropped into when the thunder hit. Behind them two more came out of the near stable.

"John," she said, leaning heavily against him, "what was it?"

"You want me to guess?" he said as he waved to Les Burgoyne.

"No numbers, okay? This ain't the time for numbers."

He knew that. He didn't like it, but he knew it.

"You remember what you told me? What your mother told you?"

"I . . . yes, I think so, but—no. No."

"Yes." He touched his chest near his heart. "No numbers, Lisse. I think he's here."

3

1

The municipal parking lot on Seventeenth Street is only half full, and there had been no problem finding a space near the exit. Thirty minutes ago that was, yet Rod still sits behind the wheel, the glare of the sun off the windshield hiding his anger from the passersby. That freak storm had almost killed him. Halfway to Annette's insurance office, the thunder nearly knocked him to his feet, and a sign ripped off a small camera store had come this close to taking off his head.

Shaken, he'd retreated to the car.

Furious at the delay, he watches the pedestrians stepping around broken glass, kicking at wings of newspaper scattered along the pavement to get them out of the way. They talk to each other and exclaim, and he reckons it's the most excitement this damn burg has seen in decades.

No.

Since *he* had scared them all half out of their freaking little minds.

He wants to be out of here by dinnertime. He doesn't want to give anyone a chance to recognize him. As it was, he'd dodged what seemed like half the cops in the country just getting across the Mississippi; and once here, every time he turned a damn corner, he saw a patrol car or a beat cop. He has no doubt there's someone with Annette right now. Some big tough-looking son of a bitch playing at hero. Don't worry, ma'am, you're safe with us.

Goddamn Arn Baer. Sneering at him during the trial. Hovering around

Annette like he was her macho Superman protector. Has probably been screwing her blind and laughing at him the whole time he's been away.

"Calm," he whispers. "Cool. Collected."

In his lap lies a gun. He touches it with his palm, breathes slowly and deeply, ticking off the plan's points as he waits.

Annette first; in and out, a bullet through her head. No torture, no lingering, no accusations. One bullet, maybe two. Gone before they know he's there.

Out to the house, then. Probably some kind of guard there, too. Take the guard, take whoever's there. No way the brat's going to be in school. Stay home, she was probably told; stay home, he's close, we'll protect you. Take her in more ways than one.

In and out, and gone again.

Phil last. Wimp Phil. Pussy Phil. No son of his, he can't be. No son of his would have testified against his own father at that miserable excuse for a trial.

Phil last.

And this time there'll be torture.

He grins, rubs the back of his hand against the pale stubble on his jaw and decides to give it another five minutes, let these idiots calm down a little more.

Then . . . he snickered . . . if they think that freak storm had been bad . . .

2

Lanyon Trask stood nervously on the grass, leaning over, peering through the limousine's open back door. "Are you sure you're all right?"

Alonse Paytrice nodded cautiously. In the driver's seat, his brother nodded as well. The rear window had been shattered, the stump of a branch had dented the left side passenger door, but otherwise the vehicle seemed to be in good shape.

He wished he could say the same for himself.

His hair was slightly mussed, just enough to make him appear disheveled, or wild eyed, and what was left of the hanging dust settled on the three-piece suit that matched the soft gray of his car.

He didn't care about that; he didn't even care about the explosive thunder.

What he cared about was that wind—it had made no sound. Wind has to make a sound, but it had made no sound.

What he cared about was the mother and child.

Alonse eased out, stretched, rubbed his eyes with his knuckles. "What happened, Reverend?"

"I wish I knew, son. I wish I knew."

The giant looked down at him skeptically, saying nothing. It wasn't his place to say anything, but Trask had known both these boys since they were less than swamp-snake high and a single glance told him Alonse believed he was lying. He still hadn't recovered from that incident behind the Royal Cajun, that much was clear. When Trask had questioned him about it, all he'd said was, "Some kind of army move, that's all. Took me by surprise."

Which was a lie in itself.

Alonse had been terrified, and in no hurry to pursue Bannock. Once they had lost him and the waitress in Baton Rouge, he'd had Sebastian drive directly to Vallor. Sooner or later Bannock would show up; sooner or later Trask knew in his heart he would learn what connection the man had with the End.

The irony was, or the sad thing, or the frightening thing, the thing was, he didn't need Bannock now.

He knew.

He had seen the mother and the child.

He knew.

"Hey," Tony Garza called from the porch. "Your boys okay there, Reverend?"

"Fine, Mr. Garza, thank you, sir," he called back with a wave. "Just a little taken aback, that's all."

"God's pissed," Garza called with a raucous laugh. "Somebody didn't say their prayers." Then he turned to the little man sitting on a chair, said something, and laughed again.

Trask felt his jaw tighten. He had suffered doubters and scoffers his entire adult life, and had done his best to turn the other cheek and forgive them. This man, however, was crude and powerful in ways Trask didn't understand. So unlike the mother of that child, but very like the other daughter, who couldn't look at him without some small indication of scorn.

"Ignore him, Reverend," Alonse said quietly.

Trask glanced at him sharply. This comment, this opinion, was against the rules. Neither had Paytrice ever voiced a thought before without a direct request from him. It had been a mutual decision some years ago—they protected his body, and he protected as best his could their souls.

This was against the rules.

Unruffled, Alonse gazed at the house, one hand drifting down the lapels of his suit. Then he broke another rule: "It's the boy, isn't it, Reverend. We come all this way after Mr. Bannock, and turns out it's the boy."

Trask was speechless.

"Got to be," Sebastian agreed. He stood by the driver's door, towering over the roof. Watching the house. "Got to be."

Trask raised a finger to scold them, remind them who they were and who he was, and let his hand fall back to his side, not arguing when Alonse took his arm and urged him to get off his feet, practically forcing him to sit in back, half in, half out. Leaning over to avoid the edge of the roof, hands clasped, forearms resting on his thighs.

They were right, of course.

Stories and legends and Scriptures aside, there was no solid affirmation that the Antichrist had to be an adult. And after all, hadn't the Lord performed his first recorded miracle when He was a child?

Hadn't He?

He stared at his hands for a long time and saw the bloodless knuckles of his thumbs, felt the points of his elbows pressing into his legs.

Alonse stood with the open door between them, one arm resting on the top. "Are you going to be sick, sir?"

He nodded, then shook his head.

Of course he was going to be sick, any fool could see that. His life, his whole preaching life, had been about the Word. Now the Word was here, and he was both exulted and near to panic. He had never doubted. Not once. But O Lord, he had been afraid. Was afraid.

But he wouldn't be sick because he didn't dare to.

How could he?

This was the Time. This was the Moment.

If he wasn't strong now, his whole life would be a sham. A hypocrisy. A blasphemy.

Fear or not, it was given to him to try to save the world. No small feat, given the opposition, and he allowed himself a quick smile.

But to save the world . . . dear Lord, to save the world, he would have to kill a child.

3

Joey steps away from the swing set and says, "Wow, Mom. Wow."

The frame had toppled backward, the swings hopelessly entangled, two chains snapped in half and lying snakelike on the ground.

"Wow."

Patty stands by the birdbath, which somehow remains upright, although the water inside is gone, leaving dark stains behind. "Joey?"

He adjusts his hat and gunbelt, dusts each boot off on the back of his jeans legs. When he takes a step toward her, she takes an involuntary step back.

"Mom?"

She licks her lips, pushes at her hair, snatching away a leaf as if it were something disgusting.

Joey sighs. "Boy, I wish I had some ice cream."

Patty starts, then looks toward the house. "I'll, uh . . . I'll go inside, okay? see if Grampa left you some."

"Too late," he tells her sadly, before she can move.

"What?"

"Too late," he repeats. He seems disappointed, but not surprised. "It's time, Mom."

Tears in her eyes, sudden and bright. She takes another step away, hands fluttering at her sides, one moving to her chin.

"Where are you going, Mom?"

She points. "The house. Ice cream. You said—"

He waggles a finger at her. "Mom, you're gonna try to call Dad, aren't you?"

"No. No, don't be silly, hon." Another step. "I don't even know where he is. Don't be—"

"Mom."

She stops, rigid except for her eyes, which look everywhere but at him.

"Mom." He holds out his hand.

Her lips quiver. "No, Joey. Oh no."

"Mom."

The tears slip out, one drop at a time.

"Joey, please, no. Don't."

"Mom."

She grabs onto the birdbath as if it were an anchor, eyes widening, lips pulled away from her teeth.

"Mom."

"Joey, he's your father." Her voice is contorted, not like her at all. "He's a good man, Joey, you know that. Please don't, honey, please don't."

He lifts his shoulders, lets them fall, and walks toward her. "He is, Mommy, you're right, he really is." The shoulders rise and fall again. "But he's going to die."

She whimpers; the tears fall.

When he reaches the birdbath, he brushes a finger around the rim, looks up at her. And winks. Reaches over and covers one of her hands with both of his. "Mom."

She looks away.

Her fingers release the granite, and he holds her hand.

Holds her hand.

Blue eyes dark; blue eyes smiling.

A moment later, he lets her go and says, "See, Mommy? It didn't hurt a bit."

She holds the hand in front of her face, turning it, examining it, flexing the fingers.

"Just like Grampa."

Turning it. Flexing the fingers.

"Just like Aunt Dory."

Tears dripping off her chin.

"Just like all the rest."

When she looks at him again, he says, "Mom."

"Yes, honey?"

"Stop crying."

And she does.

4

Sharon saw her first, racing full speed up the drive, leaping over branches, waving her arms, wired black hair sticking out in all directions. She looked as if she'd been through a war.

"Mag?"

Beside her, Kyle made an *oh great* face.

"Stop it," she scolded, slapping his arm. She didn't want to leave; she wanted to know what was going on, what made Mr. Bannock look so awful. He, Les, and Deputy Schmidt stood between the stable and the house, talking softly, maddeningly so; they had been there since Mr. Bannock had arrived and Fran took that woman into the house to fix her cuts and do something, Sharon couldn't catch what, with her hair.

Something to do with the wind.

"Come on," Kyle said disgustedly, "let's go see what she wants before she kills herself."

Mag had tripped over a branch, sprawled, and was on her feet again. Not running this time, but still waving her arms.

They met her before she reached the house, and she sagged dramatically into Kyle's unwilling arms.

"He's here," she gasped, her face alarmingly red. "God, he's here."

Sharon went cold and, for a moment, deaf.

Kyle pushed Mag away but held on to her shoulders. "What the hell are you talking about?"

Mag looked up at him, looked at Sharon's stricken face, and clamped a hand over her mouth as she shook her head. "Oh God, no," she managed when Kyle yanked the hand away. "No, no, God, no, Shar, not *him*. God, no, not him." She gestured vaguely toward the road. "I hitched, you know? Had a fierce one with the Chief, and was so mad I couldn't pay attention. I mean—"

Kyle shook her. "Jesus, Baer, who did you see?"

"Trask," she said, nearly shouting.

Sharon walked away slowly, moving under the pines that took up much of the Burgoynes' side yard. The boughs had been trimmed high to permit walking without bending, the ground cushioned by needles and too-small cones. Cool on warm days, a little chilly on days like this, and she hugged herself as she leaned against a trunk, facing away from the house.

Mag babbled apologies and excitement over by Kyle; behind her she could hear voices in the Burgoyne kitchen through the open window.

She wanted to throw up.

"Sharon," Mag said, hustling over, punching at the hair that wouldn't stay away from her face. "Sharon, jeez, I'm sorry, I wasn't thinking."

"Got that right," Kyle grumbled, trailing. He studied Sharon's face, rolled his eyes, and poked Mag hard in the side. "Slowly," he ordered. "No sidetracks."

Mag dropped to the ground, sat crosslegged, and plucked at the needles between her legs. "I thought you could use some company, Shar, that's all. I walked . . . *walked,* you understand, all the way from school, and then that awful thunderstorm or whatever nearly knocked me into a ditch." She shuddered, looked from Sharon to Kyle and saw only stares. "I saw him, Shar, up at Mr. Bannock's house. Reverend Trask himself, standing by this humongous limousine."

Kyle frowned. "Who?"

"TV," Sharon answered flatly, not caring. "He's on TV all the time."

"Right *here,*" Mag said, stabbing the ground with a finger. "He's right here in Vallor, guys." She lowered her voice. "And he's right up the road!"

Sharon didn't know whether to strangle her, or laugh, or climb up the tree and never come down. She couldn't believe how much like winter she had felt inside when she'd thought Mag had been talking about . . . him. She should have gone with Phil and her mother. She should be in Chicago now, living in a hotel, watching city cable, letting Phil fuss while Mom went into orbit.

She shouldn't be here.

She didn't want to die.

She hugged herself tighter, tucked her chin toward her chest. "I don't get it," she said.

"Get what?" Kyle asked.

"I . . ." She almost cried and hated herself for it. "I don't know, but I don't get it."

"Shar, listen," said Mag, flinging needles left and right, "this is big stuff here, you know? I mean, the Reverend Lanyon Trask is right on your street. Right in—" She stopped, looked over at the three men and jerked a thumb in that direction. "Right in his house. Can you believe it? Do you think he'd talk to me, huh? The reverend, I mean. If I went over there, do you think he'd talk to me?"

"Oh, right," Kyle said, practically sneering. "Sure, go ahead. Walk right up to that big-time minister, looking like you've been hit by a truck, walk right up and grab his hand, maybe he'll heal you from being stupid." He closed his eyes and held out his hands as if cupping them around her head. "Now listen here, Lord, we got this little lady here, she's—"

"Stop it," Sharon said, her voice low and hard.

"—got a problem maybe—"

"Stop it, I said."

Kyle looked at her, startled, then looked at Mag and the tears forming in her eyes. "Hey." He pushed a hand back through his hair. "Hey, Mag, I was only kidding. I didn't mean anything by it. Really."

Mag lowered her head, raised her shoulders. "Yeah, well, maybe I forgive you, maybe I don't. Just don't make fun, okay? You don't know what kind of man he is. You don't know what he can do. You don't—"

"You, too," Sharon said. "Quiet. Don't start."

She closed her eyes and listened: Mag shifting on the needles and Kyle poking at them with his boot; the men talking over there, their voices low, like whispers; Fran in the kitchen, saying something to that woman and laughing a little, as if they'd been friends for a hundred years; a bird singing someplace; her heart thumping in her chest, calm, and aching.

And for no reason at all, she opened her eyes and looked at her friends and said with a trembling voice, "Something's going to happen."

5

The little cowboy strolls around the corner of the house, trying to mimic the swagger of the cowboys he's seen on TV. He ignores Grampa's call from the porch, pays no attention to his mother walking slowly behind him.

He keeps his gaze on the silly, not so old man sitting half in and out of the car that's as big as a boat. He can see the two giants, but he watches only the not so old man, who sees him and pulls himself off the backseat. Pushes his hair back into place. Puts out a restraining hand when the giant by the door shifts as if to move.

Smiles broadly.

Joey smiles back as he crosses the lawn, hitching his gunbelt, touching the grip of his plastic six-shooter.

"Well, young man," Reverend Trask says, keeping his back straight, trying to look tall. "I see you have survived the storm with no injury?"

Joey doesn't answer; he keeps walking.

"Hey, Patty," Grampa calls. "Come here, look at Ari. He doesn't look so good."

"Nothing," he hears the little really old man say. "Nothing, Patty, it's nothing. This weather you got out here just took me by surprise."

"Patty," Grampa commands, "get over here and take a look. Dory is helpless."

And Aunt Dory says something really really bad.

Reverend Trask moves onto the lawn, arms down, hands folded one over the other, and the giant closes the door and stands behind him. "My, my," the minister says. "I can see by your outfit, young man, that you are a cowboy." Then he chuckles and shakes his head. "I do apologize, son. That was supposed to be a joke, but you're too young, aren't you."

Joey stops and looks up at the giant with the beautiful dark hair just like a lady's. And looks away as if he wasn't there.

"What can I do for you, son?" the minster says.

Joey pulls out his plastic six-shooter, points it at the man's heart, giggles and says, "Bang, you're dead."

6

Tony watched his grandson draw on the TV preacher, and with a smile shook his head. That kid, he thought; that kid.

"Check it out, Dad," Dory said.

He looked again, and saw the giants jump when his grandson pulled the trigger a second time, looking for all the world like they wanted to jump on the boy and pound him into the ground. His right hand patted his pants pocket, just to be sure it was there. Nobody, not even those two, would harm a hair on Joey's head.

"Yes," Ari said to Patty's question. "Another glass would be fine."

"You drink too much water," Tony said, "you're going to spend the rest of the day in the john."

"Tony!" Ari was shocked. There were, after all, ladies present.

"They're family," he answered, feigning a grunt and groan as he settled on the top step. "They know me too well."

"All the same."

"Next thing you know, you old fart—"

"Tony!"

"—you'll be telling me you want to take a nap, all the excitement's too much, you gotta lie down, rest your heart."

"It wouldn't be a bad idea. Your age, my age, it wouldn't be a bad idea."

"See?" he said, spreading his hands. "You girls see what I have to put up with every day, all day, every week of the damn year?"

"I keep him young," Ari said primly. "He looks at me, he doesn't feel so old anymore."

"I never feel old," Tony protested with a grin. "Not as long as I have Miriam."

"Tony!"

He laughed, but he never took his attention away from Joey, who had backed away from that phony son of a bitch, who himself actually wasn't looking so good. He still didn't know why that guy was here, and he didn't much care, as long as he wasn't here very long. Hit the road, he yelled silently; take your thumping Bible and hit the damn road.

Then Dory hunkered beside him, balancing herself by laying an arm on his shoulder.

"It's good to see you, child." He patted her hand.

"You, too, Pop."

"Don't call me that."

"Sure. Whatever."

Joey returned his gun to its holster, saluted the preacher, and turned away, and waved.

Tony waved back. "Hell of a kid."

"Yeah."

"Just like his grandfather."

Dory swatted him lightly on the chest. "Sure."

They watched as Joey stopped in the middle of the lawn, staring up at the sky, head cocked, squinting. Trask hadn't moved.

The door opened, and Ari said, "Thank you, dear. You're very kind."

"Any time, Ari," Patty said. "You want me to find you a sweater or something?"

"No, but thank you. Some people," and he raised his voice, "worry about other people freezing to death in the open." He lowered his voice again, a laugh there now. "I'm fine. That wind thing, it kind of shook me, but I'm fine now. The sun's nice and warm again."

"Good," Patty said. "Just let me know if you need anything."

Something about her, the tone, the cadence, made Tony look over, leaning back a little to see around Dory. When Patty looked at him with a quick smile, he smiled back and tilted his head quickly—*come on over here*—and she did, moving down the steps, turning her back on her son.

"Yes, Dad?"

He looked at Dory. "What do you think?"

Dory shrugged. "I don't know. I guess."

"Patricia," he said, "give me your hand."

Patty grinned. "Go to hell."

Dory rocked back and looked at the ceiling. "Well, hot damn, it's about damn time."

"What?" Ari wanted to know, sounded miffed he'd been left out.

"I'm sorry, old friend," Tony said, beckoning Patty to him. "It's a family thing. I don't mean to offend."

"No offense. Just so I know. So . . . do I go inside while you do your family thing?"

Patty took Tony's hand and squeezed it, bowed over it and kissed the back lightly. "Missed you," she whispered.

Dory scoffed.

"Well, I did," she insisted, managing at the same time to sound insolent and mocking.

"My daughters," he said to Ari, "know how to worship me."

Dory smacked him; Patty slapped his knee.

Ari laughed and wondered if maybe today they could go into town, walk around, see some things.

"Absolutely," Tony said, grabbing the post, pulling himself to his feet. "In fact, let's do it now. All of us. We'll find a nice place and have dinner out."

"In a minute," Ari said, standing. "I have to, uh, go upstairs." He looked sheepish. "I think I drank too much water."

"So go already, you old fart," Tony said with a laugh. "Make yourself beautiful." He shooed his daughters away as well. "You, too, girls. I want every man in town to envy Tony Garza."

"Jeans," Dory said to Patty as they went inside. "If you wear a dress, I'll scratch your eyes out."

Life is good, Tony thought as he went down the steps; life is very good.

He walked over to Joey, humming until the boy looked up at him, smiling that smile that had stolen, he was sure, a million hearts already.

"We're going downtown, Joey," he said. "Dinner out. Look around. Maybe see a movie. What do you say?" He waited. "What do you say, partner?"

Joey tipped his hat back, pulled on the strap. "I don't know, Grampa."

Tony frowned. "You don't know? What kind of answer is that, you don't know? You want to go, you don't want to go. Pick one. It's easy."

The boy crooked a finger, asking him to down to his level. When he did, hands braced on his knees, the little cowboy said, "What about him?"

Tony looked over his head at Trask. "Him? He's rich, son, he can buy his own meal. Besides, this is family only. And Ari."

Joey nodded solemnly. "And Daddy?"

"What? He's here?"

"Yes, Grampa. He is."

Tony struggled to keep the obscenities inside, said only, "He's not family anymore, son."

Joey nodded again, solemnly, and said shyly, "Grampa, do you know who I am?"

Tony didn't know whether to laugh, frown, scold, tease. So he said heatedly, "You are the one and only Joseph Anthony, my favorite grandson in the whole world, and don't you damn forget it."

Joey grinned, and hugged him around the neck.

Tony rose with him in his arms, almost laughing aloud at the urge to stick his tongue out at the preacher, who still, for God's sake, hadn't moved.

Then Joey whispered in his ear, "Grampa, Daddy's coming here soon. He scares me. Will you dance with him?"

Tony didn't blink, didn't answer.

Then Joey whispered, "Grampa, laugh."
And Tony did.

7

Rod stands by the car, his back to the street. He pulls the cotton shirt out of his jeans so it will cover the gun he's tucked into his belt. He reaches into the front seat and grabs a baseball cap, puts it on, yanks the bill low. Adjusts the shirt. Adjusts his belt. Scowling because, after all this time, after all the dreams, all the schemes, all the hassles, he's mad because he's nervous.

He makes a fist and punches his chest, a scolding for being an asshole.

You're here, he tells himself; now goddamnit, go do it.

He walks up Seventeenth to Madison, crosses at the corner, heading uptown, away from the godawful pile of stone that houses the police station across the street. Just one of scores of pedestrians on the sidewalk, his head slightly down but not too much, taking his time, noting how quickly the mess from the wind has been cleaned away, how quickly everyone seems to have gotten back to normal.

Some things have changed since he's been gone. Not, however, all that much. Still the same shitty town pretending to be big. A shoe store, sweater store, camera store, newsstand, travel agency, more dress stores than the town has damn women to support them; an antique store, for crying out loud, where the hell did that one come from?

The Rialto movie theater between Nineteenth and Twentieth, made into two now and flanked by a pair of luncheonettes, one of which was new.

On Twentieth's west corner he looks over and sees the glass front of Illinois Insurance Partners, right next to First Illinois Bank, as if they were business related. He can't see through the window, there are too many people; it's nearly four-thirty and the ants have already begun to leave their nests for home.

Time to move, he reminds himself when he doesn't cross at the change of light; in and out, Roddy, in and out, or you're dead.

At the next change, some idiot in a delivery van blocking the crosswalk, he follows a pack of women to the other side and doesn't hesitate: He walks straight to the door, pushes in, and sees Annette's desk at the back of the large open room.

It's empty.

He glares, yanks the cap's bill, and moves to the gate in the low wood rail that separates the waiting area from the desks.

Her desk is empty.

A door in the back opens, and a stout woman in a stiff white shirt and tie steps out. Graying hair in waves and curls not quite to her broad shoulders. A string of small pearls around her neck. "May I help you, sir?" she asks with a blind smile, crossing the carpet as though greeting an old friend.

Rod shifts his glare from the empty desk to the woman, who finally pays attention. Falters in her progress, although the smile holds. "Do you have an appointment?" she asks. She gestures apologetically at the five unmanned desks. "I'm afraid we're a little understaffed at the moment. Perhaps I can—oh my God, oh my God."

Rod smiles. "Hello, Stephanie."

Stephanie Zwingler immediately holds up her hands. "She's not here, Rod, I swear to you, she's not here." She backs away. "I don't want any trouble, please, okay? No trouble."

Rod is furious he's missed the bitch, but this is the bitch who talked her out of the house and into a job. It didn't matter that Annette was very good at it. It didn't matter that she made more money than God. It didn't matter, because once she had left the house, it had all gone to hell.

Zingler is near her office, and Rod sees she's ready to bolt inside, shut the door, and call the cops.

"Just go, Rod," she pleads, that perfect hair leaking unladylike sweat onto that perfectly made-up face. "No trouble, all right? Just go. She's not here."

"I can see that," Rod said in disgust, pulls out his gun and aims it at her head.

"Oh God."

"Where is she?"

"I don't—"

Rod yells: "Where the hell is she?"

"Chicago!" Stephanie shrieks back. "Chicago, she went to Chicago with—"

He pulls the trigger, barely flinching at the explosion, not really minding that people on the sidewalk can undoubtedly see in. He wants to make sure that old Steph, lying half in and out of her office now, is dead. So he pulls the trigger again, and Steph's not so perfect stomach ripples as the bullet rips through it.

Shit, he thinks, and turns, yanks open the door, and hurries onto the sidewalk, tucking the gun carefully back into his belt. What the hell is she doing in Chicago? A man, right? She's got a new man? Yeah. She has a new man, the bitch, but that's okay because there's still the wimp and the other bitch, and old Steph is gone and that takes care of that.

He pays no heed to the pedestrians round him. To the handful who gape, and the others who are running.

He crosses against the light, one hand out matador-style to keep a pickup from running him down.

When he reaches the other side, he breaks into a trot, then a full sprint, thinking maybe he ought to go down Nineteenth, cut through an alley so he doesn't have to tempt anything by heading straight for the cop shop.

Someone is screaming.

No one tries to stop him.

At Nineteenth he decides to go one more block, get him one block closer to the car. Halfway there, someone bellows his name and he looks up, focusing on a man standing at the corner. Alone. With a gun.

Be damned, he thinks; it's my old friend, Arn.

He doesn't break stride when he pulls out his gun and fires without aiming, swerves into the recessed entrance of a bookstore and fires again just as good old Arn ducks behind a lamppost.

Funny, he thinks, how fast the streets get empty. Checks his pocket to be sure he has the extra ammunition, then crouches down, a smaller target, and aims this time before pulling the trigger.

He sees that Arn is too big to hide behind that skinny pole, sees the chief jerk when the bullet hits him someplace.

Then he hears the sirens, sees far beyond Baer a handful of uniforms pelting toward him, shotguns at the ready. Since he's in the middle of the block, he can't run back, they'd get him for sure, and Arn, although hit, fires again, punching a hole in the window just over his head, sprinkling him with shattered glass.

He looks at the door, and can't believe his eyes when he sees a woman backing away quickly, panic and terror in her eyes.

Well, well, he thinks; maybe it's not so bad after all.

He fires once more to keep everyone down, then charges the door, slamming it open, raises the gun and aims it at the woman's head. "Hey, Vonda," he drawls. "You know your old man's trying to kill me?"

8

Lisse blew her nose on the tissue Fran handed her. "I'm sorry. I don't get this way, really."

"I don't blame you, dear," Fran assured her, sitting opposite her at the kitchen table, the radio on low on the counter behind her. "It's been a weird day."

Lisse looked at her, and laughed. Too loudly and too hard, but she couldn't stop. "Day?" More tears that prompted Fran to push the whole box at her. She grabbed a handful and waved it. "Day?" And didn't stop laughing until she ran out of breath. "Sorry. God, I'm sorry."

But she was more embarrassed than sorry. Coming into this nice woman's house with blood on her face, babbling all the time while Fran brushed and plucked the glass from her hair, snipping away some, with constant apologies, to make sure the cuts she found on her scalp weren't in need of more attention. Half the time neither of them made much sense, although she did learn this wasn't the first time that thunder-and-squall had happened.

John, bless his heart, had stayed away. Being in his own state, he knew he wouldn't do her much good, and for that she wanted to kiss him. Wanted to kiss him badly.

Once back in control, she smiled gamely at the other woman and checked the window on her left. She could see John, Fran's husband whose name she couldn't remember, and that cop talking. Under some trees she could see three kids talking, one of them, a girl, taller than half the men she knew.

It looked normal out there.

It looked perfectly normal.

She, on the other hand, was a perfect mess.

There were no deep cuts, just pricks and little stabs, but she did not want to see her face in a mirror. And her hair . . . she shuddered, deciding that as soon as she had the chance, she would get a cut like Fran's—short and easy to take care of.

Oh, Lord, she thought; now I'm babbling in my own head.

Quickly she pushed her chair back. "I think . . ." A look outside again.

"It's okay," Fran said, her smile friendly, understanding. She waved at the table—used tissues, strands of hair, winking glass. "I'll clean up and be out in a minute. You sure you're okay?"

"As I can be, I suppose," Lisse answered gratefully. "I don't know how to thank you."

"Easy. After all this, I don't feel like cooking. You and John take us to dinner."

"Deal," she said, and after a moment's fumbling for direction, found the back door and hurried out. John saw her come around the side of the house and walked toward her without a word to the others.

She didn't mean to do it: She just walked right up to him and wrapped him around the waist, put her head on his chest, and sighed when his arms squeezed her tightly and she could feel his breath in her hair. Then he pushed her back a bit so he could see her face.

"My, my," he said, exaggerating her accent. "My, my, don't you look something."

He had a scratch on his cheek, another that slipped under the hair that wouldn't stay away from his forehead, a third, a little deeper, on the side of his neck.

"You ain't no prize yourself."

"So I'm told," he said, the rasp in his voice softer.

She wanted him to say more, and maybe he would have from the look on his face, but suddenly the deputy cursed. They listened intently to the voice crackling on the radio snapped to his shoulder. "Gotta go," Schmidt said.

"What's up?" Les asked, unable to hear it all.

"Gillespie." The deputy looked over at Sharon. "They got him cornered downtown."

And he was gone, racing to the car, gunning the engine and leaving smoke in his wake as he shot down the drive as if ignited by a rocket, slamming over the debris and screaming left out of the gate.

"Son of a bitch," Les said.

The kids, who had scattered at the patrol car's passing, ran over, confused.

"What?" Sharon demanded of John. Her face was pale, her eyes wide. "What, Mr. Bannock?"

"Your . . . it's him," John told her, putting a hand on her shoulder. "Downtown. It seems the police have him trapped."

Sharon whipped around to stare at the road. "Oh God."

Lisse shifted to stand beside Les, watching them, wanting to say something to the girl who so obviously had a crush on John; but this wasn't her world and nothing she could say would have any weight, much less any comfort.

Then John looked at her, hesitated, and said, "What did I tell you."

9

Dory and Garza flank Ari on the porch, teasing him, flattering him, while Patty stands at the head of the steps and watches her son.

From the moment her father put him down, he has stood in the middle of the lawn. Looking at the sky. Looking at the house. Looking at the limousine into which the preacher and his giants have retreated. Fiddling with his chin strap. Pulling his toy gun in and out of its holster.

Something is not right, she thinks. She knows him too well, and she knows something isn't right.

When, at last, he looks right at her, she smiles and goes to him. "Hey, cowboy."

"Mom?"

"What is it?"

"We can't go."

She doesn't understand. "You mean, go to town, or leave town?"

"No dinner," he says, shaking his head, disappointed. "No movie."

"But we're all ready." She looks back at the porch. "Look at Mr. Lowe, he's so excited. You know," she adds, lowering her voice, "he doesn't have much back home. Only Grampa. This is a big deal for him."

"No."

"But why?"

He looks up at her somberly, one eye in a squint. "Daddy knows."

Her confusion deepens. "Joey, I don't get it. What does Daddy know? You mean, that we're here, where we are?"

"No." He turns away from her, looking at the limousine, looking at the road. Shaking his head slowly.

"Joey?"

Lanyon Trask felt small. Helpless. Infinitely weak. Faced with the biggest decision of his life, and he had failed. Mrs. Cawley would be ashamed of him. The Paytrice brothers certainly were already. But despite his best efforts to explain, they did not really grasp the significance of this day, of this moment, of what he knew was right and could not bring himself to do.

"Sebastian," he said wearily, the timbre drained from his voice, "let's go."

The engine started.

Alonse did not blink.

"Where, sir?" Sebastian asked.

"Down the road," he said. "Just get away from this house, these people."

That boy, he thought; get me away from that boy.

Joey raises his left hand over his head and wiggles his fingers. She hears voices and footsteps as the others leave the porch. Ari sounds as confused as she feels, but she says nothing until they're all beside her. Then Joey turns and shakes his head again.

"I'm sorry," he says.

"What?" Ari says. "What's he talking about? What are you sorry for, little one? You're not feeling well?" He frowns at Patty. "You're his mother, what's the matter?"

"Hush, Ari," Tony says.

"Oh. I see. Another family thing, is that it? Well, fine." Angrily he chops the air with one hand, heads back for the porch. "When you're done with your family thing, let me know, you think you can do that? Let me know."

"Pop," Dory says, "that wasn't very nice. He's your best friend."

"Yes," says Tony sadly. "Yes, you're right, he is."

IN THE MOOD

*   *   *

John walked away from the others, not stopping until he was beneath the pines. He inhaled the scent of them, brushed a hand across a trunk to feel the rough bark, picked up a tiny cone and rolled it between his palms.

He was out of his mind, of course.

Facing the truth about his split with Patty, about the lies he'd told himself and others for so many years, had sent him off the deep end. Around the bend. Over the edge.

Because if it was true, and his madness said it was, he also had a feeling he knew what Casey Chisholm meant, and what, perhaps, Casey had done.

Lisse came up behind him; he knew it was her, he could smell her, he could sense her.

"Gillespie, right?" she asked.

"No."

"No? How can it not be?" She moved to stand in front of him. "How? He's a cold-blooded murderer. He raped his own daughter and strangled her to death, for crying out loud. It's gotta be."

"I've talked to some who've murdered more. You've heard them, Lisse. They're different."

"Okay." She fingered her cheek gingerly, touching each of the tiny cuts. "Then who? Or do I say 'what'?"

"Who is good," he answered, staring over her head at the road.

"This is crazy."

"I know."

She gave him a lopsided grin. "Your ex?"

"No."

"No games, John," she told him. "No more games. I'm scared. I'm very scared, and I don't want any more games." Clearly she wanted to hold him, and clearly she was too afraid. "You can't play games with the end of the world."

"But that's the thing," he said, still looking at the road. "I don't think it's the end, either. Not yet. Not if I can—not yet."

Her face darkened. "Then damnit, will you tell me? Will you please . . . oh Jesus." She stepped away from him. "Oh Jesus, John, you can't mean Joey."

This time he did look at her, and at the boy's name he felt something inside rip open.

"Oh, John," she said, "you can't mean it."

A deep breath, a hand to his eyes.

"Levee Pete, remember? When we were fighting, he said something about 'him' promising to let the kid ride with him. His eyes, Lisse. Remember the pirate's eyes?"

"But John . . . he's your son."

"Yes," he said hoarsely. "Yes, and no."

"You're doing it again," she said, her voice low and dangerous. "You're treating me like that again."

The hand dropped from his eyes.

"Yes," he said. "Yes, I mean Joey. But no, he's not my son."

Patty slaps a hand to her mouth, smothering a cry as Joey suddenly grimaces in pain and staggers sideways a few steps.

"See?" Ari calls from the porch. "I told you he wasn't well. Why the hell don't you do something?"

Patty moves toward the little cowboy, and stops abruptly when he raises his head.

"Oh," Dory whispers.

All this time, all these years, traveling all over the country, meeting all kinds of people, watching Joey take their hands and smiling and laughing with those lips and those stunning blue eyes, she has never seen him lose his temper. Never saw him truly angry.

Until now.

"No more time," he tells them.

And she has never seen him afraid.

Until now.

"Grampa?"

"What is it, son?"

Joey points. "Dance with Uncle Ari."

"What?"

"Grampa."

Tony touches his trouser pocket, and Joey smiles and nods as the old man leaves.

Patty swallows hard. "Joey? Honey?"

"No more time," he says again. "I have to see the horses."

"Now?" Dory says incredulously.

"Now," he says sternly. "You'll have to help me. Wait here. I'll be back."

He starts for the road, stops and looks over his shoulder.

Blue eyes.

Floating.

"Now," he says to his aunt and his mother, as Uncle Ari screams, just once, "it's time to find my Dad."

And the breeze begins to stir.

4

Rod mutters to himself, searching desperately for the silver lining, but he knows that he is in seriously big trouble.

He hadn't remembered that Vonda Baer was such a hefty woman; not as big as the bitch Stephanie, but big enough. Even with the gun aimed at her temple, she struggled as he dragged her to the back of the store. At that point, all he had been able to see through the front window was a bunch of uniforms ducking and darting across the street. But Vonda kept struggling and pleading for her life, and he hadn't been able to stand it and clipped her with the barrel just to shut her up so he could have a moment's peace and do a little thinking.

A storeroom in back, filled with open and unopened cartons of books, a small desk with a computer and telephone, a small filing cabinet with a framed color picture of Arn and his brat. A back door he had opened, cautiously, sighing when he had seen the alley outside. Just wide enough for delivery trucks, and one-way left to right. Across the alley, not eight feet away was a grimy brick wall at least five stories high, without a single window. Slightly to the left was a metal fire door, and he had taken a big chance, had run across and tried it.

He hadn't been surprised to find it locked.

Back in the bookstore he reloaded his gun.

Now he begins to see things more clearly. A couple of states want to fry him by now, but it looks like Illinois has drawn the right card. No way is he going to get out of here alive. He supposes the alley is already blocked, that Baer is right now deploying what men he has. Maybe even called in the county or state.

Sure enough, when he opens the storeroom door a crack, he can see patrol cars along the curb on the far side of Madison, lights spinning, cops in uniform and cops in suits, every damn one of them with a shotgun or rifle.

On the floor behind him Vonda moans.

In a book he once read, a guy in a position pretty much like this has this something, this icy calm, settle over him, which allows him to figure the angles and the odds and ultimately the means to his escape.

Rod feels only rage. A rage so deep it makes his legs quiver and dries his throat and his lungs hard to work. It feels good, though, it feel fine. He tugs at his cap's bill. He rolls his shoulders. When Vonda moans again, he figures he has only one chance in hell.

Which is what Arn figures as well.

He has been, and knows he has been, insanely calm since Gillespie ducked into the store. He hasn't even felt the hastily bound wound on his upper left arm. What he has done is make sure there is no possible way the man can leave that place except by the front door. Two men in each of the shops on either side, cruisers nose-in at the alley entrances, even someone behind the fire door in the building behind.

Two vehicles blocking each intersection, the nearest civilians on the street are two blocks away behind sawhorse barriers.

When the call went out, every off-duty cop in Vallor showed up at the station.

"He's gonna come out," he says, looking at no one, staring over the hood of the cruiser that gives him at least the illusion of cover.

"Chief—"

"No, Rafe, he's gonna come out."

"Hands up?"

"Not likely. He has Vonda in there."

Rafe snaps his gum. "A hostage situation."

"Him? Hell no. There's no negotiations with that man. Nope. He's gonna use her as a shield and try to make it to his transportation, wherever it is."

Down the row of police cars, a man with a bullhorn urges Gillespie to surrender. He's surrounded. He has no chance. No one will shoot, no one will hurt him as long as he doesn't try anything stupid.

That's supposed to be Arn's job, but he had recognized immediately he wouldn't be able to do it without saying something to set the killer off.

In the classes he took they called it personal involvement.

Damn right, he thinks; goddamn right.

When Rafe hands him a small pair of binoculars, he concentrates on the doorway. Praying. Knowing full well she was supposed to work today, but hoping for a miracle that maybe her partner had decided to work instead, that she is home instead, having a wonderful fight with their daughter.

When he sees movement at the back—the storeroom door opening slowly—he sighs, and hands the binoculars back, passes his knuckles over his eyes. Then he leans back a little and checks on the kneeling, aiming policemen. "You men ready?" he says, just loud enough for them to hear. "It's coming, men, it's coming."

Then he stands before Rafe can stop him.

"Chief, don't."

"I got on the vest, what more do you want?"

"He can shoot you in the head."

"Maybe."

But he didn't think it was all that terrible a risk.

After a few seconds, Gillespie comes out of the storeroom, holding Vonda with one arm for a shield, the gun at her head or neck or heart. If he tries for a shot, he won't be aiming all that well. And in several of the windows on several of the stories of the buildings this side of Madison is a sharp-shooter licking his lips.

He can see them making their way up the middle aisle, his Vonda just as he thought, the gun pressed against her temple.

"Chief," Rafe begs.

Arn gives him a wink that doesn't mean a damn thing and steps around the front of the car. He raises his arms over his head, making sure Gillespie can see his .38. Then he slowly puts the weapon on the hood and steps into the street.

"Well, Jesus," Rafe whispers, "at least don't forget the signal."

Arn makes no sign he's heard, because he's concentrating too hard as the door finally opens and Rod Gillespie and his wife move out into the shadowy recess, shuffling their feet, swaying a little.

"Arn!" she cries when she sees him.

"Hang in there, Vonda," he calls. "Just don't move. You stop moving now, do as I say."

He sees it when he walks to the center line—smears of blood across her brow and down one side of her face. Spatters of it on her blouse and pale skirt.

Up and down the street, the sound of chambers being loaded, hammers drawn back. Like gunshots themselves, they echo off stone and blacktop.

"Here's the deal, Mr. Chief," Rod says, his voice raised a little, not bothering to hide the sneer.

"I already know the deal," Arn tells him. "It's the only one you have."

Gillespie laughs, and nods. "So?"

Arn holds up a hand—*just give me a second here*—and tries to think of the absolute right thing to say, the words that won't get his Vonda killed.

As he does he realizes something very strange—there is no sound on Madison Street.

No breeze, no cars, no sirens, no horns; no one shifting, no one whispering, no one clearing a throat; no radio talk or static, no whir of cameras, no doors or windows pushed open, pulled closed.

Nothing.

No sound at all.

and . . .

No sound at all on the porch of the dark-brick house around the Jackson Street bend.

George has long since stopped calling for help. His throat is sore, and his eyes sting from too much weeping.

He lies on his stomach midway between the door and the steps, where he fell when the thunder came, and the wind. And whatever it was that had slammed into his back as he tried to make it inside. He thinks now, lying there, cheek against the floor, looking out at the road, it must have been something metal. A piece of the gutter maybe, or maybe one of the flower pot stands.

Whatever it was, it hit him low, dropped him, and knocked him out for a while. He doesn't know for how long, but he does know that he can't move. He can't wiggle his toes. He can't bend his knees. He can only move his right arm.

He doesn't think there's any blood, but he wouldn't know it even if there was; he doesn't think his back is actually broken, but there's no way to tell, and no one to help him. He prays that he's only stunned, like the time the hammock that used to be here pulled away from its hooks and dropped him, landing him square on his coccyx so hard he couldn't breathe for more than a full minute, couldn't move for nearly ten, and when he could move, he had to crawl to get inside. It was an hour before the pain stopped screaming in his tailbone, several more before he was able to get up off the couch.

He does know, for sure, that his left arm is broken.

That's what made him yell and cry—when he tried to move it.

"So," he says, thinking it's all right to talk aloud to himself, because if he doesn't he'll lose his mind. "So, how long do you reckon it will take the cavalry to get here, Mr. Trout?"

His voice, strained as it is, is a comfort.

He can hear nothing else.

"I am not amused."

No one answers.

"God, I am thirsty!"

No one answers.

"All right, all right, I can take it. I am, if nothing else, able to take a little dry spell now and then."

He shifts his head, wincing at the feel of his beard rubbing over the floor. It may have saved his jaw, but it's going to look like hell when he gets back up.

"Tell you what," he tells the yard. "I'm going to recite the names of all the women who have stayed in this house, as far back as I can."

It will kill some time, it will keep his mind off his arm and the nothing in his back and legs, and it may well amuse him.

"Damnit, John, where the hell are you?"

Hating the thought that he needed anyone.

Feeling a new tear slide along his nose.

"Did you know," he tells the lawn, "that I've had every one of Marcotte Dovinsky's wives?"

Did you know, he thinks, that Kyle may well be my son?

Nothing.

No sound at all.

and . . .

No sound at all when Les Burgoyne checks the sky, makes a face, and walks over to the kitchen window. "Fran? I'm going to get the horses in. It doesn't feel right out there."

"Hang on," she says, flicking off the radio. "I'll go with you."

He takes off his hat, wipes his brow with a sleeve, and has an idea, maybe help the kid out. "Sharon?"

She stands shivering next to Kyle beneath the pines, Mag at her feet.

Louder: "Shar?"

When she looks, he tilts his head toward the pasture. "I'm going out to get the guys. You want to help out?"

Kyle gives him an *are you out of your mind* look so comical he has to grin, and beckons him his own invitation. "No time like the present to learn," he calls, taking his gloves from a hip pocket and pulling them on.

It isn't until he looks at the paddock that he remembers he only has two horses, the roan and the gray. Nice work, he thinks; nice going.

Luckily, after a heated discussion with Sharon, Kyle stays behind. Pouting. Standing over Mag and, by his gestures, demanding she stand up. Les points as he walks over to the tack room in the stable nearest the house, and Sharon nods, veering in that direction. She seems in no hurry, and he doesn't blame her. The shocks she's had today, he'd probably be in bed with his wife and a bottle, not coming out until the next century got here.

Fran beats him there and glances at the girl, asking the question with her eyes.

"I counted wrong," he apologizes.

"No sweat," and adds softly, "She needs it more than me, anyway. You're sweet." And kisses his cheek.

"That's me," he says with a stupid grin.

She grunts, and helps Sharon with her saddle and bridle. It doesn't take long to get the horses ready, although they seem to be a bit skittish.

They feel it, too, he thinks, wishing he knew what the hell "it" was. And when Fran opens the gate to the pasture, both animals pull hard at the reins, eager to move, get out with the herd.

"Boy," Sharon says, shifting in her saddle. "You give them vitamins or what?"

Her voice is shaky, her cheek gleaming, her eyes bright. Les wants to tease her about her seat and the way she's hanging on for dear life, but he suspects that if he does, she'd either spit in his face or fall into hysterics. And when her mount, the gray, rears a bit, he reaches over and pulls the horse back firmly.

"No hurry," he says, both to the animal and the girl. "The guys aren't going anywhere. We'll take our time."

"Kyle," Sharon tells him, "will help get them in the stalls." It isn't a suggestion; it's a fact, even if Kyle doesn't know about it yet.

"Sure thing," he says, twists around and waves to John.

John waves back, and with Lisse, starts a slow walk toward them.

"You know her?" Sharon asks stiffly.

"Nope. I understand he met her in New Orleans, while he was working on that book thing of his."

"Is she a writer?"

He looks over. Her spine is rigid, her hands twist the reins. Oh boy, he thinks; oh boy.

But he's pleased that the girl's come along. Taking care of the herd will keep her mind busy. She knows how to put distractions aside; she knows how dangerous these critters can be when they get a temper up.

As if he'd spoken aloud, she says, "Don't worry, Les, I'll be all right."

"I ain't worried, kid."

They ride on, slowly.

"I'm scared, though."

He nods. "Just keep your mind on your job, nothing will happen."

"That's not what I mean. I mean, I'm scared the cops won't get him."

He stops, waiting until she realizes she's alone and turns her mount to face him, its tail and ears twitching. To her apprehensive, did I do something wrong look, he says, "What I heard on the radio there, he's holed up in a store. The bookstore by the movies. They'll get him, Shar, don't you worry."

She considers what he's told her, and more than the odd wind and thunder, the smile that touches her lips unnerves him so much that he almost changes his mind and tells her to go back, she has no business out here, not today.

Then the smile fades, replaced by a puzzled frown. "Listen," she says. Looks east and west, and over her shoulder.

He's not sure what she means until the roan snorts and tosses its head.

The silence; it's the silence.

Out here under the open sky, there ought to be at least a whisper of sound, a breeze, the herd talking to itself, a bird, something.

But there was nothing.

No sound at all.

and . . .

Lanyon Trask asks Sebastian to pull over there, behind that car with the windows blown out. Once the limousine has stopped, the engine turned off, he steps onto the road and approaches the car.

"My Lord," he says to himself. "What happened here?"

"The wind."

He jumps and spins around to face Alonse. "The wind you say?"

"Yes, sir, I believe it was that wind."

"Nobody inside."

The giant looks to the ranch entrance. "Perhaps they went there for help."

Trask nods. "You're probably right, Alonse, you're probably right."

He looks at the gate, at the name carved in the arch, and walks around the giant and past the limousine.

"Reverend Trask?"

He steps onto the bridge, rests his arms on the rail, and looks down at Oakbend Creek. Shallow water and shifting shade, the silver dart of some small fish, the skip of a water spider darting over the surface. He feels

Alonse beside him, but he says nothing because he is struck by the way the water skims and ripples over the rocks in its bed without making a sound.

It saddens him somehow; it saddens him deeply.

"Alonse," he says when too much silence makes him uneasy, "I think it's time I stop this foolishness and let you take me home." He leans over the rail a bit more, up on his toes, trying to see beneath the bridge. "I have been vainglorious in my beliefs, my friend. I have assumed the weight of a cloak that has not been given to me. I . . . I am a fraud."

Only then does he swivel his head around so he can look into Alonse's face. Only then does he realize how small he truly is.

Oddly, the giant smiles, showing all his teeth. "You remember, Reverend, a day long time ago, I cry to you about the boys in school making fun of me and Seb on account of how tall we were then, how big across? How they were supposed to be afraid of us, but they weren't?"

Not quite following, but recalling the moment well, he returns his gaze to the creek. "I believe I gave you and Sebastian a lecture, am I right?" He chuckles. "Or was it a sermon?"

"You always give a sermon, Reverend," Alonse answered gently, fondly. "Even you say hello good morning, you are giving a sermon."

Trask laughs, shakes his head, takes a pebble from the ground, and flicks it into the water. "And I suppose you remember the moral of that sermon?"

"Feel sorry for yourself, you die slow and bad the whole of your life. Every day. Every night."

Trask nodded. And touched his shirt where a simple wood cross hung from a leather thong, a smaller version of the one above his office door. He reached inside and pulled it out, held it top and bottom between his thumb and forefinger. And whisper-prayed, "Lord, I don't suppose you'd mind a coward on Your side?"

A rustling, and Alonse's hand appeared over the rail, a penny in the palm.

"I make a wish," he said. "I will make a wish."

A pause before the palm flips the penny high, and when it hits the water, Trask frowns and leans over again.

He saw the splash, he can see the glint of copper, but he hadn't heard a sound.

IN THE MOOD

*　　*　　*

and . . .

John stops before he reaches the first stable, holding his hand out blindly until Lisse takes it and squeezes it.

"It's awful quiet," she says. "Makes you want to take a horn and blow so loud your brains come out your ears."

The two riders have stopped, and he wonders if they've noticed the quiet, too.

"Calm before the storm," Lisse says with a forced laugh.

He can hear the tension in her voice, see it in the way the muscles of her neck stand out, feel it in her grip. She's been this way since he told her about Joey, about how, long before he married Patty, he knew he could never give a wife children, and how, after a year, they decided to adopt, and didn't care if the child was a newborn or well into growing.

At the time, they had thought it a miracle—Joey was there, in St. Louis, the first time they went. They had no interest, not really, in who his birth parents were, and Joey took to them so fast, it was as if he'd always been in the house. From the beginning.

"So," Lisse had said, "you don't know where he comes from?"

"You have to remember," he had answered, "that I'm crazy, okay?"

She hadn't responded.

She knew what he meant.

"A penny," she says, tugging at his hand.

"I'm wondering how long he's been here, how many other parents he's had. If there really are any records of him at all."

The tug becomes a yank. "Stop it! Just . . . stop it!"

"I'm wondering," he says, unable to stop himself, "if Ruesette Argo or Stan Hovinskal have ever met him."

Lisse gives his knuckles a stinging slap, and walks away. "I'm not crazy," she insists tearfully, turning, walking backward, shaking her head. "I do not want to be crazy, John, you hear me? I—" She turns again and heads for the pines, and the drive beyond.

"Lisse, don't," he calls.

271

He can see Kyle and Mag staring at them, wondering; he can see Fran by the stable uncertain whether it was her place to intervene.

He can see everything but what he's supposed to do now, and it makes him angry, and frustrated, and makes his fingers snap at his side and his tongue work at his lips and his body sway at the waist, a slow rocking while his right heel hits the ground again, and again, and again.

And again.

"Lisse," he calls. "Lisse, please."

She slows but she doesn't stop, hints of fire in her hair and in her walk.

Suddenly she whips around, arms flying outward, hair veiling her face, and she marches back, muttering to herself until she nearly runs him over.

"Goddamnit, John Bannock," she snaps, "you're stalling again." Tears in her eyes. "You're loon crazy, and you're stalling. Standing here all this time, talking to this one, talking to that one, talking—"

"Lisse, wait."

"—to every damn person in the whole damn world, and you're stalling and you know it and if you're going to do this thing your crazy says you have to, then goddamnit, stop all this talking and *go do it* before I . . ." Tears on her cheeks. "Before I . . ." And she punches him in the chest so hard he staggers, astonished at her strength, surprised that her expression shows no regret.

"Well?" she demands.

He rubs his sternum gingerly, gauging the rise of his own temper.

"You're marked," she says in a harsh whisper. "You can't drink it away, you can't run it away, all you can do is go more crazy than you are and—"

She stops, too shocked to react, when he clamps a hand over her mouth and says, "Shut up and listen."

He can see by the way her eyes slowly widen that she hears it. Then Fran moves away from the stable, rubbing a hand nervously over a shoulder. Kyle and Mag, keeping close together, come out from under the pines, Mag hanging onto his arm with both hands.

Thunder.

At first he thinks it's thunder.

and . . .

IN THE MOOD

*   *   *

Lanyon Trask looks up from the water with an uncertain frown, looks to Alonse for an answer, but the giant is too busy scanning the sky.

"Again?" Sebastian calls from the limousine.

"I don't know, son," Trask answers, then grabs Alonse's hand and heads quickly off the bridge. "But I do not believe we should stay here long enough to find out. Turn that thing around, Seb, and let's leave. Now."

He doesn't wait for either man to open the door for him. He gets into the limousine himself, even as it's moving to face west, and pushes himself into a corner, the wooden cross in his hands.

Thunder, he thinks, but something tells him that he's wrong.

Patty races around the house to the backyard, stumbling to a halt when she sees her father digging a hole under the trees. He looks up and scowls.

"Dad?" she calls, "have you seen Joey?"

"I'm busy," he snaps. "Go away, have some respect."

Flustered, she backtracks to the front yard. Dory comes out of the house, shaking her head, shrugging. "So what do we do now?"

Patty clasps her hands and holds them to her mouth. "I don't know. He was right here a moment ago. I . . . he's never done this before. I don't know."

"Well, you'd better make up your mind quick, Sis."

"Why? What's wrong?"

"Jesus, Patty, are you deaf? Can't you hear it?"

and . . .

Arn holds his arms out at his sides, trying to look as sorry as he can. "Can't let you do it, Rod. You know I can't let you do it."

"You jackass," Rod screams, making Vonda wince and begin to sob. "I'll kill her! I swear to Christ I'll kill her!"

Think, the chief orders; think, because he'll do it.

"One more chance," Rod warns.

Arn knows there's no way any of the shooters can get him, not now. He keeps moving around in that narrow recess, turning one way, then another, Vonda always at the front.

Think, for God's sake; *think.*

But he can't, because Rafe is hissing urgently at him, and finally he looks over his shoulder and the deputy points west, up the street.

When he looks, he's not sure he understands what he sees. When he finally does, he can't help a grin.

"Hey, Rod," he calls, mopping his brow with a jacket sleeve, "I think it's gonna get cooler, huh?"

"What? What the hell are you talking about?"

"The breeze, Rod. The breeze."

"What goddamn breeze are you talking about? You trying to mess with me, Baer?" He tightens his grip on Vonda, who's struggling to keep her feet. "Three seconds, Mr. Chief. Three seconds."

Arn points to his right. "That breeze," he says.

And holds his breath.

Prays.

Trying to watch two things at once:

Rod easing out of the recessed doorway to make sure there's no trick, cops crawling up on him, maybe; and the breeze coming down Madison in the form of a faint cloud of dust as high as the tallest building. A peculiar phenomenon he'd seen once before, like watching rain come at him across a pasture.

"Wasn't lying, Gillespie," he says as the barrel of Rod's gun, however briefly, leaves Vonda's neck.

And puts his right hand in his jacket pocket.

and . . .

When it begins, it sounds like thunder.

5

1

Slowly John takes his hand away from Lisse's mouth, keeping it up, though, to caution her against speaking.

The idea that what he hears is thunder—deep and constant and rumbling and growing—is wrong. He knows it not by the sound, but by the vibrations beneath his feet.

The breeze strengthens, just enough to lift dust, just enough to turn his head slightly as he moves toward the pasture fence, uncertain, left hand moving as if searching for something to hold on to. Fran looks over at him and he shrugs; the riders in the pasture are having a difficult time controlling their mounts; a flutter of wings as some small bird flees a tree near the paddock.

"John," Lisse whispers, "is it an earthquake?"

"No," he whispers back, and asks her with a simple gesture to hold on for a minute, don't speak yet.

While the rumbling deepens and grows louder, and now he can feel it in his stomach, practically in his bones, and if it lasts much longer he's pretty sure he's going to come down with the emperor of all headaches.

The breeze is strong enough now to set smaller branches trembling in the taller trees' leafless crowns. Pine needles stir and shift. Dead leaves stir, and shift.

Deeper still, the vibrations shimmer through his legs into his stomach, and there is a terrifying moment when he fears they will affect his heart.

Lisse grabs his elbow, not to pull him back but to hold on. "Horses?" she wonders.

"Can't be," he answers. "There aren't that many of them. Certainly not enough to do that," and he points to a narrow puff of dust that rises sharply a few inches over the grass near the fence. A second erupts in front of the far stable door. From his left, over by the creek, they hear what sounds like a score of birds shrieking.

"Hey, Mr. Bannock," Kyle calls. "What's going on?"

"Don't know," he yells, but he can't help a check of the cloudless sky just to be sure there really aren't any thunderheads up there.

Louder.

Deeper.

Suddenly his right hand snaps out and grabs Lisse's arm.

The sound, it isn't constant, isn't smooth. Within that cavern-deep rumbling he can hear the rhythm that distance had masked.

"Oh man," he says.

Lisse tries to pull him away. "What? What do you mean? John, what *is* that?"

Another dust eruption in the pasture, not much higher than the highest blade of grass, but dark enough for him to see that there are others out there, swelling upward, hanging briefly, then scattered by the wind.

"John?"

"I was wrong."

And Fran races toward the fence, hands cupped around her mouth, screaming, "Les! Sharon, ride! For God's sake, ride!" Climbing the fence, screaming, "Ride, Les! Ride!" while she waves her right arm frantically, sweeping her husband and Sharon to the east.

That's all it takes.

John breaks for the fence himself, realizing what a stupid, pointless gesture it is. There's nothing he can do, and had he any sense he'd be running in exactly the opposite direction. But he has to see. He has to make sure. And he has to know that Les and Sharon will be okay. He doesn't realize he's still holding Lisse's arm until she stumbles and falls to one knee, jerking him around, nearly bringing him down, too.

She's crying, and back there Kyle and Mag are making their way toward the house, torn between curiosity and fear, neither stronger right now.

He turns.

Fran screams her warning without a breath, arm still sweeping, her voice rising to a helpless keen as Les and Sharon, struggling with the roan and gray, finally get them moving and charge toward the stables. Les's hat is gone, and Sharon leans so far over her mount she seems molded to its neck.

John thinks Sharon is screaming, too, but he can't hear her; the thunder not thunder has grown too loud.

When he sees it, he gasps.

2

The sound is like splitting glass, and Gillespie, his right shoulder exposed, jerks the arm, and his gun, out and away from Vonda, who falls immediately to the pavement.

Nothing moves but the dust cloud.

No one moves but Gillespie, whose knees buckle and he lurches against the display window, rights himself and begins to run.

Arn stares dumbly at his wife, then wheels and snatches his gun from the cruiser hood, races back to the center of the street in an awkward crouch and hopes to hell he's better here than he is on the firing range.

The breeze turned wind sweeps the dust down Madison, blurring the sun and sky.

Gillespie fires wildly, staggering toward the corner, and Arn fires back just as wildly, half blinded by the dust, shoved by the wind, wondering why in the hell the others aren't getting into the act, why does it always have to be him that does all the damn work.

Then he realizes it's his fault: Out here like he is, dust sweeping the street like rain, they don't want to hit him, and isn't that a goddamn fine kettle of goddamn rotten fish.

Gillespie fires, and a chunk of tarmac slices Arn's left ankle, staggering him to one knee.

That's all it takes.

Maybe it was Rafe, maybe somebody else, but a shotgun lets go, and Arn drops to the ground, firing, still firing, while thunder explodes around him, and Gillespie lets loose thunder of his own, rebounding off glass, danc-ing spastically, falling, getting up, a ghost in the dust that refuses to go down until Arn, choking, slammed by the wind, aims and guesses and pulls the trigger one last time.

3

The sound is like nothing George has ever heard before.

He has given up trying to crawl to the half-open front door, and uses his right hand instead to claw at the floor while rocking side to side, hoping he'll be able to get to the threshold. Once there he knows, he just knows, he'll be able to figure out a way to get inside.

His broken left arm fills him with pain so intense he nearly loses vision.

He thinks he can feel something in his legs, but they still won't obey him.

He curses himself for the tears that slide and sting into his beard, and he claws the floor again, gasping when a nail breaks, tasting blood in his mouth, willing himself to get closer to that damn door over there, it's only a couple of feet away, even a dead man could make it.

The sound grows louder. Nearer.

And something else just inside it.

He shudders a deep breath and rests for a moment, eyes closed, listening carefully, spitting blood, until, at last, he knows what it is.

It isn't thunder.

It's the rhythmic beat of a hundred wings.

4

The limousine sweeps past the house he had visited only that morning, and Trask can see the two women on the lawn, staring at him as he passes, while that large old man leans out from under the porch roof to stare at the sky.

The noise, the thunder, whatever it is, makes the limousine shudder, and he can't believe Sebastian is having such a hard time steering. The wheel jerks left, right, and the car swerves sharply left, sharply right.

Alonse prays aloud.

Trask prays as well, but silently as he watches the bend come at them.

Too fast, he thinks; Sebastian, you're driving too fast, we'll never make
it.

5

Patty races to the road, waving her arms wildly to stop the limousine, but
it has already passed her, going too fast for her to catch. She can hear the
sound that she knows isn't thunder, and she knows she won't be able to
get to the ranch in time.

To stop her son.

She doesn't understand, not really, what he tried to do to her with those
wonderful soft hands, and for a while it had seemed as if she'd been wandering in a dream.

Floating.

His eyes everywhere, smiling at her.

Mocking her.

But the dream, like all her dreams, had ended abruptly, and Joey was
gone, and the years she had spent wandering with him all over the country
tried to flood her memory all at the same time. To tell her what she'd done.
To tell her what she'd seen. But it was too much, far too much, and she
can do nothing now but concentrate on the fact that he's gone, and for
some reason that's wrong, and for some reason she has to stop him.

Louder, now, the thunder, and she runs back to the house, skidding to
a stumbling halt when she sees Ari lying on the porch, her father kneeling
beside him, wiping something on the old man's shirt.

"Pop," Dory says, leaning against the post, her arms folded sternly
across her chest.

Garza looks over his shoulder, and frowns only the way he can frown
when his children have done something terribly, terribly wrong.

Slowly, shaking, Patty climbs the steps, her arms out for balance, and
pleading.

"Pop, I don't think it worked. I don't think Joey did it."

Garza nods. "The father. Must be that damn father."

"Joey," Patty begs, looking from one to the other. "I need to talk to
Joey."

"No, you don't," Garza tells her. "And even if you do . . ." and he shrugs, and turns back to the task of cleaning off his razor.

"I hate you!" Patty screams.

"Too bad," Dory tells her, turns toward the house, then whips around again, her right arm out and rigid, fist and wrist bone catching Patty across the throat and lifting her off the steps.

When she lands on the walk, she hears something snap, and sees the sky darken, and hears nothing but the thunder, expanding in her skull.

6

Rod Gillespie falls, more blood than flesh, and Arn rests his forehead on the street, letting the wind swing over him until he pushes up to his hands and knees, rocks back onto his heels, and coughs, and spits, and rocks up to a standing.

There are no cheers, no backslaps, no congratulations.

Rod Gillespie is down, and he cannot hear the wind.

7

George Trout tries one more time to reach the edge of the open door. If he can grab hold, he can use it to pull him, since nothing else is working and there isn't much time left. But his fingers won't stretch far enough, and he can't rock anymore, and the wings have stopped beating long enough for him to open his eyes and take stock.

He laughs.

A short laugh, a scornful laugh, but a laugh nonetheless.

"And the horse you rode in on," he yells, just before the crow with the bright blue eyes brings its beak into George's eye that isn't gray anymore.

8

Over the rise.

They come over the rise.

IN THE MOOD

The palomino's bobbing headfirst, mane brushed by the wind that flows out of the north. Then its neck. Its chest. Its forelegs. Until it stands alone on the upper pasture, and the dust begins to rise and flow like dark water along the top of the grass, through the grass, bending and snapping the blades that are caught and taken with it.

Standing alone under a sky John thinks is much too large, much too high.

Standing alone, while the thunder not thunder continues to roll behind it.

He can't help it; he feels the tears, standing alone at the fence, with Fran far to his right silently urging her husband on, Lisse behind him on her knees, begging him not to leave her.

He feels the tears.

And something else.

Facing the wind and its debris, unblinking, breathing deeply, waiting for the moment when the dream will end and he'll wake up in New Orleans or Denver or Ossining or San Diego just in time to make another tape, and have another drink.

"Joey," he whispers.

And Joey, astride the palomino's back, lifts his hand and waves. Just once.

Although they're several hundred yards apart, John whispers the little cowboy's name again, and he can hear the response clearly, whispering in his ear:

"Casey's wrong, Dad, you're going to die."

6

"No," John says.

And, "No," he says again.

The palomino rears, forelegs slashing at the sky, and the thunder increases as the animal swings around to face him and begins to move.

The others come behind it, heads first, then chests, over the rise, moving slowly through the wind.

Inexplicably, Les and Sharon have stopped, and Fran is too hoarse to scream at them anymore; all she can do is pound the top of the fence in frustration and point and shake a fist and look as if she's going to climb over, run out, and drag them home.

John takes an uncertain step back as Royal shifts smoothly into a trot, and the herd follows suit, still flowing over the rise.

"I thought . . ." says Lisse behind him, "I thought you said there weren't that many."

He can't answer; he doesn't have an answer.

Not a dozen.

There were scores.

Their hooves pound the grass, raise the dust, join the wind; feed the thunder.

"John, let's get out of here."

They spread across the full width of the pasture, from a trot to a canter, and he can feel the pressure of their urgency to move faster, can see it in the way their heads move, in the way they skip a step, prance, canter on.

Waiting for the order.

Not scores.

There are hundreds.

"Les," Fran whimpers as she climbs stiffly off the fence.

Les and Sharon are still halfway to the stable, and John realizes they can no longer go sideways to escape the herd, because the herd is too wide, and their horses are suddenly fractious, fighting their bits, fighting their riders.

"Les," Fran whimpers. "Les."

John backs away, watching Royal, watching Joey, dust like amber smoke rising from the herd, swirling around it and through it, until there is only a flash of a head, a reach of a leg, a smear of flank.

Dust-smoke boiling into the sky, prairie fire, wildfire, but instead of crackling flames there is only thunder, the sound of hooves.

Sideways now, he takes Lisse's hand, resisting when she tries to pull him toward the house. "I don't think so," he says. "I don't think that'll matter."

She doesn't ask how he knows that, just changes direction toward the drive, pausing only when Fran calls to her, not for help but to catch something she tosses underhanded after digging it out of her jeans. It falls short, raises dust, and Lisse hurries over, holds up a set of keys John recognizes belong to the Jeep.

"Fran," he yells, to be heard over the thunder. "Fran, come on!"

Her hands lift helplessly—*I can't, I can't*—and she edges toward the stable door.

The palomino charges.

John's first running step is a stumble, because he can't not watch Les and Sharon, still fighting their mounts until the first of the herd reaches then, with the dust-smoke, and the thunder, and he isn't sure if Sharon falls or Les's roan is toppled because one moment they were there, and the next moment there is nothing but the smoke and the charging herd.

Still, he doesn't run again until Lisse tugs frantically at his shirt. Then he moves, not looking back, brandishing a fist to drive Kyle and Mag toward the Jeep. Mag bolts instantly, but Kyle is frozen, mouth gaping, eyes in full wide panic.

"The fence," the boy says as John reaches him and grabs for his arm. "See? The fence. Sharon will jump the fence, she can do that, she's really good, but—"

John sees the herd and nothing else.

"Come on, kid," he urges, trying to turn the boy around. "We have to go. Now!"

Lisse yells at him from the driver's seat. The engine is running, she's turned the vehicle around, and Mag is hysterical in the back, screaming for Kyle, for her father, for God.

"Kyle," John says, then grabs him around the waist and hauls him away, feet dragging while Kyle whispers Sharon's name over and over again.

The explosion stops them briefly.

Royal hits the fence in full stride, breaking through it without stumbling, as if it were paper, splinters and shards and full-length planks tumbling into the wind and carried off, dropping to the ground and trampled by the hooves that run them over.

The first stable disintegrates in sections.

Part of a wall, part the roof, the doors blow outward, adding straw and tack to the wind.

"In," John orders, dumps Kyle into the back, knocking Mag to the seat, and yells at Lisse to get out.

When she hits the accelerator, he nearly tumbles out, grabs the top of the windshield and hangs on as they jounce and shudder over the branches still littering the blacktop. At the gate she doesn't slow down at all, but swings right, tires protesting, skidding and smoking to the opposite shoulder until she regains control and heads for the bridge.

"Where?" she shouts.

"Just keep driving. The trees will slow them down. They'll have to bunch together." Then he grabs the back of the seat and checks on Kyle and Mag. They're coated with dust and dead leaves and needles, holding each other, so deep in shock he doesn't think they'd respond if he asked how they were.

The Jeep bounces as it shoots over the bridge, and suddenly he thumps Lisse's shoulder and yells, "Stop here! Stop here!"

She does, braking hard, Mag moaning panic in back as he scrambles from his seat and races around the back and across the front yard of the house that used to be his. Two people stand together on the porch, but it's Patty he needs to talk to, Patty he needs to ask.

So intent is he that he doesn't see her body until he's halfway up the walk.

He blinks, and makes to kneel, changes his mind because he sees the way her neck is turned.

Dory steps away from her father, and when she does he can see the body of an old man lying beside a chair, his chest and neck gleaming with blood. Garza has a straight razor in his hand, stained, still dripping.

"My God, Dory, why?" he says, forgetting everything else, pointing to the dead man, pointing to his wife.

She shrugs. "I don't know. I guess we felt like it."

He stares at her, searches her face for anything that will tell him she didn't mean what she'd just said.

I felt like it, stan hovinskal had told him.

it's all part of the plan ruesette argo had said.

"Patty," he whispers, part in sorrow, part in rage, then cocks his head and hears the thunder, and hurries back toward the Jeep. He has the answer he didn't want.

"Go," he tells Lisse.

Dory calls his name.

When he looks, she grins and says, "Sorry, Ace, I think you're a little late."

The Jeep jerks, nearly stalls, and as it pulls away, he watches Dory put her arm around her father's waist, pulls him close and hugs him warmly.

The razor in his hand.

Then Kyle warns, "Hey, watch the bend," and John faces front just as Lisse screams into the turn, and the Jeep skids again. Fishtailing slowly. Spinning slowly. So slowly he can see each one of the lightning-shot trees in the dry marsh across the way, each of the pines and oak George had planted to keep people from seeing his house until they reached it, the road behind, the road ahead, and the blur of all things between.

"Damn," Lisse says, grinning as the Jeep straightens and stops, facing the wrong direction. "Not bad for a New Orleans waitress, huh?"

He wants to kiss her, he wants to smack her, instead he gestures urgently, ordering her to turn around and get this thing moving again before it's too late.

It isn't until she does that he sees the limousine parked in front of George's house.

"Stop!" he says when they draw abreast.

"Again?"

"Stop, damnit!"

She balks, but they haven't yet gone to speed, so he jumps from the Jeep, runs a few steps to keep from falling over, then runs for the house. Lanyon Trask is on the porch with one of his giants, kneeling beside George, whose head is covered with blood. Trask's arms are flailing at several crows on Trout's back and legs, while the giant swings a chair leg at others swooping through the porch. Alongside the walk the second giant lies on his stomach, hands cupped protectively over his head while a half dozen more birds try to reach his face.

John doesn't think about the fact that they're not making a sound except for an occasional soft squawk.

Without thinking, he stops by the prone man and kicks at the birds, yelling at them, cursing them, stumbling back when he's joined by Kyle and Lisse, and Mag heads for the porch shrieking madly.

Within seconds the birds are gone, fleeing as he spins and punches at their faces, at their wings.

Panting, feeling the sweat in his hair and on his face, he looks to the porch. Trask, his white suit stippled and darkly smeared, looks back and shakes his head.

"Damn," John says.

Then, "Damn!" he yells.

He points at the groaning giant, then at Lisse and kids. "Help him up, get on the porch."

He points at Trask. "Stay there."

"John?"

He can't hear her, not really. All he can hear is the thunder, and a peculiar silence, a familiar silence that stays with him when he returns to the road and stands in the middle, facing the bend.

floating

he's floating

Vibrations that shake his knees, and dust billows over the trees, thunderhead dark, shot through vivid streaks of blue.

Casey, he thinks, you damn well better be right.

floating

When the palomino appears in the turn, the herd just behind and squeezed onto the blacktop, all he can think of is Levee Pete and Alonse the giant . . .

. . . and the herd stops.

He watches.

They stand at the turn behind Royal, shifting, anxious, and he can see the muscles bunch and release, bunch and release, can see the large dark eyes, the ears laid back, the froth at their mouths, the bared teeth, the raised hooves that paw and slice the road while the dust settles on their shoulders.

He can see Joey on Royal's back; he can see the boy's uncertain frown when he thumbs his hat back.

"Your mother's dead," John says.

"I saw it," Joey answers. Not a tear in those big blue eyes.

It's the silence that keeps John talking; all those horses, and not a sound.

"This is it," he says, pointing at the ground. "Right here. Right now."

"You can't stop me, John," Joey tells him, adjusting his hat, adjusting his belt. "You know you can't. You know." He strokes Royal's neck, smooths the sweep of his mane. "You gonna write about me, Daddy?"

"Stop it, Joey."

"You gonna tell everybody who you think I really am, Daddy?"

"Joey, knock it off."

"They should have killed you, you know, the big man with the pretty hair, and that silly pirate." The little cowboy shakes his head. "You should be dead."

John spreads his arms—*well, take a look, kid, because I'm not.*

The horses shift, bunched close together, and one nudges the palomino, forcing it to take a step.

John tries not to smile at Joey's startled expression—they're not supposed to do that; they're supposed to wait, because I'm boss.

"Go away," John says at last.

"Just like that?"

"Just like that."

Joey giggles; then he laughs; then he takes off his hat and slaps the palomino's shoulder; then he puts the hat back on and says, "Do you know who I am, John?"

John braces himself; it's coming.

"I'm Daddy's little boy."

And the palomino charges.

From dead stop to full gallop, and the herd is just behind.

It happens so swiftly that they scarcely seem to move, heads bobbing, teeth bared, filling the road from side to side, the dust smoke rising, Joey grinning, and pulling his sixgun to his hand.

John doesn't move.

He's *floating*.

All he sees are Royal's eyes, and Joey's eyes, and Royal's teeth and Royal's hooves bearing down on him, aiming for him, reaching out to take him down.

He doesn't move.

He's *floating*.

His arms are at his sides, and his fingers spread and curl, and he holds his breath—blue eyes—and narrows his eyes—Levee Pete—and as Joey grins and cocks the hammer, John swings his arms up violently, and in that floating second before they ride him down he sees the terror in Royal's eyes, sees it rear, sees it topple sideways into the herd, throwing Joey into the smoke, and the hooves that thunder past him, and the cloud that cloaks him with grit and dust and droplets of blood.

He can't stop himself; he cries, "Joey!" as he coughs and chokes while the dust-smoke tries to blind him, as he fights to keep his feet when a shoulder strikes him and spins him around, when a haunch slams him and something butts him and another shoulder almost knocks him to his knees.

He wants to run, but he can't; there are too many, and they're too strong, and he can't see, and he's suffocating, and he wishes, maybe prays, that he won't fall because then it's done.

And when they're gone, he still can't move.

IN THE MOOD

*   *   *

When the floating stops and the silence is normal and the dust smoke disperses and his breathing is ragged, he still can't move.

But he can weep, which he does, because the road he faces is empty.

Nothing here but him.

His lips twitch, and he gulps a breath, and he turns and sees the herd spreading across the empty field down the road, nuzzling through the dead corn stalks for something fresh to eat. Twelve of them; no more than twelve.

The palomino isn't there.

He spits dust and wipes his eyes, turns suddenly and sighs.

Nothing back there, either, but an old cowboy hat in the road, its chin strap torn and broken.

Part 5

1

1

There is a silence at Cornman Center. A respectful hushed quiet. Only the murmuring of conversations in rooms with open doors, the occasional squeak of a nurse's shoe on the polished floor, the soft voice of speakers hidden in the walls paging someone, the squeak of a wobbly wheel as a food cart is pushed down an empty hall.

Dr. Bergman, pouches and smudges under his eyes, stands at the nurses station in the psychiatric unit and scans a patient's chart before replacing it in the rack.

"All quiet?" he asks the nurse in charge, and she grins at the tone in his voice.

"Yes, Doctor," she answers patiently, as she has every twenty minutes since her shift began. "Everyone's quiet."

"Even Mrs. Grauer?"

"Especially Mrs. Grauer."

"Thank you, Lord," he mutters to the ceiling, and walks away with a see-you-later wave.

But he doesn't leave; he doesn't want to; he doesn't dare.

He knows it, he feels it in his bones that haven't had a decent rest since the beginning of the week, that as soon as he steps one foot outside, all hell's going to break loose. It's silly. It's probably crazy. But maybe one more night on the cot.

Just in case.

You never know.

2

Halfway into a dream about what it's like to fly, Kyle starts awake and stares at the hospital bed. At the wires. At the monitors. At the clear liquid in the plastic bag hanging from the IV stand. He rubs his eyes; nothing's changed.

Tomorrow, he promises himself, he's going to bring his own chair. This molded plastic garbage is breaking his stupid back. But there's no way he's not going to be here when Sharon wakes up. Even if her mother and brother get sick of seeing his stupid face, he will be here. He needs to be. He has to explain why he left her back there, and maybe she'll understand, and maybe she won't hate him.

The weird thing is, you look at her and she doesn't look that bad. Left arm in a cast-and-sling, right leg in a cast, a couple of now-fading bruises on her face, and one long bandage across her forehead that covers a gash that, the doctor said, is going to leave one beaut of a scar.

She does not look as if she was trampled by a hundred horses.

A cough at the doorway. He looks up, grins. "Hey."

"Hey," Mag says quietly, easing into the room. "Hey, Shar, how you doing?" She drags the other chair from the wall by the door and settles beside the bed, reaches out and strokes Sharon's unmarked hand. "Raining today, do you believe it?"

"She can't hear you," Kyle tells her.

Mag nods. "Sure she can. You got to talk to her, Kyle, you know. That's what brings them out of it."

Uncomfortable because he suspects she's right, he confesses that he really doesn't know what to say, that he feels a little silly talking to himself.

"Who cares? In the first place, you're talking to her, not yourself, you jerk. So tell her about the Kentucky game, how you sacrificed the one chance you ever had to meet a Kentucky blue grass chick just because of her." A sly look over, and a grin. "Hey, you're blushing."

"I am not."

"Sure you are."

"No, I'm not." A lie, because he can feel it. "So how's your mom?"

"Are you kidding? A bump on the head, that's all." Mag rubs her arm absently. "They're saying he's a hero, you know."

"Now who's a jerk? Sure he is. From what I saw in the paper, what I heard, they should give him a medal, a million dollars, and . . . and . . . I don't know, something else."

Her shoulders lift, her head turns away, and he's right beside her, touching her hair until she turns and stands and hugs him so tightly he can hardly breathe.

"He almost died," she says into his chest. "The stupid bastard almost died."

"But he didn't," he reminds her softly. "He didn't, we didn't. That's what counts."

An embarrassed moment later they break apart, take their seats, and Mag brushes her fingers over Sharon's wrist. "They're saying it was a tornado or something."

He nods; he's heard. After a week of listening, he almost believes it himself.

Her eyes are puffed and bloodshot. "It wasn't, was it? I mean . . . we know different. Right?"

He doesn't answer; he can't.

So she takes a breath, and takes another, and tells Sharon all about the storm, as if it were just a storm, and how the ranch is a mess but not to worry because the horses are okay and need her back real soon.

She doesn't tell her that no one lives there anymore.

She doesn't tell her what happened to the Fish Man.

Kyle listens, and wonders, and after a few minutes chimes in with some things of his own, eventually teasing her about her height, a few cracks about basketball and the weather up there, and desperately searches her face for a sign that she's heard and when she wakes up she's gonna deck him.

When she doesn't, he sighs, stretches, and announces he's got to get something to eat before he starves. Mag, after a kiss to Sharon's cheek, follows him into the hall.

They stand there, not moving.

It's funny, he thinks, how it's only been a week, and they've nothing left to say.

"Want to come?" he asks, not very sincerely.

"Nope. Gotta get home, listen to my mother brag on the old man."

Finally he says it: "So why aren't we bragging on Mr. Bannock? Why haven't we said anything about him, what he did for us?"

Like the storm, they have no answer, and after a fumbling good-bye, a brief hug, they part.

And he has a feeling he doesn't understand—that he and Mag won't talk much anymore.

3

Arn Baer just wants to go home. For the past six or seven days he has snapped and snarled at everyone who's walked into his office, including the mayor; he's had a couple of really dumb fights with his wife, who doesn't want him to go to work in case that Gillespie scum has accomplices lurking out there; he's talked to reporters from papers he's never heard of and networks he wouldn't watch on a bet; he's filled out more paperwork than the entire U.S. Army; his shoulder is killing him; and the goddamn newspaper dispenser across the street still won't give him back his money.

Worse; Rafe Schmidt is treating him like he's learned to walk on water.

Jesus, what a way to live.

Thankfully, the only thing left to do is go over the signed statement from that old man who killed that other old man out at the Bannock place, then get hold of the city prosecutor to find out if that woman is going to be charged as an accessory. Or maybe Patty Bannock's killer. She claims it's an accident, because of that wind, but he still isn't sure.

The weird thing is, neither of them seems to give a damn.

Gillespie he can understand. Sort of.

But the old man's daughter? Standing there doing nothing, while her father cuts some guy's throat? Maybe even shoving Patty down the steps? Then just waiting around until the police show up?

"What the hell's going on around here?" he asks his empty office.

"You call?" Rafe says anxiously, sticking his head in.

"No. I did not call. And aren't you supposed to be on the road or something?"

"Paperwork, Chief," the deputy says, snaps his gum, grins, and vanishes, and reappears a moment later.

"What?" Arn snarls, then apologizes with a grimace that was supposed to be a smile.

"Patty Bannock," Rafe says hesitantly.

"What about her?"

"Well . . . didn't they have a kid? Her and her husband?"

Arn opens his mouth to snarl again, closes it when he realizes the deputy is right. All this stuff going on, nobody's thought to ask about the kid. Which, he thinks, is funny, since neither Bannock or the old man or the woman in the cell have said a word about him.

He feels like a jerk.

"Sorry, Chief," says Rafe miserably. "I feel like a jerk for not thinking of it before." He shrugs. "The thing is, nobody's seen him. Maybe he's with a relative or something."

Right, Arn thinks; like this mess is all that easy.

Rafe waves the clipboard, his tone dropping into his own official mode. "But he's probably with his old man, right?"

"You think maybe?" he answers, not worrying about the sarcasm because Rafe seldom took the bait.

"Stands to reason, Chief. The mother's dead, his aunt and grandfather are in jail, if he's here he's got to be with the father."

"We haven't seen him there, have we? It's been a week and we haven't seen him."

"Well . . . no."

"We don't have an extra body floating around, do we?"

Rafe studies the ceiling. "Okay. No."

Arn sees the disappointment, though, and figures this could be a good way to get some peace. He clears his throat. "Look, do me a favor, take some time off from all that paper crap, take a ride out there, have another look around. Ask about the kid." He tries to look sincere as he taps the folder on his desk. "I'm so swamped, maybe I'm wrong." He adds a heavy sigh. "Loose ends, Rafe. Loose ends."

Rafe salutes, leaves, and returns, his face creased in a frown. "Suppose he's not there? The kid, I mean?"

"Don't," Arn warns. "Do not even think it. Just go. Come back. Bring me good news."

"Sure, Chief," says Rafe. And blows a big blue bubble.

4

Dory sits on the cot in her cell, knees drawn up to her chest, hands around her ankles. She ignores her father, in the cell on her left, stretched out and snoring. She ignores the guards who stroll by now and then, sneaking looks at her and the old man, looking away guiltily when she catches them at it.

Something has been missing since they brought her and Pop in, and she can't quite figure out what it is. It's important, that much she knows, and it probably has something to do with getting her out of here and back home to Philly, but she'll be damned if she can figure it out.

It'll come to her, though, she's sure of it; it'll come to her.

Meanwhile, she's bored, and she decides it's time to wake Pop up so they can talk. She wishes he would say something about what he did out there, at least listen to her as she tries to figure out how the thing with Ari Lowe can be fixed not to look like murder.

"Hello."

A man in an expensive suit stands at her cell door, briefcase in one well-manicured hand. "Ms. Castro?" he says. When she nods warily, he smiles broadly and tells her, "I'm your attorney." He looks toward Tony. "Both of you. I just stopped by to tell you not to worry, that as soon as I can I'll have you, at least, out on bail."

"How can you do that?" Dory demands, not bothering to ask where he came from.

"Because I'm good," the man replies simply. "So how are you doing?"

"Like shit," she complains. "How do you think? And where the hell have you been? I've been rotting here for days."

The attorney studies her for a moment before he says, "Listen, Ms. Castro, I realize you've been through a lot. You may not realize just how much you've suffered. Your father and sister and all." The smile turns sympathetic. "What I'm saying is, now is not the time to build walls around your trauma. You can talk to me. You can tell me anything. But I need to know the truth. You need to be honest with me."

Dory sighs a martyr's sigh, and nods reluctantly. "You want the truth, I wish I had my piano. It would make me feel a whole lot better." She stares at her knees. "I miss my music."

She feels it stir then, the something that's eluded her.

Not quite here, yet, but closer.

"I can't help you there, but that's what I mean. I need to know what's in your head. So," and he reaches through the bars, and she reaches out and takes his hand. "So, Dory, tough talk aside, how do you really feel?"

She stares at him, not knowing how to respond, not understanding what he really wants, until she hears a whisper in her ear:

"Aunt Dory . . . cry."

And she does.

2

In the spare room of George Trout's house there is a steamer trunk, brand-new, its brass trim and corners and lock gleaming and as yet untouched. Inside is a stack of papers and two briefcases filled with cassettes that John stares at for a long time before he closes the lid and turns the heavy brass key over. He sniffs then, and stands, and uses his foot to shove the trunk across the bare floor and into the closet. He doesn't look at it again before he slams the door.

"You know," says Lisse from the doorway, "that ain't going to make it go away. Just tucked under for a while."

"I know." He faces her, and smiles. "But I think I deserve a little tucking now and then, don't you?"

Her eyes narrow. "You talking dirty to me . . . Prez?"

"I wouldn't dare," he tells her, taking her arm, turning around. "I want to live, thank you."

She mutters and leads the way downstairs, out to the porch where they stand at the rail and watch the rain drip from the eaves and fill the dry marsh across the road. Although the air is damp and chilled, neither wears a sweater or a jacket; it feels good on their skin, and they want it to last.

She folds her arms across her stomach, one hand cupping her elbow. "That policeman called while you were upstairs. The chief?"

"Oh."

"He says he's sending somebody out again, to check on the whereabouts of the boy. Loose ends, he said. He's clearing up loose ends."

IN THE MOOD

John smells the rain and the damp earth and the wet grass. Good smells. It's been a long time.

"Are we packed?"

She looks over, and he's not sure about her expression, not until he sees the set of her jaw, the way the fingers of that cupped hand drum slowly, deliberately, on her elbow.

"Lisse, I'm sorry." The rasp is clear in his voice. "I just don't have a whole lot of time all of a sudden. I am not taking you for granted. Believe me, I'm not."

A reluctant nod. "All right. I'm sorry, too. So what's the plan? We can't stay here forever."

"We're leaving. Now. I'll drop you off wherever you want." He hesitates. "If you want." No reaction, and he checks the road, and the rain. "But I can't shake the feeling that I don't have a lot of time."

Without waiting for a response, he returns inside, lifting an eyebrow when he spots the suitcase at the foot of the stairs.

"We gonna walk?" she asks smugly from the door.

"George's car is in the garage. We'll take that. He won't mind."

"Probably smells like whiskey." A joke, and a comment.

And a caution.

Suddenly there's too much to do, and suddenly there's nothing to do, which depresses him because the last time he left Vallor, it had taken him weeks to get everything in order, make all the necessary arrangements for an extended time away.

Now it will only take minutes.

And he wishes he had a drink.

Within five minutes, the house locked up and swift good-byes said to George, his presence still connected to his home, they're on the road, not speeding but moving steadily, the suitcase in the backseat, John driving, checking the rearview mirror and seeing nothing but the smear of gray rain.

"What are you thinking, Prez?"

"I like Yank better."

"Too bad."

Vallor fades, and vanishes, as if, he thinks, it had never been.

"Patty," he admits. "And Joey."

"Are we still crazy?"

"God, I think so."

"Then that means he was one of them, right? The ones Momma told me about."

He nods.

"He's not dead, though."

"No, I don't think so. Stalled, that's all. I hope, anyway."

Illinois fades and vanishes, the Ohio taking them to Kentucky. Then it fades as well, as if it had never been.

"Here," she says, tapping his arm. "Take this."

"Take . . . ?" He opens his right hand, and into it she drops a small wooden cross on a thin leather thong. The surprise of it shakes his concentration, and she hisses to remind him to watch the road, it's slippery.

"When he left," she explains, "he gave it to me. He said, he was going home, do some praying, write some sermons, try to figure out where he went wrong." She shakes her head, traces a finger around a bruise on her neck. "I must be nuts, because sometimes, now, I think maybe he ain't so bad."

Trask was gone before dawn, he and his giants, no word of farewell. But they had returned a few days later, for George Trout's funeral, a simple and sad affair, no one there but John and Lisse, and Kyle and Mag. A prayer had been said by the TV preacher, whose hair, John noticed, wasn't quite so white anymore, and John hadn't bothered to wipe away the tears. Nor had he addressed the lingering fear he had seen in the giants' faces when he offered to shake their hands.

Whatever he might have said, they wouldn't have believed; whatever explanation he conjured, and conjuring it would be, they wouldn't have believed; and they certainly wouldn't have believed any protests he might have made about being anything but an ordinary man.

That he no longer believes himself.

"So what are we going to do, probably being fugitives and all."

"Well, the first thing I'm going to do is figure out that damn English of yours."

She scowls, then smiles, then shrugs and says, "You wish."

"The next thing is, when we get to Tennessee . . ." He waits a moment, making sure. "I think maybe we ought to go east, try to find Casey Chisholm."

"We're done," she snaps. "Done with it, John. I don't want anymore."

"You don't have to," he tells her softly. "I can still take you home. But I think I have to do this. I don't know for sure, but I really think I do."

"Well, damnit, then I'll have to go, too."

"No," he says. "It's all right. You don't."

She growls and smacks the dashboard. "That's exactly what I'm talking about, John Bannock. You don't know jack about some stuff, and you're gonna need me." She rubs her forehead, rubs her face. "Momma was right. I was born under a bad sign." She gives him a sour look. "Probably the Sign of the Eternal Dope."

"Why, Lisse Gayle," he drawls, "I do believe you're blushing."

"Shut up and drive, Prez, before I have your scalp."

They stop between Nashville and Knoxville, at a motel near a tiny stream. The rain's been left behind, and in the floodlights that drive the shadows from the parking lot, John sees a garden beside the entrance.

It's late, from what he knows of such things, which isn't very much, but it pleases him to see something green growing there. Lisse sees as well, lifts an eyebrow, but doesn't smile. Instead she pokes him until they go inside, rent a room, and grab some supper in the coffee shop.

"So this is what it's like," Lisse says, "from the other side of the fence."

They talk of nothing, and that's all right with him.

There's some laughter, and playful teasing, and that's all right with him.

Later that night, lying in bed with Lisse snuggled in his arms, and he finds himself smiling, and that's all right, too. A reward, he hopes, for things he still can't understand.

And as he drifts and holds her closer, she murmurs something in his ear, and he can't help but grin and whisper, "Yeah, me, too, hon, me, too."

3

In his dreams he's *floating.*

And Joey whispers, "You're gonna die."